I0663808

Whatever It Takes

Bridgett Henson

Empowered Publications, Inc.
Leroy, Alabama
www.empoweredpublicationsinc.com

© 2013 Bridgett Henson

Scripture quotations are taken from the King James Version.

Original cover photo provided by SAILob.com. Final art produced by Empowered Publications, Inc.

This novel is a work of fiction. All characters are a product of the author's imagination. Any resemblances to actual people or events are purely coincidental.

Published by Empowered Publications, Inc.
529 County Road 31
Millry, Alabama 36558

ISBN 978-0-9895857-2-9

In loving memory of
Charles Devin Giles.
July 10, 1988
to
March 25, 2013

Acknowledgements

I thank God for saving me, calling me, and giving me a work to do. He provided the venues for research, and great friends to keep me going when I was ready to give up.

This book would not be possible without the encouragement of Tyler Chastain. Thank you for supporting me through three rewrites and countless revisions. I truly couldn't have done this without you.

A big kiss sent to Nicholas Henson for holding down the fort while his mother sailed away on a research adventure. You are the real hero in this story. And a huge applause goes to Captain Ryan at Sail OB in Orange Beach, Alabama, for a great sail and for providing the cover picture. Also, thanks to my sailing partners, Colby Chastain, Tyler Chastain, Adam Henson, Holly Henson, and Samantha Robinson.

Shout out to Justin Nace of Sidewalk Prophets for taking the time to answer a few drumming questions. Thanks to Bobby and Fonda Horn, and Willie and Twila Long for having a heart to help those recovering from addictions, and for sharing your experiences with me.

Thank you to Carl and Joyce Hunter for letting me borrow your "Little Lulu." The world needs more people willing to rescue the forgotten children.

Every book needs good proofreaders. Amber Stokes, and Diana Lesire Brandmeyer, thank you for lending me your eyes.

May God bless each and every person that had a part in the production of this story. The list is truly too long to name everyone. But I must mention my own superhero, Ernie Henson. Thanks for allowing me to bring my imaginary friends into our home, thanks for ignoring the dirty dishes in the sink while I was writing, and thank you for answering all my girlie questions.

Chapter One

Cindy McDuffie gasped and sat straight up in the bed. Clinching the covers with both hands, she sucked in a breath. "I'm okay." *Breath out.* "Just a dream." *Breathe in.* "I'm fine." *Breathe out.* "I'm safe."

Her own voice soothed her fears, and the welcoming breeze from the air conditioning duct cooled her perspiring brow. Yet, the dark memories gripped her mind as her heartbeat tattooed inside her tight chest.

She inhaled. Counted to three. And slowly released her breath.

The nightmare slowly receded. Through the window, the midnight sky had turned a dull gray. Curling onto her side, she snuggled into the soft comforter Joni had placed on the guest bed last night. A luxury compared to the scratchy blankets in jail.

She pushed the lingering images of the familiar nightmare to the back of her mind.

The next three months were going to be the best of her life. Her friend Joni had picked her up from Mobile Metro Jail, and brought her to the ritzy Eastern Shore. Here, Cindy was safe, and she was free.

"How could you bring her into our home?" James's angry voice echoed through the thin bedroom wall. "Visiting her in jail is one thing, but she can't stay here."

Joni's muffled whispers answered her husband in the next room.

But they only escalated the frustration in James. "I know you want to help her, but Cindy has to answer for her crimes. And she will. Her court date is set. You can't undo her past. You can't keep her out of prison."

He was right. In desperation to survive, Cindy'd destroyed the lives of many.

Fully dressed, she eased out of the covers. Joni had lent her a flimsy nightgown, but Cindy hadn't worn the thing.

As she slipped into her ragged tennis shoes, her friend's singsong voice became clear, "Yesterday, the doctor heard one heartbeat, James. Yet, you insist God promised you twin boys. Why can't you trust Him to save her? It's up to us to show her the love of Jesus, and to teach her that God wants to give her a better life. Let her stay. Please, James. For me?"

James growled his consent. "Ah, beautiful, I'd do anything for you. She can stay, but lock your jewelry in the gun safe."

Cindy couldn't blame James for being leery, but she wouldn't stay here knowing she wasn't wanted. Besides everything he said was the truth.

As she tiptoed into the hall, Joni's giggle floated under the master bedroom door. Unlike Joni, no man had ever cared for Cindy without a selfish motive, but God did love her. Of that she was certain. He had proved it in the darkest night.

She crept down the carpeted stairs. The Lord promised her a good life—one without fear. Determined to find it, she paused with her hand on the brass knob. Which way should she go?

"Jesus, I don't want to be who I was. Change me. Make me worthy of Your love. Lead me. Make me who You want me to be." She sucked in a breath. "And help me sell my stash at the pawnshop. Amen."

With a flick of her wrist, the deadbolt disengaged. She unlatched the security chain, but glanced toward the stairs. Joni had said that James would cook omelets. Cindy ignored her rumbling stomach, opened the door, and stepped into unfamiliar territory.

Unseen birds chirped in the hazy morning, as a gentle breeze flowed through the rip in her jeans, chilling her knee. Come noon, she'd crave the cool. She descended the steps.

She needed to hurry and get her stuff before the users and dealers arose and tempted her to stay. She didn't want to live in that world, but she wouldn't leave the merchandise she'd hidden away either.

The sidewalk ended, and she stepped in the fresh-cut grass. Luxury homes hid behind iron gates and tall shrubs. Would she ever have a life like Joni's? Would she ever know a love like James's? Would she ever be good enough? Maybe when she got out of prison…

Cindy shook the daydreams out of her mind. Downtown Mobile was a long walk from the Eastern Shore. Without her new friend's sponsorship, Cindy would still be locked in her cell. She stumbled on a rock and wondered how Joni had talked her cynical husband into posting bail.

೮ഠൡ

Cole Maxwell made good time in the early morning traffic, but the meteorologist had warned of dense fog on I-10. He crossed the bypass and took the scenic route spanning the Mobile Bay as a new voice from the radio admonished husbands to love their wives.

Cole punched the knob and silenced the voice, but the longing in his heart couldn't be ignored. Despite his earlier prayers, he consulted his savior. "Lord, is it too late? Did I miss her somehow? Is that what happened yesterday? If You show me who she is, I'll love her forever, but I'm so tired of waiting. Where's the one You promised? Where is *my* wife?"

Along the edges of the bay, the rising sun painted the oyster grass a brilliant gold. Cole passed a deserted building destroyed by a storm years ago. The causeway was a dangerous place during hurricane season, yet the beauty of the waves lured both tourists and locals to its marshy banks.

"Forgive my impatience, Lord."

A girl walked alongside the road. Sunbeams inflamed the back of her long red hair as it danced with the wind.

The Spirit within him fluttered, and Cole suppressed an urge to help her. He needed to reach his office early and prepare for his father's staff meeting.

Take her home.

His heart quickened at the sound of God's still, small voice. But he must be mistaken.

"Lord, she's a hitchhiker and I'm late."

Turn around. Take her home.

Never in his life had Cole offered a stranger a ride. Good Samaritans ended up on the five o'clock news, and he had no desire to become a statistic. He drove on.

From the cup holder, his phone sounded a drum roll. Grateful for a distraction, Cole answered James's call. "Hello?"

"Hey man, sorry to call so early, but did you see Joni's friend Cindy, on your drive across the bay?"

"Who?"

"Hold on." James's voice grew louder. "Cole didn't see her." And then it lowered. "By the way, Sara said you could have my old apartment. I'll text you her number."

Cole sighed toward heaven. "That's an answer to prayer. Thanks."

"You're welcome. See you Sunday." The call ended.

Moving above Sara's garage would cut his commute in half. Even as Cole doubted, God was good.

Turn around. Offer her a ride and take her home.

He could no longer ignore the voice of the Spirit. God had blessed Cole in abundance. He couldn't disobey a direct command. So at Battleship Parkway, Cole signaled left and waited for the traffic to clear. "Forgive my lack of faith, Lord. But please don't let her be a serial killer."

⁝⁝

The constant wind tangled her hair, but at least it cooled the hot summer morning. She was free! After being cooped up in jail, her legs weren't used to walking. Her muscles ached, but she kept moving. Another quarter mile and she could rest on the seawall.

A horn blared, and a small hybrid zoomed past. She glanced over her shoulder as a white BMW pulled alongside her. She quickened her pace.

Music drifted through the window as it lowered. "Good morning. You need a ride?"

Something in the cheery masculine voice beckoned her, but she shook her head and kept walking. She'd known girls who'd accepted a lift and were never heard from again.

"Are you sure?" A tan hand reached across the leather seat as another horn blared behind them.

He was blocking traffic. She didn't like the attention from angry drivers. One call and she'd land back in jail.

Beautiful laughter sounded as an arm clothed in grey material beckoned. "Come on. Save me from angry commuters and get in the car."

An import and a blue minivan zoomed around them.

Accepting his offer was practical and time-saving. She slung her hair out of her eyes and snatched the door open. Besides, she only had three months of freedom before her trial.

Dressed in a suit and tie, Mr. Persistent smiled across the tan leather seats. Dark waves haloed his head. "Isn't it a beautiful morning?" The light in his silver eyes sparkled.

Her heart lurched as the window crept up, sealing them in together, but the cold air from the vents felt like heaven. She ignored his question, wiped the sweat from her forehead, and then wiped her hand on her worn jeans.

The Clark Kent/Superman look-a-like drummed his fingers on the wheel in perfect time with the beat playing through the speakers. With his good looks, he probably had his choice of girls. He didn't need to pick up women off the streets. Why had he stopped for her?

"I've never offered anyone a ride before. I suppose you have a destination in mind?"

The scent of his aftershave mingled with the air freshener clipped onto one of the vents. He was too clean to enter her neighborhood. She shouldn't have accepted his offer.

"If you lean any closer to the door, you might splatter on the roadway. I assure you, I'm perfectly harmless." After another minute of silence, he released a slow whistle. "Let's start with introductions. My name is Cole Maxwell and you are…?"

"Lulu." She spoke the nickname her brother had given her years ago. Long before he'd abandoned her.

The driver tilted his head, and deep laughter filled the car. He glanced her way several times while keeping one eye on the road. "Interesting name, Lulu. You have no idea how long I've waited to meet you." He slowed in a line of traffic and turned in his seat. His elbow propped on the windowsill, and a fist cushioned his head. Gentle eyes cherished her from her unbrushed hair to the rip in her shoe. Unlike the men in her past, the desire flickering in his eyes treasured. Full lips curled, and his eyes closed briefly. "Thank you, Jesus."

His words intrigued her. Comforted her. Why?

Thankfully, he turned his soul-searching gaze back on the traffic. "My sweet, precious Lulu, where would you like to go? Anywhere in the world. California? New York? Italy? Name it, and I'll take you there."

Who was this guy? People didn't really help others. They used and took what they could, then abandoned you when you were left with nothing. "Why are you helping me?"

"You wouldn't believe me if I told you."

She glared until he relented.

"God told me to."

At least he was original. His was a line she hadn't heard before. She studied the hand holding the wheel. His words sounded similar to Joni's logic, but Cindy wasn't convinced. She turned toward him. In her cell, she'd felt a comforting presence, and she'd known Jesus was with her. Whispers of reassurance breezed through her mind, but the words couldn't be understood. "Tell me His exact words."

"He said to take you home. That's what I'm doing."

Really? Maybe God did talk to him. But how far was he willing to go? "Texas."

A curious smile peeked from the corner of his full lips. "Dallas or Fort Worth? Or perhaps Austin? I haven't seen my college buds in a while."

The sun broke through the haze, and two white, puffy clouds floated in the sky. If this guy were a real superman, he'd fly her to the clouds, away from the hell that waited where she had to go. "Not Texas. Downtown Mobile. Houston Street."

His brows arched. "You live in a dangerous area."

"I didn't say I live there. At least, I don't anymore. I need a few things I left behind."

He glanced her way. "Okay, but after that? Where *do* you live?"

She cleared her throat, battling against the longing she'd heard in his voice. Reality set in. She was homeless. Where could she go? It depended on how much of her life savings survived her six-month stay in the Metro jail. Her sister and her friends probably helped themselves to her possessions. No hard feelings. In her world, people did what they had to in order to survive. "Drop me off at Houston and Government Streets. My life isn't your problem."

"We'll get your things, and then I'll take you home."

The snazzy beat of his music danced around them. Pretending an interest in the beautiful scenery of the Mobile Bay, she let the lyrics about God's mercy and grace wash over her. "Is this a CD?" She fumbled with the controls, determined to hear the entire song.

A masculine hand chased away her fingers. His soft laughter sent waves of warmth through her soul. "The driver controls the radio."

Laughter bubbled somewhere inside her. She bit her lip, refusing to let the small bit of happiness escape.

They waited at a red light for the on-ramp to the interstate. There were two ways across the bay: Battleship Parkway and I-10. The light turned green and her head lolled against the seat as he merged with the interstate traffic. She stared at his profile. Her fingers itched to touch his square jaw.

Impossible. She hated men. Feeding them the poison she cooked was her chance at revenge. She hated their touch. She hated their crude words, their foul bodies, their wicked thoughts. Was Cole any different from the others?

One hand left the steering wheel and rested on the console between them. His forearms held power. Would he hurt or protect her? Long, masculine fingers spread, clenched into a fist, and then relaxed.

Without looking at his face, she placed her pale hand beside his. The contrast was startling. His hand was strong. Hers was weak. Her nails were jagged and her cuticles overgrown.

His pinkie finger extended toward hers, sending her heartbeat into spasms as he traced the outline of her knuckle, seducing her hand to relax. Hooking around hers, his finger held her safe. She closed her eyes and enjoyed the warmth of his simple touch.

His palm rolled under hers. Her breath quickened as the hollow cavity in her chest ached. Tingles spread up her arm as her hand became weightless. With a whisper of his lips, the shell around her heart shattered as his breath danced across the back of her hand.

A whimper escaped her. She exhaled slowly as he lowered their entwined hands to the soft leather.

Reality returned with the eerie echoes of the deep, as the car entered the tunnel submerged underneath the Mobile River. Concrete walls and rows of florescent light surrounded the West bound traffic. Tons of water and countless ships lay between her and the surface. She held her breath until the car emerged into the morning sunshine. Cole exited onto Water Street. She stared out the window as he maneuvered through the many twists and turns of downtown. She sucked in a breath as he turned onto Houston Street.

The brief dream vanished. "Which house?"

She freed her hand from his. "The green one."

He parked near the curb.

With one hand paused on the handle, she memorized his facial features, especially the cute dimple on his chin. "Thanks for the ride."

Before she could open the door, he touched her arm. "This isn't home. I'll help you retrieve your things."

She couldn't allow Cole's apparent goodness to be tainted by the contents of the house. "Wait here." She didn't think he'd obey when he reached for the door. "I'll just be a minute."

He nodded, released the handle, and leaned against the seat.

She forced herself to step out of the car and trudge up the walkway. Bitterweed had overtaken the broken concrete path. Her hand trembled as she pushed the door open and quietly entered. A girl she didn't recognize was crashed on the couch. Cindy stepped around the filth and into her past.

The shattered bedroom doorframe rendered the deadbolts useless. In her closet, the gun safe stood bare. The boxes that held the jewelry she'd accepted as payment were also empty. Her shoulders sagged. All her hard work would be for nothing.

A snore snapped her attention to the bed. Elliot! Her heart jumped into her throat, stealing her breath.

If he saw her, she'd be trapped. She eased out of the room and ran toward Cole. Her hoard of merchandise was gone, but hopefully Elliot missed her hiding place at Granny's.

She jumped into the car and slammed the door. "Go down the street."

Cole frowned from the driver's side, but shifted into gear. "Are you okay?"

"Drive across the tracks." He followed her direction as she gnawed on her lip. "Stop here." Once again her hand paused on the door handle. "Will you wait for me?"

His smile seemed genuine. "I've waited years. I'm not going anywhere now that I've found you."

"Cole?" Her voice trembled. She swallowed. "Thank you." She stepped out of the car and jogged up the sidewalk into the old house.

Her half-sister jittered around in the living room. Maria looked like death. Shaky hands lifted a cigarette to cracked lips. "Cindy, I'm so glad you're here. Elliot's back."

The deep lines on her face revealed the truth. Her sister was up on meth—or some other homemade remedy. Elliot had indeed returned.

Cindy knew what it was like. She'd been there. But never again. "I'm not staying." She rushed into her Granny's old bedroom. The brass bed held five children sleeping sideways across the bare mattress. "Whose kids are these?"

Maria's chin flexed left to right, a sure sign of drug use. She whispered, "I reopened Granny's daycare."

With her back to her sister, Cindy twisted off the beveled top of the brass bedpost. Her fingers dug inside the pipe. Her breath gushed as her fist closed around the nylon sock.

"What are you doing?"

She shoved the bundle in her front pocket and hid the bulge with her shirt. Over her sister's shoulder, through the dirty window, Cole leaned against the door of his BMW talking with someone out of her view. "I'm starting my life over." Could God save her sister from drug addiction, or was His power limited to those who'd decided to go straight? "Come with me. God loves you, too."

Her sister's empty eyes widened. "God? Girl, are you trippin'? He doesn't care about people like us. Don't leave. You're the only one who can handle Elliot's moods."

Cole looked down at his gold watch, and then turned toward the sidewalk. Cindy needed to hurry. "I have three months of freedom. I intend to enjoy them, without Elliot or his drugs."

"But where will you go?"

Slipping past her sister, she whispered over her shoulder. "Home. I'm going home."

Chapter Two

"You buying? Or selling?"

Cole flinched and turned his attention from the door of the rundown house to a guy with two teardrop tattoos on his cheekbone. "Excuse me?"

Dark eyes narrowed, and the boy stepped closer. His voice hardened. "This is the boss's turf and he ain't into sharing. I said, are you buying or selling?"

"Neither, I'm waiting for a friend." Should Cole call the police? The boy couldn't be more than sixteen, but the bulge in his shirt outlined a large handgun. "And she isn't buying or selling either."

"You stealing the cook from her old man?" Course laughter shot into the morning. "That's good. The boss is gonna love that. See ya 'round, dude." The boy lay three fingers on his own forehead, turned them perpendicular, and then saluted. He swaggered down the street and disappeared around a huge oak tree.

A door slammed.

Lulu sprinted down the broken steps, her hair fanning in the wind. She grabbed his arm and rushed him toward the car. "Come on." Cole reached for the passenger door, but she waved him to the driver's side. "We need to go, before she tells him I'm here." Fear flamed her blue eyes.

He jogged around the hood and slid under the wheel. "Are you all right?" He wouldn't let anyone hurt her.

"Go." She pressed the door's lock button. "I'm fine."

He turned the car around and drove back toward Government Street. As he neared the green house where they'd first stopped, she slunk down in the seat and hid her face from the window. A shirtless, middle-aged man stood on the curb with a scowl on his face.

Cole accelerated past the unkempt man. "Who was that?"

"No one important."

Although his office was only a couple of blocks away, he'd never entered this neighborhood and didn't intend to return. If he could prevent it, neither would she.

She glanced out the back-glass. Her shoulders relaxed as she exhaled. "Thank you, Jesus." Her brief laugh relieved his anxiety. "I did it." Her eyes sparkled. "I'm free, Cole. I'm free." She laughed again and tugged a man's sock from the front of her jeans. Steady hands flipped a rubber band off a roll of money. Nimble fingers shifted through dozens of hundred-dollar bills with the proficiency of a bank teller—or a drug dealer.

Did she steal the money?

Or earn it illegally?

Was he guilty of accessory after the fact?

Probably. He shouldn't ask too many questions. She'd been in jail, but she was his Lulu and their future was all that mattered. "Have you ever thought of using a bank?" His suspicions tripled as she poured a ring into her palm.

Slender fingers closed over the gold stone. Long lashes fluttered closed. "Thank God. He didn't find it."

Cole slowed on the causeway. Fishermen waited to launch at the boat ramp. Bait shop parking lots overflowed so he pulled over next to the seawall. As the waves crashed into the concrete, thousands of dollars fanned Lulu's lap. He didn't want to know about the money. Did he want to know about the ring? From his brief glimpse of the size of the yellow stone, it was either a fake or worth a small fortune. "Nice ring."

She turned her head and blue eyes flickered. "Thank you. My brother sent it to me. At least, that's what Granny said." She slid the ring on her finger and spun it around. "If Elliot had found it, he'd have sold it like everything else." She removed the ring and shoved it in her pocket.

His sweet Lulu deserved a better life than the one she'd obviously been living. She folded the bills in a wad and stuffed them in the other pocket of her worn jeans. Her shirt was missing a button, and the soles separated from her shoes.

Her flawless beauty blinded him as she faced him. "The bail

bondsman said I couldn't leave Alabama." Doubt clouded her eyes. "Since I don't have another option..."

Her chin lifted. "I'll go with you. So, take me home."

His heart hammered in his throat as he visualized the picture she painted. "We have to take care of two little problems first." He reached over and claimed her hand. Tingles of awareness heated his palm. "One, if we're going to live together, I should know your full name."

Amusement sparkled in her eyes. "Cynthia LouAnn McDuffie. My brother called me Lulu, but everyone else calls me Cindy."

"And two, we need to get married." His sentence hung on stagnant air.

Sweet, feminine laughter broke the silence. "Sorry, that's not gonna happen."

His Lulu wasn't what he expected.

"Don't get all huffy. You offered me a place to stay. I accepted. But I intend to enjoy every day of my freedom, so just drop me off at the next hotel."

His stomach clinched. He couldn't lose her. "I can't leave you alone. There are sick people in this world."

Her gaze focused somewhere beyond the concrete wall, toward the choppy water. "I couldn't have escaped Elliot without your help, and I thank you. But I've been living on my own since I was fifteen. I can take care of myself."

He leaned close and claimed her hand. To his delight, she didn't shrink away. "Where do you *want* to go? Anywhere in the world. I'll take you there."

Her long lashes fluttered against creamy skin, shutting out the window to her soul. He suppressed the urge to hold her as she leaned into the headrest. Her full lips parted. "Geography doesn't matter. I want to sleep in peace and not wonder who's picking my locks from the other room. I want friends who aren't thieves. I want to eat until I'm full. I want fresh air and sunshine."

Her lips turned upward. "One night in Metro, some of the inmates started a ruckus. To punish them, the jailer turned off the electricity breakers." Her body shuddered. "I've never experienced total darkness until then, and I never want to repeat it. Grown men cried in the night. Without the a/c, we couldn't breathe. It was so hot. I almost lost my mind, until I remembered that Joni said God loved me. I prayed. There on my cot, I squeezed my eyes shut and saw a beautiful light. In the middle of a stone building with no windows, a breeze blew through my cell and wrapped around me."

Tears slipped down her cheek as she described God's presence.

"I don't know if I had a heat stroke and hallucinated or what, but no drug on earth brings a high like that. I want to experience it again." Her head turned toward him and her blue eyes captured his. "The next morning, I called Joni. Two months later, I was released." Her gaze dove toward the floor. She tugged her hand free. "You must think I'm crazy for craving a feeling." White knuckles gripped her shirttail.

"God's presence is real and it's very addicting. But even when you don't feel Him, He's there."

Her stomach growled and broke the heavy tension in the air. "Sorry."

James's earlier reminder about Sara gave Cole a new purpose. He pulled onto the causeway and drove toward the Eastern Shore. "I know a place you might like to stay. My friend has an apartment available. I have to warn you though it's above her garage. The bedroom is nothing more than a corner, and it takes up half the living space."

Lulu turned toward him. "Does it have a kitchen?"

Cole laughed. "Yeah, but it's more of a kitchenette."

"How much is the rent?"

He glanced her way. Sara's apartment was a God-send. "I don't know. Let's find out?" Keeping one eye on the traffic, he reached for his phone. Sara was happy to show them the apartment but she asked that they wait until nine. He disconnected and relayed the message to Cindy.

Her brows furrowed as she shifted in her seat. "That gives us time to stop by a thrift store. I don't want to meet my potential landlord in rags."

Her clothes were a little worn, but… "If you need clothes, the mall opens at nine. I can call Sara back and delay the appointment?"

"No that's okay. Is there a Walmart around here?"

§©CR

How much would the apartment cost? Cindy didn't get her hopes up. Even with her life's savings, she would never be able to afford a place on the ritzy Eastern Shore. Too bad, because no one from her past would find her amid the private yacht clubs and pricey boutiques.

Cole had said he lived on his boat. She had a feeling it wasn't a dilapidated old shrimper.

Hedged trees lined the highway and multi-colored flowers decorated the median. Cindy swallowed and surveyed her surroundings. Three law books, a leather briefcase, and a tie lay scattered on the backseat. Her throat tightened and sucked the moisture out of her mouth, leaving a stale taste. She covered her face with both hands and groaned.

He braked for a red light. "What's wrong?"

"You're a law student?" She peeked between her fingers, and his triumphant grin sent shivers of dread down her spine.

"No. I passed the bar last year."

It was worse than she thought. "I've been indicted on two felony charges. An attorney can't be friends with me."

Cole turned into a Walmart parking lot. The short sign hadn't been visible from the road. "Don't be silly. I'm in corporate law, not criminal. Besides, I doubt anyone will recognize you here."

He parked near the grocery entrance. "There's a McD's in here. We'll grab a bite to eat, and then you can shop for the basic necessities."

After breakfast, they entered the attached store.

He walked beside her until they reached the ladies lingerie department. His cheeks turned bright red. "I'll be in the electronics. What's your number and I'll call when I'm done?"

"Phones aren't allowed in jail. No biggie since my old one was a prepaid. I figured I'd buy another one later." She tossed the cheapest underwear her size into the cart.

A cough came from the center aisle where Cole averted his gaze. "I'll be back." Long legs carried him away from her.

"Wait." She swallowed as he stopped and turned. "After I find some jeans, I'll be in the pharmacy. I need a toothbrush."

His lips curled into a deep smile. "I'll meet you there."

Being alone never bothered her, so why did she worry they'd become separated? The buggy wheels clicked against the bare floor as she chose two complete outfits and then the basic toiletries.

As she waited in the checkout line, a lady in the next lane glanced at Cindy's ragged shirt hem and frowned.

"Excuse me." A touch landed on her shoulder as Cole squeezed around her to the front of the buggy. He grabbed handfuls of clothes and dropped them on the conveyor belt. His face glowed as he transferred the undergarments.

Cindy hid her smile as the cashier totaled the purchases.

Cole reached for his wallet, but Cindy stopped his hand. "Don't even think about it, unless you're in the habit of buying panties?"

Every guy she knew would've made a raunchy comment and asked her to model them. But Cole averted his scarlet gaze and placed the bagged items in the cart.

Why did he hide his desires? A man who looked as good as Cole probably had several choices in women. If she was interested in that sort of thing, she'd be first in line.

"Is there a truck-stop around here, where I can take a shower and change?"

His head tilted at an odd angle. "I-I don't think so."

"No problem. I'll change in the bathroom." She grabbed the receipt, a pair of jeans, and a shirt. After she changed, she found Cole waiting near the customer service desk. She looped her arm through his and snuggled against his shoulder as he pushed the buggy outside. "I've discovered your kryptonite."

One masculine brow arched as he stopped at the trunk.

She watched him closely, waiting to see his face light up. "You're afraid of satin and lace."

The beautiful glow appeared, but this time he didn't look away. His eyes darkened and his gaze burned a path down her body and slowly back up again. "I'm not afraid." Heat flooded her own face as his voice caressed her battered soul and stirred an unfamiliar longing in her heart. "But those thoughts and images have no place in my mind unless you're willing to stand before a preacher and say, 'I do.'"

Surely he was joking about the preacher, but for once, she'd met a man who didn't think she should fall naked at his feet. Or one that would force her there if she dared to object. Time would tell if he was for real. "Thank you." Breaking away from his invisible hold, she got in the car and waited.

Chapter Three

Forgive my lustful thoughts, Lord. Cole silently prayed as he drove to Sara's. He glanced across the seat at Cindy. He feared the spectacle he'd made of himself would create an insurmountable distance between them, but for some reason the opposite happened. Instead of pressing against the door, she now propped her arm on the middle console. Her eyes had lost that hard suspicious edge as she studied him. If she knew his thoughts, she wouldn't feel so secure, but how could she not know?

He turned into an azalea-lined driveway and parked in front of Mark and Sara's garage. "We're here. The apartment stairs are in the backyard."

She hadn't waited for him to open her door while he removed his coat and draped it across the backseat. Instead she stood beside the car. Her quick hand snatched a forgotten tag off the sleeve of her shirt as she shifted in her old tennis shoes.

"You're beautiful."

Blue eyes blinked in surprise. Hadn't anyone ever complimented her before? He circled the car to her side and motioned her around the garage. Thick, green foliage from Sara's flower garden towered above the path, which wasn't wide enough for both of them, so he let Cindy go first. She paused and stared. Around her shoulders, Sara's seven-year-old son splashed into the pool. "That's Andrew. Go ahead." Cindy didn't budge so he nudged her lower back. "Go on."

She whirled around, and her forearms pressed against his shirt. "What if she doesn't like me? What if she doesn't want to let me stay here but she does because of you? What if—"

He pressed a finger against her soft lips silencing her protests. Small hands gripped his wrist as he stared into the wonder of her eyes. Her fear overrode his desire for a kiss.

Wrapping her in his arms, he held her near his heart.

Minutes passed before she relaxed against his chest. "I'm okay now. It was just a moment's panic."

He released her and turned her by the shoulders, grateful she couldn't see his face. His protective instincts would send her running. His hands trailed off her shoulders and down her arms. Linking their fingers together, he didn't let go as she walked forward. Until they came to the fence. He released one hand, reached around her, and opened the creaky gate.

"Cole." Andrew spotted them first. "Swim with me."

"Sorry, buddy. Can't today. Maybe next time."

Sara's chair faced the pool. Her back was to them. She rose from the cushioned wicker and turned to her visitors. "Co—" Her greeting halted and her mouth dropped open. Wide eyes flickered from their joined hands to Cindy's face. "You're a girl."

Cindy's gaze flew to his. He squeezed her hand for reassurance as it stiffened in his palm. Her chin lifted. "Is that a problem?"

"Oh no." Sara smoothed the front of her sundress. "No problem. I'm a little surprised, that's all. Cole's never brought a girl around, and I assumed his friend was a colleague. When he called this morning, I thought that…"

Cole cleared his throat. "Sara, this is my friend, Cindy McDuffie. Cindy, this is Sara Doyle, who also happens to be the assistant pastor's wife. If you move here, you won't have to worry about having thieves for neighbors."

Cindy scowled and tilted her head. "Cole."

"Never mind him." Sara pulled her into a quick hug.

Cindy's eyes widened and then narrowed. Had her past life held so little affection that a friendly 'hello' put her on guard? He vowed then to hug her at least once every day for the rest of his life.

Sara smiled. "Come on up. I'm airing the apartment. Cole can watch Andrew while I show you around."

The stairs were only twenty feet away, but he didn't want Cindy to feel abandoned. He touched her arm. "Do you need me to go with you?"

Cindy shook her head as Sara answered, "You can't hold her hand forever."

ഇൻരു

Never mind the beautiful couch or glistening pool table. The studio apartment had central air conditioning. Cindy loved the small galley kitchen with its electric stove squeezed next to a midsized refrigerator. A painted screen separated the twin bed from the living area. The wood panels appeared Oriental, but she wasn't certain.

Sara opened the only interior door, revealing a huge tub in a small bathroom. "There's no stand-up shower, but there is an adapter under the sink for the faucet."

"Can you use bubble bath with the whirlpool jets?" Cindy longed to soak for hours.

Sara laughed. "A girl after my own heart. Yes, but don't use too much or you'll have a mess."

Cindy forced herself away from the tub and crossed the room to look out one of the two windows. Sara's house sat on a hill in a secluded subdivision. Through the many oak limbs, Cindy glimpsed a body of water several streets over. Mobile Bay? She loved this tiny apartment, but she could never afford a place like this. "How much is the rent?"

Sara patted the sofa beside her. "Before the business side of things, let's sit and chat."

Cindy dragged her feet across the plush carpet and perched on the edge of the leather cushions.

Sara spread her hands. "Does the apartment suit you?"

"I'm a little concerned about the distance to the store, but the view is worth a short walk. How much is it?"

"We'll talk about that in a minute. Where are you from?"

Cindy hesitated. "Houston S—"

A ring blared from Sara's dress pocket, cutting off Cindy's answer. "Sorry for the interruption." Sara took out a phone and pressed the screen. "Hello, my love."

Cindy detected a male voice on the opposite end of the call, but couldn't make out his words.

Sara stood and crossed the room as she spoke into the phone. "I'm showing the apartment. Cole recommended a friend. Cindy's from Houston." Sara's joyous laughter filled the room. "*She* is. I'll call you back when I'm done." She laughed again. "Me, too." She pocketed her phone. "That was my husband. Mark's anxious to meet you. We've always wanted to visit Texas. I guess you met Cole in school? Well, it doesn't matter. When do you want to move in?"

Cindy couldn't let her believe a lie. "There's been a misunderstanding. I didn't go to college with Cole." Intimidated by Sara's frown, Cindy stood. "I didn't go to college at all." She hadn't graduated high school either, but she kept that secret.

Sara reached for Cindy's hand. "My brother doesn't have a degree, but I love him anyway. Do you need help moving?"

"How much is the rent?"

"Oh. Well…" Sara shrugged. "We're not in this for the money. My brother renovated this empty space. It's a shame to waste it. We thought Cole was tired of driving to the boat, and offered it to him, but… If you need a place to live, we have one. That's all there is to it."

"How much?"

"How about…$400 a month. All utilities included." Sara dipped her head. "Is that too much?"

The amount was about five times less than what she should ask for. "No. I'll take the apartment. And thank you."

"You're welcome." Sara reached out and Cindy endured a second awkward hug.

Stepping back, Cindy dug in her pocket and separated four bills. Sara's gasp announced Cindy's mistake. Never let anyone know you have money. But surely Sara didn't need to steal her meager savings.

"Goodness, why on earth do you have that much cash?"

Cindy shifted her weight from one foot to the other. "I, uh… liquidated some assets before moving here." She swallowed the lump in her throat under Sara's suspicious stare.

"If you don't mind my asking, why haven't you already made other living arrangements?"

"Oh. Um. That's because…" She searched for an acceptable excuse that wouldn't be a complete lie. "Cole." It really was his fault. "I had planned to live somewhere else, but he talked me into moving here."

Sara tilted her head, and slowly the corners of her mouth curled. "I saw the way he looked at you. I imagine he was very persuasive."

The mention of Cole's name brought a smile to her lips. She remembered his persistence when he offered her a ride. Was that this morning? It seemed like a lifetime ago. "He's like no man I've ever known." She shook the longing aside. "But this move is temporary. I have somewhere else to be in three months."

"The apartment's yours for however long you need it." Sara surveyed the small living space. "I hope there is enough room for your things."

"Plenty. I only have what I bought this morning."

Sara spun on her heel and tilted her head. "What?"

Cindy bit her lip. "Unfortunately, most of my things were… stolen." Not exactly a lie.

"You poor thing." Sara laughed. "Last year on a trip to the mountains, my luggage was lost. By the time the airlines located them a month later, I'd already replaced everything." She glanced at Cindy's new clothes and sighed. "Although you're a bit taller and I'm a mite rounder, if you need to borrow anything, I don't mind you raiding my closet."

Cindy squashed the guilt at allowing Sara to believe yet another lie. "Thank you, but I need a new wardrobe anyway."

Sara laughed again. "Don't we all." She stood and held out a key. "You can move in as soon as you want."

"Cole picked me up this morning. I haven't checked into a hotel yet. Is today too soon?"

Sara turned toward the door. "Not at all, dear. About the pool, feel free to use it, but I do ask that you wear modest swimming apparel, and use a wrap whenever you aren't in the water."

Cindy followed her down the blue wooden stairs. The pool wouldn't be a problem. On the rare occasions she'd gone swimming, she'd worn cut-offs and a T-shirt. She'd never owned a swimsuit, modest or otherwise. These people were so different. Maybe she shouldn't stay here.

Cole stood by the pool. A huge wet spot outlined his gray shirtfront. "Well? What did you think?" The late morning sun brought out the silver in his eyes.

She wanted to believe in the hope she read in them.

She held out her hand, palm up. "I need the keys so I can bring my things in."

His smile lightened her heavy heart. "I'll help." She shouldn't have been surprised at his offer. She could get used to having him around. He turned to Sara. "Thank you."

Sara held out a towel for her son. "You're welcome." She glanced at Cindy. "Let me know if you need anything."

Cindy thanked her again. This was really happening. A place of her own. She followed Cole down the path. Her steps grew lighter and faster. She needed some sheets for the pillow-topped mattress and some scented candles for the bathroom like Joni had. A foreign giggle escaped her as she ran the rest of the way to the BMW. Behind her, Cole laughed and heavy footfalls gave chase. As she circled the trunk, he caught her around the waist and lifted her off her feet. Laughter freed her arms to embrace him. She held tight to this newfound freedom and never wanted to let go.

A gentle breeze blew. Cindy closed her eyes and silently thanked God for giving her a safe place to live. Cole whispered near her ear, "Thank you, Jesus, for my sweet Lulu." His hands folded tight against her back, but he didn't grab and grope with expectations.

If her new apartment didn't wait for her, she'd be content to stay in his arms forever. "I've figured out who you really are." She leaned back against his arm. "You're my guardian angel."

His perfect lips curled. "I'd like to think that I'm God's messenger, but if you look behind me, you won't see any wings." His gaze lingered on her lips and she waited for his kiss. "I'm sorry to disappoint you, but I'm just a man." He released her and reached in his pocket. Using the keyless entry, he opened the trunk.

The one guy she wouldn't mind kissing was a gentleman.

He cleared his throat and lifted out several bags.

She closed the trunk and followed him down the path. "I wished I'd have bought a few groceries. How far is the nearest market?" She'd wait until evening temperatures cooled the humid air. That would make the walk bearable.

"Couple of blocks. We'll go after we unpack your things."

She stumbled on the bottom step. We? Was he planning on

staying in the apartment? She liked having him around and enjoyed his hugs, but she didn't want to share the twin bed.

Sara said he was tired of living on the boat, and he did find this place. She should let him stay. But there was no door to the bedroom. That meant no sturdy lock. Cole wasn't like other guys. At least she hoped he wasn't. He could sleep on the couch. Once up the stairs, she entered the kitchen and opened a cabinet. "Look. There're dishes in here."

He leaned around her and frowned. "We'll buy you a matching set later. For now, I'll bring in the rest of the bags."

She leaned against the pool table and soaked in the apartment. *Thank you, Jesus.*

Cole tapped the door with his foot. She let him in and noted the phone pressed between his shoulder and ear. "I'll have her call you. Everything's fine." He rolled in a small suitcase and dropped the plastic bags on the table. "She's fine. Quit worrying. It won't kill me to stay on the boat for a while longer." He propped the suitcase against the door, placed the bags on the pool table, and ended the call. "Joni wants you to call her. She thinks I've abducted you for nefarious reasons."

"I forgot to buy a phone." She pointed to the suitcase. If he wasn't staying here, why did he bring that up? "What's in there?"

"Oh." His cheeks reddened. "I hope you don't mind if I change out of this wet shirt."

"Go ahead." Relieved and at the same time disappointed, she turned to the bags he'd brought in, and found the body wash and shampoo. Would it be rude to disappear into the tub now? The other bags held her new clothes. She wanted to change before shopping again. "Cole?" Where was he?

"One minute." His voice came from the bedroom corner.

Curious, she stepped around the screen. "Why are you hiding back here?"

He scrambled and clutched his wet shirt to his bare chest. "Lulu."

One...two...three. His face turned crimson. She shrugged and pretended not to notice his modesty. "What?"

"You said you didn't mind if I changed."

Reclining against the oak headboard, she inspected what little she could see of him, which wasn't much. "I don't mind."

He lifted his clean shirt and escaped into the bathroom. The view of his sculptured back and shoulders along with the brief glimpse of his chest was worth his disapproving frown.

A few seconds passed.

The bathroom door opened.

Cole's gaze caressed her, but then he shook his head and walked into the living area.

The soft bed invited her to relax, but she shoved off and found Cole sitting on the couch. She smiled. Her couch.

A drumroll broke the silence. Cole stood and answered his phone. "Hi, Dad." He rubbed a hand over his brow. "I'm sorry. I completely forgot the meeting. I know. I'll be there in twenty-five minutes." He disconnected and turned to Cindy. "I'm needed at the office."

"I understand. Thanks for your help." She stretched on her toes and brushed her lips against his cheek.

Despite the urgency in his voice during the call, he froze. Like the wind after a brisk afternoon rain shower, he smelled clean and fresh.

"Knock, knock." In the open door, Sara held a stack of towels and washrags.

Cindy stepped away from Cole.

"I'm sorry to interrupt." The sparkle in Sara's eyes said differently. "I've brought bed linens and bathroom towels. These should do until you purchase your own colors."

"Oh, thank you so much. I can't wait to soak in the tub." A soft groan came from behind her. She turned.

Cole sucked in a breath. "I'll see you in a few hours." In a blur, he whirled around and disappeared out the door. His suitcase clunked down the stairs behind him.

&⊃⊂&

The meeting endured for one hundred, twenty-three minutes and eight seconds. Cole swiped his phone screen and stood.

What was Lulu doing now? Was she thinking of him? She needed a phone. He could call Sara, but longing to hear Lulu's sweet voice wasn't exactly an emergency. In the previous weeks, his cell provider had texted several promotions for adding a line. Cole could buy her a phone, but would she accept it as a gift?

"Son." His father blocked the exit. "I want to see you in my office."

All eyes flickered toward him. He suppressed the urge to ignore the summons and return to Cindy's apartment. Not wanting to cause a scene in front of his dad's law partners, Cole nodded his consent.

Dusk had fallen by the time he knocked on her door.

"Cole." Her smile erased the weary hours spent away from her. "Come and look what I found buried in the cabinet above the refrigerator." She opened the door and against his better judgment he walked in.

Stripes and solids were scattered across the pool table. A cue stick rested on the rail. A game was in progress. "You play nineball?"

Delicate shoulders shrugged. "It's been a while. I'm a little rusty, but I'm slowly remembering the game."

During his college years, he'd spent a lot of time playing with the billiard club. The phone he'd purchased was in his car. This was the perfect way to make her accept it. "Care to make a wager?" He didn't gamble, but he was determined to lose. "Loser buys dinner and pays a forfeit."

Her smile grew as she racked the balls. "You're on."

₮₧

Cindy bit back spontaneous laughter as she sank the nine ball for the fourth time. "I win, again." She couldn't remember ever having this much fun. And to think they'd played without a roll of quarters or a pack of straws to fill the coin slots of the pay-per-game tables she was used to.

Cole swallowed a bite of pizza and grinned. "And I was worried about winning. I've been hustled. You understated your abilities and now I have to pay the price."

If he was anyone else, she'd gladly collect her winnings. But he'd already ordered and paid for the pizza. "I can't take your money."

He'd reached for the door. "Nonsense, I have something in my car that's just what you need."

While he was downstairs, Cindy ate another slice of pizza. Cole had offered to help however she needed him. Her plans to walk to the shopping center and buy a prepaid was interrupted by his visit, but she needed to call Joni and let her friend know that she was okay.

The door opened and Cole walked in holding a small plastic bag in one hand and his phone in the other.

Cindy sucked in a breath of courage. "Can I borrow your phone?"

"No."

She withdrew her hand and hid it behind her back. Joni would be worried, but Cindy wouldn't beg. The call could wait until after he left. Then she'd walk to the nearest store.

Cole opened the bag and winked. "You can use your own." His gaze caressed her. "Do you know her number?"

She shoved off the pool table as Cole opened a small white box. "What are you doing?"

"Programming your new phone. I bought this earlier today when I wanted to call you."

As much as she appreciated his thoughtfulness, she couldn't accept it. That brand cost a fortune. "Where I come from, nothing is free. Why did you buy that?"

He flashed his little boy grin. "I didn't say it was free. I bought it. So it cost me something. As for you..." He extended the hand holding the phone. "I programmed my number in there. You have to call or text when you need me. Preferably, once a day."

His smile was genuine. Was his offer? She shouldn't accept such an expensive gift from a stranger. But he was a friend. The sizzle that flew from his hand to hers couldn't be ignored, and she glanced into his serious eyes. "What kind of plan do I have?"

His lips twitched. "Unlimited."

ॐ

The excitement on Cindy's face added new depth to her beauty Saturday night.

Cole focused on the sailfish tacked to the rustic wall behind her as she told Joni about her new apartment and the things she'd bought while they'd shopped today. Well...she gawked at the price tags and he enjoyed her company.

James swirled the ice in his sweet tea, creating a whirlpool that threatened to spill. "Sara's my sister."

Cindy dropped her fork into her coleslaw. "You're the brother that installed the tub?"

Joni leaned back in her chair and rubbed her gently rounded stomach. "Oh, the tub." She frowned at James. "I never got the opportunity to soak in it. Did you use aromatherapy candles?"

"No, but..." A hint of a smile tugged at Cindy's lips. "...after months of showering in a mold infested stall, I'm surprised Cole could drag me out of there."

James choked on his tartar sauce, and for once Joni was speechless. A vision of Cindy floating in bubbles, swam in Cole's wicked mind. James punched him in the shoulder. "Do we need to step outside?"

"I wasn't there. I was—" Cole swallowed the crab claw stuck in his throat and covered his smile with his napkin.

Cindy gawked at James. "You're defending my honor? Even though you know better than anyone at this table what a horrible person I am?"

James eyed Cole as he answered. "Used to be." Then he turned to Cindy. "If Jesus set me free from the guilt of sin, He did the same for you. What you do now is what matters."

Cindy lifted her chin. "Does it bother you that I rented your sister's apartment? Or that Cole and I are friends?"

James leaned back in his chair. "I'm glad the apartment is going to good use. But as far as Cole is concerned..." He turned and glared at Cole. "How good of friends can you be after two days?"

The barest of smiles lit Cindy's face. "Excuse me." She stood, and likewise Joni came to her feet. Using the unspoken language of women, they walked toward the restrooms.

Cole waited until they were out of hearing. "Cindy's my Lulu."

James's laughter ended abruptly when Cole didn't blink. He rubbed a hand down the side of his face. "That's absurd. Lulu is an innocent promise of God." An agitated hand waved in the air. "And Cindy is..."

"One and the same." Cole folded his napkin beside his plate.

James leaned across the table and whispered, "She was a drug dealer. She has two felony indictments against her.'"

Cole clenched his jaw and hid his temper. "And because she's so bad, she's beyond redemption?"

"No." James's shoulders rose. "Before I met Joni, I tried to help Kathy, but even Jesus can't save someone who doesn't want to be saved." James guzzled his tea, and then rubbed a hand down his face. "Actually, Cindy rescued Isaac once. Are you sure this isn't a result of Thursday's appointment?" He leaned across the table and lowered his voice. "I know the doctor scared you, maybe if you talked to your dad about—"

"No." Cole straightened in his chair. "One thing has nothing to do with the other. I confess that I doubted God, but I prayed. And then there she was."

The women's appearance ended the awkward discussion. The talk turned to the songs planned for morning worship.

Cindy's eyes narrowed as her brow arched. "You play the drums?"

Joni reclaimed Cindy's attention. "So, you'll come to church in the morning?"

Cole's heart swelled when she looked to him for the answer. He reached under the table and squeezed her hand. "Church is a good place to find that feeling you told me about yesterday."

Her fingers weaved with his. "Have you felt it there?"

"Many times." He drowned in the waves of fear and hope battling in her eyes.

Her lashes fluttered and then spread like butterfly wings taking flight. "I'll go with you."

James cleared his throat as Joni's gaze darted from Cole to Cindy. "What feeling are you talking about?"

Cole leaned back in his chair and listened to Cindy's musical voice as she told their friends about experiencing God's presence in the dark jail.

Joni propped her chin in her hand. "I can't wait until tomorrow morning's service."

Cindy's brows arched. "Why?"

Joni glanced at James. Cole knew it was time to say goodnight as his friend winked at his wife and said, "Because, God always keeps his promises."

Chapter Four

Why, today of all days, did her hair rebel against the humidity? Normally, a ponytail would solve the problem, but not today. This was Cindy's first visit to Cole's church. She wet her hands, and using the full length mirror in the church bathroom, she threaded moisture through her frizzed hair.

The door swung open.

A pretty girl about Cole's age entered. Blond curls were artfully arranged atop her head. She stepped closer. Her complexion was flawless. "Good morning."

The girl placed a large purse on the counter and unzipped the top. "My hair never cooperates on Sunday mornings. I think it keeps a calendar and dooms me on the important days."

Cindy ran her brush through her now-damp tendrils as the girl repined perfect hair. What was in all those spray cans and bottles? If Cindy used them, would her hair shine as the girl's did?

If Cole hadn't come to the church early to pray and if he had driven this morning instead of Joni, she could have talked him into stopping for the hairspray she'd forgotten to purchase yesterday.

When they arrived, Joni had dashed into the church, but Cindy asked for directions to the bathroom. She needed to summon the courage to face Cole.

What if he'd changed his mind last night? What if he didn't want to be her friend? What if he regretted giving her a ride and helping her find an apartment?

Was that the real reason he'd sent Joni?

The girl smiled in the mirror. "I'm Rachel. You're welcome to borrow this."

Cindy took the offered can. Her hair must really look bad if a stranger was offering to help.

"Thank you. I'm Cindy. I need to make a good impression, and my hair poofed."

Rachel laughed. "I love the color. Turn around. I'll fix it."

Other than her few trips to the free cosmetology school, no one had ever fixed her hair before. Cindy endured the awkward silence as Rachel worked a miracle. Then she choked on the fumes as Rachel emptied half a can of hairspray over Cindy's head. "There. Beautiful."

Cindy's hair looked better than it ever had. She needed to remember Rachel's technique. "Thank you. I don't know how you did it, but it looks pretty good."

An older lady stepped into the bathroom and spoke to Rachel, who had turned the spray to her own head. "Don't worry, dear. You look gorgeous as usual."

Rachel packed her bottles of hair potions into her oversized purse. "Tell that to your son."

Cindy trashed a paper towel as the elder woman patted the girl's hand. "He's been frowning at the side door that leads in here for several minutes. I wondered why. Now that I see you, I know. It may take him a while to show his affection, but it's obvious to everyone in church that you belong together."

In the mirror, the girl preened. "Thank you for the encouragement, Mrs. Maxwell. If he doesn't propose soon, I'll have to change the date, and I'll lose another wedding deposit."

Mrs. Maxwell? Cindy's heartbeat stalled in her chest. Cole's mother? The older woman frowned at the short hem of Cindy's borrowed dress. She wanted Cole to marry Rachel? Rachel already had the date set? Cindy clamped her lips together and turned toward the door. In her haste, she bumped into the garbage can. The door swung closed behind her and she released a shaky breath. She had to get out of here.

Moving back the way she'd come, she passed a table with Christian literature. Music came from the inner section of the church. Her frantic heart pounded with the rhythm of Cole's drums.

Should she leave? Rachel had been so nice to her.

Cole's previous text told her to sit in the second pew from the front on the far right side. He'd join her after the worship service.

She peeked through the crack between the double doors. It seemed as if all the rows except the one Cole had directed her to were occupied. Rachel and Cole's mother entered through a side door. The girl slid in and sat in the middle of the once empty pew. From the stage, Cole frowned at Rachel, and then glared at his mother on the other side of the church.

No way could Cindy sit beside the girl destined to marry Cole, no matter how nice she was. Cindy had been looked down on and cast aside all her life, but somehow she'd thought church would be different. How could she sit with Cole when everyone knew she wasn't good enough for him? When the whole church wanted him and Rachel to be together? Cindy couldn't, but she wouldn't leave without saying goodbye either.

She inhaled every ounce of courage she possessed, but her feet refused to move. A family with three small children entered the foyer behind Cindy. She quickly stepped aside.

The young mother smiled. Cindy stumbled as she found herself locked in a friendly embrace. "It's nice to have you here."

"There isn't room for me." She turned to go, but the lady tugged on her hand.

"Nonsense. My name is Andrea. This is my husband Derek. You can sit with us. We have plenty of room."

Cindy nodded and followed the whirlwind of a family into a pew four rows from the back. She'd stay for the service, but only to tell Cole goodbye. An elderly couple slid down to make room.

The red carpet had tiny flecks of gold, something she hadn't noticed before. The cushioned pew was comfortable. Straightening the back of her borrowed skirt so it wouldn't wrinkle, she kept her arm inside the wooden armrest. Why didn't she have the foresight to walk in first? Now, curious eyes darted her way. Did everyone know she didn't belong?

Was Cole disappointed she hadn't sat in his pew? Or relieved? Was he even aware of her presence? Her eyes lifted to the front. He smiled from behind a large set of pearl drums. Her heart lightened. He wasn't mad.

Joni's angelic voice sang of amazing grace. Cindy shouldn't be surprised. Everything about her new friend was perfect. And James sounded good too. Never would she have believed it two years ago, when he banged on her door looking for Isaac.

Images from her past overshadowed the upbeat music. Bet Rachel didn't have a clue about the sin in the world, much less, been a part of it.

A little girl from the whirlwind family toddled close. A purple-and-yellow bow pinned brown curls away from her sweet face. Cindy never had a mother to fuss over her hair. *God, why couldn't I have been born into a family like this?* Down the pew, the father cradled an infant in one arm and raised the other hand high in the air, while the mother smoothed the ruffles on the dress of another girl slightly older than the toddler. All were standing. Cindy stood too. Her view of Cole was blocked by scores of people between them.

Closing her eyes, she listened to the beat of his drums. He was good, like every part of him. No matter how much she wanted the circumstances to change, she would never be enough. After church, she'd thank him for all his help and catch a bus out of town. She'd go north. Move to a big city with a transit system. Birmingham or Huntsville.

The music trailed off, and a man wearing a suit prayed into a microphone. Cindy bowed her head along with everyone else. After the "Amen," he added, "You may be seated."

The toddler wandered closer, and Cindy sat on the end of the pew to avoid the little girl. Her arm pressed against the wood. The musicians left the stage and entered the second row. Except Cole.

Her heart caught. He followed the others, but lifted a Bible from the seat and reversed his steps toward the stage. He crossed the church in front of the middle rows. His steel, gray eyes held hers as he walked up the left aisle with deliberate strides. He was the last man standing. Every head turned and followed him to her side. She held her breath as long arms reached over and lifted the toddler.

Cindy scooted down the bench, giving him room to sit beside her. The little girl patted his cheek. "Dole." She snuggled against his shoulder. A thumb went into her mouth and her eyes drooped.

The preacher's voice directed all eyes back to him. Cole leaned near and whispered, "I'm sorry. I should've met you at the door."

His thigh pressed against hers in the crowded pew. One arm rested on the wood behind her. The concern in his eyes revoked her plans for goodbye. She wanted to be by his side. It didn't matter if she wasn't worthy.

"Lulu? What's wrong?"

A huge weight lifted from her shoulders. Jealous of the little girl in his arms, she briefly pressed her head against his muscled arm. "It doesn't matter."

ℴℴℴ

"The devil wants to change the glory of God into clouds of gloom." The pastor paced in front of the pulpit as he preached.

Cole wondered what Cindy thought of the sermon.

Her head turned and followed the pastor's every step as he continued. "He'll use the guilt of your past to steal God's gifts of today. You think you've had a rough life? What about Paul? Five times he received thirty-nine lashes with a whip. He was beaten with rods three times. Stoned once. Shipwrecked on three different occasions. Endangered! Naked! Hungry!"

Cindy whispered to Cole. "Is that true? Did someone survive all that?"

It was strange sitting this far back in the rows, but Cole was glad Cindy's presence didn't hinder him from getting into the service. At his nod, she refocused on the preacher's words.

"If the devil did this to such a great man of God, he will certainly do it to you."

Like many others, Cole added his "Amen" to the preaching.

The pastor paused, and tear-filled eyes pleaded with his congregation. "Now that you know the enemy's intentions, the choice is yours. Are you gonna let the devil steal what God has given you? Or will you stay and cling to your blessings?"

Cindy stood to her feet with the rest of the saints. "Can we go pray now?"

He smiled at her eagerness. "Yes, we can go pray." Cole gently laid the sleeping toddler on the pew and followed Cindy to the front.

At the altar, he knelt to pray but peeked at Cindy. Joni and Sara were on her other side. He focused on God and thanked Him for bringing Lulu into his life. "Forgive me, Lord, for all the times I wanted to give up. Forgive me for doubting Your promise. Bless her, Lord. Let her feel Your presence like she's never felt it before. Fill the hunger inside her. Fill her with Your power…"

A rough hand shoved his shoulder, rousing him from his prayerful stupor. James grinned and nodded to the right. "You'll never believe it."

Several ladies surrounded Cindy. He heard several of them pray in the Spirit. "Thank you, Jesus. She's experiencing God's glory."

"It's more than that." James tugged him toward the women. "Listen."

A hush fell over the crowd. Expectancy filled his heart in the seconds that followed. The air grew heavy. And then he heard angelic tongues spoken with Cindy's voice. Cole pushed his way through the crowd of women to her side. Never had he heard a more beautiful sound. Joy burst from deep within him, and he couldn't be still. He paced the front with both arms aimed toward the heavens. He praised God with all his soul. His feet grew wings and wind rushed passed. Promises and dreams from long ago emerged. The years of waiting evaporated in the midst of God's glory.

A voice strong and sure echoed through his soul. *Rejoice in the wife of your youth.*

Energy surged through him, and his feet moved faster until he ran with his full strength. He circled the inside of the sanctuary once, and James joined in his celebration. The house burst with praise. Phillip leapt off the platform and made a victory lap with them.

Cole caught his breath in front of the communion table. James grabbed him by the shoulders and laughed. "God's promises are real! They are real!"

Cole's knees buckled in awe of his Great God. He collapsed onto the carpet, thanking his Savior for the wonderful gift he'd received this morning.

Time ceased to exist. He blinked as the light shifted and the chandelier focused. The euphoric aftereffects of God's glory lifted slowly. The floor vibrated as the door opened and closed several times. A swish of fabric brushed his hand.

Movement turned his head to the right.

Cindy's beautiful face stared at him from the platform step. Her chin propped in her hand and her lips turned into the brightest smile he'd ever seen. "That was the most amazing thing that's ever happened to me."

Joy bubbled in his throat and escaped in a chuckle.

"That was a new kind of high, but I loved it. You felt it too?"

"Yes." He struggled to catch his breath. "Give me a minute."

"You're still coming down, aren't you?"

He leaned against the platform next to her. "I'm good." Few people lingered inside the sanctuary.

James and Joni waved from the first pew. "You hungry? Sara invited us to lunch."

Freshly empowered, Cole surged to his feet and held his hand out toward Cindy. She slipped her smaller one in his and whispered, "Can we stay here for a while longer?"

He understood what she wanted. "You can take God's presence with you."

Surprise illuminated her beauty.

"That's the best part." He turned to his friends. "But, I promised mother I'd be there for lunch. She's probably holding the meal for us."

Joni pressed her lips together, and he heard her mutter, "What a way to kill the Spirit." James nudged his wife's side, but she didn't flinch. In a louder voice she said, "We'll see ya'll back here tonight for Bible study, right?"

"Right."

Cindy was quiet as they descended the outside steps. He waited until they were alone in the car before asking, "Are you okay about lunching with my parents?"

Her smile never wavered. "I think after that experience I can face anything. Including your mother."

Her words reminded him of her decision not to sit with him. "What happened this morning? Did Mother say anything to you?"

"No." Cindy threaded her fingers through his.

He held tight to her hand as he drove the few blocks to his parents' mansion. A red Mercedes was parked in the circular drive.

Cole's stomach rolled and spewed out sarcasm. "Great, Rachel's here."

Cindy straightened in the seat and removed her hand from his. "You know what? I'd better go help Sara. Can you drop me off at the apartment and then come back for lunch?"

He shifted into park and turned toward her. Something definitely happened this morning. "You're not the type of coward that runs away. Tell me what happened."

Cindy sank into the seat. "I overheard your mother and Rachel talking in the bathroom."

Of all the people she could have met this morning, why Rachel and his mother? Imagining the subject of their conversation, he rubbed his forehead and bit back a groan. He had to put Cindy's mind to rest. "No matter what you heard this morning or what you may hear in the future, I've never wanted to marry anyone but you."

Her eyes rounded. "That's crazy. You've just met me."

"But I knew you were out there somewhere." He reclaimed her hand and lifted it to his lips.

Her gaze flickered to his and then trailed to his mouth. Her lips parted.

He didn't need a verbal invitation. Turning in his seat, he caressed her cheek, and then slowly leaned in. She met him halfway. His hand moved to the back of her head as her arm slid across the top of his shoulder. She tasted sweet and he hungered for more, but he wouldn't cheapen God's promise.

He ended the kiss and cradled her close to his heart. He blew out a breath as she trembled in his arms. From here on, he'd exercise extreme caution. The liberty to hold her, touch her, and love her made no sense. It was as if God had removed the restraints and said, "Here, she's yours." They definitely needed to marry soon. He kissed the top of her head and relaxed his hold. "Let's go eat."

80C3

Eyes targeted Cindy as Cole led her into the dining room. She gripped his hand as she took in the gilded mirror and the silver candlesticks on an elaborate buffet table behind Rachel. Cole stopped at the end of the table-for-eight and kissed Mrs. Maxwell's cheek.

From the opposite end of the table, his father spoke. "We were about to give up on you."

Cole pulled out the chair next to his father and tugged on Cindy's hand. She hesitated. The peach plate trimmed in gold and the many wine glasses were probably worth more than the entire contents of her tiny apartment.

The hand holding hers went to her shoulder. "Everyone, I'd like for you to meet a special friend of mine, Cindy." He nodded to his father. "Cindy, this is my dad."

Mr. Maxwell held out his hand and Cindy shook it. His welcoming smile put her at ease until Cole stepped behind her and turned her by the shoulders. "This is Rachel. She and Mom are forever working on some secret project."

Cindy didn't know what to say. "We met this morning."

Rachel's greeting was more of a snarl. "Yes, but you didn't tell me you knew Cole."

He then introduced her to his mother, Beverly. Cindy waited for a polite greeting.

None came.

Cole pushed her into the chair and then massaged her shoulders as if apologizing. When he was seated next to her, a maid appeared and exchanged the empty plates for full ones.

His father said a short blessing and then addressed Cole. "You should have told us you were bringing a friend."

His mother folded a linen napkin in her lap. "Although we would never turn anyone out, you need to warn us before you bring one of your little friends over."

Cindy mimicked Cole as he laid a napkin across his lap. The maid reached for her glass. "Tea, ma'am? Or do you prefer coke?"

"Tea's fine. Thank you." She didn't listen to the conversations around her as she concentrated on following Cole's movements. She didn't want to embarrass him by saying anything inappropriate, so she kept silent and focused on not spilling anything. She turned the fork in her hand and gulped at the fine silver marking. She tested the weight in her hand. Twenty dollars easy, not counting the antique value.

She mentally shook herself. She was here as a guest.

Mrs. Maxwell didn't need to trade the silverware for pills.

The fork cut through the tender meat. Chicken? She couldn't be certain with the sauce piled on the top. The delicious bite melted in her mouth.

Mrs. Maxwell's voice rose to a whine. "Cole, I wish you'd settle down and start a family. I'm not getting any younger, and neither are you and Rachel."

Cindy had missed something. She searched Cole's face for clues. He must have read her confusion. "Mom is forever trying to marry me off."

"Oh." Cindy knew this from the bathroom.

Across the table, Rachel dabbed at her mouth. "Thank God you didn't marry Michelle. She giggled entirely too much. And that cheap perfume choked anyone within five feet of her."

Once again Cole clarified. "She was a good friend and a better colleague. I'll introduce you someday. She lives in Montgomery. You'd like her. She always speaks her mind."

His mother glared from her end of the table. "Well, you have to marry someone. I want to be young enough to enjoy my grandchildren."

Cole lowered his glass and draped his arm on the back of Cindy's chair. "You don't have anything to worry about, Mom. I'm gonna marry my Lulu."

Cindy choked on the delicious green stuff. She swallowed several times and reached for her tea. Clumsy fingers slipped. She barely caught the glass with both hands before it spilled. She gulped the liquid, freeing the tightness in her throat.

Rachel laughed, but his mother clearly didn't like the joke. "Coleman Maxwell, I want real grandbabies. Not imaginary ones."

Mischief sparkled in his eyes. "You'll have real grandbabies. As soon as I convince Lulu to say yes."

Heat flamed Cindy's face. She couldn't look at him. What was he doing? And why wasn't anyone else worried about his statement?

She peeked at Rachel, who gloated as if she held a secret. "It's a family thing. You wouldn't understand." A graceful hand waved daintily.

Cindy flinched at Mr. Maxwell's touch.

He quickly removed his hand from her arm, and she hid her hands in her lap. "When Cole was a kid, he had an imaginary girlfriend, Lulu. He brought her home from school one day when he was about six. From then on, everywhere Cole went, Lulu went. For a while there, his mother and I were seriously worried, especially when he started requesting prayer for her at church."

Rachel added, "And through the years, Cole used the Lulu excuse to escape all relationships." She giggled. "More than one girl thought of changing her name. Personally, I think he's afraid of commitment." She tilted her head and smiled at Cole. "But the right girl will wait as long as it takes."

Cindy turned to find Cole's gaze locked on her. She pushed the words out of her dry throat. "You prayed for Lulu?"

Underneath the table, his hand covered hers. "Every day. I still do. Does that bother you?"

"It bothers *me*." Mrs. Maxwell threw her napkin on her plate. "My son is in love with his imaginary friend. And worse wants to marry her."

Cole's gentle touch found Cindy's ring finger and drew circles between her knuckles. "Does it bother you that I intend to marry Lulu?"

She drowned in his smile and she forgot the others. "I think you deserve more happiness than Lulu can give. She doesn't live in your world."

"Maybe not when I was six, but she's here now."

Chapter Five

"She's from Houston."

Cindy cringed inwardly as Joni raised both brows in response to Sara's statement. She couldn't let the ladies decorating the kitchen part of the church believe a lie. God didn't like liars, and Cindy didn't want to upset Him. He'd done too much for her. "Actually…"

"Where you're from doesn't matter." Joni grabbed her hand and squeezed. "I'm glad God brought you here. I wish he'd send James and me somewhere new for a fresh start."

"Poor thing." Sara stapled a cartoon cowboy and his twirling lasso onto the wall. "The airlines lost all of her luggage."

Cindy tugged her hand from Joni's and whispered, "Thank you."

Joni nodded to a bale of hay. "Help me move this over to the corral area."

Andrea nudged Joni out of the way. "No heavy lifting for expectant mothers."

Joni laughed and stepped aside. "You're as bad as James."

The square hay bale wasn't heavy. Cindy helped Andrea carry it across the room, away from nosy ears. Andrea kept her voice low. "We're almost done decorating for the kids crusade. Can I give you a ride home? My house is on the way to your apartment, and there's something I'd like you to help me with."

Wariness sprang up inside Cindy. "What kind of something?"

೮೦೦೪

Who knew there were so many different brands of hairspray? Cole slipped his phone from his pocket and called Cindy.

She answered before it rang. "Where are you? We're gonna be late."

"Did you know that there're at least fifty thousand varieties of hair products? Not to mention the variation in dispensers. What's your brand?"

"The one Rachel had was in a gold can."

At least five brands fit her description. "What's the name?"

"It don't remember. Grab whichever one is on sale. And hurry. Wait. Can you pick up some lotion? I'll pay you back when you get here."

"Anything for my sweet Lulu." He disconnected and searched the aisle. He could do eenie, meenie, miney, moe, but chances are he'd choose wrong. Or…? He flipped through his phone contacts and pressed the green button.

Rachel's voice was a little too cheery. "Cole, I'm so glad you called."

"What kind of hairspray do you use?"

The brand she named was in the front. He snatched a bottle and went in search of the lotion. "Thank you."

Before he could disconnect, she called out, "That's all you wanted?"

"Well, yeah. Cindy mentioned she liked the type you use."

"Good grief. You can't ask another girl to recommend hair products for her competition."

Maybe calling Rachel had been a bit tactless. He didn't want to hurt her feelings, but he had to be honest. "I'm sorry if I've let you believe otherwise, but Cindy doesn't have any competition."

"Maybe not now. But I have better hair."

That was not the smartest call he'd ever made. He pocketed his phone and stared at the lotion bottles. He sighed with indecision. A man gave him a sympathetic look. "I hate buying things for the wife. No matter how hard I try to please her, I always buy the wrong one."

Cole didn't know how to respond. He chose the closest bottle.

"Not that one." The man shook his head. "Read the label. It's for severely dry skin. You take that home and your wife will be in tears because she'll assume you think her skin is ashy."

"Oh." Cole replaced the bottle. Church started in twenty minutes. The few times he'd touched her skin, it was perfect. He chose another bottle.

"Don't do it, man." His new ally held a plain white bottle. "That one's for oily skin. Here, take this one. It's your basic lotion." He shrugged. "Of course, you can bet it's not the one either of our wives want, but at least we won't be scratching fleas in the doghouse."

Cole accepted the offering and the words of wisdom from the retreating stranger. "Thank you." Alone in the aisle, he grabbed the other two bottles, as well. He wanted Cindy to have what she needed.

When she opened the door to the apartment, he held out the bag. "For the record, your skin is perfect. Not too dry. Not too oily. But you asked for lotion, and I bought you lotion. And I totally messed up the hairspray thing."

One perfect eyebrow arched, and Cindy peeked into the bag. Sweet laughter relieved his anxiety. "It's perfect, and any of the three lotions would have suited me fine." She dug into her pocket and laid a ten-dollar bill on the arm of the chair. "Here's your money." Clutching the bag, she disappeared behind the screen.

Leaving the door open, he stepped into the apartment. He didn't bother taking the ten, and he didn't bother telling her the hairspray alone cost more than that.

Clothes were strewn on every surface. He turned toward the kitchen area. They were actually divided into stacks. Denim skirts on the pool table. Long-sleeves on the couch. T-shirts on the floor near the window. Socks and—he averted his eyes from the lacy slips and counted twelve pairs of shoes arranged against the wall. Most had heels.

Cindy stepped around the screen with a bottle of lotion in her hand. Her faded jean skirt stopped below her knees, and she wore one of those tank-top things with lace at the top and bottom. Unlike the girls at the church, she didn't have anything over it.

He struggled to breathe as she flounced over to the couch and smoothed the lotion over her long legs. Backing out of the apartment, he turned in time to grab the railing before he tumbled down the stairs. Concentrating on the calm water in Sara's pool, he waited.

"Cole?" Her voice came from behind him.

He was afraid to turn around. "I'll wait out here."

"How do I look?"

He braced himself and turned.

She snapped the last button and tugged down the hem of an orange button-up. The lacy edge of the undershirt clung to the denim hugging her curves. The lotion had shined her legs, and peach toes drummed against the carpet. "You're beautiful."

The toes stopped their dance. "Come help me decide on a pair of shoes." She crossed the room and held two pairs. "These?" One in each hand. "Or these?"

He leaned in the doorway. "Where did you get all this stuff?"

"I bought them from Andrea. She and her sister were gonna have a yard sale, but never got around to it. Pretty nifty, huh?"

About half a dozen dresses hung on the curtain rod. All of them wrinkled. Lulu deserved new things, not someone else's hand-me-downs.

The excitement on her face broke out in a wide smile. "Now, I don't have to wait for you to take me shopping. I have clothes to wear to the kids crusade this week, without borrowing from Sara. Isn't God amazing?"

She was thankful for so little. "Yes, He is amazing."

Cindy slipped into a pair of brown casuals and lifted her beautiful chin. "I'm ready."

ଚଉ

In the front rows, hordes of kids laughed at the antics of the cowboys on stage. The youth group did a great reenactment of a horse theft. A sheriff chased the bandits on foot while the thieves rode away on the horses—which were bridled mops—around the back of the makeshift stage.

The evangelist stepped on the platform and quoted the commandment, "Thou shalt not steal." A long rope knotted inside Cindy's stomach as he blended in with the shadows. The thieves appeared once again and sold the stolen horses for fifty dollars each.

The knot tightened as Cole glanced her way.

Sweat pooled in her palms, and she wiped them on the pew.

Cole knew about her sock full of money. Did he think she was a thief? She couldn't bear for God or Cole to think badly of her. She'd bought the pills she resold. No doubt, some of the guns and jewelry she'd accepted as payment were stolen, but she didn't steal them. Was she guilty? No. Jesus forgave her previous misdeeds, and she would never return to that life. As for the money…she needed to eat, and to pay the rent. Surely, God understood. After the service, she'd explain everything to Cole.

☙ℭ

The pretzel sticks dipped in white chocolate looked like miniature haystacks. Cindy gladly helped the women serve the snacks as the children passed through the line. She wanted to try one of the delicious-looking treats, but Cole had said they would go eat somewhere tonight after they left the church.

A little boy peered with soulful brown eyes. "Can I have two?"

Andrea answered before Cindy could form a reply. "One for now. If we have extra, you can come back for more."

"Yes, ma'am."

Andrea sighed as the boy accepted a juice box and turned toward the long row of tables. "Lord, what am I going to do?" She turned her head and wiped a tear on her shoulder. The plastic gloves rendered her hands useless for such a task.

Cindy placed haystacks on a paper plate for a group of giggly girls. She'd never seen Andrea so emotional. Not that she'd known her very long. But the ever-present smile was sadly missing from her new friend's face. Cindy waited until all the children were served and the cleanup began before asking Andrea, "I noticed you were upset. Anything I can help with?"

"Only if you can find me a week's worth of camp clothes for Robby and his brother by next week. The clothes I have that size are in various shades of pink." Andrea sighed again.

"Is Robby the boy in the green T-shirt?"

"Yes. He and his little brother are on the bus ministry. Summer camp is next week, and everyone is ready but those two. We couldn't get a parent's signature on the application, and thought they couldn't go. The other children were outfitted from previous donations, but at the last minute—yesterday to be exact—their dad drove his eighteen-wheeler in and signed the form. I hate to tell them they can't go, but they need a twin sheet, pillow, comforter, and other necessities to stay in the dorms."

The sock of guilt-wrenching money was at Cindy's apartment. "The church won't buy the things they need?"

"I hate to ask the members to do that. They've already paid the camp fee." Andrea tugged the plastic gloves off and tossed them in the garbage can. "But the Lord always provides. I just wish He wouldn't wait until the last minute."

The knots in Cindy's stomach returned, and she knew what God wanted her to do.

Cole was outside waiting with some kids until their parents arrived.

She turned to Andrea. "How long are you gonna be here?"

She stretched her back. "Long enough to help clean this mess."

"I'll be back." Cindy rushed out the door. If someone had taken the time to send her to church camp, would her life be different?

80CB

Cole gritted his teeth and breathed in slow. Blaine needed to go home. He deliberately taunted his height over the three ten-year-old boys. Cole stole the ball mid-dribble and passed it to Robby. "Take the shot."

The ball sailed toward the hoop. It was close. Maybe it would have been a ringer? Maybe not? But Blaine blocked the shot at the last minute. "Ah, come on, Shorts. You can't lag airtime." Blaine danced around the outside court with some fancy dribbling.

Cole snuck the ball back to his side and once again passed it to Robby.

With his arms held wide, Blaine immediately surrounded the little boy.

Cole's limit was near. "Back off and let him shoot."

"Naw. He's gotta learn the right way."

Thomas, another ten-year-old, circled around, and Robby passed the ball.

"Huh." Before Blaine could recover, Cole stepped in between him and the boys. Blaine narrowed his eyes. "Dude? You're on my team."

Cole stood his ground. "We're out here to teach them. Tame your game."

Blaine's attention focused on something over Cole's shoulder.

"Looks like your new girlfriend has a few enemies."

Cole turned. Cindy approached Rachel and Mrs. Briggs. "Have you seen Cole?"

Rachel rolled her eyes and turned her back. Mrs. Briggs continued talking and ignored Cindy's question.

Her steps faltered until her eyes met his across the pavement. She rushed across the court, and he met her halfway. "Cole, can you drive me to the apartment real quick?"

As concerned as he was for her, he couldn't leave the boys with Blaine. "I can as soon as the boys are done."

Her face fell. "That will be too late. I need to give Andrea something from the apartment, and she'll be gone by then."

He stepped between her and the busybodies. One touch to her arm brought her gaze to his. "What do you need?"

She chewed on her lower lip and then whispered, "Money."

He reached for his wallet. "How much?"

"Cole, I can't take your—" She stopped in mid-sentence. "Three hundred?"

He had two forty-five. He pressed the bills into her waiting hands. "This is all I've got. If it's not enough, you can take the car to the ATM."

His hand was behind him, replacing his wallet, when her lips brushed his. "Thank you." Soft arms enfolded around him in a quick hug followed by a second kiss. "I'll pay you back later."

Before he could regain his bearings, she disappeared into the fellowship hall. Two young girls giggled from the sidewalk, and Mrs. Briggs coughed disapprovingly behind her hand. Rachel's eyes bored a hole through his chest.

Cole didn't care. Cindy's kisses had surprised him, however he loved her spontaneity. He didn't try to hide his smile as the boys' voices called from the court.

"Ooooh." Robby and his friends made kissing noises.

"We're gonna tell the preacherrrrr."

"You was kissiiiiing."

Too late. He hadn't seen Rachel moving his way. She stood with one hand on her hip. "There's a name for girls who accept money for sexual favors."

"Don't go there. It was a simple kiss. She didn't realize..." Cole stopped mid-sentence. Cindy may not know the rules, but Rachel had no right to judge her.

"It's obvious that she's worldly. She doesn't know how to dress, or how to fix her hair." Rachel jerked her head about, causing the huge curls to bob and sway at the back of her head. "She doesn't know how to talk. Nor what to do. She doesn't belong here, Cole. You've been deceived."

He threaded his fingers behind his head to keep from slapping the smirk off her face. "You're right. But the deception wasn't Cindy's. Where's the nice Christian girl that helped her Sunday? Where's the friend that I grew up with? When you hurt her, when you insult her, you insult me. She doesn't deserve your harsh judgment, and neither do I." He turned his back on her and returned to the game.

"Cole?"

He kept walking.

"Fine!" she huffed. "Keep seeing the little tramp. You'll regret it."

Her words were like a knife between his ribs. He called a warning over his shoulder. "Stay away from Cindy."

The church bus pulled into the parking lot, and Pastor beeped the horn signaling the second and last group to board.

Cole put away the basketball as the boys abandoned the game and scrambled for the bus. "See you guys tomorrow night." He ignored Rachel and Blaine as they whispered their way through the parking lot.

Lord, forgive my anger. If people knew the hell Cindy had survived, would they admire her courage? Or would their judgment become harsher? So she didn't own a closet full of long dresses. So what? His Lulu was real. Genuine in her love for God. She didn't dress up and play I'm-holier-than-you spiritual games. His anger vanished as he thought of her sweet kiss. She'd meant to say thank you. He jogged toward the side entrance. If he was lucky, she'd still be in a gracious mood.

She and Andrea were leaving the fellowship hall. A huge grin lit Cindy's face when her gaze met his.

Andrea locked the door. "Thank you again, Cindy."

"You're very welcome. I'm glad I could help."

The three of them walked to the parking lot together. Andrea's car was parked in one of the first spaces. "I can't wait to put my feet up. Maybe I can talk Derek out of a foot massage. Goodnight, you two."

As Andrea's car pulled away from the church, Cindy leaned her head back and held her arms wide. She twirled in a circle and squealed. "That felt so wonderful." She halted mid-twirl, and her hair brushed over her face. "Thank you, Cole."

He pressed the unlock button on the keyless entry and opened her door. "You're welcome. What did I do?"

Chapter Six

The next night, the knots in Cindy's stomach tightened along with the hangman's noose. On stage, the bandits were caught and the townspeople wanted them hung for their crimes. And why not? They were guilty.

And so was she.

In three months, a jury would decide her punishment. How long would she go to prison? Drug manufacturing carried a sentence of five to twenty years. That wasn't counting the charge of possession with the intent to sell. Pain knifed through her and she flinched. She wouldn't be hanged, but unlike the thieves on the stage, her crimes wouldn't be pardoned. Yes, Jesus forgave her, but the district attorney demanded justice.

Cole rubbed her back and whispered. "You all right?"

Guilt stole her breath. She nodded as the children ran to pray at the altars. She wanted to follow them, but Rachel smirked from the front of the church. Cindy needed fresh air. Ignoring the curious stares, she walked out the double doors, not stopping until she reached Cole's car in the parking lot. She gulped in air and struggled to breathe. The streetlamp highlighted her position. Collapsing against the passenger door, she buried her face in her hands.

Who was she kidding? She couldn't have Cole. Luxury was an illusion that would disappear with the pounding of a judge's gavel. There was no escaping her punishment. What would Cole do while she was in jail?

He should marry Rachel. It was obvious the girl wanted him. Rachel's past would never embarrass Cole. The only thing a marriage to Cindy could bring would be long, lonely nights waiting for his wife to serve time.

Was it fair to him? To let him think she was his innocent Lulu, when in truth, she had a few months freedom before being bound inside prison walls? A low moan escaped her.

"Lord, I don't want to go back to that sinful life. Oh, God. I have no choice." When Cole's friends found out who she really was, what would it do to his reputation? She couldn't do that. "I don't belong here."

The crunch of gravel sounded behind her. "No, you don't." Rachel crossed her arms in front of her. "I should've known Cole found you on the streets. He always brings home strays." One hand patted her curls. "But not without consulting me. Did you enjoy the hairspray that I sent you?"

Cindy couldn't believe it. Was Cole with Rachel last night? Is that why he was late? She'd dealt with jealousy before, and she refused to believe Cole was guilty. There was a way to test Rachel. "Yes, but the toothpaste wasn't my usual brand."

Rachel tossed her head. "Oh, well. Can't have everything in life now, can we?"

"No, you can't." Cole's voice came from the darkness. "And it's time you realized it."

The streetlight reflected on the newly formed tears in Rachel's eyes. "When you come to your senses, you know where to find me." She pivoted on her heel and strutted toward the church.

Cindy remained silent as Cole came around and opened the passenger door. He drove them away from the church, but neither spoke. When he turned into Sara's drive, she found the words she wanted to say. "What are we doing, Cole?"

Instead of answering her, he got out of the car and met her on the passenger side. He led her by the hand to the pool. Near the water's edge, he lifted her hand and pulled her close. "I don't want to think about losing you. Trust God, Cindy. He'll make a way."

"But Cole, we both know I'll be gone soon. Why set ourselves up for disappointment?"

"Whether God gives us three months, three years, or three lifetimes, I intend to cherish every moment." He released her and toed off his shoes.

Her brain was a tangled mess of emotions. "What are you doing?"

"The kids crusade is over, but with snack time Sara and Mark won't be home for at least another hour." He shrugged out of his button-up and pulled off his socks. His white T-shirt stood out against the dim light surrounding the pool. He emptied his pockets and tossed his wallet and phone in the nearest lounge chair.

She squealed when he lifted her in his arms. "Cole."

"It's time to have some fun." He stepped onto the diving board. "We're going swimming."

He couldn't. He wouldn't. "Don't you dare." She squealed again, and laughter erupted like a dam bursting.

He moved to the end of the board and grinned down. "Truth? Is there anything in your pockets that shouldn't get wet? Say for example, an expensive electronic device used for talking and texting?"

Her phone was in the apartment. She searched for an excuse to stall him, but she couldn't think while cradled in his arms.

He bounced. She squealed again and buried her face against his T-shirt. The warm water drowned her laughter. Cole released her and they surfaced a few feet apart. The denim skirt threatened to drag her back down. Choking on the water, she fought her way to the shallows. Cole pulled her near and she caught her breath.

"Are you okay? I only meant to have fun."

Her legs were tangled in thick fabric. She reached down and pushed the offensive garment off her legs. Cole released her as if he'd been burned. Here was her chance at revenge. He had no way of knowing what she wore underneath. She shrugged out of the three-quarter sleeve, button-down shirt. Wearing her cami and spandex shorts, she closed the distance between them. How she wished the lights were bright enough to see the hue of his face.

She laughed as he dove under the water and swam toward the deep. She wasn't as fast a swimmer as he, but she could dog-paddle pretty good. She treaded water in the middle of the pool searching the shadows. Under the water something brushed her leg. "Cole?"

"I'm right here."

She swiveled around to find him grinning from four feet away. She didn't want him to keep distance between them. "Andrea taught me to wear shorts under my skirts. It makes me feel less naked."

A grin split his face. "That's good to know." He pushed a full-body float between them and propped on the edge. He kicked toward her, and she folded her arms on the air mattress. They were inches apart. He held both her hands. "Do you feel better now?"

"Yes." His touch soothed her frazzled nerves.

"Why did you leave the church? Why did you go outside?"

"I couldn't breathe. It was weird, but I felt as guilty as the horse thieves."

His thumbs caressed hers. "Conviction is a powerful thing to resist."

The word was foreign to her. "Conviction?"

"Are you withholding something from God? Is there anything you don't want to let go?"

"Of course not." The money-filled sock floated through her mind. Did God want her to give it away? "I don't want any part of my old life, but I need money to live on."

His thumbs drew circles on the inside of her wrists. "Ah, the money."

She wrestled her hands from his and gripped the side of the float. "What's that supposed to mean?"

"Maybe He's asking you to trust Him, to let Him take care of you without the money."

"Give away all my hard-earned cash?" She couldn't do that. "And then what? Starve? Be at the mercy of others? I've been there. Done that. It's not a time I want to repeat."

Under the water, Cole's foot nudged her leg. "A judge can't stop God's will. But disobedience can. If He's prompting you to do something, you'll never find peace until you comply."

Who did Cole think he was? "That's easy for you to say. Have you ever lived without necessities? Food? Water? Electricity? You don't understand. Could you trust Him if you didn't have your family's money? I don't think so, Cole. Don't preach what you can't live yourself." She swam to the steps and hoped he drowned in his self-righteousness.

"Cindy, come back."

Headlights flashed in the driveway. Sara and Mark were home. Cindy grabbed her skirt and hurried up the stairs.

ઇ૦ઉ

Late that night, her body hummed from head to toe in anticipation of raw pleasure, but even if she had a line she couldn't give in to temptation and hit it.

She belonged to Jesus. She was a child of the King. Chills racked her body and she curled into a ball. Sweaty palms clutched the sheet as perspiration soaked her brow.

Muscles tensed. She knew what was coming next. "God, help me." The shakes racked her body as ten thousand devils crawled under her skin. Gasping for breath, she flung off the sheet and surged to her feet. Rushing from one end of the tiny apartment to the other, she desperately searched for a cure to her ailment.

The Bible Joni had given her lay on a corner of the pool table. Cindy snatched it in her arms and collapsed to the floor. Violent, trembling hands wouldn't open the sacred book, so she cradled it against her breast and rocked back and forth.

Why now? Why, eight months since she'd had her last fix, did she struggle with the cravings? Her phone caught her eye. One call to Elliot and it'd all be over. The cravings would stop. The doubts. Why was she holding on to Cole anyway? Wouldn't it be better for him if she let him go now? She dropped the Bible and grabbed the phone. Trembling fingers punched the screen. One ring. Two. Panic slammed her and she tossed the phone across the room—the phone Cole had given her.

Self-disgust claimed her. Her chest tightened and she struggled to breathe. She'd kept clean for months by sheer determination, before one chase of the dragon had landed her in jail. She didn't want to be the person she once was. She had two and a half months before prison. She intended to live them clean.

The dark walls closed in. She needed to escape, but she had nowhere to go. Forsaking the phone, she stumbled into flip-flops and ran into the night.

ઇ૦ઉ

Cole balanced the coffee tray and the box of bakery Danishes and knocked on Cindy's door. Without looking up, he knelt on one knee as the door opened. "I am an insensitive jerk and I beg your forgiveness. You were absolutely right. I have no idea what it's like to go without, and if you forgive me, I'll share breakfast."

His hands emptied.

Beautiful toes tapped against the carpet. Naked legs had him gasping for breath. His dress shirt barely covered the tops of her thighs. He fell onto both knees. Blood rushed to his head, and a rapid pulse beat near his temple.

Cindy yawned and stretched. "I forgive you, Cole. Come in."

He stood and brushed the dust off his pants. "You're wearing my shirt?" *Only* his shirt? The green fabric opened at the neckline. He swallowed. The sleeves rolled to her elbows.

She opened the box and selected a donut. "I found it near the pool when I got back from the store last night. It smells like you."

Her teeth sunk into the sugary confection and Cole shook the thoughts from his brain. Did she say…? "You walked? At night? Last night?" She could have been robbed or killed. "What were you thinking? Why didn't you call me? Do you know how dangerous that was?" He didn't want to think about the dangers. Thank God she was safe.

"This is the nicest neighborhood I've ever lived in. It was after midnight and I didn't want to wake you. Besides, I wouldn't have been good company." She licked powdered sugar from her lips and shrugged.

He tore his eyes away from her mouth and met her tired eyes. "Why? Were you sick?" He moved toward her but bumped into a garbage pail. A large, empty box of instant mashed potatoes and two empty jumbo jars of peanut butter fell to the floor.

She redeposited the trash. "I'm okay now. Actually, I'm proud of myself."

Along the counter some kind of peanut butter balls lined waxed paper. "What are these?" He popped one into his mouth. "Mmm, delicious."

She moved behind him and leaned around his shoulder. "Poor Man's Candy. Do you like them?"

"Yes." He ate two more and ignored how close she was standing. Or what she was wearing under the shirt. Her arm brushed his as she claimed one of the bites of candy. "Mmm. They are delicious."

He reached for more and she slapped his hand. "Stop. I'm

taking them to church tonight. For the kids. As a thank you to God for helping me last night."

He turned and leaned against the counter. She'd slept in his shirt. What would it be like if she slept in his arms?

Her lips bowed and her eyes darkened. "I'll get dressed."

"Don't." It was wrong to stand so close to temptation, but he couldn't deny himself this pleasure.

Her eyes widened, but she stood still as if giving him permission to admire her.

His eyes caressed her long legs. Unfortunately, the baggy shirt hid most of her. A freckle below her collarbone teased him from the shirt's opening. The curve of her jaw would fit perfectly in his hand. And her lips would meld with his. The desire flowing through him could be tamed, but the pale skin under her eyes couldn't be ignored. With one step she was in his arms. Her heated breath tickled his neck. Fragile arms encircled his waist and curled around his shoulder blades. He pulled her close, resting his cheek against her temple. "I'm sorry you couldn't sleep. I'm sorry for not understanding. I'm a spoiled rich kid without a clue. Forgive me?"

Her giggle was priceless. "I'm fine, Cole. I had a weak moment. But with the Lord's help, I made it through."

He leaned back and caressed her cheek with one hand. His Lulu was stronger than she knew. He suspected she'd never given her cares over to the One who could meet all her needs.

Blue eyes darkened. Her hands traveled up his chest, along the side of his neck, and buried in his hair. She smiled and pulled him down. Her lips nibbled his—tasting. The fragile thread of control threatened to snap as she kissed him full on the mouth.

Gently, he removed her arms and lifted her hands to his mouth. Closing his eyes, he kissed her knuckles. "Sweet Lulu. How I wish the circumstances were different." He brushed her lips once more, enjoying the sweet torture. "Guess I'll be fasting today."

Delicate brows furrowed. "Fasting? Like, not eating? Why?"

He bent his head and tasted her confusion. His thumb caressed her jaw. "It's the only way to overcome my flesh. When my body craves pleasure but my spirit is waiting on God, fasting helps me keep control."

Leaning back against his arms, she smiled. "So, if my body wants one thing, but my mind wants something different…I can fast, and those urges will go away?" Her eyes glowed as he nodded. Her soft gasp whispered through his soul. "Teach me how."

಑ಞ

Hours later in the safety of his office, he couldn't concentrate. He mentally calculated the time it would have taken to walk to town and back to the apartment. Then he factored in preparing and baking. The faint circles under her eyes testified to her lack of sleep.

During the hour he normally enjoyed lunch, he drove across the bay. She wasn't at the apartment. Or the church. Did she leave town? Was that why she insisted on paying him back the money he'd lent her? Her kiss had hinted of desperation. He should've never left. He slammed his fist against the steering wheel as he stopped for yet another red light. *Please, God, help me find her.*

He searched his surroundings. Four car lengths in front of him, Cindy hurried across a busy intersection. Where was she going? She'd walked from the direction of the church, but that was four blocks away.

She needed her own car.

The traffic prevented him from merging into the turn lane, but at the next light he signaled left and raced back toward her.

She was gone.

He turned into the street where he'd seen her and circled the block—twice. Finally, he spotted her leaving the pawnshop. What had she done in there?

She wiped her cheeks with both hands and tilted her face toward heaven. Head down, she entered the bank next door.

Curious, he parked between the two buildings. His eyes darted from one building to the next. Which one should he enter? Snatching the keys from the ignition, he dashed into the pawnshop.

Fishing gear lined the walls and cases of jewelry created a barrier from the back where a short, thin man scribbled on a notepad. "How can I help you?"

On the glass countertop, Cindy's ring glistened. The day they'd met, she'd cradled it close. Why did she sell it? Cole lifted the heirloom and pushed it on his little finger. "I want to buy this."

The man scratched his goatee. "Beautiful, isn't it? Just bought it, too." He grinned and bumped Cole with his elbow. "You wouldn't happen to know the girl that was in here?"

Cole reached for his wallet. "How much?"

"Twelve thousand dollars."

He flinched. "How much did you pay Cindy?"

"That's not any of your business. If you don't want the ring, get lost. Otherwise, I'll take that gold card you're waving around."

He shouldn't have appeared so eager. Now, he'd have to pay the price, because the guy figured out why Cole needed the ring. He slipped it in his pocket and signed the sales slip.

It needed to be downsized, but by someone he trusted. Cole adjusted his sunglasses as he stepped into the sunshine.

Crossing the parking lot, he entered the bank. A teller shook her head and handed Cindy a check. "I'm sorry, Miss McDuffie, but you can't open an account with a check drawn on a different bank. Take this across town, cash it, and then we'll be happy to open your account."

Cindy's shoulders slumped as she turned. Her eyes widened in surprise. "Cole."

His footsteps echoed as he crossed the massive room. The vice president of accounts watched warily from an open office door. Cole deliberately stepped close to Cindy and caressed her cheek. "What are you doing here?"

She kissed him, and panic ensued throughout the small branch of his family's bank.

He should caution her about public displays of affection, but for now her actions suited his purposes. Her kisses weren't a hardship either. "Taking your advice. Why aren't you at the office?"

"I have some banking to do." He plucked the check out of her hands. "Five thousand dollars?" He didn't intend to speak the words, but he'd paid almost three times that amount for the ring in his pocket.

The paper jerked from his fingers. She folded it in half. "When you're finished, will you drive me across town? I need to cash this." Her smile sent quivers down his spine. "I'd buy you lunch, but we'd both better not."

So she was fasting, too. Good for her. *Draw her close to you, Lord.* "We don't have to drive across town." He pressed a hand against the small of her back and led her to the teller's cubicle. To Cindy, he said, "Give me the check." He scrawled his signature underneath hers, and then passed the document to the teller. "Cash this, please."

The young woman blanched. "Yes sir, Mr. Maxwell."

Beside him, Cindy huffed in disbelief as the teller stepped away from the high counter into the vault. "How did you do that?"

He winked and whispered, "Spoiled rich boy. Remember?" Her musical laughter flowed through the high-ceilinged building.

The teller returned and held out a fat envelope to Cole. "Will there be anything else, Mr. Maxwell?"

Cole passed the money to Cindy who, to his amazement, opened the envelope and counted the money. Twice.

The teller stammered multiple apologies. "I assure you, Miss McDuffie, the money is all there."

Cindy faced the girl. "Yes, it is. Thank you."

"Is there anything else I can help you with today?"

"Well…" Cindy turned to Cole. "I need to open an account. Do we have time?"

"Go ahead. I need to see the branch manager about a funds transfer." To his disappointment she didn't kiss him, but followed the teller to a small alcove. Cole leaned against the counter as Cindy was given VIP treatment. Why did she sell her brother's ring? And why didn't she use the sock money to open the account?

"Mr. Maxwell." The branch manager held out a hand.

Cole shook it and followed the woman to her office. There he initiated a fifteen thousand dollar transfer to his general checking account. He needed the money to pay off the gold card after purchasing the ring.

A quiet knock sounded and the office door slowly creaked open. The head teller peeked in the room. Sweat beads shined from his bald forehead. "My apologies for interrupting, but Miss McDuffie insists on waiting for your advice before selecting an account type. It seems the choices have her a bit confused."

Cole pictured Cindy randomly making a selection. He should have chosen an account for her. "Tell my fiancée to open an interest-bearing account. One without a service charge."

"Yes sir, Mr. Maxwell."

He read the man's nametag. "Mr. Avery?" The head teller turned back in the doorway. "Thank you for helping Cindy. I hope you'll treat her with the same reverence when I'm not at her side."

"You're most welcome, sir. And of course. I'll let her know I'm available if she should need anything. Might I add that I admire her unique perception of finances?"

Cole could imagine how Cindy's previous selling experiences affected her opinions of the banking world. The door closed, and the bank manager pushed a transfer requisition across the desk. Cole signed and stood to his feet.

"Congratulations on your upcoming marriage."

"Thank you, ma'am. However, until we've made an official announcement, I know that I can count on your staff's discretion."

Chapter Seven

Good-natured chatter surrounded her. Cindy dried a glass serving platter and passed it to Sara, who added it to the stack in the church's kitchen cabinet. The people here sure loved to eat. Not that she cared. Cindy liked listening to the women. Most of them were friendly, even after Rachel told them Cindy was from the streets. Some claimed a sinful past, but she didn't believe the godly women could have committed real sins.

Andrea's youngest was up all night with an earache, but thankfully Joni's morning sickness had ebbed. Across the room, she waddled toward James. The ladies wouldn't let Joni help clean after the final service of kids crusade. She'd been told to put her feet up.

Mrs. Briggs returned from the tables with an armload of silverware. "Look at that disgusting display. In the church house, no less."

In the far corner, James kissed Joni's cheek. Though not a quick peck, there was nothing lewd about it.

Another lady scolded the older woman. "I know it must be hard for you seeing a happily wedded couple since your Thomas passed on, but I wouldn't judge so quickly. The Bible does say for husbands to love their wives."

"Yes." Rachel's tone was dry. "At least we know James loves her. It's disgusting when a girl hangs all over a guy. Especially when it's clear that he doesn't want her." To Cindy's shock, Rachel rolled her eyes toward her and sighed. "Some girls take a simple gesture of friendship and build a complete fantasy relationship."

Was she serious? Cindy bit her lip to keep from commenting.

Andrea patted Rachel's hand. "One day, when you're married, you'll understand the bond that a husband and wife share. Derek can look at me across the room and I know what he's thinking."

Cindy's eyes found Cole at that moment. He was sitting with a group of men. Probably talking about golf or sailing. Their eyes met, and his lips twitched in the barest of smiles.

"Cindy?"

She shook the silly thoughts from her mind. "I'm sorry. What else needs to be done?"

A knowing sparkled in Andrea's eyes. "You look like you have other things on your mind. We'll finish this."

Beside her, Rachel huffed. "Cole always plays basketball with the men after fellowship."

Cindy ignored Rachel and thanked Andrea for the reprieve. Cole's gaze followed her to the sanctuary door. She hurried to the pew for her purse and their Bibles, then she walked to his table.

His eyes scanned the items in her hands. "You ready to go?"

"Yes." She twisted her purse strap as the guys begged him to stay and play basketball.

He slapped Derek across the shoulders. "Maybe next time."

Though they didn't touch, an electrical current buzzed between them as they left the building. They descended the steps and were almost to the parking lot when the door opened behind them.

"Cole."

His dad's voice didn't stop their progress, but a groan slipped past Cole's lips before he called over his shoulder. "Sir?"

"Your mother wants you to come to dinner tomorrow evening." Mr. Maxwell rushed toward them but stopped at the edge of the gravel.

Cindy's hand froze on the passenger door handle. *Please God, let him say no.*

Over the top of the car, Cole cleared his throat and held her gaze. "Sorry, Dad, but we have other plans." He pressed the remote's unlock button and they slid in opposite sides of the car.

The doors shut out the outside and cocooned them in their own world. With one hand on the steering wheel and another on the ignition, Cole smiled her way.

What was he thinking when he stared at her like that? Except for that one time in his parents' driveway, he hadn't kissed her. She'd kissed him, but did he want her to? Had she misread his intentions?

Did he offer simple friendship? She leaned over the console and lined her mouth up with his. At the last possible moment, he turned his head. Her kiss landed on his cheek. Maybe Rachel was right. She pulled away and stared out her window.

His hand wrestled her fingers into his, confusing her further. "Are you okay?"

She determined to forget about Rachel and her snarky comments. "I'm fine." She released one more sigh and relaxed against the leather seat. "Thanks for not ratting me out earlier." Her heart had panicked when the pastor described the sock full of money found at the church with a note indicating it should go to the camp.

Cole turned into Sara's driveway and cut the engine, killing the headlights. "You're welcome, but why did you give the money away?"

"What was the word you used? Conviction? Anyway, I guess the Lord knew what he was doing. Imagine. Eight thousand six hundred dollars and ten cents, the exact amount the camp needed for new bunks in the girls' dorm."

Full lips curled upward. "He is amazing." His white knuckles gripped the steering wheel and he cleared his throat. "Come on, I'll walk to your door."

His fingers did their familiar tease against her palm before entwining with hers. Without letting go of her, he led the way up the narrow steps. Light from Sara's patio and the smell of chlorine faded as they climbed higher. Cole's steps slowed.

"I forgot to leave the light on." Immersed in total darkness, she squeezed his hand, afraid to let go.

"I'm here." His words reassured her. "Where's your key?"

His closeness confused her thoughts, and his body heat burned, though only their palms touched. She released his hand and fumbled in her new purse. The single key was hidden in a zippered compartment. Clutching it, she reached for the doorknob and bumped against him. "Sorry."

Male energy surged through her shoulders as he maneuvered her around the landing. With Cole pressed against her back, the key trembled in her hands as she struggled with the lock.

The door opened. Dim light flowed from the lamp by the sofa. Cole's breath zinged across her neck and she turned without stepping into the room. Propped on the doorframe, he hovered mere inches above her. She swallowed her fear of rejection. "Do you want to come in?"

His lips curled. "That's not a smart idea."

"Oh." He wouldn't kiss her goodnight, though she needed his reassurance. She wanted him to drop his mask of control. Her fingers reached out and caressed the pulse beating at the base of his throat. Something flashed in his eyes. A warning maybe? Stretching on tiptoe, she slid her hands up his shoulders and closed her mouth over his bottom lip. He tasted like the wind. Clean and fresh.

His breaths came faster. Short and quick.

"Thanks for walking me through the dark." Her raspy whisper dried her throat, and she wet her lips. Hungry eyes focused on her mouth. He stood still as she kissed him. Gentle hands rested on her waist. Yet, he didn't return her kisses. She gave up. The man was immovable. A sigh escaped her. Maybe, Rachel was right. Maybe Cole only wanted to be her friend. "See you tomorrow?"

Bands of iron held her captive. Smoky eyes blinked. In anger? Or desire? She couldn't tell. Her fingertips played in the soft waves of his hair while his eyes surrendered.

His head lowered in slow motion. She thought she'd die when his mouth hovered above hers. She opened to him and they melded as one. *Oh my heavens.* Her knees turned to jelly and stars burst in her head. There was no mistaking his desire now. His kisses drugged her into a state of euphoria.

He tilted his head, causing his lips to hover next to her mouth. "Marry me." His plea rocked her. "Mark is ordained. He's downstairs. He can say the words and tomorrow we'll buy a license."

"You can't be serious."

His kiss stole her breath. "Marry me and put us both out of our misery. I want to stay the night. I want to know biblical love in your arms. The bonding of spirits and bodies. Say yes, Cindy."

"Ye—" What did he say? "Wait." She fought her way out of the fantasy and stepped inside the door, out of his reach. "You'd marry me for sex?"

"Yes, but no. It's more than that." He linked his fingers behind his head. "Come back out." The smoke in his eyes cooled. He held out his hand, and she grabbed hold of the lifeline. He turned to the stairs. Would he pound on Sara's door? No. He sat on the top step and she on the second. His knees and arms embraced her. She leaned back against his chest. She twisted again, but he held tight. "Don't look at me. One glance from those ice blue eyes and I forget we're not married yet."

She heard the smile in his voice.

"Your kisses drug me. For once in my life, I have no power to resist temptation. I'm afraid of my own actions and reactions." His arms hugged her tight. "You can't seduce me again until after you say yes." Soft lips pressed against her temple.

Surely he'd slept with a girl before. "How many girls have you lost your head and proposed to?"

"Only you. You're the first."

The implications of his words shook her. "And so you've never..."

"Nope."

That's how the Bible said it should be, but Cindy didn't know any who'd made it past puberty. Until Cole, she'd never thought of sex as special. It was something you did, because the consequences of not giving in were too painful. Cole was a virgin. "How is that possible? Girls beg for your attention. I could name several, right now, who are more than willing to let you flip their skirts over their heads."

His laughter rumbled through the night. "I see I'm gonna have a jealous wife. I like that." He kissed her shoulder. "I never said I didn't have offers. It wasn't easy, but I'm glad I waited for you." His arms tightened around her. "I love you, Lulu."

She sagged against him. He didn't love Cindy, reformed drug dealer. He was in love with an illusion—an innocent. He deserved God's promises. Not a jaded sinner like her.

His lips nudged her ear. "Will you marry me?"

"I can't."

He tensed behind her. Hurt laced his voice. "Why not? Don't you love me?"

Cole deserved the truth. "How I feel doesn't change my past." She smoothed a hand down on his arm. "It won't change my future. You shouldn't have to wait twenty more years to claim a wife."

"Marry me now. We have months before your court date. Who knows what could happen? Lulu, say you'll marry me?"

"Stop it!" She scooted out of his arms and stood. "I'm not Lulu. I've never been Lulu. I'm Cindy. A horrible person who can't remember ever being innocent. I've lied. Cheated. I've ruined people's lives for money. I'm no good for you."

He threaded his fingers through hers, and she turned. The hurt in his eyes stabbed her. "Lulu was a promise. The woman standing before me is the reality of that promise. I don't want an innocent little girl. I want you."

Pain pricked her heart. "Marry Rachel. She knows how to dress, how to talk, how to act. She fits in your world."

The muscles in his jaw tightened. "I don't belong to her."

She threw up her hands. "It's time to be reasonable. You are a brilliant attorney. I have not one but two felony charges pending against me. Maybe God intended for us to be together, but that was before I messed up and got arrested. You deserve someone your equal."

Anger entered his eyes. "What about you? Do you deserve someone your equal?"

"I deserve the flames of hell, but Jesus saved me from that. I don't need anything else."

He stood and towered over her. "That's ridiculous, Cindy."

"Lower your voice."

"Marry me!"

"No! What will you tell people when your wife is serving time? What will they say? I don't fit in your life. There's no way I could measure up to your standards. In the end, I'd disappoint you."

Hard steel entered his eyes. "My standards?" His jaw ticked. He was a bomb waiting to explode.

She pushed passed him, stumbled inside, and bumped into the end table. The contents of her purse spilled to the floor.

Cole closed the distance between them and raised his voice. "Because your sins are so horrible and mine are like stealing flowers from Mrs. Briggs' garden?"

"Yes." The whispered word enraged him.

"That is such a load of crap!" He loomed above her, and she took another step backward.

The inside wall pressed against her back. She turned her head and stared out the open door. "You can't change the past, Cole."

His body flattened against her, but anger, not desire, held his muscles taut. "Marry me." The challenge in his eyes rendered the words a threat.

"No."

"Fine!" He shoved away from her. "Have it your way. I'm tired of waiting. So here's what I'm gonna do. You're right, I can't change your past, but I can change the present. Congratulate yourself. I'm going to Gulf Shores to pick up the first prostitute prowling the beach. And then, after I've spent the night *naked* in a stranger's arms, maybe, just maybe, I'll be sinful enough for you. Then my standards will be on your level!" He strode out the door.

She gasped and hurried after him. "Are you crazy?" She ripped the car keys from his hand and held them behind her.

"You said it yourself, there are plenty of girls who want to—"

She slapped her hand over his mouth. "Shut up! No one is touching you but me. No one! Especially not some floozy down at the beach." The thought of someone else touching Cole, kissing Cole, made her nauseous. She backed him against the door. His arm knocked over the broom. "If you go…if you do what you said…" There was nothing she could threaten him with. "Don't do it. Please, Cole. I can't stand the thought."

His eyes softened, and he quit reaching for the keys. She released the pressure against his mouth and his kiss grazed her palm. His face turned into her hand. "It's your touch I crave. Yours and yours alone. Touch me, Cindy." Her hand traveled his jawline to the back of his neck. She pulled him down into her kiss. The fear of losing him made her desperate.

He lifted his head. Determination steeled his eyes, "Marry me and become the only woman to know my touch."

Her lungs squeezed against her heart and she couldn't breathe. The keys slipped from her fingers. "I can't."

She sank on the step and buried her face in her knees.

She waited for comforting arms to surround her.

She waited for his kisses to calm her fears.

An engine roared from the driveway.

"Cole?" She ran down the steps and around the garage. "Wait!" Taillights faded down the street. He wouldn't do what he'd threatened. Would he? She stumbled along the path and collapsed in a chair, hoping the concrete would swallow her.

"Are you okay?" Sara's one-piece swimming suit dripped with water. The door to the main house closed behind her.

Cindy should drown herself in the pool. "Did you hear all that?"

"Not everything, but some of it was hard not to."

Cindy's face burned with embarrassment. Would Sara ask her to move out now that she knew the truth about her past? The lights from her apartment spilled onto the pool. No doubt her landlords witnessed the whole thing.

"Do you want to talk about it?"

The one time Cindy had confided in a stranger resulted in her stay in Metro. Thanks, but no thanks. She shook her head.

Sara settled in a lounge chair. "How about I talk and you listen?"

Wrapping her arms around her middle, Cindy bent at the waist. Where was Cole? Would he carry out his threat?

"I've known Cole my whole life. He and James pestered me to no end when we were kids." Compassion rang in Sara's words. "I love him like a brother and I don't want to see him hurt. So if you don't return his feelings, I'll ask you not to string him along."

Cindy jerked her head up. "What?"

Sara scooted her chair closer. "Do you love him?"

"I—" She hadn't said the words to Cole.

"Then why not marry him? Are you married to someone else?"

"No." Sara must not have heard everything. Cindy didn't like talking about her childhood, but her love for Cole was being questioned. "My past isn't pretty and my future is…uncertain."

Sara smiled. "No one is promised tomorrow. If I gave you a gift and someone stole it, what would you do?"

"Take it back."

"Jesus has given you the gift of salvation. Your sins are gone. There will always be people used by the devil to remind you of your past mistakes. But don't let them steal God's blessings. Isn't your love for Cole worth fighting for?"

ജ൭

Cole turned left on Scenic Highway 98, determined that Cindy would see things his way come morning.

Turn around.

He ignored the still, small voice of God and drove on.

Turn around.

He increased the volume on the CD. A small dog ran out in front of him and he slammed on the brakes. Who was he kidding? He couldn't go through with it. He turned left.

His phone rang in the empty seat. He shouldn't answer Cindy's call. He should make her wonder where he was, who he was with, and what he was doing. But he couldn't deliberately hurt her. He turned down the volume and snatched his phone. "What?"

"Cole?"

Unspoken questions dominated the silence. She wanted to know where he was. He wanted an answer to his proposal.

"I love you." Her soft declaration was balm to his soul. Did she know how much those words meant to him? "Please don't go to the beach."

"I couldn't. I'm on my way to the boat."

She huffed a sigh. "Did you know that Sara and Mark often swim at night? We had an interesting conversation."

Cole groaned at the image the assistant pastor and his wife had witnessed. Mark wouldn't call him out as he'd done nothing officially wrong, but there would be several prayers on Cole's behalf tonight. That could be a good thing. "Did Sara lecture you?"

"No. But she did give me some helpful advice."

"How helpful?" Cole parked at the marina, and then relaxed against the driver's seat.

"She said things that made me think. About God and his blessings. His promises to me."

Cole didn't want to push her too far. "Breakfast tomorrow?"

"I don't know. We've seen each other every day since we've met. Maybe we need to take the day off."

He didn't want to spend one minute away from her, much less a whole day. The clock was ticking. "If that's what you want. James and I have plans Saturday morning, but we're on for Mom's party, right?"

"Well…your mother never invited me."

He got out of the car and pocketed the keys. "You'll be with me. You don't need an invitation."

Chapter Eight

Cindy baked three dozen sugar cookies and cleaned the apartment top to bottom before six a.m. Though her body was exhausted from fighting the cravings, her mind refused to rest. Her last load of laundry would be dry in thirty minutes.

After another three games of nineball, she descended the stairs and rounded the garage. Sara shrieked and pressed a hand to her throat. "Cindy. You scared me."

"Sorry." Cindy had never seen Sara's hair down. "I'll move my clothes out of your way." She folded denim skirts and jeans into the plastic tub Andrea had given her.

Sara loaded the washer. Her curls flowed past her waist. "I'm running late for work as usual... And you're awake early. Did you patch things up with Cole? Is he bringing breakfast?"

"Thankfully, he didn't do anything stupid. We talked, but I thought I needed some space to think about where this is leading. I did all my thinking last night. I miss him."

"Well...if you need something to do, my laundry baskets are overflowing, the kitchen's a wreck, and who knows when the bathroom was scrubbed last." Sara closed the top-load washer and leaned against the machine. "The pay is good too."

After a morning of cleaning, the noon sun sparkled off the pool. Cindy was beyond exhausted. She placed her iced-tea glass on the small table and stretched out on the lounger. The sun warmed her legs and arms. Her lids grew heavy, and drifted as her phone rang. Only Joni and Cole had her new number.

Joni was in class. Eyes closed, Cindy smiled and fumbled with the phone. "We said we needed a break."

Elliot's coarse laugh shivered down her spine. "The caller ID said Cole Maxwell, but I'd know that sweet voice anywhere."

She leapt from the lounger and stared at the empty path leading around the garage. "How'd you find me?" She stuffed her arms in Cole's shirt and hurried up the stairs.

"I'm returning your call. Who is this guy who stole you away from me?"

She ran into the apartment and locked the door. "I was never yours to steal. It was a mistake dialing your number." She wanted to hang up, but he'd call back. "Forget I called."

"Tsk, tsk, tsk. You always thought you were better than a little bit of Tina, but I've got something sweeter than Molly. A bag of your favorite powder, snow white."

The Bible lay open on the coffee table from her morning devotions. She clutched it to her breast and rocked back and forth on the sofa. "I'm done with that stuff."

"Good," Elliot snorted. "Your sister's habit eats up most of the profit. We don't have much to sell. How soon can you set up a kitchen?"

"I'm not cooking. I have a new life now. I won't be back."

"Ha! Don't forget, girl. My blood flows through your veins. You've got your old man's sweet tooth and when it calls...you know where to find me."

"Forget it and don't call me again." Trembling fingers disconnected, and she dropped the phone to the floor. She held tight to God's word and prayed.

⁊

The letters on the document swam before him. Cole couldn't concentrate. He missed Cindy. Did she sleep last night? He should have stopped by the apartment this morning, but she wanted space.

How much time did she need? It was after lunch. Was she home? He didn't want her walking all over town. It was dangerous. Maybe he should rent her a car. That is, if her stubborn independent streak allowed it. Then he wouldn't worry about some wacko abducting her off the streets.

The papers failed to hold his attention. He reached for his phone.

"Cole?" He heard a sniff and a gulp as she answered. She sighed. "I didn't think you'd call today."

"Are you okay? I wanted to hear your voice, but you sound like you're crying."

He could almost hear her smile. "I'm fine now that you called. I miss you."

Leaning back in his chair, he closed his eyes. "You miss me?"

"Yes, I thought about you all night, and I've come to the conclusion that I don't want any space between us. My freedom is short. I want to spend it together with you."

Thank God. "Good. I'll come over tonight. And since tomorrow's Saturday, we'll have the whole day together."

Her sigh echoed through his ear. "You forgot your fishing trip with James. Joni asked me to go shopping."

"Oh, yeah. That's right. Forgot about that." Could he cancel the plans? Maybe James would let the girls go with them? No. Joni got sick on dry land. No way could her stomach survive rough seas.

"Guess what? Sara hired me to clean her house. Now I don't worry about running out of money before court."

"You're working for Sara? As a maid?" His Lulu didn't need to work. He'd take care of her. And she most especially didn't need to clean other people's messes.

"Is that a problem?"

"No, but…I could give you money. You don't need to work."

Silence bounced off the walls of his small office until she said, "The church is full of enough gossip. If you paid my rent, they would assume I was your mistress. There's nothing wrong with working. And Sara is one of the few friends that I have. I offered to help her for free. She's the one who insisted on paying me."

He sucked in a breath. She was insulted. That was not his intention. "I'm sorry. Guess my spoiled-rich-boy mentality is showing. Forgive me, again?"

"Yes. Always."

80Q3

Shopping and fishing trips cancelled. Morning sickness has struck again. James insists on babying me. No hardship there. He treats me like a queen. I'm loving it.

Yes. Not that she wished Joni ill, but now Cindy could spend the day with Cole. She quickly replied to Joni's text. *Sorry you're sick.*

Saying a prayer for you.

Cindy looked out the apartment window for that tiny stretch of bay water and prayed for her friend. Using her phone, she searched for the marina address on the internet and then slipped on flip-flops and flew down the stairs. Three blocks away from the apartment, she regretted wearing her favorite jeans. Cole's sailboat was docked in Orange Beach. There was no way she could walk thirty miles. Why didn't the Eastern Shore have a bus service?

As she arrived at the closest strip mall, an advertisement for a taxi company caught her attention. She made the call. She'd never ridden in a cab before, but she'd seen others do it on TV. Faking a confidence she didn't feel, Cindy opened the back door and slid into the seat. After she gave the driver the marina address, he ignored her and talked on the phone. She paid close attention to the road signs. She wanted to remember this route. Forty-five minutes later, they crossed a huge bridge. The driver turned and the road curved into a large marina. He stopped at the boardwalk. "That'll be forty-two ten."

"Dollars?" Seriously? She reached in her pocket. This would be her first and last taxi ride.

She scrambled out of the cab and smiled at Cole's BMW parked near the ropes. Despite the early morning hour, boats and people were everywhere. Which one was Cole's? She moved toward the entrance and pretended she knew where she was going. Hopefully, Cole's boat would have his name on it.

A man stepped into her path, blocking the entrance into the maze of boardwalks. "Can I help you, miss?" His white polo and navy cargo shorts complemented his dark tan, but his frown set off the deep wrinkles on his face.

She ignored the panic in her heart and faked her best smile. "Yes. Which boat belongs to Cole Maxwell?"

He unclipped a mini-tablet from his side. "Your name?"

"Cindy McDuffie." She held her breath and waited.

A beefy hand thumbed over the screen. "Sorry, ma'am, but you're not on the Maxwells' guest list. I can't allow your entrance unless the owners give you permission." He turned and walked toward the security booth.

"Wait." The one word got his attention. "What if I call Cole? Can he give me clearance?"

"Of course." He flipped through his electronic device.

She dialed Cole's phone and sighed when his voicemail answered. Where was he? She tapped the device against her palm. His car was in the parking lot, so he must be on the boat. Given the morning hours, he was probably praying. Cole's prayers tended to be lengthy. She loved to hear them, but she wanted to see him, now. She dialed again. He didn't answer. Great. She wasn't paying good money for a ride home only to return when he was done. The security guard shook his head.

He was doing his job, but why couldn't he bend the rules? She bit her lip, and tilted her head. "So, I'm not on the list, but if you show me which boat it is, I'm sure Cole will be happy to see me."

Muscled arms folded across his chest. "I can't let you in, but I'll give Mr. Maxwell a call."

She rolled her eyes. "Thank you, but I've already tried that. He isn't answering."

The guard lifted the phone to his ear. "Mr. Maxwell, there is a young lady wanting directions and entrance to your slip?" He held the receiver away from his mouth and spoke to Cindy. "What was your name again?"

Come on, seriously? If this was Cole's idea of a joke, he was in deep trouble. "Lulu."

The security guard repeated the name and then snapped to attention. "Yes, sir. You've described her perfectly." Whatever Cole said on the opposite end of the line must have satisfied him. "I understand, Mr. Maxwell. I'll escort her personally. Of course, sir. She'll be added to the database."

Cindy propped a fist on her hip and waved the guard in front of her. "After you."

He led her down to a wooden boardwalk and then turned. "Watch your step. Floating dock."

The planks moved beneath her, and she grabbed hold of the rope stretched along the side. The security guard glanced over his shoulder. "You good?"

Cindy nodded and let go of the lifeline. "Fine."

Stepping careful, she followed him down a long row of boats. Most were white fishing charters, although some had sailing masts. They walked straight toward a large white yacht. She swallowed. It was at least fifty feet long. *Please, don't let that be the one.*

The guard turned and kept walking. Relieved, her feet quickly caught up. He stopped in front of a nondescript sailboat. Three masts stood proud and tall. Large white letters spelled out "Lulu" on the blue bottom half.

The security guard pointed. "This is the Maxwells'. Watch your step as you board." He unsnapped a chain and held it while she stepped onto the deck of the boat. "If you need anything else, let me know."

"Thank you." She picked her way around the canopy-covered bench seat adjacent to the wheel, and found a ladder leading down into the boat. "Cole?"

His phone rang from farther away.

She wasn't the only one trying to reach him. Calling his name again, she climbed down into a small kitchen of sorts. A dining table was built into the wall. She turned in a circle. Behind her, a small opening led into a cramped living area. The cushioned benches could be used for sleeping or lounging. The phone rang again from the opposite end of the ship. Cindy crept past the swinging stovetop as the boat rocked. A large bed dominated the room. Running water from behind the wood-paneled door proclaimed Cole to be in the shower.

His phone rang again from the top of the dresser. She peeked at the screen. Rachel? What was she doing calling on his supposed "boys day out"? Sara's words from the other night returned. This was one battle Cindy would fight for Cole. She slid her finger up the phone and held it to her ear. "Hello."

"Who is this?" The outraged feminine voice dripped with honey.

Butterflies took flight, and Cindy pressed a hand to her stomach. Would Cole be upset she'd answered? Sucking in a breath, she gathered her courage and forged on. "He isn't available at the moment. Would you like to leave a message?"

"Nooo. I want to speak with Cole. He always takes my calls."

Which meant the hooch had been calling him at work too. "Sorry, not this time."

"Who is this?"

"Cindy." She hardened her voice. "And like I said before…Cole isn't available, but I'll tell him you called."

"I insist you hand him the phone."

"Well, if you insist…" Cindy blew out her frustration. "Hold on a minute." She walked to the wood pocket-door she assumed was the bathroom and knocked, holding the phone so that Rachel could hear. "Cole." Something crashed on the other side.

"Cindy?" The water flow ended with a squeak, and she pictured his glowing face as he probably scrambled for a towel.

She leaned her forehead on the closed door. "Your phone rang and I thought it might be Joni, so I answered. Now Rachel *insists* that she talk to you. I didn't know how to tell her you were in the shower." Cindy spoke the last word into the mouthpiece.

Cole's nervous chuckle came through the teakwood loud and clear. "If you open that door, I will not be held accountable for my actions."

A giggle escaped Cindy at his playful tone. "What do you want me to do?"

His voice turned husky. "You know what I want."

The hiss in her ear told her that Rachel heard every word.

Cindy stuck her tongue out at the phone and pronounced her words carefully. "What do you want me to do about Rachel?"

"Tell her I've got the papers drawn up and she can come by the office and sign them Monday morning."

One glance at the phone proved that Rachel had disconnected. Ha. Mission accomplished. With a smile, Cindy climbed topside.

∞∞

Cole whistled to himself as he heard dainty footsteps above. He threw on jeans and brushed his teeth in a flash, then climbed the ladder two steps at a time. Cindy stood near the bench that ran the length of the stern, her profile visible. His throat constricted. Because of his stupid pride, he'd almost lost her. He couldn't live without his Lulu. He walked through the cockpit, eased down the narrow deck, and then wrapped his arms around her. "I missed you."

Though separated for only a day, the wait had seemed like a lifetime.

She turned and lifted her face. "I'm sorry, Cole. I don't ever want to fight again."

He brushed his lips across hers and lost himself in her sweetness. Water lapped against the boat, rocking it gently. A loud clang from the next slip brought him back to reality. The neighbors could clearly see and be seen. "Let's take the boat out for the day."

Her eyes widened. "In the ocean?"

"No, the Gulf of Mexico. What do you say? Spend the day with me?"

She stepped back and frowned. "I've never sailed before. What if we sink?"

He laughed and massaged her tense shoulders. "We won't sink." In Sara's pool, he'd been shocked by her inability to swim. She'd barely kept her head above water. He crossed the deck and selected a life vest from a storage compartment. "Arms out." She rolled her eyes but complied. Careful to touch only the life preserver, he zipped the vest and snapped the buckles.

Movement from the pier behind her caught his eye. The security guard lifted a hand in greeting. "Making sure you knew the lady was onboard, sir."

"Yes, thank you for helping Cindy." Cole tugged on the straps, making sure they were tight, and glanced over her shoulder. "And can you add her to the guest list? Give her all access."

"Already done, sir. Have a nice sail."

As the sound of whistling faded, Cindy's arms flexed at her sides. She spun around. "Cole?" Her eyes rounded and she pressed a hand over her mouth. "Oh, no. What did I do?"

"When? Was the guard rude to you?" Cole was surprised they'd let her in the marina. The security was very tight here.

The frantic shake of her head confused him further. "The guard called you. You knew I was here, because he called and then you got into the shower. Right? Please, Cole. Tell me you talked to the man on the phone."

What was she so upset about? He scratched his brow. "Nope. Sorry."

With both hands on top of her head, she paced across the deck.

"Ugh. This is great. Just horrible. That was your father." She stopped and spun on her heel. "Oh good grief. What did I say?" She gasped. "I told your dad my name was Lulu. Cole, what must he think? I have never been more embarrassed." Her hands fisted on her hips as he pieced together her jumbled bits of dialogue. "Don't you dare laugh. This is horrible. This is beyond horrible. This is…"

He captured her hands. "It's okay. Dad knows how I feel about you. He doesn't have a problem with it. He's happy for us."

A delicate brow arched. "He is?"

He kissed away her frown. "Yes." He led her into the cockpit and nodded to a bench seat beside the wheel. "Sit here beside me until we hit open water."

Her smile reminded him of unfulfilled promises. Using the radio, he requested the help of dockworkers to untie the boat. The teen boys stared as Cindy slipped off her flip-flops and curled her feet onto the cushions. Cole yelled his thanks and then motored into the open bay. An egret dipped into the water and reemerged with a catch for her baby chicks. Cindy gasped, and her parted lips were too tempting to resist. He kissed her again and had trouble ending contact. He shook himself and concentrated on navigating through the bottlenecked pass.

With her bail restrictions, they couldn't sail The Intracoastal Waterway. Or could they? There was nothing between them and Mexico but water. No judge and no jury. The wind blew her hair onto his shoulder. He cut the engine, and then unfurled the sails. Running from her court date was tempting, but he didn't want to hide. He wanted the freedom to love her forever. God ordained their time together. Man could neither shorten it nor prolong it.

When they were clipping along, Cindy tilted her head back, and the wind whipped through her hair. She smiled over her shoulder. "This is fun."

Seagulls cried overhead. He piloted them to Sand Island and dropped anchor.

"What are we doing?"

He nodded to the water. "Swimming."

She frowned at her pants. "I don't have anything to wear."

They were the same ragged jeans she'd worn the day they'd met.

He fell at her feet and ripped the hole around her pant leg.

She bopped him on the head. "These are my favorite jeans."

He glanced up and winked. "Mine too." Using a knife from the storage bin, he cut the seam and turned to the opposite leg. The back of his hand caressed her soft skin. His hand trembled as he sliced through the denim fabric above her knee. "Wait here while I go below and change."

He needed a minute to clear the thoughts from his mind. Out here in the open water, Cole didn't worry about protecting his eyes from the half-naked bodies of sunbathers. He hurried into his swim trunks and thought about leaving on his shirt, but he didn't like the way salt stuck between the fabric and his skin. One day, Cindy would become his wife. It wouldn't hurt for her to see him shirtless.

Pausing in the galley, he grabbed a bottle of sunblock. Her fair skin needed protecting.

She let out a long whistle as he emerged. "Nice abs."

He noted the appreciation in her eyes and was glad he'd left off the shirt.

"What, no red glow today?"

Biting back a grin at her compliment, he held out the sunblock. "Put this on. On the water, you're doubly exposed."

Her lips curled. "Yes, sir. Anything else, Captain?"

He winked, enjoying her playful tone. "I'll let you know." He turned his back but froze at her touch. Alabama temperatures soared as her hand brushed across his shoulder blades. Cole struggled to find his voice. His heart tripped as she faced him, bottle in hand. "I don't need sunscreen."

"You don't want to burn, do you?"

His skin was naturally tanned. Every now and then he might turn pink, but by the next morning it would blend in with the rest of him.

Her palms brushed lotion over his collarbone and he shivered. "Is it cold?"

Unable to speak, he shook his head. Her fingers blazed a trail up his throat. He opened his eyes as his sunglasses lifted from his face.

Standing on tiptoe with one hand on his shoulder, she smoothed her fingers over the bridge of his nose. "Sit down. I can't reach."

As if in a trance, he obeyed without question.

Sweet arms reached around him and placed the sunscreen in the cup holder. His heartbeat thundered in his chest. Her hands slid up his shoulder and he melted. Leaning his head forward, he closed his eyes and enjoyed the sensation her fingers spread through him.

She massaged his shoulders and neck. Cole tilted his head back and her hands slid down his throat to his chest and back again. Her fingers danced around his ears and skimmed over his face. Cindy leaned over him and kissed his cheek. "I'm done. Now you won't get burned."

Too late. Her touch had scorched him. In danger of spontaneously combusting, Cole stood and dove over the side. He shook cold water from his hair after he surfaced. *Jesus, help me.* "This would be a good time to discuss the rules."

Her sly smile didn't fool him as she propped on the seat he'd just vacated. "What rules?"

"Except for the occasional boat, we're alone out here." He waved his hand. "No distractions and no interruptions. That's not a good thing, since one of us stubbornly refuses to attend a wedding."

"Cole." She straightened and tilted her head.

"So…no kisses. No caresses. And no looking at me with that look that's on your face right now."

To his delight, she laughed. "Can I admire you from a distance?"

"Absolutely not."

Hours later, Cole maneuvered around the deck as Cindy waved her phone in the early afternoon sun. "Joni and James aren't gonna make it to your mom's party tonight. The smell of seafood makes her nauseous."

"Everything makes Joni nauseous." He reclined on the cushioned seat at the bow of the boat. "I hope you aren't sick when we are expecting."

"Cole." Beside him, she lifted the shades he'd lent her and frowned.

He reached out and claimed her hand. "I meant in the future. When the courts are satisfied, and you're ready. Don't panic."

"I didn't panic." A musical giggle floated in the breeze as her hand gripped his. "This morning, I read about a woman in the Bible that had a baby when she was ninety."

White clouds floated overhead. Cole turned to see her profile as she contemplated the heavens. "That happened because of God's promise to her husband."

Cindy rolled on her side and faced him. "Do you believe that God promised James two babies? Twin boys?"

"Yeah, I do. Just as He promised Abraham's seed would outnumber the sands of the sea."

Her groan of protest surprised him. Sunglasses hid her eyes, but a pink tongue darted out and wet her lips. "How many children did he promise you?"

His joy couldn't be contained, and his laugh boomed through the air. Finally, she was thinking of him and babies with forever written on her expression.

"Don't laugh." She flopped on her back. "It's not funny."

He gripped her hand and stood pulling her to her feet.

"What are you doing?"

"You'll see." He pulled her atop the cabin roof and sat. "Lie down." He followed his own command and folded his arms underneath his head. "Come on. I want to show you something."

He noted the caution in her eyes. She kept a few inches between them but lay by his side. "Now what?"

"Look up." Cumulus clouds floated across the sky. "What do you see?"

"Is this the game where we find different shapes in the clouds?"

He turned his head long enough to frown at her. "No. Concentrate. What do you see?"

She slowly exhaled. "Clouds. All sorts of clouds. Cottony. You can almost reach out and touch them."

"Keep that picture in your mind and close your eyes."

He followed his own instructions. The wind rushed past. "Spread your arms. Hold them out like wings." Her arms brushed his shoulder.

A wave lifted the boat and her gasp delighted him. "It feels like I'm floating. I'm floating through the clouds. This is awesome."

"I prefer the term, swim. We're swimming in the clouds."

"Whatever you call it, this is amazing." Sweet laughter mingled with the wind.

"I've heard that joyful sound before." He wanted her to know the depth of his promise. "I know people think I'm strange, but I couldn't have held on to God's promise without a vision of you. When I'd get discouraged, I'd come out here and swim— through the waves or the clouds. Sometimes, I could hear you laugh. Now that I've met you, I picture a new Lulu. A little version of you and me. She giggles and calls me Daddy. We hold hands and swim from cloud to cloud. She's my new promise." He rolled on his side and caught Cindy's gaze. "I can't wait to meet her."

Cindy's finger slowly circled the underside of his wrist. "Cole, if there was something that I wanted more than anything, would you give it to me?"

"Absolutely. What do you want? A new pair of jeans?" He stretched out his foot, and his big toe nudged her ankle.

She lifted her shades and flexed her foot.

His toe drew swirls along the silky skin of her calf. He stopped at the knee and suppressed the urge to explore higher.

"You're definitely buying me a new pair of jeans, but I'm talking about something momentous."

"Momentous? That's a big word." His hand caressed her cheek as he stared deep in her eyes. "I don't care how big or how small. If you want something, name it, and it's yours."

Her smile outshined the sun. "Thank you, Cole. You've given me so much. I could never repay you. You've given me love, laughter, a home. You've shown me how to find God, and I'll never forget it. My father took me to the family planning clinic when I was twelve, but in jail they didn't allow unnecessary medicine so…"

He ached for the girl she used to be. "I'm sorry your father didn't treasure you."

She shook her head. "I don't want your pity. The girl I used to be died at an altar." She leaned over and kissed him. "Thank you for your thoughtfulness though. I love you, and I want to give you something to show you how much."

He brought her hand to his lips. "I don't need anything to know you love me. I see it in your eyes."

She pulled his hand to her and pressed his palm flat against her belly. "Before I go to prison, I want to give you little Lulu."

His ears popped as the boat rose on an open swell. "You'll marry me?"

"We don't need a marriage license to have a baby together." Her finger landed on his lips, stifling his protest. "Lots of people do it. I've got two months until my court date. I'm guilty. I know it. The cops know it. The lawyers know it. If God works a miracle and the judge gives me the minimum, the most I can hope for is to serve both five-year sentences consecutively." Her touch trailed fire and ice down his chest. "That gives us two months to get me pregnant. When I go to prison and the baby's born, you can raise her. Most kids are lucky if they have one parent. You'll be a great dad."

He swallowed and fought against the workings of his brain. He'd never imagined the two Lulus together. Could he settle for one? Is that all God would allow him with the time they had left? "There's no guarantee you'll become pregnant."

She rolled onto her back and pulled him with her. "Maybe, but you'll have fun trying."

Her shirt had ridden up slightly. His forefinger chased the water droplets on the warm skin around her navel, hypnotizing his sanity. "God's laws say no."

She ran her hand through his hair and tugged him down. "He'll forgive us. That's what He does."

Her lips were soft, yielding to his.

He lost himself in her touch and his hand grew bolder.

The smell of salt breezed through her hair, and her unique fragrance drugged him. Visions of blue-eyed babies swam through his mind and ended with a picture of the bed below.

From a distant fog, a voice called his name, but the pleasure of her touch drowned out the sound.

Cole silenced the conviction with his mouth and tasted her sweet kiss once again. His arms held her captive.

Somewhere in the far recesses of his brain, he knew he should release her, but his body refused to let go.

A feathery caress brushed his jaw. She was his to do with as he willed.

No. What was he doing? Cindy was right. Lulu deserved to grow up with at least one parent. He swallowed and struggled to catch his breath. His heart hammered against his ribs as his body violently shuddered. "I can't do this."

Blue eyes blinked in confusion as he released her.

"God won't bless sin. But if we follow Him, He'll make a way for us to be together."

Her swollen lips beckoned. He leaned against the bow's lifeline. From several feet away, her wet cut-offs and T-shirt clung to her skin. He could feel its warmth next to him. He needed a distraction. "What did you do yesterday?"

She open her mouth but no words formed. The heat of her gaze said it all.

"For mercy's sake, Cindy. Talk about something, anything to take my mind off…"

Her smile reignited a fire within him, and he fought for control of his wayward flesh. Shimmering lips drew him in to their sweetness.

He reached for the anchor. "We need to go."

Chapter Nine

The warmth of Cole's hand gave her the courage to smile and nod as he introduced her to countless influential people. From across the lawn, a white-haired gentleman approached them with an iced drink in his hand. Cole's brows furrowed in the sunset and his expression went blank. He didn't greet the man by name. "Good evening. Have you met my girlfriend, Cindy?" His hand pressed on her lower back.

She accepted the hand offered. "Nice to meet you, sir."

Being introduced as his girlfriend sent tingles down her spine, but when the gentleman had moved on to another group of people, she elbowed Cole's side. "Why didn't you tell me his name?" Not that she would remember it.

He leaned down and whispered. His breath tickled her neck. "He's one of Dad's clients. I've known him all my life, but I forgot his name."

She turned her cheek into his. "And I thought you were perfect. How many more flaws are you hiding?"

"Stay with me for the rest of my life and you'll slowly figure them out." Intense heat burned in his gaze. She broke eye contact and stared at the green grass. His warm hand slid from around her back and reclaimed her hand.

She glanced over at him.

Determination replaced the heat in his eyes. "I won't give up. I'm praying and fasting that God will make a way for us to be together."

The corner of his lips curled and lightened the weight of her heart. "I know. And I'm praying too."

Over his shoulder, the sun dipped, painting the bay a brilliant gold. Since that episode on the boat, she craved Cole's kiss. She'd never longed for a man's touch. Maybe there was hope for her yet.

His full lips parted. "Stop that." How could he read her thoughts? His jaw ticked as the muscles in his arms tightened. He tugged on her hand. "Come on. Let's go in the house."

Three times they were stopped and he introduced her to someone new. Each confirmed the fact that she didn't belong here. The mayor, a doctor, and a marine biologist. How could she ever fit in his world? Even after she got out of prison, she couldn't compete with these people.

"Excuse me." She didn't know the proper etiquette, but she knew better than to announce her need to pee. She broke Cole's hold on her hand, and then forced herself to walk slowly toward the house.

A maid directed her to a discreet half-bath designated for the ladies' use.

Moving through the crowd, she spotted Mrs. Maxwell and Rachel. Cindy had almost managed to dodge them when a hand touched her sleeve.

"Miss McDuffie?"

She turned toward the familiar voice and blinked.

It was the lady from the bank. "I hope my staff met your financial needs sufficiently."

Behind her, Mrs. Maxwell headed their way. Cindy answered quickly. "Yes. Thank you for all your help. If you'll excuse me, I ha—"

"Cindy, dear." Cole's mother glided to her side. "I'm so glad you could make it."

Yeah, right. "Good evening, Mrs. Maxwell." She redoubled her smile.

Mrs. Maxwell glanced at the banker. Cindy could see the wheels in her mind turning as the woman removed a business card from her purse and held it out to Cindy. "In case you weren't given one at the branch Thursday. Mr. Maxwell asked that I handle your account personally."

Cindy shifted her feet and accepted the card. "Thank you." What did she do now? As the lady turned her attention to Cole's mother, Cindy stepped aside.

"Congratulations on your engagement, Miss McDuffie."

Mrs. Maxwell paled and swayed on her feet. Cindy reached to steady the elder woman, but Mrs. Maxwell swatted Cindy's hands. "Don't touch me. You've done enough. Where is my son?"

"He's out on the lawn, discussing golf with some other gentlemen."

"Well, I do hope he makes it in the house. I have a few things to say to him." She flounced away, leaving the unsettled banker with her mouth open.

"Was it something I said?"

Cindy took pity on the lady. "No. You're fine. Thank you again for your help. Excuse me." Fighting her way to the bathroom, she leaned against the wall and waited her turn. The other women in line held stiff postures and stared at Cindy's slouched shoulders. With a sigh, she heaved herself off the wall and wished she'd worn a pair of sandals instead of the heels that matched Andrea's dress.

In the bathroom, the soap smelled of gardenia. She hated gardenias. The embroidered towel was too pretty to touch. She shook her hands dry as the small handbag on her shoulder chimed.

She could almost hear Cole's voice as she read his text. Meet me out back, past the gazebo, take the trail. Don't worry about getting lost, I'll find you.

Darkness had fallen by the time she descended the marble steps. Wanting to avoid another run-in with Cole's mother, she stepped onto the lawn. Once again her heels sank into the grass. She imagined the holes in the beautiful landscaping come morning, and paused to slip off her shoes. No one could see her feet if she kept to the shadows. With a soft sigh, she wiggled her toes in the soft grass, and then made her way around the side of the house. Stringed lights illuminated the white gazebo.

Rachel stood alone in its center.

"Cindy?" Cole's faint voice called from the wooded area beyond. Rachel turned and ran toward it.

Great. Cindy didn't want to compete for Cole's attention. But what would he say to Rachel when he thought no one else was around? A lot of guys were players. She refused to believe he was in those low ranks, but she had to make sure.

On silent, bare feet she followed until she heard Rachel's soft cries. "Please, Cole. You don't know what you're saying. She's enticed you away from biblical principles."

"Stop." Through the moonlight, Cole reached into his pocket and offered Rachel a handkerchief. "I hold to the same standards."

The whine of Rachel's voice intensified. "I heard the water this morning. You were showering. With her."

Cindy pressed her lips together to keep from defending him. He rubbed his chin and tilted his head toward heaven. His sigh echoed through the roses. He dragged Rachel by the arm to a nearby stone bench. A not-so-gentle shove forced the troublemaker to sit. Cole knelt beside her. "I don't understand. Why are you doing this?"

"Because." Rachel reached for him and Cindy gritted her teeth.

"Stop." Cindy flinched at Cole's tone. He stood and paced in front of the bench. "Have I ever asked you on a date?"

"No, but—" Rachel's smile disappeared.

"Have I ever declared any feeling toward you?"

Rachel dabbed her eyes. "Not audibly."

"Have I ever promised you a future?"

"No." Rachel's sobs came in great waves now.

"I'm sorry to cause your tears, but you've always been like a sister. I care about you, but I'm in love with Cindy. She's my future wife. You need to accept that."

Rachel leapt to her feet and sniffed. "Never. I will never let you marry her. And neither will your mother. Cindy is using you, and when she breaks your heart, I'll be here to pick up the pieces." She sashayed toward the house.

He collapsed on the bench and rested his elbows on his knees.

Cindy stepped into the clearing. "I'm sorry. Your mother and Rachel overheard the banker congratulate me. I have no idea why she thought we were engaged."

"That would be my fault." Cole stood and fought his way around the saplings. "I wanted the branch manager to know you're special to me. And eventually…" Crickets sang a love song into the night air. He hugged her close. "Forgive me?"

Cindy closed her eyes. Beneath her ear, his heart beat steady and sure. She may not belong in his material world, but she never wanted to leave his arms.

The wind blew in between them, and Cole relaxed his hold. He reached for her wrists and held them against his heart. Her pulse drummed against his touch. "I wanted to show you my treehouse, but now I'd better not."

She couldn't catch her breath long enough to speak. He tugged her hand and they followed the path around the gazebo toward the back entrance. When they hit the paved sidewalk near the in-ground pool, she scraped her toe. "Ouch. My shoes?"

"I like naked feet."

"Cole." She didn't try to hide her irritation. "I can't go inside barefooted."

"Wait here. I'll find your shoes. Don't go in without me."

He didn't need to worry about that. As he jogged back the way they'd come, footsteps sounded behind her.

Mrs. Maxwell descended the steps. Her overly-friendly smile raised Cindy's defenses. "Just the person I wanted to see." She glanced into the night. "Where's Cole?"

"Um, he'll be back in a minute."

"Good. We have time for a chat." Mrs. Maxwell sat in a wicker chair and patted the cushion of its mate. "Have a seat, dear."

She wanted to refuse, but Cole's mother had never been this nice before. Maybe she wanted to apologize for her earlier outburst. Cindy neared and perched on the matching chair. She forgot to hide her toes.

Mrs. Maxwell's smile morphed into a disapproving frown, and Cindy fought the urge to squirm in her seat.

"I'm not sure where you're from, and I doubt it's Houston, but we both know you don't belong in this social setting. Cole, on the other hand, was born to replace his grandfather in the Senate."

He hadn't said anything to her. Was it true, or was Mrs. Maxwell making it up? "The United States Senate?"

"Yes. I see this is news to you. His infatuation won't last forever, but it may endure long enough to destroy his future. You're another of his adventures. But he always comes back to his senses." Mrs. Maxwell folded a slip of paper in her lap. "If you care for him, you'll want his happiness. Can you imagine yourself as a politician's wife?

Parties? Public appearances? Media coverage?" Judgment crossed her face. "Shirt and shoes are required."

Cindy didn't want to hear more. No one had to tell her she wasn't good enough for Cole. Never would she do anything to cause him harm. It didn't matter if he was a senator or a local attorney. If anyone was to learn of her criminal record…how would it affect his career? She pictured the headlines and cringed.

"Here's some money." Cole's mother held out the folded check. "If you're genuine in your love for Cole and God, you'll take it and start a new life somewhere else. A good moral life. One without enticing young men into illicit affairs."

Cindy swallowed her outrage and remained calm. "I haven't enticed anyone."

Mrs. Maxwell stood and offered the check once more. "I don't blame you, dear. My son is very easy to love. Take the money. Don't ruin Cole's future."

Cindy would never accept the ridiculous offer. With as much dignity as she possessed, she rose to her feet. Shoeless, blinded by unshed tears, she walked into the night.

Chapter Ten

She wasn't at the apartment. Driving slow, scanning the ditches beyond the sidewalk, Cole continued his search for Cindy.

When he'd exhausted the area between his parents' and Sara's he gunned the motor and raced toward the beach. Her shoes lay on the passenger floorboard, along with the crumpled check for $50,000 he'd found on the patio. He parked at the marina and jogged past the sleeping security guard. The ropes creaked as he stepped onboard. "Cindy?"

"I'm on the deck."

He smiled at her terminology as he made his way to the stern of the boat. She lounged against the cushions. Streetlamps illuminated her swollen, red eyes.

His stomach clenched as if someone had sucker-punched him. His mother had hurt her.

Cindy had overcome a powerful addiction, withstood losing her home, survived an abusive father and the criticism of the overt righteous. Yet he'd rarely seen her cry. He lowered to the seat beside her and opened his arms.

She fell into him as sobs shook her body.

He tucked her head under his chin and brushed a kiss against her hair. *Lord, help me help her. How can I show her how much she's loved when others put her down? Comfort her, Jesus. Let her know what a wonderful creation she is.*

Cole continued to pray as she cried. When her tears were spent, she sniffed and lifted her head. He had no handkerchief to give her. Instead, he untucked his shirt and wiped her eyes with his shirttail. "You are beautiful. Smart. Funny. A wonderful person."

"No, I'm not." She sniffed again. "I'm horrible and selfish, but I don't care anymore. I couldn't go."

Fear swallowed him. "Please, I know our time is short, but don't ever leave me."

"I can't. I'm too selfish." Using the backs of her hands, she wiped fresh tears. "Everyone knows I don't belong here." She buried her face in his side. "Everyone knows I'm not good enough for you. Rachel. Your mother. James. Even Joni and Sara. But I want you." Her head lifted and her gaze met and held his. "God gave you to me, and until He sends me away, I'm gonna keep you."

He kissed the stubborn tilt of her chin. Finally, she was ready to fight for their relationship. He couldn't win the battle with his mother and Rachel without her. "It's about time."

"I won't do anything to ruin your chances of becoming a senator. So stop asking me to marry you. And when I go to prison, you need to forget—"

"Shhh." Cole liked studying the law. It was like a giant puzzle. But he'd never figure out the way Cindy's mind worked. He stood, distancing himself from temptation. "Let's clear the air tonight, shall we? One, I don't want to be a politician. Unless God himself appears before me and commands it, I will never run for public office. Two, I will quit proposing when you say yes. Three, you don't have a selfish bone in your body. And four, if you ever left me, not only would you rip out my heart, but I'd search the whole world until I found you again."

He fell on his knees in front of her and clasped her hands in his. "I'm not letting other people dictate our life. God put us together, 'till death do us part."

Her blue eyes misted.

"I love you, Cindy. Will you marry me?"

Silent tears breached her long lashes. "Not yet."

Her forehead rested against his, and he swallowed a victory shout. Her answer had changed. It wasn't quite a yes, but it gave him hope.

"I love you, Cole." The whispered words danced over his soul, leaving him dizzy and disoriented. "If I wasn't bound for prison, I'd say yes in a heartbeat."

"Tell me again."

Her lips hovered a breath away. "I love you."

He was drowning in her essence, yet he didn't care to surface. His lungs burned for air. They were seconds from exploding.

He cursed his weakness. He didn't want a sleazy affair with the woman he'd make his wife. But, like Paul, he somehow managed to do the things he didn't want to do. And the things he wanted to do, he didn't. *Oh, wretched man that I am.* He needed to place some distance between them. He was out of breath, his voice gruff. "Here're my keys. Take the car and get out of here while you can. I'll catch a ride to church in the morning."

℘℧

Cindy pulled out of the marina's parking lot and her phone rang. An unfamiliar number flashed across the screen. She'd exchanged numbers with a few of the girls at church. "Hello?"

Her half-sister Maria's voice surprised her. "Does your new friend have a car? I need a ride to the store."

"How did you get this number?"

"Elliot said you called. He left me here without a dime to go find you, and now I'm sitting here with four hungry children. Come back. I need you to take me shopping."

Cindy didn't have a driver's license. Driving Cole's car home was one thing. Taking it to Mobile was another. What if a cop stopped her? "What's wrong with Granny's Buick?"

"You should know, Miss High and Mighty. You were the one who ran it out of gas."

Cindy hadn't driven the car in months, but arguing with her sister's drug-induced memory would do no good. Maria obviously had the munchies. "I'm sorry, but I can't."

"Fine. I'll sit here and die. The world will probably be better-off without me. But these poor kids don't deserve to starve."

At a red light, Cindy tapped her toes against the brake. It would take her forty-five minutes to reach the city of Daphne, and then another twenty minutes to drive across the bay. Maria needed her help. Cindy couldn't say no. "It'll take me an hour and a half to drive there, but I'm not getting out of the car, and if I see one sign of Elliot, I'm gone."

"I haven't seen the old man in days. I'm worried about him."

Cindy was worried about him too, worried that he was setting her up. But she couldn't let her sister go hungry. She disconnected and concentrated on the traffic.

Lord, please don't let the police stop me. Don't let me wreck Cole's car. And please, please don't let Elliot be there.

She prayed the entire drive.

When she arrived at Granny's house, her paranoia was unfounded. Maria sat on the curb, waiting. Her sister's cheap perfume polluted the inside of Cole's car. Cindy pressed a button and opened the sunroof.

Her sister popped a wad of gum and gawked at the interior. "Your boyfriend drives this? He must be loaded." For once, Maria was sober.

Cindy relaxed against the seat. "Cole lives a blessed life."

Her sister swore and then laughed. "My sister has a sugar daddy." Maria made kissing sounds and fish faces. "You kiss him, and he gives you some sugar."

Cindy laughed at her sister's antics. "It isn't like that. Cole is a good Christian man. He wouldn't do anything sinful."

"Does he have a brother? I might be willing to sacrifice my freedom for a ride like this."

"No, he doesn't. But I want you to meet him. He helped me find a private apartment. You should come stay with me."

Her sister's phone chimed and her fingers ticked away as she answered a text. "I don't know. I wouldn't want to embarrass you in front of your new friends."

"You won't." Cindy hoped not, anyway. "You're my sister and I love you."

"I'll think about it." Maria pulled a stack of EBT cards from her purse and unwrapped the rubber band holding them together. Each one had a four-digit number written in the corner.

"Where did you get those?"

Maria smiled in triumph. "Payment for services rendered. Granny had the right idea about this babysitting gig."

Cindy kept her comments to herself and drove to the nearest 24-hr market. Once there, she parked beside an older import hatchback. Despite the late hour, four little kids were arguing in the backseat. Cindy hated it when Granny or Elliot made them stay in a hot car.

She turned to Maria. "Go on in, I'll be there in a minute."

Maria hurried toward the automatic doors as Cindy walked to the vending machine near the corral of buggies. She bought four cheap sodas and returned to the children. Their eyes brightened at her offering. "I thought you'd like something to drink." She handed out the sodas and hurried away. Her heart expanded, and she had a renewed purpose.

"Hey, lady!"

She turned.

One of the kids sat in the car's open window and yelled, "Next time, can you buy me grape?"

Cindy waved, and walked around a pile of trash and crossed the parking lot. An old man lay against a wood bench between the generic coke machine and the door. Once inside the grocery, she searched for her sister.

As she moved up the aisle, her shoes stuck to the dirty floor.

The swoosh of the automatic door turned her head. Maria disappeared outside into the night and dread crept under Cindy's skin.

No way. This was not happening. Please God, don't let her be selling. Cindy rushed toward the front of the store.

Through the large glass windows, her sister leaned inside a blue sedan parked in the pedestrian crossing. Straightening, she slipped some folded money into her back pocket.

Cindy blinked and unclenched her fist as she reached for her phone. She wasn't about to let anyone jeopardize her future with Cole. "Start walking, little sister. It's a long way home."

Maria looked through the glass and paled. Her sunken cheeks made her eyes look like saucers. She shrugged and spoke into her phone. "What are you talking 'bout? I ain't done nothing wrong."

Aware of the bystanders and other shoppers, Cindy kept her voice low. "I know exactly what you did, and I don't want any part of it. I'm clean and I intend to stay that way. Have one of your friends give you a ride. I'm done."

Cindy disconnected and hurried toward the car. What was she thinking, coming here? Her sister didn't want help. Cindy should've learned her lesson by now.

Maria tapped on the window. "You can't leave me here. I don't have a car. How will I get home?"

"Use some of the money you made and call a cab."

"Wait! Please." The look in Maria's eyes would forever haunt her. Cindy lowered the window. Her sister leaned in and whispered, "I wasn't selling drugs. I needed some money, so I rented out one of the cards."

"You're selling food stamps?"

Maria glanced over her shoulder and then continued. "Why not? They were given to *me* for payment for babysitting, and the cut-off for the lights is tomorrow. It's not a bad thing. Look, I loan out the cards. People return them and pay half the amount used. It's a great deal. I'll have cash and they buy twice the groceries, plus they don't pay taxes."

The headrest cushioned Cindy's head as she fell against the seat. "It's illegal."

The shadows under Maria's eyes stole her youthful appearance. "Go live your own life. Just abandon me."

Her sister's tears melted Cindy's heart. "I'm not abandoning you, but being in this neighborhood makes me feel like a criminal. One wrong move and I'm back in jail. That can't happen." Cindy dug into her purse and pressed a few bills into her sister's hand. "Pay the utilities and see about fixing Granny's car so you'll have a way to go. If this isn't enough, tell the repair shop to call me."

Maria snatched the money and counted it. "How did you get this?"

"I sold the ring."

෨෬

If God performed all the miracles in the Bible, could He make a way for her to stay with Cole? If He could, would He?

Cindy's phone chimed the next morning as she found an empty spot and parked the BMW on the back side of the church. She'd lost track of time while praying for her sister this morning. She dug through her purse and read Cole's text. *Where are you? I need my extra sticks from the trunk.*

She grabbed her Bible off the front seat and shut the door. Using the remote key, she locked the car and popped the trunk. At least three dozen drumsticks lined the carpet. She replied to his text. *Im here. Which ones?*

She tapped her toes and waited for his reply.

The new ones. In the blue bag.

Cindy grabbed the bag and checked the contents. After slamming the trunk, she sprinted into the foyer. During her mad dash, her skirt had twisted. She straightened it and pushed through the double doors.

The worship service hadn't officially begun, but the musicians were playing. She suspected they were stalling for time. This was confirmed when James waved her forward. She mouthed the word "Now?" to Cole.

He nodded.

She blew out a breath. Though she kept near the wall, all eyes followed her to the front. She didn't look into the congregation as she crossed the platform. Mrs. Maxwell and Rachel were out there somewhere, watching.

The stick in his right hand was fine. The one on the floor next to his pumping foot was split into pieces. She released the bag to his outstretched hand and turned.

"Wait." He exchanged the bad sticks for the new ones, while his foot never stopped moving on the pedal. "Here. Take the broken fragments with you. I'm afraid one of the kids will find them later."

She accepted the bag. "As long as I can leave this stage."

The stick in each of his hands pounded the various parts on the drums. He tilted his head back and laughed. "Ah, Lulu. Don't you want to stay here and keep me company?"

She'd never be jealous of Joni standing on the platform again. "No, thanks. I prefer worshipping from the comfort of my own pew."

He winked. "Save me a seat."

৶ଙ

Blue circles decorated the pink envelope that Cindy accepted from Andrea after the service. "My house. Saturday at eleven. Allison's birthday party. Bring Cole with you. He can help with the slide." Andrea moved through the crowd issuing similar orders as she handed the invitations to her friends.

A longing stung her eyes, but Cindy refused to give in to the foreign emotion. Tomorrow was her birthday, and she'd never had a party. If she ever had kids, she would rent the biggest slide made.

Cole stood in the doorway, waiting. She hurried to his side, and they walked into the quiet night together.

Comfortable silence reigned on the short ride to her apartment. She couldn't stop thinking about her past birthdays. Her best and worst was when she, her brother, and Maria, had spent the day at Granny's house. She could taste the sugary icing on the cake. The first she remembered having.

Cindy swallowed. She didn't want to relive the memory of that night, but her mind wouldn't cooperate. She'd turned nine that day. Her father hadn't celebrated her milestone, but had instead thrown an adult party as usual.

The lock on their bedroom door didn't prevent a drunken reveler from finding the two little girls huddled in the closet.

Her fourteen-year-old brother had tried to protect them. During the attack, he'd been knocked unconscious and then tossed out of the house. She hadn't seen him since. Elliot insisted that he'd run away, but Cindy believed he'd been killed. No one reported him missing. Not the school, and certainly not his wicked stepfather.

That night was the first in a long list of bad memories. She shook her head and put the brakes on those thoughts. Six years later, after Elliot got busted, Granny had given Cindy the ring. She said it came in the mail, addressed to Cindy from her brother. The ring gave her hope that one day he would return. She wished she hadn't pawned it. It was all she had left of him.

Cole squeezed her hand and brought her back to the present. "Are you okay?"

They were at a red light. She nodded. She hadn't been able to stop her father's friends from hurting her, and she couldn't protect her little sister, but she didn't want to remember.

"Cindy?"

Her vision blurred, but she blinked away the tears. Why couldn't she have been born in Andrea's family? With birthday parties and slides? Church camp and Sunday school? Her chest heaved. Deep sorrow threatened to overflow. "Jesus, I need your blood to wash the memories away. Help me, Lord. Make me new." She didn't know she'd said the words aloud until Cole joined his prayers with hers.

Prayers for peace, comfort, and love flowed from his lips and surrounded her. She inhaled his comforting scent.

She raised her eyes. Love reflected back at her. Real love. Godly love. Love that would take care of her no matter what—past or present. His gaze searched her face and landed on her trembling lips. "Better?"

Her mind cleared and the memories faded. Her heart swelled and blood warmed her veins. No longer would she be the ice dealer. She wanted to make new memories. Good ones. Memories with Cole. Esther redeemed her time, and so would Cindy. She leaned over the console and rested her head against his shoulder. "I want to do something special tomorrow."

His arm wrapped around her and held her tight while he drove with his left hand. "I can manage an afternoon off. What did you have in mind?"

She curled into his side. "I'm not sure. Something I've never done before. Somewhere I've never been. Somewhere I can feel the wind on my face." It would be her best birthday ever.

He turned into Sara's drive and cut the ignition. Mischief twinkled in his eyes. He tilted the steering column and pulled her into his lap. "Fast or slow?"

The driver's window pressed against her back. "Both."

"I'll pick you up around noon. And I'll bring you a present."

She flexed her foot on the passenger seat. There was no way he could know about her birthday, and she didn't have the courage to tell him. "A present?"

"You'll need it for where we're going. I don't trust myself to take you out in the boat. So we'll do something different."

Not a gift that came with bright paper and a bow, but she'd treasure it the same.

„→ ℳ

The attorney was gone. The drummer from church hid behind mirrored shades. His black leather jacket matched his boots. Cindy had forgotten how good Cole looked in jeans.

She'd waited for him on the bottom step and jumped in the car when he arrived. She leaned over and accepted a quick kiss. As he backed out of the driveway, she asked the question burning on her mind. "Where are we going?"

"It's a surprise."

On the backseat, a huge orange bag was splashed with the name of a famous motorcycle maker. "Is that for me?"

"It depends. Do you promise to trust my judgment today? I had a friend who took a big spill when his girlfriend fought the balance."

Her eyes strayed to the sack. If she didn't count the doll her second-grade teacher had given her, this was her first birthday present. Along with the doll, the teacher had given her a large multicolored lollipop with ribbons wrapped around the stick. She had hid the candy in her pillowcase and had shared the treat with her brother and sister each night. Until the ants found it.

He frowned in concern.

"I'm okay. It's perfect, Cole. Thank you."

He laughed. "You don't know what's in there."

Whatever he had bought would be treasured. She could hardly wait to see what it was.

They arrived at the gate to a storage facility. He reached out the window and punched in a code—"Five, eight, five, eight—for my Lulu. You might need to remember that."

A few aisles down, they parked in front of a garage-type door. She reached for the bag, but he playfully snatched it off the seat as he got out of the car. She laughed and followed him.

He held the bag behind his back. "It'll cost you." He tilted his head and tapped his cheek.

Kissing Cole wasn't payment. It was a reward. One she gladly claimed.

He smiled and surrendered the gift.

Black leather similar to his was smooth against her fingers. She reverently lifted the lightweight jacket, and the bag thumped to the pavement. "It's beautiful." She'd never owned anything so fine.

"Try it on. I hope it fits. If you're joining my secret life, you need to look the part."

She slipped her arms in the butter-soft leather. "Secret life?"

"My folks don't know about the Harley." He winked. "Will you be my biker babe?"

"And ride away into the sunset?" She reached up and kissed his other cheek. "Yes."

"Then you'll need this too." He lifted a black helmet out of the discarded bag. He stepped near and tugged it over her head.

"I should complain that you are messing up my hair." Her heart was too light to do anything but soar.

"You should be glad that I love you enough to keep you safe."

Cindy slipped off her helmet and finger-combed her hair away from her face. Cole locked the car inside the storage unit and wheeled a shiny motorcycle into the sunshine, while she slipped on her helmet and fumbled with the straps.

The sun reflected in his glasses, and the corners of his mouth curled up. In two seconds he had her helmet secure. "Better?"

She nodded. "Yes, but I've never ridden a motorcycle."

He claimed her hand and led her to the bike. "I've never had a passenger. Remember what I said. Relax and ride. Trust me."

"I do."

His smile grew. "Too bad I can't convince you to say that in front of a preacher."

She laughed at his persistence. She was glad he didn't give up.

"No pressure, today. Just fun." He stole a kiss, and then straddled the bike. He grabbed the helmet strapped to a mirror and secured it on his own head. With one push of a button, the motorcycle purred to life. The engine wasn't too loud. It was smooth. "Climb on." He flipped down rear foot-pedals.

She swung her leg over. He held the bike steady as she placed her feet on the chrome and black pegs. Four inches separated their torsos, but her knees cradled his thighs. The heat that flashed between them had nothing to do with the exhaust. Cole's back muscles flexed against her palms. "Don't lower your feet to the ground until I say you can, not even when I stop for a red light."

"Okay." She shifted on the seat and rested her hands lightly on his shoulders.

He turned. "Hold tight to me. Don't let go."

Her hands slid down to his waist. He turned forward and

leaned against her. Slowly they moved across the payment. Panic assailed her, and she fought the urge to feel solid ground.

"Trust me." He yelled back to her.

She swallowed the urge and slid her arms around his chest, plastering her front to his back. The bike surged forward and she squeezed her eyes tight. The open air, on either side of her, jump started her heart.

Cole slowed at the gate. Powerful legs held the bike upright as he keyed in the code. The gate lifted and they were off once again.

Slowly, she relaxed her death grip and opened her eyes. She loved holding him close. His body blocked the wind as they headed east out of town. At a red light, a woman driving a convertible glanced over and lifted her shades. Cindy smiled, savoring Cole's nearness.

The light changed and they rode through a rural area. She peeked over his shoulder. The wind cooled her face. It was wonderful! She tilted her head back and laughed.

Cole reacted, and accelerated.

She kissed his shoulder, and his hands peeled one of hers from around his waist. Soft lips teased her knuckles. Their speed slowed, and warmth kissed the center of her palm. The jolt traveled to her toes as his teeth scraped the inside of her wrist. She shivered. He placed her hand over his heart and left it there.

The freedom on the back of his bike was intoxicating. When a small town appeared out of nowhere, he pulled into the parking lot of a rustic restaurant. "Hungry?"

୨୦୯୧

Cole missed her closeness as he stared across the table. His Lulu had ordered a hamburger and fries in a steakhouse known for its prime rib and coconut shrimp. "Are you having fun?"

"This is the best day I've ever had. Thank you." She sipped her sweet tea, and her phone rang. She frowned at the caller ID. "My sister. I need to answer."

He nodded.

Slurred words echoed from her phone across the table. "Happy birthday, Big Sis!"

Birthday? Cole forced a chunk of ice down his throat.

Cindy's eyes shifted down and to the left. "Thank you. It was good. The best ever, thanks to Cole." Slender fingers twisted her napkin. "No, I'm not working for him and I'm not coming back. Or you could leave him and start a new life here with me." Graceful hands smoothed the napkin flat against the tabletop. "Then leave me out of it. I gotta go." Cindy rolled her eyes and ended the call.

He reached across the table and caressed her hand. "Why didn't you tell me?"

She shrugged. "Surprise, I have a sister, and a brother, though he disappeared years ago."

"Why didn't you tell me it was your birthday?"

"Oh. You heard that?" At his nod, she continued. "I don't know. You've done so much already, and I meant what I said. Today was the best birthday I've ever had. Thank you, Cole."

He squeezed her hand. "I should've bought you a cake."

"I'm used to not having one." She laughed. "This hamburger probably tastes better anyway."

What kind of childhood had she endured? Who was the "him" she and her sister had spoken of? Her father? Did Cole want to know? "Your mother never made you a birthday cake?"

"I never knew my mother, and my father isn't the domestic type. My life drastically improved the day the cops hauled him to jail." Sadness clouded her eyes. "I don't want to think about the past. I prefer to concentrate on the future."

He wanted to restore the happiness of the day. "As long as that future includes me, I'm good with that."

Her trembling lips smiled, and then she excused herself to the ladies' room.

He blew out a breath. How many times had she walked to town? Now, he had an excuse to solve her transportation problems. He signaled the waitress and paid the bill. "Can you can find me a birthday cake?" He slipped her a large tip. "I don't want any fanfare and nothing that would embarrass her. Just a cake."

The girl grinned. "Give me a minute and I'll see what I can do."

Cindy returned, and he leaned close and whispered. "So how do you like your alter ego?" Her brows rose. "Biker babe?"

Her laughter was music to his ears. "I love it."

The sweet torture of having her plastered against his back would be forever etched in his mind. The first intimacy in what would hopefully end in a godly union.

Her eyes widened. A flash of light caught his peripheral vision. The waitress rounded their table and placed a small sugary confection in front of Cindy.

"Oh. You shouldn't have." The sparkly candle lit up her smile.

"Happy birthday." He winked and nodded to the cake. "Hurry and eat so we can go shopping for your gift."

"You've already given me a present."

"I want to buy you another one." He needed to protect her. "I have my own selfish reasons. I know you are used to walking, but I worry about your late-night jaunts to town. It would set my mind at ease if you had your own vehicle." *Jesus, please let her say yes.* "When you finish your cake, we'll drive to town and buy you a car."

She coughed and shaking hands reached for her sweet tea. She guzzled half and licked her lips. "I appreciate the thought"—she blinked three times—"but the church ladies gossip enough. If you buy me a car, there's no telling what they'll say."

He wasn't giving up that easily. "Then we'll rent you one."

"I-I can't." She leaned close. "Not while I'm out on bail."

Why couldn't she accept her blessings? "Fine, I've always wanted a truck. Let's go buy me one. And if I choose to let my girlfriend borrow it?" He captured her gaze and smiled. "That's between me and her. Let's go." Walking out of the restaurant, he determined he'd have his way.

They rode the Harley back to the storage unit. She didn't say a word until he parked the BMW in front of a new car showroom at a local dealer, and jogged around the hood to open her door.

She remained in the seat and stared at her hands. "Cole?"

"Yeah?"

"I like this car." Blue eyes met his. "Please don't trade it in."

With a triumphant grin, he knelt in the open door. "You like this car?"

Happiness peeked from the corners of her lips. "Yes."

"Then it's yours." He stood and held out his hand. "Come help me pick out a truck."

Chapter Eleven

2.79 carats. Natural. Fancy. Vivid. Yellow. VS2.

Cole leaned back in the chair. Last week, he'd dropped Cindy's ring off to be sized. As an afterthought, he'd asked the jeweler to appraise the stone. His pride had been chafed at having discovered that he paid a seven thousand dollar profit to the pawnbroker. Now, he drew in a steady breath. He placed the gemological report on the desk between him and the jeweler, hoping his ignorance didn't show. "The yellow stone is a diamond?"

"Yes." The reed-thin man leaned across the wooden desk and tapped the folder. "We've also appraised the smaller stones, although you may consider them insignificant in value."

"How much value?" The money didn't matter. He didn't like being cheated.

The jeweler straightened his gold cuff links. "If I were to place this ring in my store, I'd price it at $86,010."

Cole let out a long whistle. "Wow." To think Cindy had pawned it for a mere five grand. And he'd bought it for twelve. Ha. He'd gotten the better deal over the stingy pawnbroker after all. "That's good. Real good."

"As you requested, we've chosen a selection of wedding bands that would complement this ring, but might I suggest you choose a more nondescript stone for an engagement setting?"

Cindy could never know its appraised value or she'd refuse to wear it. "My fiancée is worth every penny. Yes, I want the bands."

Cole stood and held out his hand. "Thank you."

The diamonds on the jeweler's hand flashed. "Mr. Maxwell, might I suggest you at least insure the ring before the future Mrs. Maxwell wears it? I've added a few business cards to the folder."

"Of course. Call when the bands are ready." Cole accepted the report and placed the square velvet box in his pocket. He could secure it in the family safe until Cindy said yes, but he wanted to have it ready. On his way out the door, he sidestepped a couple wrapped in each other's arms. He began the short walk to his office. He loved this part of downtown Mobile. The old historical buildings, the small cafés that catered to businessmen, and the variety of people. Since the day he'd met Cindy, God had opened his eyes to the beauty around him—beauty he'd taken for granted.

As he neared the courthouse, the ring in his pocket burned against his thigh. Cindy would never agree to marry him with the court date looming over their heads. After her offer on the boat, he wasn't so sure they should. She was right. Little Lulu should have at least one parent.

Would God make a way for them to be together? For the past several nights, Cole researched her case. Her court-appointed defense was a joke. Harry Buruger, the district attorney, was good friends with Cole's uncle, but he'd been no help. Judge Pierson was the toughest in the district, but he also played golf with Cole's dad on occasion.

His spirit quickened. Should he ask for his dad's help? God prompted Cole in that direction. But if he did, he'd have to share everything. Cindy's childhood. Her arrest record. His father might help them. But what if he didn't? What if he turned against them after learning the truth about her past? His father once persuaded a judge to hand down a maximum sentence. Could he influence the judge for a lesser charge?

Cole adjusted his sunglasses and waited for the "walk" signal. The risk was great, but what choice did he have?

Peace filled him as he crossed the street and strode into the law office. He'd talk to his dad this evening. Right now, he had a meeting scheduled with a potential client in ten minutes.

The new temp the agency had sent to serve as his secretary wasn't at her desk. Would he ever find the right person for the job? He couldn't hire someone fulltime in a permanent position, not while his own future was uncertain, but someone out there was competent and capable enough to run his small office. He hoped.

He placed the box and the gemological report on the desk and then settled into his chair. He wanted to go over Mr. Worthington's profile before the meeting. As an afterthought, he texted his wayward secretary. *Please return to the office for the one oclock meeting.*

Zack Worthington was an investor based in Atlanta. He grew up in Georgia's foster system as a ward of the state, attended college on scholarship, and made his first million before he turned twenty. In the four years since, he'd acquired quite a portfolio. According to his personal assistant, who'd contacted Cole, Mr. Worthington wanted to expand into the import business.

"Mr. Maxwell, I'm so sorry I'm late." His breathless secretary burst into his office. "I had car trouble, and then the line at the bank was awful. I'll make it up to you, I swear."

He lifted a hand. "Please, don't swear. Just prepare for Mr. Worthington's arrival."

"Yes, sir." Footsteps echoed from the reception area. Her face paled. "He's here."

Cole blinked at his now animated secretary. "Darcy, calm down and send him in."

"Yes, sir. Right away, sir."

Cole stood and offered his hand. "Mr. Worthington, I'm Cole Maxwell. Nice to meet you in person."

The man's grip was firm, but his hand was cold. "Mr. Maxwell, call me Zack. I anticipate a long working relationship."

Unease churned in Cole's gut as a second man, also dressed in a suit, ducked his head in order for his massive frame to enter the office. The man wore shades. His bulky suit couldn't disguise the muscles bulging underneath the business exterior. A petite gray-haired woman followed in after him. The plain woman scurried to a chair along the wall and flipped open an electronic notepad.

"Mr. Maxwell, meet my team. I believe you've spoken with my personal assistant, George." Mr. Worthington waved a hand toward the man. "And my secretary, Mrs. Calloway."

The woman didn't glance up. The man, who looked more like a bodyguard than an assistant, stood behind the leather chair Mr. Worthington had settled into.

Cole cleared his throat and lowered into his own chair. "Mr. Worthington, I understand you're looking to expand your enterprise.

How exactly can I help your efforts?"

The velvet box claimed Mr. Worthington's attention. "May I?"

Cole didn't see any harm in showing off Cindy's ring, but before he could answer the request, George's beefy hand claimed the box and offered it to his employer. A chill ran down Cole's spine as manicured hands flipped the lid. "Ah. A yellow diamond. An interesting find. Wouldn't you say so, George?"

"Yes, sir." The deep voice echoed through the office.

Mr. Worthington's serious expression darkened. "May I ask where you found this?"

Cole suspected the ring was stolen, but he had a legitimate bill of sale. "I bought the ring from a local pawnshop."

"Would you be willing to part with such a gem?"

The question was asked innocently enough, and maybe the man was curious, but Cole reached across the desk and gently reclaimed Cindy's ring. "I'm sorry. It's not for sale." He dropped the ring into his desk drawer. "Mr. Worthington, why did you choose to employ my legal services?"

The man the media dubbed as "the gentleman gambler" tilted his head. "I want to work with someone near my own age. I like your youth and your exuberance. I also admire your caution, but the deciding factor came in discovering our mutual friend. Let's just say you come highly recommended."

Michelle? Cole wanted to ask, but he didn't want to scare off a potentially lucrative client. "All right. What's first on your agenda?"

The meeting continued as any other would have, although a bit lengthy, as some discussion was needed to determine Mr. Worthington's expectations. Somehow, by the grace of God, Cole was the attorney they'd chosen to contact first. He agreed to work on a for-hire basis, and hopefully this opportunity would prove to his father that he was a capable attorney.

After the meeting, Cole prayed that he hadn't misinterpreted God's direction as he pocketed the box and climbed the stairs.

The secretary's chair was empty, but his father's inner office lights glowed from the open door.

His dad rubbed his forehead as he stared at some document. Cole rapped on the door frame. "Hi, Dad. You busy?"

"Cole." Startled, his father crossed his arms over the papers covering his desk and removed his glasses. "Uh, come in. I was going over something." His father stacked the papers and flipped them down on the desk. A corporate takeover?

"I need your legal advice." Cole sat in a chair in front of his father's desk and breathed one more prayer. "I love Cindy. She will be your daughter-in-law. But…" His father lifted his brows and Cole squirmed in the seat. "She didn't have a good childhood, and she's made a few bad decisions."

"In Houston?"

"She's not from Houston, Texas. She grew up on Houston Street, Midtown Mobile."

His dad folded his hands behind his head. "I see. And you want to marry her?"

"Yes. She's not…she doesn't belong on those streets. She's compassionate and loyal. And she's given her life totally to God."

His father clicked his pen. "Does she love you?"

"Yes." Cole didn't try to hide his smile from his father. "Without a doubt." Cole swallowed. *Here comes the hard part.* "The consequences of her sins are a bit different than your average sinner."

His father leaned forward and placed his elbows on the desk. "How so?"

Cole forged ahead. "She has two felonies pending against her."

His father blinked. "What do you intend to do about that?"

Cole sank into the chair and folded his hands behind his head. His breath gushed out in a sigh. "I don't know, Dad. What can I do? She has Judge Pierson, and the district attorney won't plea bargain. Even after I offered him the use of the boat, Harry wouldn't talk about her case. I'm not the attorney on record."

"That's easy enough to change. What about Cindy? Can she pass a drug test now that's she's been out of jail for a month?"

Warning bells sounded. Cole planted both feet on the floor. "Wait. How do you know the charges are drug-related?"

His dad's brows quirked. "Answer my question first. Can she pass a drug test?"

"Absolutely."

For the first time since Cole walked into the office, his dad smiled. "Then pull up a chair, Son. We'll compare notes."

He scooted the chair close to his father's desk and accepted the stack of papers previously hidden from his view. The name of a private investigator was at the top of the first page. Cindy's full name was listed above a file number. "Dad! You investigated her?"

There was no remorse in his father's clear gray eyes. "I wasn't looking for dirt. I hired the firm after I learned she was your Lulu. Forgive me if I overstepped, but I don't relish my grandchildren born in a penitentiary. But…" His father came to his feet and paced in front of the large window. "There is something in there that you need to know. Quite frankly, I was unprepared for what I read. Take a look, and if you want to marry her after you have all the facts, you have my support."

There was nothing that could alter his love for Cindy. Nothing. Not her childhood abuse or her previous drug indictments. She was reborn, a child of the King. Her past didn't matter.

Until he read page four. The words blurred before his eyes.

He knew she wasn't an innocent, but he didn't have a name to go with the faceless men that taunted him. Men that knew his Lulu more intimately than Cole had ever dreamed. But he never imagined. He never suspected. Did Joni know? How could she and claim Cindy as a friend?

Cole rubbed his eyes, but he couldn't erase the words swimming in his mind. Could he live with the cold, naked truth? That a little over a year ago, Cindy had an affair with James?

"Keep reading, Son." His father's head tilted. "There's more."

Cole blew out a breath and pressed on. He read of her arrest and the evidence against her. The signature on the bond freeing her blurred.

He blinked.

The bail money that freed Cindy was paid by his new client, Zack Worthington.

Chapter Twelve

She was going to prison. There was no way around it. *Jesus, help me.* Cindy dialed Cole's phone while her attorney fumbled through his documents on the small, dusty table. Once again her call went straight to voicemail. "Cole, it's me. Again."

Her attorney lifted his head and stared wide-eyed across the consultation room in the courthouse.

She turned her back and spoke perhaps her last words to the man she loved more than anything. "I don't know what's happening, but it can't be good. My attorney called and asked for a meeting. I'm going before the judge." She paced the scarred hardwood floor. "If I don't see you again…don't wait for me. Remember that I love you." The phone beeped, indicating she'd reached the time limit. "Ugh!"

It wasn't fair, especially since Cole had worked late the past few nights. If she didn't know better, she'd think he was avoiding her. She pocketed her phone and prayed. *Cole, where are you?* She would not cry in front of the judge. She wouldn't.

Rough hands landed on her shoulders and spun her around. She broke away from her attorney's pitifully weak grip.

"Cole Maxwell? You know him?" Her attorney ran a hand through his thinning hair. "Great mother of night, I knew the Maxwells were in deep, but this is…very surprising."

A knock sounded and a uniformed officer opened the door. "They're ready for you."

The attorney walked close to her side and whispered, "Listen to me. You do not know Mr. Maxwell. Don't smile. Don't look at him. Pretend he doesn't exist."

Her breath quickened. "Cole's here?"

"Yes. I suspect he's arranged this whole affair. Especially if you and he are *friends.*"

Cindy's mind whirled as she followed the man down a long hallway. Cole had said he was working on a special case. Her case? But why go before the judge now? Why not wait until the original court date? Was he trying to get rid of her?

Her attorney opened a solid wood door and stepped back, indicating she should precede him. Her eyes found Cole the moment she stepped into the room. She frowned at the district attorney sitting next to him at a long table that filled the small space. What was going on? Cole stood and crossed to her side.

Her attorney repeated words of caution. "Don't look over."

She ignored them and stepped into Cole's open arms. "I was so worried. Why didn't you answer my calls?"

He hugged her tight. "Phones aren't allowed in the judge's chambers."

Her attorney coughed into his hand. "Mr. Maxwell, I've advised my client not to reveal her association with you."

Cole frowned. "That would have been a very big mistake." He led her by the hand to the other side of the table, leaving the court-appointed attorney standing by the American flag.

He quickly rounded the table. "Mr. Maxwell, I've sworn to defend Miss McDuffie."

Cole's fingers flexed on her hand. "If you must stay, fine, but let me handle this hearing."

"All rise." The security guard opened an inner door, and a gray-haired gentleman entered wearing a suit and tie. He settled at one end of the table. "You may be seated."

Cole pulled out the chair closest to the judge for her and then took the next seat. The weight of his arm fell across her shoulders. His other hand gripped hers on the table, in view of all the room's occupants. So much for pretending.

The judge smiled down the table. "Miss McDuffie, I hope you know what a great guy you have?"

She swallowed. "Yes, sir. He's the greatest man I know." Though she was afraid of today's outcome, she'd never regret loving Cole. Would he regret loving her?

The judge flipped through a folder. "You have two serious charges against you. How do you plead?"

Knots twisted her intestines. Cole's hand massaged her shoulder. She couldn't lie. God didn't like liars. "I was guilty, sir." She blew out a breath.

"Your Honor, my client is under duress."

Cole turned in his chair. "I told you not to speak!"

Cindy drummed her fingernails on the table and prayed. What happened to Cole's restraint?

The judge peered over his glasses. "Miss McDuffie, are you under duress? Because if you are, this hearing can't continue."

"No, Your Honor. I'm not under duress. I hesitated with my answer because I'm not guilty of those crimes any longer." She dropped her voice to a whisper. "Jesus forgave me."

The judge reclined in his leather chair. "Many influential people have written letters of recommendation regarding your change of lifestyle. One of them being Mr. Alexander Maxwell. Do you know him?"

"Yes, sir. Um, I mean." She swallowed. "Your Honor. He's Cole's father."

"He asked the court for leniency. Does this surprise you?"

"A little, but he's a good man, too."

"Yes, he is." The judge leaned forward. "Are you a good person?"

No, she wasn't. "I didn't used to be, but I'd like to think that I am now."

"Can you prove it?"

She looked down at the table, breathed, and lifted her gaze to the meet the judge's once again. "No, sir, but I'd like the opportunity to try."

"That's exactly what I was hoping you'd say." The judge turned to the district attorney. "Harold, I believe the six months previously served by Miss McDuffie is sufficient for her crimes."

"The state concurs with that assessment, Your Honor, but respectfully requests a period of five years' probation."

"Five years?" Cole glared across the table. "Come on, Harry. Isn't that a little much?"

"My client accepts the offer, Your Honor." Cindy's court-appointed attorney spoke.

Cole slapped the table. "No she doesn't. No probation!"

The judge pounded the gavel. "Calm down, Cole." He blinked and then smiled at Cindy. "Where were we? Oh, yes." He cleared his throat. "This court hereby sentences Cynthia LouAnn McDuffie to three years' probation with time served." The folder closed. "Miss McDuffie, God and this court have given you a chance at redemption. I feel that it is my duty to remind you that you are the product of your decisions." He nodded at Cole. "It has been my past observation that successful rehabilitation occurs more often with a support group. You seem to have found one. It is my greatest wish that you become a productive citizen. Often when we overcome insurmountable obstacles, others look up to us. And then we are able to come alongside our fellow man to encourage and edify." He steepled his hands and leaned forward. "Let me be blunt." He nodded to her and Cole's joined hands. "If in the future you have access to large sums of money—by legal means—this court asks that in remembrance of the leniency shown to you today, you invest in community."

He wanted her to give to charity?

"And might I commend you for your previous donation."

How did he know about that?

The judge rose and added, "I'm sure one of your legal counsels will petition my office for a probation liaison."

Cole answered, "Yes, Your Honor, and thank you. You have no idea what this means to us."

The judge smiled. "Actually, I think I do."

Once the judge disappeared behind a closed door, a whirlwind of activity surrounded her. The court reporter gathered his things. Cole scraped back his chair and stood. The latch on his briefcase sounded like a shot. He held out his hand and tugged her out of the chair. In a daze, she followed. Why wouldn't he look at her?

In the elevator, he reached for her, but two janitor ladies entered the old relic and he shoved his hands in his pockets.

When the door opened, Cindy struggled to keep up with his long legs. He strode out of the courthouse and into the sunshine.

She paused in front of the paralleled parked BMW near the curb, but he reclaimed her hand and tugged her along the crowded sidewalk. "Cole, where are we going?"

"My office." He rushed up the steps of an older house, hurried through a carpeted reception area, and navigated around a staircase. The hall opened into a small office space.

He nodded at a lady standing near a fax machine, and opened a solid wood door that stood between a copier and a narrow desk. He waved Cindy forward and stepped in the room behind her. His eyes shut as he sagged against the closed door. "Thank you, Jesus." His chest rose and fell.

"Cole, what just happened?" Did she dare to hope?

Silver eyes met hers with a shimmer of emotion she couldn't name. Relief? Desire? Both? "Come here."

She stepped near, and he rested his forehead on hers as his hands settled at her waist. "Do you know what the judge's ruling means?"

"I hope I do. It all happened so fast. My head is swimming. I don't have to go to prison?" Could it be true? She walked into the courthouse a frazzle of nerves less than two hours ago. Was she dreaming? "Do miracles normally happen this quickly?"

"My sweet, precious Lulu, God has given you a second chance. What are you going to do with it?" He pushed off the door, and she went into his arms. Their mouths met and Cole swept her away on a wave of pleasure.

"Uh-hum." Mr. Maxwell cleared his throat in the opened doorway. "Excuse me for interrupting, but I heard congratulations are in order."

Cole released her and hugged his father. "Dad, thanks for everything."

"It was a God thing, Son. I had little to do with it."

Cindy stared at the man who believed in her without asking for anything in return. "Mr. Maxwell. I didn't know…that you knew… that I—" She stiffened as he pulled her into a fatherly hug.

"Dad." A warning rang in Cole's voice.

"Oh hush, Cole." Mr. Maxwell stepped back but rested his hands on her shoulders and stared at her with a twinkle in his gray eyes. "I've always wanted a daughter, but Beverly needs time." His sigh was one of resilience. "She loves Cole, and once she realizes that you love him too, well, she'll come around."

"Thank you, sir." Cindy smiled. "I do love him."

"I know." He glanced at his watch. "I'm late for a meeting." He bent toward her and she didn't flinch as he kissed her cheek. "I'd invite you over for a celebration dinner, but I think we need to wait on that." He shut the door on his way out, but not before Cindy caught the secretary peeking from the outer room.

Cole glared at the closed door. "I'm gonna have to talk to the old man about kissing you."

Cindy burst into laughter as reality hit her. Thanks to Mr. Maxwell's connections and God's grace, she was free.

For the first time she could remember, the threat of prison didn't hang over her head. She could think of a relationship with Cole without risking his career. She leaned up and kissed him. Laughter flowed from deep within her. "Did that really happen? Or am I dreaming?"

৪৩

Most of the children invited to the birthday party were gone home. Cole searched for Cindy, ready to escape from the watchful eyes of their friends. The ring burned in his pocket. With the charges against her settled, would she say yes? Across the backyard, the women cleaned the party mess. Cindy folded a paper tablecloth and then shoved it into a garbage bag while Rachel flitted nearby.

Judging by Cindy's clenched jaw, she needed rescuing.

He hurried toward her, but slowed at Rachel's words. "I've had the wedding planned for a few years. When James got saved and married Joni, I made a few adjustments to include her in the wedding party. And when Cole interned in Montgomery, it threw the timeline off, but I'm confident that after he recovers from his current obsession, he'll propose. And when he does, the wedding will be all planned."

Cindy rolled her eyes and pressed her lips together. Her chest heaved, and then she whirled around to face Rachel. "I wouldn't hold my breath waiting for him to pop the question, since he proposed to me the day we met."

Cole bit back a shout of hallelujah as silence descended on the small group. He shoved his hands into the back pockets of his jeans and silently cheered Cindy on.

Andrea and Sara exchanged an indecipherable look.

Joni's mouth closed with a snap. "Why didn't you tell us? What did you say?"

Rachel glared into the sun. "Obviously she said no, since her finger is naked."

He wished he could see Cindy's face, but her back was to him. Her shoulders straightened. "I didn't say no, but I haven't said yes. Yet." She lifted a rag and scrubbed the clean table with a vengeance.

Joni pushed her way to Cindy's side. "The other day when he was at our house, a jeweler called and said his rings were ready."

Cole's hand rubbed against cool metal in his pocket. He closed the distance between them.

Andrea sighed. "This is so romantic. Hurry up and say yes. It's been way too long since we planned a wedding."

Rachel's face lost all color as she noticed his approach. "Cole, how long have you been listening?"

He ignored the troublemaker and leaned over Cindy's shoulder. Whispering in her ear, he asked, "You okay?"

She turned and met his gaze. Her expression said she could handle herself, but her eyes reflected appreciation of his support. "I'm fine. I lost my temper and said something I shouldn't have."

"I heard." He focused on Cindy and ignored the busybodies stretching their necks toward the private conversation. "Anything you want to tell me? Any question you want to answer?"

Her smile peeked out. "Not now. Go away, Cole. I'm busy."

What was she thinking? He wanted everyone to know that it was Cindy he'd given his heart to. "I love you."

Gasps echoed behind her. Her lips curled and his heart swelled as she said, "I love you, too."

He winked and offered his hand. "The kids are gone inside to dry off. Come slide with me."

Her eyes sparkled as she glanced at the slide. "Seriously?" Her expression fell. "I don't have anything to wear."

Her jeans were new, but he could easily replace them.

"Don't even think about it. These are my new favorites since you ripped my other pair to shreds. You aren't touching my pants."

Over her shoulder, Andrea's face paled. Joni's mouth dropped, while hatred beamed from Rachel's eyes. He leaned close and whispered, "You have no idea how lewd that remark sounded."

Cindy's cheeks turned a deep red. "You knew what I meant."

He laughed quietly. "I did. They didn't. Rachel's eyes are about to pop out of their sockets."

"Good."

With the charges against her taken care of, Cindy had grown bolder. He liked it. "Come slide. We'll borrow some towels from Andrea." He held out his hand.

"Yes, go on." Andrea removed the rag from Cindy's other hand. "I'll clean this mess. Go have fun, answer questions, and be merry or married, whichever you prefer."

෪රඊ

Cindy kicked off her flip-flops. She'd been eyeing the slide ever since they'd arrived at the party. This would be another first for her, but she didn't want to appear overeager. She tapped her toes on the soft grass and waited for Cole to peel off his socks.

He held out his arm for her to go first. The blowup slide rocked beneath her as she climbed the steps. She'd almost made it to the top when something slapped her behind. She turned. Cole blinked, but the telltale curve of his lips gave him away. She couldn't believe it. "Did you swat me on the bottom?"

Merriment sparkled in his eyes. "Who me?" He looked behind him and feigned innocence.

"I cannot believe you'd do something like that. What's got into you?" Laughter threatened and she ran the last few steps. Bouncing at the top, the giant slide swayed side to side.

Cole sat at the top and patted the slide. "Race you down?"

She flopped beside him. "You're on." She shoved off and laughed through the sprinkle of water. With a splash, she landed in the small pool at the bottom. "Haha, I win."

He barreled down the slippery surface and collided with her. "You cheated."

She scrambled to her feet and they raced up the slide again. On the fourth trip down, Andrea joined them. Then her husband and James played "king of the mountain." Thankfully, Rachel was nowhere to be seen. Cindy hoped she'd gone home.

Joni pouted on the grass below. "I cannot believe grown adults are acting like children."

"You're jealous, 'cause you can't slide." Andrea and her husband splashed into the pool and then crawled off the side. Hand in hand they walked toward a table of towels.

"I could if I wanted to." Joni attempted to climb on the slide.

James pointed from the top. "Don't think about it." He slid down and crawled toward Joni.

Cindy shook her head. "He's so bossy. You'd think she was made of china."

James softly spoke Joni's name and led her to a lounge chair, leaving Cindy and Cole alone once again.

"As long as he stays away from you, I don't care what he does." He sounded jealous, but why of James? "Cole?"

Cole laughed. "It's all right. I prayed through over it. And I promise never to hover when you're expecting our child."

She couldn't speak. Since the judge freed her, she'd been thinking about marrying Cole, and Rachel's remarks had strengthened that desire. What would their child look like? Would little Lulu look like her? Or would they have a boy with dark, wavy hair and silver eyes? But Cole hadn't asked her to marry him since her court hearing.

They were sitting side by side at the top when her jumbled thoughts untangled. "Don't do that, Cole."

"Don't do what?"

She sucked in a breath. "I'd want you to hover. It shows you care. When God gives us a baby, I'll probably need the reminder."

He reached for her but slipped. Gravity took control and dragged them both down the wet plastic. Red, blue, and yellow blended together and ended with a splash.

She landed on her back.

Her laughter drowned as Cole scrambled to his knees and reached into his front pocket. Cindy's breath hitched as he crawled over and leaned close.

He'd captured her without physical touch. "I promise to hover. I promise to remind you every day how much I value you. To tell you I love you every morning and every night as I lay by your side." His lips curled and love shone in his eyes. "My sweet Lulu, will you finally marry me?" Water cascaded down the side of his face. Soaking wet, he'd never looked more perfect.

Her answer was a simple one. "Yes."

"Awe." Andrea and Joni clapped and cheered from a dozen feet away as Cole rose and pulled her to her feet. Cindy wrapped her arms around his neck and held on tight. She vowed never to let go. Until he whispered in her ear, "Do you want your ring?"

Joy bubbled in her throat. Her laughter was spontaneous. "No, I want you."

"I'm yours, and so is this." He knelt on one knee and held out his hand. Her brother's gift glistened in the afternoon sun.

Love surged through her. "Cole? All this time? You've had this? How much did it cost you?"

He shook the water from his hair as he laughed. "Don't worry. It's worth more than I paid." He lifted her left hand. "I had it sized."

The lingering doubt vanished as he slid the ring on her finger. A perfect fit. "I love you, Cole."

Her feet left the ground as he hugged her tight. Never a patient man he asked, "How long does it take to plan a wedding?"

ഗ്രര

"What a wonderful surprise." Cole's mother waved him inside her private sitting room. "I'm so glad you dropped by. You should've come for dinner." She looked over his shoulder and sighed with relief. "You're alone. I take it you and Cindy broke up?"

This wasn't going to be easy. He needed to be tactful but unrelenting. If she sensed any hesitation, she would pounce. "Mom, do you love me? Do you want me to be happy?"

She settled into the sofa. "Oh, honey. Of course I do. And that's why I'm concerned with your decisions of late. I don't want you to wake up some tomorrow and regret today's life choices."

He dove right in. "I've asked Cindy to marry me."

His mother sucked in a breath and her eyes rounded.

He quickly crossed to the wet bar and filled a glass with tap water. "Here, drink this."

His mother's hands trembled as she pushed the glass away. "You can't do this to me, Son. Why? She isn't one of us."

Why had he never seen his mother's prejudices? "I've waited

my whole life to marry her. There is no second choice. If Cindy never agreed, I'd stay single until the day I died."

"But I thought that you and Rachel would eventually marry."

He steeled himself against his mother's tears. "Why, Mother? What did I do to give you or her that impression?"

She dabbed her eyes. "We've planned the wedding. She said that she was waiting for you to graduate law school. I thought...I hoped..." His mother closed her eyes and sighed. "She's a lovely girl."

"I used to think so, but now I'm not so sure. Who plans a wedding without a proposal? That's scary. And I don't love her. Cindy will be your daughter-in-law. If you want to know your grandchildren, then I suggest you forget this crazy notion of Rachel and beg Cindy's forgiveness."

His mother gasped and clutched a hand to her throat. "I've never begged for anything in my life."

Cole smiled. "Tonight is a good time to start. Cindy and her friends are making wedding plans at Sara's. I want you to go and offer to help. Be nice to her, Mom. Welcome her into the family, and maybe she'll add you to the guest list."

ଚ୍ଚେର

Andrea's girls splashed water at Andrew in the shallow end of Sara's pool. A breeze blew across the water, making the evening sun bearable under the huge patio umbrella. Cindy's head swam with all the details as Joni scribbled in a notebook. "Zoe's Photography is the best for engagement photos." She gasped. "You and Cole should shoot some out on the boat. That would be gorgeous."

"His office." Andrea jumped in. "No wait. In his father's office, in front of the large bookcase. You should dress up and show your support of his law career. The boat can be more casual."

"The drums." Sara propped her chin in her hand and smiled. "I can picture him sitting and you leaning over his shoulder with your arms wrapped around him." She sighed. "Perfect."

"James and I would love to throw ya'lls engagement party but..." She rubbed her rounded belly. "I'll have my hands full with the twins in a few months."

"Let's have it at the fellowship hall." Andrea and Sara nodded at each other. "That way the whole church can be included."

"Next." Joni tapped her pen on the page. "Save-the-date cards. What day did you and Cole settle on?"

All eyes turned to Cindy.

She swallowed. "We haven't, but we both want to be married as soon as possible and at the church. Pastor gave Cole a list of available Saturdays."

Joni frowned. "I wish we had that list. Where is Cole?"

"He's talking to his mother."

"Oh."

Children's laughter and splashes sounded from the pool as the women around the table observed a moment of silence.

And then Joni inhaled deep. "Well." One hand covered Cindy's. "The Lord will see you through this. As the groom's mother, Mrs. Maxwell will no doubt take care of the rehearsal dinner and the reception. With Andrea and Sara organizing the engagement party, that leaves you with the wedding ceremony. What's your budget?"

Why did everything come down to money? Cindy quickly calculated her spending. She had $4,800 in her account. "Around four thousand."

Awkward silence ruled again.

"Maxwells do not hold such paltry weddings." Mrs. Maxwell stood behind the gate. A thick three-ring binder occupied both hands, and she struggled with the latch. Sara rose and let the older woman in.

Cindy closed her eyes and breathed a prayer for strength. She peeked at Joni and was grateful for the support flickering in her friend's eyes. At least Mrs. Maxwell was no longer protesting the wedding.

With a huff, Cole's mother settled in a chair and placed the binder on the table. "Cole insisted I help, and it looks like I arrived in time to save the family from abject humiliation."

"Would you like a glass of tea, Mrs. Maxwell?" Sara reached toward the center of the table for an empty glass and poured.

Cole's mother accepted the drink. "Thank you, dear. I assume I have your help and cooperation with the planning of my son's wedding."

Joni thumped her notepad. "We're here to plan Cole and *Cindy's* wedding."

A long, exaggerated sigh told everyone at the table what his mother thought about his choice of bride. "Yes. I'm aware. If I'm to pay for the ceremony—an unexpected expense, but I believe I can scrounge up seventy-five thousand—I should have final say in the preparations." She looked at Cindy for the first time since her arrival. "Agreed?"

Seventy-five thousand dollars for a wedding? She didn't want to agree to Mrs. Maxwell's demands, but what choice did Cindy have? She knew nothing about planning a society event. And she didn't have that kind of money.

Cole deserved the best. His career demanded it. His mother was rude and stuck-up, but she would plan the perfect wedding.

Cindy nodded.

Mrs. Maxwell's smile was overly bright. She opened the binder and tore out the first few pages. "Let's begin, shall we?" She blinked in Joni's direction. "What do you have so far?"

Cindy swirled the ice in her glass as Joni filled her in.

"No, that won't do. If the wedding is to be at the church—something Cole insisted upon—then the engagement party must be held elsewhere." She tapped a manicured nail against her chin. "We'll have it at the house."

Andrea shifted in her chair. "But we wanted to host it."

"Nonsense." A wave of her hand dismissed Andrea's offer. "You two can focus on the bridesmaid's luncheon. Speaking of which…" She turned to Cindy. "Who are your attendants?"

Cindy lifted her chin. "I haven't asked them yet, but Joni, Sara, Andrea, and my sister." *If she's sober enough to attend.*

"And…?" Mrs. Maxwell's brows arched into a deep V. "You need at least six." When Cindy didn't answer, Cole's mother continued. "My niece, Felicia, needs to be included. And so does Rachel."

Gasps echoed into the night.

"No." Cindy held Mrs. Maxwell's unwavering stare. She'd seen too many movies where the bridesmaid ran off with the groom. "Rachel will not be in my wedding."

Cole's mother blinked first.

"Fine. Since the wedding will be late fall, we'll use the colors brown damask and lemonade."

Joni's eyes widened and her lips pressed into a fine line. Andrea coughed and Sara patted Cindy's hand while Mrs. Maxwell laid out the wedding plans. "Of course we'll use a local wedding director, but Atlanta has the best dress designers. It's an hour flight. I'll make an appointment and we'll make the day of it. That's where Rachel bought her dress."

Cindy gritted her teeth and breathed a prayer. Thankfully, her phone rang and she escaped from the table. "Cole."

His voice calmed her fluttering nerves. "I thought I'd call and see if mother was behaving. Is she helping you? Or do I need to have another talk with her?"

She didn't want to cause trouble between him and his parents. "She offered to pay for the wedding and…" Tipping the phone away for a moment she exhaled slowly. "She's making tons of suggestions."

"Great. That's a relief. I'm glad she's accepted you into the family."

"Cole?" Cindy swallowed her question. She should be grateful for God's blessings. What did the ceremony matter if in the end she was married to Cole? "Never mind. Joni's calling my name. I think she has some concerns."

Chapter Thirteen

The next day, after playing maid for Sara, Cindy relaxed in the pool wearing the swimsuit and using the float she'd bought at the twenty-four hour Walmart the night before. Now that she had Cole's car, the trip hadn't taken long, but she preferred walking. It helped to clear her mind.

Lying on her stomach, she propped her foot on the step to prevent herself from floating into the deep end. She wanted a tan for her wedding, but the sky was overcast. She swirled her hand in the water.

How could she keep her sister sober enough to attend her wedding without embarrassing Cole or the Maxwells? And how would she ever find one hundred and fifty friends to fill the bride's side of the church?

She sighed and closed her eyes. *Jesus, please help me.*

The float jerked out from under her and water surged down her nose. She found her feet and stood from the water, sputtering and wiping the wet tendrils from her face.

Rachel's crazy eyes stared with hatred. "How could you? I was nice to you, and you repay me by not only stealing my groom, but you've hijacked my wedding." Her chest heaved with fresh sobs and tears poured down her pale cheeks.

Cindy truly pitied the girl, but not enough to give up Cole. "I'm sorry that you were hurt by my engagement, but Cole was never yours to steal."

"I'm not talking about just Cole. I'm talking about the wedding I've dreamed about my entire life. Wedding ceremony at The Grand Hotel. The reception at The Venue. The cake, the colors, everything down to your invitations was selected by me. I've planned this wedding since I was twelve years old."

Everything Rachel said made sense. Cindy walked out of the pool and grabbed her towel. Mrs. Maxwell insisted on certain social standings, but there was one discrepancy. "Cole and I will be married at the church."

Rachel's eyes narrowed as Cindy wrapped the towel around herself. "Yes, because The Grand has been booked for three years, in the bride's name—mine."

℘ℛ

What was Cindy doing at this moment? Cole had called her phone a couple of times, with no answer. He envisioned her in the pool and wished the wedding was over and done. He wanted to cancel everything and surprise her at Sara's, but he had a lunch meeting scheduled with another potential client.

Cindy's voice rounded his secretary's desk. "Is Cole in?"

"Do you have an appointment?" The new temp was strict.

"Er, no, but…" Relief struck her eyes as her gaze met his. She was so beautiful when she smiled. "Cole, are you busy?"

He didn't have long or he'd be late. "I'm never too busy for you." He held the door, and she entered his office. "You smell like coconut." He shut them in.

"I was in the pool earlier." Her arms hugged his waist and she buried her face against his chest. A deep sighed raised and then lowered her shoulders. She tilted her head back, and he kissed her. "I need a sanctuary from all the wedding plans."

"Stressful?"

"A little bit." Her smile vanished into a tight line. "I checked in with my PO. She's nice. My probation is conditioned on passing a monthly drug test. I'm on my way to the clinic, but I wanted to talk to you about the wedding."

The clock was ticking. "Can it wait until tonight? I'm late for a meeting."

"Oh." She sprang away from him as if burned. "I'm sorry. You said you weren't busy."

"I'll always make time for you." He kissed her again. "I'll come over after work." Something wasn't right. Was it his mother? Or Rachel? Whatever it was, he'd handle the problem tonight, after he landed this account.

ഔൻ
Meet me at Granny's in 45mins. Cindy had sent the message an hour ago. Hopefully, her sister was waiting. She wanted to do this as quick and painless as possible.

She parked the BMW on the curb. Someone had trimmed the weeds around the front steps. She eased onto the porch. Beyond the box fan rumbling in the entryway, Maria and another girl sat around a scarred wood table and played gin rummy. Cindy squeezed in the door and waved smoke from her face. The smell of tobacco teased her nostrils, and she inhaled the sweet fragrance. Clamping her fingers together, she fought the craving.

"It's about time you came home." Maria thumped ashes into an overflowing tray. "Come around and we'll deal you in."

"Gin." The girl fanned her cards on the table and stood. She crossed the backside of the kitchen. "I need to feed the kiddos." She opened the door and yelled. "Jermaine! Craig! Get in here and eat!"

Cindy shook the ringing from her ears.

Three small children ran from the backyard where Granny had always let her young'uns out to play. Since Maria had taken over Granny's babysitting business, did she keep their grandmother's strict rules? The kids could only come in for lunch. A water hose provided a cool drink when they were thirsty. Cindy had drunk from the hose plenty of times as a child.

A baby cried and she followed the sounds to the couch. Precious ringlets surrounded the cherub face. The poor little girl's diaper was soaked. A diaper bag lay on the floor.

Cindy changed the baby, wincing at the pink skin. "Maria, do you have any baby powder?"

"Nope." Her sister shuffled the cards. "We're fresh out."

Having no choice, Cindy finished the diaper change without the needed medicine. The baby continued to cry. Lifting her under the arms, she carried her to the kitchen. "She's hungry, too."

The girl plunked the crying baby on her hip while she washed bowls and cups and served ramen noodles to the three children sitting on the kitchen floor against the wall.

Cindy walked around the table and lifted the cards out of Maria's hands. "I'm getting married."

Her sister gawked, and then put out her cigarette. "What do you want a husband for? I've never known you to need a man. Rosetta, did you hear? My dumb sister's getting shackled."

Rosetta passed Maria the baby and a bottle. "What's wrong with that? I'd marry Danni's daddy in a minute if he'd ask me."

Cindy held out her hand and wiggled her ring finger. "Cole had it sized."

"Couldn't afford to buy you a real one?" Maria deposited the baby on the couch and propped the bottle with a pillow. "The cheapskate."

"If Cole hadn't rescued it, the ring would belong to someone else. I wanted this one."

"Hmph. Whatever floats your boat." The chair scraped across the floor despite Maria's skinny frame. "When's the big day?"

Cindy smiled as Cole's image crossed her mind. "September 9th. That means you are gonna have to clean up your act. First things first. You need new clothes. Come on, we'll drive to the mall, my treat."

Her sister's hair was matted together, and her eyes had that overbright hue. Was she coming down, or going up?

Cindy held her gaze. "I need you to stay sober until after the wedding."

"Yeah. Right. I am sober." Maria rubbed her hands down the legs of her holey jeans. "But I could use some new digs."

"Then let's go. Rosetta can watch the children." Cindy's sister followed her out the door.

"Can I have my hair done? And my nails?"

෨൙

The gate to Sara's backyard was open. Cole recognized his mother's voice, and his steps slowed. Unashamed, he listened to the one-sided conversation.

"Here's a sample of the invitations I've chosen. I need your guest list as soon as possible. It'll take a miracle to plan this wedding in less than four months. That's why I've cut the guest list to three hundred. Cole has many social obligations, so I'm allotting you a hundred guests to free two hundred for the Maxwell friends and family. It's only fair, since we're paying for everything."

Cindy's smile tightened. "I need one invitation, for my sister."

His mother tapped the paper's edge against the table. "Fine. Cole has plenty of friends and family to make up for your shortcomings." She huffed. "Now, during the cocktail hour, I'm serving shrimp and oysters, Cole's favorite."

"No." Cindy lifted her hand. "Absolutely no alcoholic beverages allowed."

From where he stood, his mother's laugh sounded like a rebuke. "We're having a dry bar, dear. But my guests need to be entertained while the photographer takes pictures of the bride and groom."

Cindy slumped in the wicker chair and rubbed her forehead. "Whose wedding is this?"

His mother fidgeted with the pen. "Pardon?"

Cole stepped forward to rescue Cindy. Her words—"Rachel came to see me today."—made him pause.

"This..." Cindy waved her hand over the many pamphlets and papers. "Is this the wedding she planned? Is this her dream wedding? With Cole?"

"What does it matter? She'll certainly want to start over now that you've seduced Cole away from her. And I *am* paying for the wedding, so I *should* have the final say."

So, that was the problem. Ignoring his mother, Cole crossed the patio in three strides. He leaned down and kissed his bride-to-be. "I love you."

"Cole, thank God you're here." Pink tinge colored her cheeks. "I mean." Her chin lifted. "Your mother is here helping me plan the wedding."

"So I heard." He frowned down at his mother and then focused on Cindy. "Unfortunately, Cindy hasn't managed to seduce me." He winked at her girly smile. "Yet."

"Coleman Maxwell." His mother's outburst demanded his attention. "It is not polite to eavesdrop."

He rounded the table and kissed her cheek. "It's not polite to take over other people's weddings, either."

"Yes, well. As I'm paying—"

"You're not." His simple statement stole her exclamation.

His mother's eyelashes fluttered so fast they could've taken flight. She smacked her lips and sighed. "Excuse me?"

"Mom, you are no longer paying for the wedding. Cindy is the bride, my bride. She has the final decision, not you."

She huffed several breaths and stood. "If that's the way you want it, who am I to interfere? Obviously nobody. I'm just the groom's mother. You're my only son."

Cole ignored the bid for sympathy and gathered the papers scattered across the patio table. "Here, mom. Don't forget your things." He kissed her cheek again. "I love you. Drive home safely."

Her shoulders squared and she sniffed. "I can't believe you are throwing me out of your wedding."

He ignored her dramatics. "I'm not throwing you out. You'll be the first person on our guest list—mine and Cindy's. I'll walk you to the gate."

When he returned, Cindy lounged in the double hammock. He rolled in beside her sending them swinging. Through Sara's glass double doors, Mark laughed at something on the television. Cole stretched his arm, and Cindy snuggled into his shoulder.

"Thank you for saving our wedding."

He kissed the top of her head. "You're welcome. Why didn't you tell me she'd taken over?"

"I tried." Her hand toyed with the buttons on his shirt. "How was your meeting?"

He caught her hand and kissed her knuckles. "Great. The Lord's blessing us."

He loved the way she smiled at him. Like he was a true superhero. "I never doubted you."

He cleared his throat. "About our wedding…is tomorrow too soon?"

Precious laughter rang into the night. "I hope you're joking. With the engagement party, the wedding, the reception, and something for the bridesmaids—not to mention cocktail hour—I have no idea where to start."

"How about we start with me saying 'I love you,' and end with you saying 'I do.'" Her lips drew him in and he claimed a quick kiss, one she returned quite willingly.

He pulled back and cleared his throat. "Back to the wedding."

She propped her foot on his. "According to Joni, you work around a budget and theme. What's your favorite color?"

"Blue, like the deep ocean. What's yours? Please don't say purple or any shade of pink." He closed one eye and peeked at her smile. "Unless it's really your favorite."

"Yellow." Her brows arched into a frown. "Like the flowers that grew alongside the road the morning we met."

He lowered his voice to a near whisper. "That was the best day of my life."

"Yes." Her curt answer surprised him. She squirmed a few inches away. Not an easy feat in an oversized swinging net. "What about a budget? Your mom said seventy-five thousand, but I don't think we'll need that much."

"Good. We're not poor, but we'd have to make a few sales to produce that much cash." His wink freed her laugh. "Seriously whatever it cost, I'll come up with the money. Don't skimp." He pulled her flush against his side. "Tomorrow, we'll add you to my accounts. But as far as I'm concerned, we can skip the decorations, detour to the courthouse, and jump straight to the honeymoon."

"Not tonight, you won't."

"Mark?" Cole hadn't heard the man sneak up in front of them. That's why Cindy had wanted distance between them.

Sara emerged from the shadows and chose the chair beside her husband. "So you have your colors. Have you set a date?"

ဆာငာ

Blessed beyond measure, Sunday after the altar service, Cindy was overwhelmed. Being able to feel God's presence was enough reason to praise Jesus forever. The pastor leaned on the pulpit as, one by one, individuals stood and thanked God for healings and miracles. Her gaze found Cole behind the drums.

The beautiful apartment they'd found yesterday was more than she'd ever dreamt possible. They'd both signed the lease, and he would move in the first week of July.

She wanted everyone to know how grateful she was. For the first time, she wanted to testify in church. Could she do it? How could she not? She wiped her sweaty palms on the pew and stood on shaky legs.

All eyes turned toward her. The pastor nodded. Cole winked, freeing the words from Cindy's throat. "I want to thank God for giving me a church family and a godly...fiancé." She released a ragged breath as she collapsed into the pew. Though her heart beat out of control, she smiled. She'd done it. Her burden lifted, and she felt as if she could fly.

Cole's heated gaze never left her as he twirled his drumstick. The pastor turned to him and raised his eyebrows. Cole stood behind the drums. "I want to thank God for keeping his promises. Like Abraham, when everyone is laughing and saying it's impossible, God is ever faithful. I love Him, and I'm extremely grateful for my beautiful wife-to-be."

Movement brought her eyes to the congregation. Many husbands nudged wives as a few wiped tears. Cindy's chest threatened to explode as Cole recaptured her gaze and mouthed the words, "I love you."

Pastor cleared his throat, silencing the "awe"s. "Yes, God is always, faithful in keeping his promises. And in case you didn't hear, there's been an engagement recently. Cole and Cindy are to be married..." He turned to Cole. "Have you set a date?"

"She said September, but I'm praying for next week."

Laughter flowed through the congregation. Pastor held out a hand. "Let's congratulate the happy couple. I hear there are plans for a bridal shower, but we don't want to spoil the ladies' surprise."

Chapter Fourteen

"People were starving!"

Cindy flinched as the preacher pivoted on his heel.

His voice boomed through the sanctuary. "A circle of military force prevented any outside contact with the city. Donkeys' heads were sold for eighty pieces of silver." He stopped and stared at the congregation. "Most of us can't imagine real hunger. In fact, we complain about slow service at the drive-thru."

Cindy shifted in her pew and shook away the lingering images that haunted her. She'd tasted the pangs of hunger. Almost died when her father had locked her in the root cellar for slapping one of his perverted friends. Ten days without food or water, and she could barely stand. When her father had finally left the house, her sister freed her. Raw spaghetti noodles gave her the strength to walk to Granny's. She'd learned a valuable lesson.

The next time she'd been punished, she'd survived on the food hidden in her closet.

Tears streamed down the pastor's face as he stopped in front of their section. "In the latter part of chapter six, we're told about two women. Starving, desperate women. We can't fathom their actions because we've never experienced life-stealing hunger. They boiled one of their own children and ate him. This would never happen in today's society, but I want you to understand. Starvation makes people desperate. Desperate people do crazy things."

The preacher was wrong. Mothers sacrificed their children every day to feed their hunger for drugs. Maria's stack of cards testified of the women that sold food stamps to buy a line or hit, never caring that their children were hungry. In crackhouses around the country, people died of starvation. Adults, crazed for a new high, prostituted their own bodies and the bodies of their children.

At thirteen, Cindy's own father had pimped her out for the first time. She'd learned to hide when he was home.

She'd been desperate.

She'd lived with crazy.

She leaned back and closed her eyes. Pressing her head against Cole's arm, she fought against the flooding memories.

Pastor preached on. "But there were four leprous men outside the city. They were ostracized, because they were different. They were stuck between the Syrian army and the crazed city. What are they gonna do? They're hungry, but if they go into the city, they'll starve. If they stay where they are, they will die. Out of desperation, they decided to go to the Syrian army and beg for mercy. They didn't know that God had performed a miracle.

When the lepers reached the camp, they found that the army had fled, and all provisions had been abandoned. The lepers gorged on food and hoarded treasure until one of them stood and said, 'Wait!'"

Pastor flashed a palm. "They realized they were doing wrong. People were starving in ignorance. Food lay waiting, but no one in the city knew about it. They couldn't keep the good news to themselves, so they returned."

A finger pointed at the congregation. "Can you? You were once like those lepers. You benefited from others' desperation. God has miraculously provided beyond anything you could've ever imagined."

Cindy squeezed Cole's hand. He smiled and winked.

The pastor slammed a hand down on the communion table. "And while you are pigging out on God's blessings, your family is in the wicked city. Starving!"

℘℃

Cole's truck was in the shop having his specially ordered rims installed, and Cindy refused to pay another inflated taxi fare. She should have told him that she needed the car when he'd asked to borrow it this morning, but it was his. So, she'd begun the long walk to Mobile shortly after he'd left Sara's. Thankfully, in the middle of the causeway, a fisherman and his wife had given her a ride to Government Street and DIP. From there, she'd walked the tracks.

Weeds grew around Granny's car tires. Maria hadn't fixed the car. As she climbed the broken steps, Cindy wiped the sweat from her brow and decided to pay the taxi fare to the mall.

A raunchy talk show blared from the TV. "Are you ready?"

Maria waved a hand. "My story will be over in five minutes."

In the kitchen, Cindy searched the refrigerator for something to drink. She washed out a glass and poured herself some tea. Through the kitchen window, the children played outside. "Where's Rosetta? Is she coming to watch the kids while we go shopping?" She returned to the living room.

"Ain't no need in wasting all that money on clothes." Maria's new haircut hung limp around her face. "I took back the ones you bought the other day. But I can't pay you back, 'cause I done spent the refund."

"Why did you do that? I want you to look nice for the wedding." Cindy sat beside her sister on the couch and looked into over-bright eyes. "What did you do with the money? You're high. Why Maria? I want you to have a better life. Why won't you let me help you?"

The screen door slammed.

Elliot's tall, skinny frame blocked the fan, and a wave of heat inflamed the fear in Cindy's gut. "Hello, my darling daughter. Have you come to invite me to your happy day? Or have you asked someone else to walk you down the aisle?"

She stood and met her father's hard eyes. "You're not invited. I can walk by myself." She refused to cower as he strode deliberately toward her.

"Miss High-Society flaunting all that money around. Buying clothes and spa days. Where's my share of the loot?" His hands landed on her shoulders. It could have been an embrace except for the pressure against her collarbone. "Didn't I raise you and your worthless brother? You owe me, girl. Now hand it over."

Cindy refused to whimper as the hand squeezed and his thumb dug into her flesh. "Let go of me." She snatched out of his arms and hurried into the kitchen. Her plastic tea glass bounced in the sink. No matter what he did, she wouldn't hand over the four hundreds in her pocket—the money she'd intended to spend on her little sister, who was ignoring the commotion in the living room.

Elliot grabbed her hair and yanked. "Give me the money."

She closed her eyes. *Jesus, help me.* "No."

He slung her against the countertop. The side of her head caught the corner of the stove as she went down. Her vision blurred, but she managed to scramble to her feet in time to see his flying fist. The blow to her stomach stole her breath. She staggered back into the window as her phone clattered to the floor.

Elliot twisted her arm behind her back and pressed her cheek against the dusty glass panes. She kicked and struggled, but she was no match for a man's brute strength. Merciless fingers dug into her pockets and found the money he sought.

She cringed against his bad breath as he cooed in her ear. "There's a good girl." Her stomach heaved as saliva dribbled down her neck. "Come back and see daddy again sometime."

He released her, and she slumped to the filthy floor. He paused in the living room and spoke to her sister. "See you later, sweet girl."

Cindy's shoulders sagged with relief as the screen door slammed. Stunned, she trembled on the sticky floor.

Maria appeared and scolded, "He took my money, didn't he? Why do you always provoke him? Now what am I supposed to do? Starve?"

⋆⋆⋆

Mr. Worthington signed the last document and lay the pen down as Cole's phone sang Cindy's ringtone. He touched the screen and sent the call to voicemail, intending to return her call after the meeting ended. "I'll have the other contracts ready by the end of the week."

Cindy's ringtone sounded again. Was something wrong? He should answer.

Zack slid the paper towards Cole and leaned back in his chair. "Go ahead and answer. I can tell by your face you want to. Is it your fiancée? Tell me, did she like the ring? If not, my offer stands."

Cole didn't want to talk to Cindy in front of his current audience. He stood, signaling the meeting's end. He hoped Mr. Worthington took the hint. "She loves the ring. It's not for sale. It was a gift from her brother." Cole didn't say more. Did he want to know Cindy's association with Zack Worthington?

Or was her past better left alone?

The gentleman stood, and his ever-present attendants came to attention. "Perhaps I'll be lucky enough to meet her someday."

"Maybe." Over his dead body. Cole didn't want Cindy around the man. "The next time you're in town, we'll have dinner."

The phone rang a third time as the trio slipped out of Cole's office. When the door closed, he answered. "Cin—"

Her sobs halted his greeting.

"What's wrong?" He should have answered her first call. Never again would he place business before her. "I can't understand you. Take a deep breath."

Short heaves scratched through his phone. "I need you." She whimpered, and he grabbed his keys.

His latest secretary played solitaire on her desktop. "I'll be back later." In the reception area, Mr. Worthington sidestepped to allow Cole to pass. "Are you hurt?"

Through her sobs, few words registered. He pieced together her incoherent babbling. Someone named Elliot had robbed her. "Shhh, baby. I'm on my way."

Worthington's bodyguard opened the outside door, and Cole ran down the steps. "Where are you?"

Her weak voice cleared. "My granny's house."

Cole yanked open the car door and slid under the wheel. "The green house? Where we went the first day?"

"No. The second house we went to. Across the railroad tracks. Third house on the left." The call ended. He tossed his phone on the passenger seat and shifted into drive.

Mr. Worthington's beefy giant stepped in front of the hood. "Sir, do you require assistance?"

Cole didn't have time to chat. "I don't know." He drove around the man and sped through town. He prayed. The closer he got to his destination, the more trash clogged the gutters. Maybe he should have accepted the giant's offer. Cindy's safety came before his pride. He reached for his phone.

James answered on the second ring.

Cole explained quickly. "Cindy's in trouble. I may need help."

"I'll call Joni and head that way. Be careful, Cole. Wait for me.

Getting yourself killed won't help Cindy."

He drove passed her childhood home. A few houses later, a scraggly man waved and yelled for Cole to stop. Was he Elliot? Cole kept driving. In his rearview mirror, the drunk turned and headed back the way he came. Toward Cole. Toward his precious Lulu.

An old, rusted-out sedan occupied the driveway. He parked on the curb and hurried up the broken sidewalk. "Cindy!" He didn't bother to knock, and stepped over the fan in the open door.

"Quit hollering." A skinny girl with stringy hair stood from a plaid couch. "Ooh. Who have we here?"

"Cole." Cindy swayed and grabbed the kitchen doorframe.

He hurried to her side. "Oh Jesus help me." He caressed the bruise on her temple, and a seed of murder planted itself in his heart. "He could've killed you. Who is this Elliot person?"

"My father stole my money." She fell in his arms.

"It's okay, sweetheart. Don't worry about the money. I can replace it." A quickening stirred his soul, reminding him of the outraged man coming toward them. "Let's get you out of here."

The girl followed them to the car. "You all right, Cindy? He didn't hurt you that bad. Dad can't control his temper sometimes. You should've given him the money."

Cole shut the passenger door and glared at the sister. She couldn't be more than eighteen. "Don't you dare defend him. He could have killed her. And for what? A few lousy dollars?"

Jogging around the hood, he hurried into the car and sped away from her crazy family. If he had his way, she'd never be back here.

Across the railroad tracks, a black Hummer limousine was parked haphazardly on the curb. Had Mr. Worthington followed him? Where was the wild-eyed drunk man?

Cindy curled into his side and reclaimed his attention. Each sob squeezed his heart. *Jesus, speak peace to her battered soul.* Why had she come here? Something about the wedding. She'd told his mom she needed one invitation. For her sister? No wonder she hadn't invited her father. Her cries turned into hiccups as he entered the Bankhead Tunnel. He remembered James and reached for his phone. "I've got her. We're on our way home."

Cindy whimpered beside him, and he forced himself to listen as James said, "Joni's with me. She's worried. If you think Cindy's up for it, we'll meet you at Sara's in forty-five minutes."

Cole gave the suggestion serious thought. Cindy needed all the support available, but was Joni the one worried, or was it James? "There's no need to come over today. Joni needs her rest." He disconnected before James could object.

He pulled over on the causeway. A sudden urge to hold Cindy consumed him. He parked and got out of the car.

She must have read his mind. They met at the hood. He opened his arms and she stepped into them.

The wind blew around them as waves crashed against the seawall, reminding him of the day they'd met. Seagulls cried overhead. Content to simply hold her, he lost track of the time.

Until she lifted her head and said, "I can't marry you."

His heart stopped beating.

"Wait. That came out all wrong. I love you. I want to be your wife, but I don't know how to plan a wedding. I tried to make my family presentable, but I failed. And Elliot…" She swallowed and lifted her chin. "I have no one to walk me down the aisle. I have no guests, no friends. I know you were joking the other night but…can we skip the wedding and detour to the courthouse?"

The swelling along her hairline now held a blue tint. He brushed his finger gently over the bruise. He didn't want to wait months to have the privilege of holding her in the night. To protect her from her past. "Are you sure this is what you want?"

"I want you for my husband. The wedding itself isn't important."

If she were his wife, then his mother would have no choice but to accept her into the family. And her father would have no authority over her.

Cole could hold her each and every night, but she deserved so much more than a hasty ceremony by the justice of the peace. "If we went to the courthouse, Mom and Dad would know the minute the marriage license was issued."

Her smile faded.

He bent his head and kissed her. "We'll drive to another county. Another state if we have to."

Sparkles lit in her eyes, and the sun danced in the fire of her hair. "Thank you, Cole." Her arms slid around his neck, and he tasted her gratitude.

Her ringtone broke them apart. She reached in her back pocket and answered the phone. Cole heard Joni's voice through the earpiece. "We're so worried about you. Are you okay? What happened?"

As Cindy reassured her friend that she was safe, Cole regretted calling James. Why was he worried about Cindy? What was their relationship? His thoughts tossed about like the churning of the bay water. He had to break past this. He was no stranger to Satan's tricks. Would the truth set them free, or confirm his worst nightmare?

His sweet Lulu ended the call and snuggled against him. She winced in pain and shifted to his side. "They're waiting for us at Sara's so that Joni can see for herself that I'm okay."

"They can wait a while longer." He kept her wrapped in his arms and leaned against the car. "I want to ask you something. Your answer won't change how much I love you, but I want the truth."

Her face tilted upward. "Okay."

He brushed his lips across the bruise on her temple. "Whose house was that?" He held his breath and waited, knowing the answer and praying that she would tell him the truth.

She shrugged and then winced. "I don't know who owns it now. It belonged to my granny. I've always thought of the house as a sanctuary. After she died, me and some friends moved in, but I used Elliot's place as a business."

"And Elliot is your father and not an ex-boyfriend." He should have trusted her, but what about James?

"Wait." She turned to stone in his arms. Her head tilted back and one brow lifted. "You thought that Elliot was my boyfriend?" Sweet laughter floated on the tide. "Ouch." She touched her collar. "Don't make me laugh. It hurts."

"I'm sorry." Now that she was out of danger, he longed to return to the house and beat her father senseless, but her sweet lips kissed his.

And then she smiled. "I thought the attorney in you didn't want to know about my past crimes, but allow me to set the record straight." She kissed him again. "You already know my mother abandoned me with Elliot when I was a baby. He was a dealer, and when he went to prison, I took over his business at sixteen. I was good at selling. I had my own recipe for meth and other homemade drugs. There's no telling how many lives I ruined. I never touched that poison, but I had my own addiction—cocaine.

Then Granny died of an overdose. I decided to straighten my life out, but I needed money to start over. Kathy used to distribute for me. She attempted to go clean too, but neither one of us could find a real job. She blackmailed James into moving in to pay the bills. When he split, I was desperate."

James left her penniless?

"I reopened my former business. Crazy thing was, when I quit using and concentrated on the profits, I got greedy. College students love pills. I expanded and became a regular pharmacist. Money is a precious commodity for a druggie, so I traded for goods. Guns. Jewelry. Electronics. More pills."

He rubbed her back, and she continued.

"I was afraid of thieves. So, I moved back to Elliot's to protect my investments. No big thing, since he was locked up. Then Kathy knocked on my door again, this time with Joni. Kathy had traded me a rifle that belonged to some of James's ancestors, and Joni was determined to buy it back. I sold her the rifle." Her shoulders rose and fell. "At an exceedingly high profit." Blue eyes met Cole's. "Kathy would've killed her. Until you, James was the only decent guy I'd known."

So she had loved James? He couldn't ask that question.

"I snuck Joni out the back. I'll never forget what she said, 'God loves you.'

After all the bad things I'd done, I clung to those words. Shortly after her visit, I was arrested. You know the rest."

"The money in the sock came from selling drugs?"

"Yep. And I would've had more, if someone—I suspect Elliot—hadn't stolen my hoards of merchandise."

Cole laughed at the outrage in her voice. "I love you."

She leaned back in his arms. Tears misted her eyes. "I promise you, I will never go back to that lifestyle."

ॐ ॐ

She was a fast healer, but the bruises would linger for at least a week. Cindy didn't want to be married looking like a deformed plum. She washed her face and pulled her hair forward. Over the years, she'd learned how to hide the bruises in the shadow of light, and thankfully her shirt hid the ugly bruises on her shoulders and collarbone.

She stepped from behind the bedroom screen in time to hear Cole's clipped tone. "I'd rather we were married at an altar."

James leaned forward. "I'm sure Uncle Pete won't mind us using the country church, and Mark's licensed."

"What church?" Cindy wrapped her arms around Cole from behind and kissed his cheek. "What are we talking about?"

Joni's voice was a bit too cheerful. "Your wedding, silly." She stared at Cindy's face, and tears sprang into her eyes. Several rapid blinks, and the extra moisture vanished. A bright smile appeared. "Do you want to be married in a church or the courthouse?"

Her friends avoided questioning her about the bruise, but she'd overheard Cole's earlier explanation. God had given her good friends. People who cared. Cindy moved around and sat on the arm of the couch beside Cole. He hugged her close, resting his hand on her waist. "We're just tossing around ideas. Texas is still an option."

"Texas?" Joni recoiled into the leather cushions. "That won't do. The doctor said I could no longer fly. Unless you want to wait until after the twins are born?"

"No." Cindy shook her head, and then leaned down and whispered to Cole, "But I want to wait until the bruises fade."

His thumb fiddled with the diamond on her finger. "What do you think of a small country wedding? One with a few friends, and no announcement in the society pages."

Nerves churned her stomach inside out. "Your mother?"

"No." Joy bubbled in her heart at his answer. "As much as I love my mother, you deserve a peaceful ceremony." He turned to James. "Call your uncle and see if the church is available next week."

Joni gasped. "Next week?"

Cole met Cindy's gaze and lifted a brow. "Too soon? How long do you need to plan a simple ceremony?"

She smiled and fluffed his hair. "I want to be married on June thirteenth." Her original court date. "But your mother said a weekday wedding was unheard of."

Cole grinned. "I think that's a perfect day to start our new life together."

"I need to buy a dress and a few other things. Maybe some flowers. I like flowers."

"Then we'll have tons of flowers. I own a couple tuxes, and the wedding bands are at the office." His arm tightened around her. "If we invite James and Joni, Derek and Andrea, and Mark and Sara, that's three guests each. Mark can perform the ceremony and Joni can play the piano."

Old self-doubts resurfaced. "I'm sure they can't drop whatever they're doing for us."

"We'll be there." She'd almost forgotten Joni and James sitting on the couch. "And I'm sure the others will be honored to be included."

Cole brushed a kiss across her knuckles, and she focused on him. "People care more than you think. Ask and let them decide."

The stone sparkled on her finger. Of all the years she'd had it in her possession, she'd never worn it on her left hand. Now she vowed she'd never take it off. She should have refused Cole. He was good. She wasn't. He was light. She'd hid in the dark for as long as she could remember. He'd seen her at her worst. Yet he loved her anyway. *Jesus, thank you for saving him for me.*

A knock sounded, and Sara peeped in the door. "Can we come in?" She and Mark didn't wait for an answer. Cindy silently counted her blessings as Cole invited them to perform the private ceremony while James called his uncle to check the availability of the church. Sara wiped a few tears. Cindy wasn't sure if it was because of her bruised temple or nostalgia, but soon excitement crowded into the apartment as plans were quickly made. The men agreed to babysit so the women could go on an impromptu shopping trip.

As everyone headed downstairs to wait for Andrea and Derek, Cole gently pulled her to the side. "We'll be down in a minute."

"Yeah, right." Mark tapped his wrist watch. "I'm timing you." He left the door open on his way out.

Cole's laugh confused her. "Keep watching the clock." Then he shut and locked the door.

"Why'd you do that?" He never stayed in the apartment alone with her. What was wrong with him?

His Adam's apple bobbed as he swallowed. "Because. I don't want anyone to see what I'm about to do." He crossed the room and claimed her hand. To her shock, he led her around the screen to the bedroom area.

"Cole?"

"Shh. Don't speak. I might lose the nerve to do this." He didn't stop at the bed, but gently pulled her into the bathroom.

She stood mute, unable to speak at his strange actions, especially when he closed the bathroom door and locked it, as well. Ignoring the pain, she lifted her arms around him, but he shook his head and lowered them to her side.

"Don't distract me." Deft hands aimed for the buttons on her blouse. Had Elliot pushed Cole over the edge?

He undid the first three and gently pushed the fabric off her shoulders. The bruises on her collarbone? How did he know? Puddles of love formed in his eyes but didn't fall. "I'm sorry I didn't protect you."

She closed her eyes as his lips brushed across her lower neck and collarbone, the places where Elliot's fingers had hurt her.

Cole's breath caressed her neck once more. "I promise, he'll never hurt you again." He straightened her shirt and fastened the buttons. As if he hadn't just seen her half naked, he led her out the bathroom and toward the door.

They were halfway down the stairs when she found her voice. "Cole."

Pausing on the step below her, he turned. "Yes?"

"I love you."

His smile grew until it sparkled in his eyes. One foot crowded her step, and he leaned close. "I certainly hope so."

She tasted the passion in his kiss. It was a good thing he didn't kiss her like this in the bathroom, because she didn't want it to end.

"Hey!" James and Derek glared from the bottom of the stairs. "None of that until after the wedding."

Cole's face turned bright red in the evening sunshine. He reached in his back pocket and pulled out his wallet. "Here. I'd marry you in rags, but I'm sure you want a new dress. Use this to buy everything you want for the wedding."

She stared at the offered gold card.

He pressed it into her hand. "And not just for the wedding. Use it to buy anything you need. Hairspray. Lotion. Peanut butter."

She couldn't prevent the giggle from escaping her lips. "Peanut butter? You'll spoil me."

He kissed her again. "That's what husbands do."

James and Derek pulled them apart and playfully hauled Cole up the stairs. "Not before the wedding, they don't."

Cole winked. "Hurry back. We're gonna shoot a few games of eightball while we wait."

Chapter Fifteen

Cantina music danced from the hidden speakers. Cindy entwined her arm in Cole's and linked their fingers together under the table. His leg pressed against her thigh in the crowded corner booth. While on her other side, Joni scribbled notes on a pad of paper. Andrea dictated their last minute errands before they could decorate the church. To Cole's left, James and Derek rehashed yesterday's sermon and munched on chips and salsa. A festive sombrero hung on the wall above their heads

Cole's gentle squeeze made her smile. In the midst of the different conversations going on around the table, his reassurance gave her hope that this wasn't a dream. Tomorrow, they'd be married. This morning, she and Cole had driven to the courthouse in his new truck and bought a marriage license. Cole's whispered breath landed near her ear. "Are you sorry we invited them?"

The other occupants of the table were oblivious of them. "No. Let them have their fun." She peeked into his smoky eyes."

His gaze dropped to her lips and he leaned closer. If they were alone he would kiss her, but the crowd at the table held him inches away. Her fingers caressed the smoothness of his jaw, and her thumb traced his bottom lip.

He glanced at his watch. "The courthouse is still open."

A tortilla chip bounced off his eyebrow. "Bite your tongue." Spunky Joni was backed by the brooding Andrea. "Cindy will have a real wedding."

Andrea's arms crossed. "So cool your hormones."

Joni giggled. "At least until tomorrow night."

Nausea bubbled up Cindy's throat. She swallowed. Cole had waited twenty-eight years for the perfect night. She craved his hugs and kisses, but the thought of sex turned her stomach.

His arm tightened around her. "Lulu?"

"I'm okay." She forced a smile, and reminded herself that Cole wasn't like the men from her past. "Wedding jitters."

Two waitresses arrived with their food.

Cole said grace and thanked God for bringing them together. She could listen to his prayers all day. "I love how you pray for us."

His hand squeezed and then released hers. "Good, because I intend to thank God for you every day for the rest of my life."

෨෬

Cole paced the front of the church and tugged on his tuxedo sleeve. Yesterday, Cindy was skittish. What if she changed her mind? He should've never suggested this wedding. They should've gone to the courthouse. She'd be his by now.

James slapped his shoulder. "She'll be here."

Cole stretched his arms behind him and then shoved his hands in his pocket. A door slammed. He flinched. They hadn't seen each other since they parted at the Mexican restaurant. He'd knocked on the door of the fifth wheel RV at James's family farm last night, but the girls kept her hidden from view. What was taking so long?

"You're a nervous wreck." Derek shook his head. "Chill."

Joni appeared in the entryway. Where was Cindy?

Mark stepped through the baptistery door and stood in front of the communion table. "I believe we're ready to start."

Cole tugged on his jacket and brushed a piece of lint from his sleeve as Joni walked the aisle and settled at the piano.

James stayed his hand. "You're good."

Music softly played as first Sara, and then Andrea, entered. Their blue dresses were the identical to Joni's. The double doors opened and Cindy stood in the foyer. Cole's breath caught. Shimmery white fabric draped from her shoulders and then poofed from her waist down. The smile she wore was his. Soon she would belong to him like no other. She was more than beautiful. *God, I promise to love her forever.*

The music changed and she moved forward. Stitched blue flowers decorated the bottom of her white dress. Pink toes appeared as she walked. Why didn't she buy shoes? Sara and Andrea blocked his view. When they stepped to the side, Cindy was halfway to him.

What was taking her so long?

His feet moved. He found himself in front of her.

She whispered fervently. "You were supposed to wait."

Was she mad? Her pretty dress was too puffy. He couldn't step near her without trampling it. "Sorry. Do you want me to go back?"

Her smile lit up the heavens. "No. Walk me down the aisle."

He nodded, but his feet didn't move. Instead, he lifted her hand and brought her knuckles to his lips. Blue stuff was sewn into the V below her neckline. He needed a distraction until after the ceremony. "Where are your shoes?"

She blinked. Her lips parted and then she swallowed. "The dress was too short with them. Does it bother you?"

Her hair was different. Shinier, but he couldn't reach it. "No. You're beautiful." His finger traced the jeweled pin on the silky blue fabric. She had two freckles below her throat. The bruises had faded. *Thank you, God, for my sweet Lulu.*

"Cole? Do you want to marry me?"

The softness in her blue eyes matched the flowers in her hand. "More than anything."

Her glossy lips twitched. "Then move. We need to reach the altar before you forget that we're in a church."

She would soon be his.

Her voice hardened. "And our friends are waiting."

James's cough echoed through the empty pews.

"Oh." Cole snatched his hand away from her satin skin, marched to the front, and froze. Wait! She wanted him to walk beside her. He hurried back up the aisle and reached for her hand. "Sorry."

A knot lodged in his throat and he forced himself to breathe. The dizziness faded, and he focused on his beautiful bride.

෨෬

The dreaded wedding night had come, but the sun shone outside the hotel window. Cole said they'd waited long enough and had booked them a room in the nearby town of Jackson.

It was the longest thirty-minute ride in her life.

Cole carried her into the room and kissed her sweetly. Then he returned downstairs for their luggage.

She fell back against the firm bed and inhaled. The dress cut into her side. She exhaled, sat up, and reached behind her. Joni had said this happened when you bought off-the-rack. Cindy stood and twisted right then left. The tiny hooks and loops wouldn't budge.

Lord, please don't let Cole be disappointed.

The door clicked, signaling the use of a key card. Looking over her shoulder into the mirror, her eyes met his. Her husband. He was so beautiful. Powerful. He, too, had shed his jacket, and his dress shirt stretched across his muscled chest.

She wanted to touch him. Shocked at her own desires, she turned toward him. He deserved so much more than she had to offer, but he was now hers. She wasn't about to let fear ruin his wedding night—or day, since it was afternoon.

He placed his phone on the dresser, and soft instrumental hymns played. His smile jumbled her thoughts. He neared. "Will you dance with me?" The first two buttons of his shirt were undone. His outstretched hand waited. She latched onto him and they moved with the music, but the fullness of her dress kept them apart.

He stopped in the center of the room and touched her skirt. The husky sound of his voice mesmerized her. "Take this off."

She turned her back. "I can't undo the stupid hooks."

Breathing came easier as his hands worked their way down her spine until she was free from her restraints. She stepped out of the pool of fabric, and stood in her strapless slip.

The gentleness of his touch soothed her frazzled nerves.

She relaxed against his chest as they swayed with the music.

"Thou hast ravished my heart, my spouse." The raspy whisper near her ear drained the strength from her knees. "Thou hast ravished my heart with one of thine eyes." He turned her in his arms and captured her gaze. "How fair is thy love, my spouse."

She closed her eyes and shivered as he inhaled her hair.

"How much better is thy love than wine and the smell of thine ointments than all spices." His mouth hovered mere inches out of reach. "Thy lips, O my spouse, drop as the honeycomb; honey and milk are under thy tongue;"

Her fear drowned in his kiss. How was she to know, that love could be so wonderful?

ဆၢ

Although Cole seemed happy enough to run around in his boxer briefs—and she was happy enough to watch him—she tightened the bathrobe around her waist and perched in the upholstered chair. "I'm starved."

He lifted a bottle of sparkling grape juice and filled two plastic flutes that were sitting on the bedside table. "If they have no bread… let them eat cake." He whisked open a white pastry box.

She could almost taste the sugary confection but… "I thought Andrea said we had to eat that on our first anniversary?"

His eyes caressed her bare legs. "Do you want to eat stale cake a year from now?"

A giggle escaped her and she scooted the chair close. "No."

Cole sat on the bed, broke off a small piece, and offered it to her.

The sugary smell made her mouth water, but at the last second his hand veered off in a different direction. Cole devoured the bite and licked the icing off his fingers.

Her empty mouth sagged. "You tease." She rose on her knees and claimed the box. The dessert melted against her tongue. He lunged, and they wrestled to the bed. Their playfulness ended with cake smeared in her hair and on his chin.

She nibbled his jaw and smacked her lips. "Now look what you've done. I'll have to wash my hair before supper."

His eyes darkened. "I'll wash it for you."

She hid her smile. "Thank you, but no."

"Yes." He trashed the empty box. "Such are the obligations of a gold band and a beautiful wife." He smacked his lips. "But being the dutiful husband that I am, I'll have to suffer through it."

He slung her over his shoulder and strode for the suite's bathroom. She laughed all the way to the shower.

ဆၢ

Cindy rolled onto her side and propped on her elbow. Her eyes followed the sounds in the predawn light until they landed on her husband across the room.

He knelt in front of the upholstered chair. "Father, thank you for my beautiful wife. Bless her, Lord, with happiness. Make me a godly husband, one both she and You will be proud of…"

Her eyes misted as his prayers continued. She wanted those things too. Cole would be the best husband. Her wifely skills, she wasn't so sure of.

Rolling onto her stomach, she buried her face in her pillow and added her prayers to his. "Lord, thank you for yesterday. I never dreamed love could be so perfect. Thank you for sending Cole to rescue me. Thank you for saving me out of the hell that was my life. Make me a good wife. And a good mom. Fix me, Jesus." She prayed until the bed dipped with Cole's weight. She rolled on her side and propped on an elbow. "Amen."

෨෬

The sun streaming through the lobby played with Cindy's hair as she nibbled on a pastry. Though they were seated at a small table for two, he dared not touch her. He reached for his coffee.

Dainty hands clenched her napkin and then hid in her lap. "I feel your thoughts, Cole. Stop it."

There was no way she could read his wicked mind. "Prove it. What am I thinking?"

Their eyes met, and her smile answered his. A sweet memory from hours ago passed between them. Her gaze dipped and color infused her cheeks.

He leaned across the table and claimed her reappearing hand. "We need a bigger tub. Have you ever been to Colorado?"

"Not counting yesterday, I've never left the Mobile Bay area."

The world waited. He wanted to share it with her, but she couldn't leave the continental United States until after her three years' probation. He couldn't wait that long. "When I was a kid, we'd vacation in the Rocky Mountains. The cabin we stayed in had a hot tub so big, I swam in it."

"But you're all grown up now."

"Yes, I am." His thumb drew circles on the inside of her wrist. "You love to walk, and where we're going has some great hiking trails. It'll be fun taking a break from the summer heat. Our plane departs at two."

The color drained from her face. "I-I don't have the right clothes." She shook her head. "I've never flown before…and what about your new client? Your mom said your career is important."

His phone rang and he regretted turning it on. "James, you shouldn't call a friend during his honeymoon."

Laughter flowed through the earpiece. "Joni wanted to call last night. You can thank me for stalling her. She wants to post pictures of your wedding. Have you told your parents yet? I'd hate for your mom to find out through social media."

Cindy paled. She must have heard James's comment.

"We've been busy."

James laughed again. "Yeah, I bet."

Cole knew how to convince Cindy to go away with him. "Give me thirty minutes to tell Mother. Joni can post the pictures in an hour. And thanks for all you did for us yesterday."

"That's what friends are for."

Cole disconnected the call and reclaimed his wife's hand. The rings on her slim finger branded her as his. "Joni wants to post pictures."

Her smile vanished. "I heard."

"I'll give Mother a call, and by the time we return from our trip, she'll forget all about not being at the wedding. You'll see."

"Are you trying to convince me or yourself?"

"Both." He stood and tugged on her hand. "Let's go somewhere more private."

Her musical laughter flowed. "Why? So the other guests can't hear her scream?"

He led her through the maze of tables. "Mother doesn't yell."

A rose garden stood on the south side of the hotel. Cindy perched on the stone bench and nodded at his phone. "Go ahead. Let's get this over with."

He dialed his parents' number and pressed the speaker after the first ring. *Please let Dad answer.*

His mother's shrill voice came on the line. "Cole. Where are you? I was so worried. When you didn't answer your phone, I called your office. The firm's receptionist said you'd be out all week. What's going on, Son? Are you in trouble?"

Cindy's shoulders rose and fell.

"I'm not in trouble, Mom. In fact, I've got some great news.

Cindy and I were married yesterday."

Silence thundered through the speaker.

"Mom? Are you there?"

"No. You. Were. Not! Coleman Alexander Maxwell, if this is your idea of a joke…"

"Joni will post pictures in about an hour. You can see for yourself."

"Joni was there? Oh, for the love of God. And you didn't invite your own mother? Wasn't it enough that you married a heathen, but you invited them to the wedding?"

Cindy flinched. "Mrs. Maxwell, Joni isn't a heathen."

"Cole, I demand you take me off speakerphone this instant."

"That's not necessary, Mother. I called to let you know we were married, not to hear you complain about our friends."

Sobs and wails burst through the phone. "Son, you can't do this to me. We need a society wedding. All my plans for your future… they're ruined. What about your grandfather?" The wails intensified.

Cole had never hung up on his mother in his life, but he needed to end this drama show. "I love you, Mom. We'll see you at church next Sunday." He disconnected and ended his mother's pleas.

Cindy slumped against him, and he wrapped her in his arms. "See, that wasn't so bad. Was it?"

"At least she didn't disown you."

"Mother, could never do that. I'm the Maxwell heir. When the shock wears off, she'll come around." Sitting on the bench, he pulled Cindy down on his knee and then called his dad's office. They needed some support for their side. Cindy's arm draped around his shoulders, and her fingers teased the back of his neck.

He winked at her as his dad answered. "Your mother's crying on the other line. You could've at least invited your parents to the wedding."

"It was a spur-of-the-moment thing, Dad. Mom owes Cindy an apology."

His father's sigh was long and loud. "I warned you that your mother needed some time, although your happiness means everything to her. Give her a few days to adjust to the news, and welcome Cindy into the family."

෩ඬ

Cocooned in her husband's arms, Cindy found perfect sleep. Their honeymoon had been a piece of heaven on earth. She woke Saturday morning, rested and happy. The twin bed in the apartment she'd rented from Sara was small, but Cole didn't complain last night as she cuddled close to his side.

Sunlight lit the room beyond the screen. She rolled onto her stomach and traced Cole's lips with her finger. His nose wrinkled and his lips puckered. Then both relaxed in sleep.

Cindy stifled a giggle and lightly touched his lips again. Quick teeth captured her finger, and she shrieked while his lips twisted. He gave a sinister laugh. She tugged on her finger and he laughed again, openly this time, freeing her.

He smacked his lips. "Yum, tasty." He leaned down and growled, sending delicious vibrations that tickled her nape. Cindy laughed and wiggled, but her arms anchored around his neck.

A click sounded beyond the screen, and she froze. "Listen." The door knob rattled and clicked again. "Someone is trying to pick the lock. I told you it needed a deadbolt."

His smile mocked her. "I don't hear anything. No one would want to break in here. They'd have to brave Sara's backyard, and it's full light outside."

The door hinges creaked. "Cole?" His mother's voice drove Cindy under the covers.

She peeked at his stricken face and whispered, "Please tell me your mother isn't inside the apartment."

Mrs. Maxwell's voice came closer. "Cole? Are you awake?"

"Mom! Stop right there." Cole leapt out of bed and yanked jeans over his boxers.

Mrs. Maxwell moaned. "Are you sleeping with Cindy?"

The absurdity of the situation hit her, and Cindy burst into a fit of giggles.

Cole held his arms out and shrugged. To his mother he said, "We weren't exactly asleep, but that's allowed between *married* people."

His mother gasped as Cole stepped around the screen. "You're naked."

Cole reappeared, eyes rolling for a brief moment, and then stepped out of her sight again. "Cindy's wearing my shirt, our luggage is in the car, and normal parents don't visit their children while they are on a honeymoon. So if my lack of attire offends you…there's the door."

"Coleman Alexander Maxwell. How can you speak to your mother like that? I raised you to respect your elders."

"What about respecting me, Mom? Or my wife?" The anger in Cole's voice was foreign.

Cindy gathered her clothes and retreated into the bathroom. She brushed her teeth until they shone and then she brushed them again. When she couldn't stall any longer, she sucked in a breath and stepped onto the battlefield. Thankfully, Mrs. Maxwell had retreated.

On the couch, Cole's elbows rested on his knees and his head hung low. He lifted his stricken gaze as she crossed the living area. "I can't believe my mother barged in here."

Cindy took pity on him. "It could've been worse." She moved close and sat on his lap. His arms encircled her waist, and her forearm rested on his shoulder. "Why don't we install a deadbolt?"

He smacked her lips with a kiss. "I have a better idea. Let's go buy a bigger bed and see if we can move into our new apartment complex early. It's gated and has the latest security."

Chapter Sixteen

The firm's receptionist had directed Cole's calls to voicemail while he'd been on his honeymoon. Unless a client had an emergency, then his father stepped in and handled the situation. The problem was, Cole didn't know which messages had been relayed to his father and which calls he needed to return.

"Mr. Maxwell?" The temp the agency had sent smiled timidly from the doorway. "I've made a fresh pot of coffee. Would you like a cup?"

"Yes. Thank you." Cole needed a good dose of caffeine. Cindy's cooking tasted amazing, but her coffee was strong. He swallowed as he remembered the bitter taste from yesterday morning. If this shy, timid girl could brew a decent pot, he'd hire her permanently.

But for now, he needed to call his father. He lifted the office phone and buzzed his dad's office.

His father's paralegal was like part of the family. "Good morning, Cole. And congratulations on marrying your sweetie?" She'd started out as a receptionist and moved up the ranks when Mrs. Bevin retired. "When will I have the privilege of meeting her?"

He pictured his wife as he'd left her this morning, curled in the twin bed, asleep. "I'm not ready to share her with the rest of the world yet."

Laughter flowed from the other end of the line. "You can't keep her hidden away forever."

"Yes, ma'am." Enough small talk. "Is my father available?"

Cole's secretary slipped in and placed a napkin on his desk followed by a large mug of coffee. The delicious aroma rolled over his tongue. He nodded his thanks while his father lectured on business etiquette.

"It wouldn't have killed you to wait for a real wedding. Both clients and family should've been included. Mr. Worthington was quite upset when I explained about your elopement. The man became enraged. He stormed out of my office, grumbling about family missing the wedding. I'm worried about losing his business. And at the same time wondering if we should just cut our losses. That man is definitely hiding something. Now that you're married, you need to focus on building your career, not jeopardizing it. You need to be able to provide a future for your family."

"Dad, life's short. I don't want Cindy to look over my casket and wish we'd spent more time together. And when God blesses us with our little Lulu, I want her to know her daddy loves her."

"That's all well and good, Son, but you need to find a balance between your personal life and business."

"Thanks, Dad. Speaking of business, I'm sure you have pressing matters to attend. I won't hold you any longer." Cole disconnected. He'd received the necessary information from his father. He hadn't asked for a lecture. He stood and went to refill his cup.

The girl bounced out of her chair. "Mr. Maxwell, let me get that for you."

Marrying Cindy had changed his whole outlook on life. He wanted to forget the office and return to the little bed in her apartment. But his father was right. He needed to provide for his family. He clicked the computer mouse and opened a file as his secretary discreetly placed the refilled mug on his desk. Time to work. Hopefully, there'd be plenty of time to spend with his wife this evening.

₧₧

Andrea spread chicken nuggets out on the paper-covered highchair. "Here you go, sweetie pie."

Cindy leaned across the table and ignored the excited screams of the dozen or so children running wild in the play area.

Andrea's daughter wailed. "Mom, I told you I don't like ketchup. My burger's ruined and now I'll starve."

Cindy frowned at the complaining kid. If she was truly hungry, she would eat the burger anyway and be thankful for the extra bites.

Pastor's sermon about the women that boiled their children surfed on her brainwaves.

And then the Scripture she'd read that morning flashed through her mind. Jesus had told Peter, "Feed my lambs."

How many children in her old neighborhood were hungry? The thought squeezed her heart, and she couldn't eat another bite of her chicken ranch club. She tossed the offensive sandwich on her tray and pressed a hand to her queasy stomach.

How could she have forgotten the pit Jesus saved her from? *Is this what you want me to do, Lord?*

"Cindy?" Andrea's blurry image cleared. "Are you okay?" Her friend smiled across the table. "You look pale."

"I don't feel good. I'll see you later. Okay?"

"Sure thing. Go home and rest. And call me if you need me."

Cindy nodded and gathered her purse. After emptying her tray in the garbage, she thought of the children at Granny's. She couldn't eat another bite without feeding someone less fortunate.

She ordered five kids meals with juice boxes and then drove to her old neighborhood.

A black Hummer limousine idled across the tracks. The windows were tinted dark. Was the driver lost? She slowed, intending to turn into Granny's drive, but spotted Elliot.

He glanced over his shoulder and then ran up the steps as if the hounds of hell gave chase.

Her breath caught and she accelerated. Shaken, she made a U-turn down the street and headed toward home. She jumped the tracks and the limo swerved into the street behind her. The vehicle followed until she entered the Bankhead Tunnel.

The smell of hamburgers drifted from the backseat. What would she do with all this food? She couldn't bring herself to throw it away, but she couldn't chance meeting Elliot.

There were other poor neighborhoods in the downtown area. An idea took root, and she took the Bay Bridge to Africatown.

Trash littered the rundown streets. Under an oak tree, a group of children played with sticks in the sand. Cindy pulled the BMW to the curb.

As she stepped out of the car, the oldest of them—probably around ten years old—pointed his stick in her direction. "What do you want, white lady?"

She felt eyes watching from the shotgun houses, but she refused to cower. "I brought you a present."

"It ain't Christmas."

"No, it isn't." Keeping eye contact with the leader of the group, she rounded the car and opened the rear passenger door.

The boy's eyes widened. "Whatcha doing with that food?"

The others crowded around but stayed behind the leader.

Cindy set the paper sacks in between them and smiled. "God sent me to deliver your lunch."

"We ain't got no money."

Careful not to turn her back on the children, and keeping a watchful eye out on the surrounding porches, she eased toward the driver's door. "Jesus paid the only price needed." She got in and pressed the lock button. Her hands and feet trembled as she drove.

In the rearview mirror, the children dug into the sacks.

Back on the Bay Bridge, she looked down at the many boxcars on the railway and the huge, cargo ships sitting idle in the port. How many other children were out there, hungry? On the highest point of the bridge, she glanced out into the gulf and marveled at the tiny puffs of white cloud that dotted the horizon.

Inhaling, she pictured the look on Cole's face when she told him how she had fed people. It wasn't five thousand, but she couldn't wait to do it again.

ཀ

A loud crash sounded from outside his office door. His new secretary shrieked. Cole jumped to his feet and ran toward the commotion.

"I want to see him. Now!" The man who'd been on the street in Cindy's neighborhood leaned over the trembling girl's desk.

"Step away from my secretary and lower your voice, or I'll have you bodily removed."

The man straightened and turned toward Cole. "Is that anyway to welcome your father-in-law? By threatening him?"

Cole swallowed his disgust at the stale, cigarette smell coming from Cindy's father.

Elliot.

The one who'd left bruises on Cole's precious wife.

Was he the one who tortured her dreams? Anger like he'd never known surged within him and threatened to strangle his reason. *Jesus, help me.*

Cole suppressed the urge to beat the man to a pulp.

"Answer me, boy."

Cole unclenched his jaw. "Lucky for you, I answer to God and God alone. As for you, you're not welcome here."

"You steal my baby girl and deny an old man a few bucks?"

"Get out and don't come back."

Mr. Worthington's assistant ducked his head in the door. He didn't wait for permission, but grabbed the old man by the collar. "I'll take care of this problem, sir."

Cole followed them into the atrium.

A small crowd had gathered in the reception area. Cole's mom frowned from the top of the stairs. He couldn't meet her gaze. She rarely came to the office. Why did she have to be here now?

Elliot's puny attempts failed to free himself of the giant's grip. His eyes narrowed on Mr. Worthington. "I should've known you'd get to him first."

Mr. Worthington held the door as his bodyguard threw Cindy's father out on the sidewalk, and then met Cole's gaze. "We all have that one relative we wish we could hide under a rock." He nodded, and the giant followed Elliot out the door.

How did Zack Worthington and Elliot know each other? And what did it have to do with Cindy? Now that he was safely married to her, Cole wanted answers. "Let's talk in my office."

The best secretary he'd ever had wiped tears and stood, her purse slung over her shoulder. "Mr. Maxwell, I can't work in this hostile environment." She walked out the door.

Cole had a sinking feeling that she wouldn't be back. In his office, Mr. Worthington settled in a chair and smiled. "A good employee is hard to find. Like family, they should be loyal and discreet."

Cole fell back in his chair and folded his hands behind his head. Then it hit him. Zack Worthington's eyes were the same color and shape as Cindy's. He'd wasted money by hiring his dad's private investigators.

The answers to his questions stared him in the face. "You're her brother."

Zack cracked a knuckle against the chair's armrest. Silence confirmed Cole's suspicions.

Cole reached for his phone. "Why haven't you told her? She'll be so excited to see you. She thinks you're dead."

"Don't call." The impersonal business façade of Zack Worthington vanished as his face crumbled. "The brother she knew died eight years ago." Unshed tears filled his eyes. "The old man told me he'd sold her to a Vietnamese massage parlor. I tried to save her, but...I can still hear her scream."

Cole didn't want to know the details.

"I was fourteen, no match for two grown men. They left me for dead, but I woke up in a dumpster. I thought Lulu was dead, so I ran away to Atlanta. A couple of months ago, I heard her old man was out of prison. I came back to settle the score with him and learned she was locked up. I posted bail, but she disappeared. Took me a while to find you." Mr. Worthington rubbed a finger across his chin. "I'll never forgive myself for failing her."

"You were a kid. You're not guilty of the crimes against her." Cole leaned across the desk. "It wasn't your responsibility to protect her."

Zack's jaw flexed and his gaze hardened. "It is yours. Do you know how close she came to another run-in with Elliot? How can you protect her if you don't know where she is?"

෧෮

Cole blinked at his wife as his mind processed the consequences of her actions. "What did you do today?"

She twirled in front of the pool table and giggled. "I fed half a dozen children. I never thought helping someone could feel this great. I can't wait to go back tomorrow."

Cole's head reeled. She could've been killed. What if Elliot found her? His wife flitted near the sofa. He placed both feet on the floor. "You can't go back there tomorrow."

She fell into his lap with a smile. Her arms crept up his neck. "I know, but there are other neighborhoods in the same condition. Each day I'll choose a different location and then I'll—

"No!" Didn't she realize the danger she'd placed herself in? "Thank God you're safe, but Cindy, what you did was dangerous."

Her condescending frown plucked at his already strained nerves. "I was raised on those streets. I wasn't in danger. I stayed by the car the whole time."

He ran a hand through his hair. How could he make her see? "You drive a BMW. That isn't a car that belongs on those streets. That car says money. What if someone would've stolen it?" He turned away from her kiss. Her safety was too important to let her distract him. "What if they had hurt you?"

"They didn't. And the judge said to invest in community."

Desperate, he placed a hand on either side of her head and pinned her with his stare. "I don't care what he said. Tell me you won't go back there. Promise me."

℘○℘

Legal documents littered the twin bed Saturday morning. Cole propped on the headboard and focused on his laptop screen. He'd have more room to work on the pool table, but then he'd miss watching his wife dress.

She stood in front of the long mirror attached to the wall. A dozen different dresses hung from the folding screen. She released a long sigh. "I hate this dress." She'd said the same thing about six others.

"Then don't wear it."

She frowned into the mirror and tilted her head. Her hands fanned out the wide flowered skirt. She squinted. "I'm running out of options."

Why did it never occur to her to go shopping? Every lady in church always had a new dress for every occasion—weddings, Easter, Christmas, homecoming. The pastor should declare a new-dress holiday. "You've got a few hours. Buy a new one."

"Cole, this is new. Mrs. Briggs picked it out. I want the ladies in the church to like me."

He sat on the edge of the bed but held her gaze. "And Mrs. Briggs opinion means a lot?"

She shrugged. "No. I saw her at the mall, and she was all friendly and clingy. It made me nauseous. But she knows how to dress churchy, so I let her help. Ugh! What was I thinking?"

His heart ached for her. "Churchy?"

"Like the other women." She flashed her flirty smile. "Their clothes are different from what I'm used to." Turning back to the mirror, she straightened her shoulders. "Honestly, how do I look?"

He closed his laptop. "Is this a trick question?"

She shook her head.

He didn't want to hurt her feelings. "You are so beautiful, but that dress is worse than ugly. It's not you, and I don't like it." He braced himself for tears, but Cindy's threw off the offending garment and smiled in her satin slip.

"That's a relief. What else? If you could choose my clothes, what would you pick?"

"In the bedroom, or in public?"

"Cole." A hand landed on her hip.

He liked this game. "I don't want other men lusting over you, so no low-cut, sexy tops." He remembered the baggy skirt. "But it's okay for them to be envious."

She stepped in front of the mirror.

"When we're at home, you can wear that slip."

She smiled at him over her shoulder. "Concentrate." She bit her lip. "Not too tight. Not too loose. What else?"

He didn't care about colors or fabric. He simply liked to look at her. "Everything else doesn't matter. I love you no matter what you wear. What did God say when you asked Him?"

Her new husband had lost his mind. Cindy's mouth dropped, and then she laughed. "I'm sure God has more important things to concern Him than my clothes."

Cole stood and stepped behind her, catching her gaze in the mirror. "You're wrong." His fingers caressed her hair. "Every hair on your head is numbered." He winked. "You are the apple of His eye. If the lilies are clothed more splendidly than Solomon in all his glory, how much more do you think God wants to dress you, His precious child? Ask Him." His hand trailed off her shoulder, and he disappeared into the living area.

She turned back to the dresses. She had three hours before her wedding shower at the church. Andrea would be more than willing to shop with her, but Cindy wanted to do this on her own. Andrea liked flowers and patterns. Pastels. Cindy wanted colors. Like the azaleas that bloomed in the spring, or daisies. The colors of the sky. She threw on the flowered skirt and its matching pearl blouse, then slid her feet into a pair of jeweled flip-flops.

In the recliner sofa, Cole balanced a bowl of Froot Loops. She should learn how to cook omelets like James. Cole pointed the remote, and the morning's news anchor froze. "Thought you didn't like that dress?"

She leaned over and kissed his forehead. "I don't. I'm going shopping for another one."

"Do you need money?"

"No. I've got some leftover from last week." She'd never be able to spend the pocket money he'd given her.

"You can use the card." He stood and followed her to the door. "I may give James a call and hang out while you're at the church."

She lifted her face for his kiss. "Have fun, and I'll see you this afternoon. I love you."

Guilt washed over her as she started the car. She should've told Cole that she hadn't gotten her license, but her pride couldn't take many more blows.

Joni had promised to drive her to the DMV next week to take the permit test. Six weeks after that, she would be legal. Taking extra precautions against other vehicles, she drove to historic, downtown Fairhope. She'd seen a cute boutique when she and the girls had shopped for her wedding. There was a cream and blue suit in the window that reminded her of the day she and Cole cloud-watched from the boat.

A lady unlocked the door as Cindy maneuvered the BMW into the nearest parking place. Perfect. No one else was around to pressure her into buying something she didn't like. A bell tinkled as she walked in. The suit hung on a rack near the window. Beside it, more flowers and pastels.

"Honey, I hope you don't mind my saying, but that skirt does nothing for you." Heavily made-up eyes couldn't disguise the wrinkles on the elegant face. "I'll put the coffee on and be right out."

Cindy smiled in spite of the lady's insult. She selected her size in the outfit that had propelled her to visit this store and found the fitting rooms along the back wall.

The cream skirt's blue-embroidered eyelet hem landed below her knee. The soft folds flared slightly, but it was nothing you could build a tent with.

The matching jacket was the problem. The small eyelet holes in the beautiful cutaway neckline revealed too much cleavage. Remembering Joni's lesson about layering, she searched for an undershirt. She found a cream color, but it didn't match the skirt. White was too obvious.

"Are you finding everything you need?"

Cindy turned to the saleswoman. She didn't want to be pressured, but she needed some help if she didn't want to be late for her own wedding shower. Her hand covered her chest. "Do you have something to wear under this?"

"Oh, honey." A graceful hand swiped the air. "Don't hide what the good Lord gave you."

Cindy smiled at the exuberance of the woman. She liked her. "If I left the house dressed like this, my new husband wouldn't be pleased. Neither would my Heavenly Father. And I'm not comfortable with this neckline either."

"If you must cover up…" She sashayed a few racks over and returned with a yellow silk tank top. "Try this on. White or cream would take away from the ornate stitching. This will bring it out."

Back in the dressing room, she slipped into the shirt, then the jacket, and reemerged. Three more patrons browsed the aisles. Remembering Cole's words of love gave her the courage to step in the mirrored slot despite the onlookers.

The saleslady whistled. "Now, that is gorgeous. What's the occasion? Just because it's beautiful doesn't mean it's appropriate."

For the first time, Cindy felt confident about attending the shower without Cole. "My wedding shower at the church."

"Oh my goodness. When you said new husband, you weren't kidding. Who's the lucky groom?"

The thought of him made her smile. "Cole Maxwell."

A soft gasp echoed throughout the boutique. "Beverly Maxwell is your mother-in-law? Well, bless your poor little heart. I shudder to think…Oh well, I don't like to gossip, but she wouldn't dare set foot in my place. Girl, I could tell you stories from her younger days to make a drunkard blush with envy." She held up a hand. "But I won't." Her chin lifted in mischief. "Unless you want to know?"

"No, thank you. I'm better off not knowing."

A sigh rang with disappointment. "Sad, but true." Her face lit up. "But Cole, now there's a cutie, and an attorney at that. How did you land him?"

"God sent him to me."

"Oh, pooh." The hand waved again. "Keep your secrets. Wait. I didn't see a wedding announcement. It must have been a whirlwind courtship. Oh, how you must have upset Beverly's little world. How wonderful. Okay." She propped on hand on her hip and the other on her chin. "Turn."

Cindy obeyed.

"Yes. This is the perfect style for your shape, and appropriate for a ladies' church-get-together. That blue brings out the color in your eyes."

"Thank you. Blue is Cole's favorite color."

"Mm-hm." Painted fingers tapped ruby-red lips. "Wonderful. You change out of that and I'll choose another outfit for you. Or did you only want to look good on one occasion?"

The lady must make a fortune in commission. No wonder jewels decorated her fingers. Cindy liked her straightforward approach. She didn't disguise that she was selling something. "I need a complete wardrobe. But I don't have time today."

"Nonsense, every woman has time to shop."

ॐ

The two hundred dollar suit and eighty-five dollar shoes gave her the confidence to walk out of the apartment, but her reflection from the new wax coat on the car pronounced her as a fraud. *Oh Jesus, help me. I don't deserve this.*

What was it that Mrs. Maxwell called her? A heathen.

Pastor had announced the shower after Sunday morning services. That was almost a week ago. What if all the ladies forgot? Or worse, didn't want to come? They probably thought the same as

Mrs. Maxwell. Was Cindy a heathen? She, Joni and Andrea would probably be the only three in attendance.

She should call and fake a headache. Ugh. Mrs. Maxwell would witness her humiliation. She shuddered and pivoted on her heel.

"Cindy." Sara's voice called from the driveway.

Cindy took a deep breath, squared her shoulders and turned. "Good morning."

Sara opened the driver's door of her Suburban. "If you need help transporting your gifts to the apartment…I let the backseats down. I've got plenty of room."

Cindy pasted a smile on her face. "I doubt I'll need it, but thank you for offering."

"Anytime. See you at the church."

Careful not to wrinkle her new outfit, she slipped into the driver's seat. If Sara was going, that made five people. With any luck, Sara's mom would be there as well for a total of six guests. Cindy started the car. Six was a good number.

She adjusted the volume of the music and drove with the traffic. If the wind wouldn't muss her hair, she'd open the sunroof and enjoy the sun on her face. She signaled right.

Oh my. Vehicles lined the parking lot. A blue and yellow wreath designated the closest parking place for "the bride." Were all the people here for her? The church was large. Some other function must be taking place at the same time as her shower.

Andrea stepped out of the crowd of ladies and smiled in welcome as Cindy entered the fellowship hall. "There's the guest of honor." She lifted a white corsage and crossed the room.

Cindy cringed as Andrea pinned the flower to the expensive jacket. "This is beautiful. Where did you find this?"

Curious but kind eyes surrounded her. "In a shop downtown. Charlotte's."

"Have mercy." The groan of disgust led to Cole's mother.

Rachel stood near her. Why was she here? It was no secret that she longed to be the bride at this party.

"Maxwells do not lower themselves to enter that establishment. Find a decent place in which to shop."

"Sorry I'm late." Joni waddled in holding a large gift bag. Her friend sent her a conspiratorial wink and set the gift bag on the floor in between two gift-laden tables. "Good grief. Look at this. This is beautiful. Ya'll did a great job. And Andrea, those pictures turned out so good."

"What pictures?" The sea of women parted, and Cindy crossed the room. Beside Joni, a round table had been decorated with a lacy tablecloth, daisies and blue glass stones. A pedestal cake was the center piece, but Cindy lifted one of the silver picture frames. The photo was taken in the Mexican restaurant the day before their wedding. She remembered the moment well. Cole was leaning near and her face was upturned to his. Her hand caressed his cheek. The photographer captured the love radiating between them. She turned to Andrea. "You took this? I thought you were too busy with the wedding plans to notice us."

Andrea laughed. "You're kidding, right? You two couldn't keep your eyes off each other. We might as well not have been at the table."

The next picture was of Cole and Cindy at the top of the slide. And another one of their wedding. Cindy had a duplicate on her bedside table. She'd been so nervous that day. She replaced the frames in their places and waved a hand through the entire fellowship hall. "I can't believe you guys went to all this trouble."

A dozen round tables were decorated with lace cloths. In their centers, vases with blue stones held daisies.

Joni giggled and then explained. "We didn't. James doesn't let me leave the house much. If it wasn't for Cole calling this morning, I would've had to sneak out for the shower." She rolled her eyes and popped a cream-filled strawberry in her mouth. "Oh, these are so delicious." Joni licked the creamy confection off her fingertips. "Thank the ladies of the church. They wanted to make you feel welcome."

Chapter Seventeen

"The apartment will be ready week after next. Let's wait to open the kitchen and bath products then." Cindy pointed to an empty corner. "Stack everything over there."

Cole and James emptied their arms and made a second trip to Sara's Suburban. When they returned, Joni waddled in the doorway behind them. "Whew. I'm glad James doesn't live here anymore. I don't think I could carry these babies up the stairs every day."

Cindy led her friend to the sofa as the two men raced down the stairs yet again. "Babies? You had your sonogram. Did the doctor see two?"

"No. Unless there is a medical reason for it, James doesn't want to have the test done. God's already told him the results." Joni sighed as she sank onto the cushions. "I have my doubts, but James's faith is so strong, and my stomach is so huge. I'm beginning to believe him, despite what the doctor says."

Cindy had dealt with disappointment all her life. The birth of a child should be special. "Maybe God meant that you would have two boys separately."

James came through the door carrying an ironing board and a huge gift bag. "Nope. Twin boys. That was my promise, and I won't settle for anything less."

"Me either." Cole entered and deposited a stack of boxes on the pool table. "God doesn't do anything halfway." A tiny gift bag bounced on the carpet. "What's in here?"

Heat infused Cindy's cheeks. She snatched the bag before he could open it. "Nothing." She looked to Joni for help.

Her friend smiled prettily. "It's time to go, James. Help me up from this couch and then down the steps."

James ran to his wife's side, and Joni winked behind his back.

೮೦ೄ

The frilly, pink and white gift bag was no bigger than Cole's fist. Cindy hid it behind a large green box. "What's in there?"

Her red face gave her away. He barely heard her whispered words. "A nightgown."

Small enough to fit in his hand? His lips twitched, and she slapped his arm. He reached for the bag, and she sprinted around the table. He laughed and chased after her. "Let me see."

"No. Stop it."

He vaulted over the table and landed in front of her. "Haha." He snatched the bag and opened it. Shimmery bronze fabric slid across his wrist. Cindy's cheeks flamed when he held the garment by tiny straps. He could see straight through most of it. Thin swirls of solid bronze were strategically woven through the transparent fabric. His breath quickened. "You got this at the church?"

"From Mrs. Thomas."

"The old lady that sits in the fourth pew? Whose husband is on the deacon board? *She* gave you this?"

"In front of about fifty ladies. It was awful. Mrs. Briggs spewed punch across the room." She placed her hands on top of her head and paced. "Cole, I'm sorry, but I could never wear that. It's…it's…"

"Beautiful. Just like you." Panic danced across her face, and he hid his disappointment. "But you don't have to wear it. Not if it makes you uncomfortable."

Her shoulders sagged. "Thank you, Cole." Her phone rang and she hurried to answer.

He held the nightgown up one last time. Lace lined the deep V neckline. He pictured it on his wife. He swallowed and carefully folded the garment back into the tiny pink and white bag.

೮೦ೄ

"Hey, Big Sis." The words slurred together.

Cindy considered hanging up. "What do you want?"

"Is that a way to treat your sister?" The cheery words rang false.

"Yes. What did you and Elliot do with my money" Cindy already knew the answer. Maria hadn't helped her during their father's attack, and that cut deep. Deeper than she'd thought possible. "Forget it. I'm over it."

"I'm sorry, Sis. I'm sobering up, and if you want me at your fancy shindig, we'll go shopping tomorrow." The slur in her voice testified to the lie of her words.

"I don't think so." Her sister probably would have ruined the wedding anyhow. Cindy should count her blessings that her sister bailed. "It doesn't matter. The wedding was last Tuesday."

"Whatever." Her sister blew into the phone. She must be smoking. "Dad wants to see you."

"Too bad. I don't want anything to do with his life."

"He's an old man. Some thugs beat him near 'bout to death the week before last, and again a few days ago. You'd know that if you'd have answered your phone."

She didn't care about him. "Good. He probably deserved it."

"He needs you. His hands are shaky."

Which meant that Elliot wanted her to cook. "Well I don't need him, okay? I found a place I want to be. I have a husband who loves me. I don't want anything to do with Elliot. Tell him to stay out of my life."

₭ℛ

"Mr. Maxwell?" Juliet, his new secretary, tapped on the doorframe. Why couldn't she use the message system on the computer network? "I'm going to lunch now."

"That's fine. Have you printed the power of attorney papers for the Sinclairs?"

"Yes, sir. I'll bring them in." She disappeared before he could tell her that it could wait until after lunch.

Juliet's heels clicked against the hardwood floor. She'd be an excellent paralegal if she dressed properly. He was praying for the words to tell her without getting sued for sexual harassment.

She returned and leaned over his desk. Her fingers skimmed his forearm as she placed a folder on the surface. He lifted the folder and shielded his eyes. "Close the door on your way out."

The dismissed secretary pouted in the entryway. "Do you want to join me for lunch? Or can I bring you anything back?"

"No, thank you. My wife will be here any minute."

Her pouting lips formed an O. "I didn't realize you were married."

Thank God. Now maybe she'd keep her distance. He held his left hand and wiggled his finger. "Yep. Happily married for almost three weeks."

"Congratulations." She tilted her head and closed the door.

Cole lifted his phone and called Cindy. "Hello, my sweet wife. How would you like to have lunch?"

Her laugh danced in his ear. "I would love to. In fact, I'm outside your office now. I was coming to see you."

"Stay out front. I'm on my way out."

෧෬

"So, how's the furniture shopping going? Did you buy anything?"

The look in Cole's eyes replaced the awkwardness of wearing jeans in the midst of designer suits and skirts. "I did." Remembering the antique couch, she bit back a squeal. "I found this amazing lounger at Goodwill. It's got to be Queen Anne. The feet and armrest—"

"Did you say Goodwill?"

"Yeah, the one in Daphne. You won't believe the price I paid. They almost gave the thing away. Of course, we'll reupholster—" Cole's frown stopped her. "What's wrong?"

"Nothing." His eyes darted around the room, and then he reached across the table for her hand. "I thought you were going to the furniture gallery where we bought the bedroom suite."

She'd been shocked at the prices. "I did, but…"

His hand covered hers. "Couldn't find anything you liked?"

That wasn't the problem at all. "I liked everything I saw. I couldn't choose, especially when I realized how expensive everything was. Cole, we could feed an entire block on what you paid for the bedroom. I feel guilty for spending so much."

His thumb caressed her knuckles. "Tell you what. You buy new, quality furniture, and then make a donation to the Bay Area Food Bank." His smile sparkled in his eyes. "We can afford new furniture. We don't have to settle for someone else's used junk."

"But Cole, the couch is beautiful. And I found an amazing dining table and matching china cabinet in Saraland. Two of the chairs need repairs, but when I'm done they'll look good as new."

His jaw ticked, and he had her hand in a death grip.

"Okay, fine. I get it." She broke free. "Your rich-boy mentality needs new furniture. No problem."

His shoulders rose and fell. "You know, I could hire someone to help you. Mom redecorates every few years. I'm sure she'd give you her designer's number."

Pain stabbed her chest. Cindy didn't want anything from his mother. She leaned forward and whispered, "I can't believe you don't trust me to buy furniture for our apartment."

He recaptured her hand. "Of course I trust you, but you're used to settling for lesser quality. We deserve so much more."

She twisted her hand out of his. "Maybe you should've married someone else. Then you wouldn't have to settle for lesser quality."

He leaned back and sighed. "I'm sorry. You're right. It's your apartment. Decorate however you like."

A man in a suit stopped in front of their table. While he spoke, Cindy smiled past the hurt, especially when Cole didn't introduce her. He must have realized his mistake after the man walked away. "I forget you don't know people."

She couldn't eat the delicious food on her plate. Cole would never understand what it was like to go hungry. What he considered necessities were luxuries. Cindy faced the truth. Her husband lived in a fairy-tale world where everything was rainbows and roses. He didn't have a clue to the poverty that surrounded the city or the children that suffered the brunt of abuse.

He signaled for the check. Once they were in the car, he drove back to his office and parked out front. A girl in a short skirt eyed them from the sidewalk, and then flounced up the steps. Cindy rolled her eyes away from the floozy and back to Cole. He did deserve nice things.

Her husband lifted her hand and kissed her ring. "I love you."

She blew out a breath. "Don't say that while I'm mad." Cole lived a life clean from the filth of the world. She didn't want to taint him.

"I'm sorry."

She couldn't quite forgive him for siding with his mother. "For what?"

"Hurting your feelings. Being a jerk. Erasing your smile." His fingers tickled her palm, and her traitorous lips curled. She pressed them together and reminded herself that he was ashamed of her. She opened her door and walked around to where he stood on the driver's side. "Go to work, Cole."

His wink teased her fluttering heart. "Am I forgiven?"

She looked away before she gave in. "I'll let you know."

"I'll take that as a yes." He leaned in and kissed her. In the roadway, with pedestrians watching? He must feel guilty.

She could kiss him all day, but…"Cole, I have to go. The bedroom suite is being delivered this afternoon." She knew he hadn't intended to hurt her. What was she thinking? Buying used furniture for a luxury apartment.

Slivers of love sparkled in his eyes. "Can we move in this evening?"

She couldn't prevent her laughter. "Weren't you listening this past hour? We don't have any furniture."

He winked and grinned. "We'll have the bed."

ဢဢ

Cole didn't know what to expect. Cindy's text had directed him to their new apartment. Her car occupied their one-car garage, so he parked in the space behind it. As he exited the elevator, the delicious smells coming from the apartment hurried his steps.

The empty living room dashed his hopes of miracle furnishings. Off-key humming came from the kitchen. Cindy stood at the stove with her back to him, stirring something in a pot. He walked behind her and nuzzled her neck. "Hmm. You smell good."

She giggled, and his burden lifted. "It's the meatloaf." She turned in his arms and lifted her face. He claimed the kiss she offered. "Forgive me for being a jerk?"

"No." She stepped out of his arms and swept potato peels into a small stainless-steel garbage can. "Sara was right. I need to learn how to accept God's blessings." Slipping on a thick, red oven mitt she pulled a miniature cast-iron skillet from the oven. The small loaf of cornbread was golden brown. "I'm used to doing without and stretching every penny till Lincoln surrenders Gettysburg." She waved her hand over the bar that separated the kitchen from the dining area. Fine china and crystal glasses set two places. "Be patient with me. I'm a fast learner, but we'll have to eat standing up. I didn't have the countertop dimensions and couldn't decide on barstools."

He turned. Shopping bags lined the walls of the dining area. "Did you move all our gifts by yourself?"

"I bought this stuff today." She wrapped her arms around his waist. "The interior designer is meeting me here at eight in the morning. Don't worry. From here on, I won't complain about spending your money."

☙❧

Peace may have cost him a small fortune today, but Cole loved making up to his wife. She curled on her side and snuggled close. Wrapping the wedding quilt—a gift from Sara—around them, he drifted off to sleep.

Until a shrill ring pierced the night.

Cindy rolled out of bed and raced to her phone. Who could be calling at this hour? At the dresser, she frowned at the screen.

Cole rubbed his eyes and blinked the sleep from his brain. "Is it Joni? Is something wrong with the babies?"

"No, it's not Joni." Cindy ended the call and crawled in bed. "Go back to sleep."

He had almost dozed off when her phone rang again. "Should I be concerned?" She rolled in his arms and the ringing faded in the distance. An hour later, it rang again.

Cindy shoved her head under her pillow. "Why can't they leave me alone?"

He slipped out of bed, intending to power off the device, but the name on the screen stopped him. "Maria McDuffie." A muffled groan sounded from under the pillow. He pressed send and dove on the bed. "Hello."

Cindy peeked out from the pillow. "You're gonna regret answering that."

A rough feminine voice cackled. "You must be my new brother-in-law. Yeah? Where do you have my sister hid? I need to talk with her. It's serious."

He'd never talked to an inebriated person and decided to have some fun. "And you must be the new sister-in-law. You'll have to talk to me. Cindy isn't allowed phone privileges after midnight."

"Where is she?"

"I threw her in the harem with my other wives."

Cindy gasped and stuck her head out from under the pillow. In the moonlight, her blue eyes widened. "What are you doing?"

He waved her hand away. He'd missed Maria's comment. "What was that?"

"I need to talk to my sister. She married some good looking, rich guy, and I need to borrow some money."

Beside him, Cindy shook her head. "Don't give her any. She'll buy drugs."

He spoke into the phone. "Sorry, she spent her allowance for this week."

Cindy snuggled close and giggled. "You wish."

An exaggerated gasp flew through the earpiece. "Was that Cindy? Let me say just one thing to her."

"No. And before you call her again—make sure the sun is up."

A sigh deflated the short-lived hope in her voice. "You must be one of those bossy men."

"Yeah, I am. I'm about to bring out my whip." He slapped the lump of covers playfully. Cindy yelped and then giggled. He ended the call and tossed the phone on the floor. "You have some crazy siblings."

Cindy rolled over. The moonlight illuminated the question on her face. "Siblings? Plural? You barely know my sister. Why would you think Zack was crazy?"

Uh-oh. He scrambled for a reasonable excuse.

She sat up in the bed and faced him. "You've met my brother haven't you? How is that possible?"

Cole would keep his promise to her brother, not out of loyalty to Mr. Worthington, but because it would hurt Cindy to know that her brother didn't want to see her.

"Cole, you look guilty. Why?"

One day he hoped she'd forgive him. "I hired a private investigator a few weeks ago." Which was true.

Her breath caught and wide eyes misted. "Is he dead? Is that why you didn't tell me?"

He pulled her into his arms. "No. He's not dead. He…um. He ran away to Georgia and grew up in the Atlanta foster system. He changed his name. That's all I can tell you. But I'm hoping to have some additional information soon."

"You're looking for my brother? Oh, Cole. Thank you so much." Kisses showered his face. "And you're sure he's alive?"

The wonder on her expression tangled the web of deceit in his soul. "Yes, I'm pretty sure." Unless Elliot killed him in the last twenty-four hours. "But I don't understand something. He's your brother and Maria's your sister…but they're not related?"

"No. Elliot isn't Zack's father and Maria was born after my mom took off. I don't have a real family."

"Yes you do." He pulled her against him and wrapped the quilt around her. "You have me, and one day we'll have Lulu."

୨୦୧୫

Charlotte waved Cindy into the small boutique. "You sure like to shop early. Come on in, honey. Tell me about the shower. How was it?"

"It was wonderful." Cindy twisted the purse straps on her shoulder. "Thank you for your help. I got several compliments on my outfit, and Cole loved it. But the other day, we went to lunch and well…I didn't fit in"

"Say no more. I understand." Charlotte clapped her hands and then frowned at Cindy's jeans. "We'll transform you into a butterfly. Wait and see." She moved into a sitting area. "Would you like some tea or coffee?"

She didn't like coffee. "Tea will be fine."

"What's your flavor?"

What brand had Mrs. Maxwell served? "Um, whatever you have is fine."

"How about Earl Grey?"

Cindy nodded mutely and hoped the stuff wouldn't taste horrible. She liked sweet tea. How bad could it be hot?

୨୦୧୫

Cole slammed the file folder on his desk and rubbed his chin. This was the second estate probated this week of the same nature. Because the husband didn't have a will, things didn't go so well for his wife. Without a will, each heir received a child's portion. Fifty years of labor beside her husband was stolen from the widow by her greedy children. The once prosperous pecan farm would be sold to condominium developers, and the widow would probably end up forgotten in a retirement home.

Blue-embossed paper stuck out from under the folder. Cole slipped the title to his new truck from under the pile.

Since they weren't married when he'd made the purchase, Cindy's name wasn't included on the title. Neither was her name on the car.

What if he died tonight? Since they had no children, would the judge rule that Cindy was his heir and next of kin?

His fingers drummed against the legal document. He inhaled the smell of bound leather and faced reality. As he'd seen this past week, the worst of people surfaced when they were grieving.

His mother would never accept her new daughter-in-law as the owner of family properties. Not without a will. Even then, she may fight his last wishes in court.

In order to be certain Cindy would be taken care of, he'd give her half-ownership now—of everything. He buzzed his paralegal. "I need you to work late."

☙☙

The cost of the mani-pedi could purchase twenty kids meals. Cindy pushed the guilt aside and flexed her toes in the warm water. She promised Cole she wouldn't give out more food, but…

A thought breezed through her mind. *Feed my lambs.*

Her phone sounded a drumroll. She tapped the screen with the pad of her finger. "I'm having my nails done, so you're on speaker."

Cole's voice wavered. "Uh…okay. I'm glad you're having fun. I hate to do it, but I've got to work late tonight. Then there're a few things I need from Mom's house. Do you want me to pick you up before I go to my parents'?"

The petite, foreign girl scrubbing Cindy's feet paused and then frowned. "Ugh. Mother-in-law bad."

Cindy stifled a giggle and hoped he hadn't heard. "No thanks. I have to return to the upholstery shop for the barstools. I may be late, myself. I'll grab a burger on the way home. Do you want one?"

"No. Marquetta will probably try to feed me. I'll see you tonight. I love you. Have fun."

"Love you, too." Cindy pressed the screen with the pad of her finger and leaned into the seat.

The girl wrapped Cindy's feet in plastic. "He sound like good man. No?"

"Yes." She wiggled her soft toes and sighed with pleasure. "Cole is a very good man." She wouldn't deliberately do anything to upset him, including feeding hungry children.

Later that afternoon, idling in the drive-thru, she admired the reupholstered barstools in the backseat. God had richly blessed her.

"Feed my lambs."

She whirled around, looking for the man who spoke with such authority. The drive-up window opened. "Here you go, ma'am."

The scent of hamburger turned her stomach.

Feed my lambs.

Cole was the one who taught her to recognize the voice and the conviction knotting her stomach. Cindy couldn't eat while others hungered. She turned to the window. "I need twenty kids meals."

ೋ೦ೞ

The cardboard box of documents wasn't a hardship to carry up the stairs, but after his parents' inquisition, Cole was exhausted. He rolled the kinks out of his shoulders and opened the door with one hand.

The lamplight highlighted Cindy's hair as she slept on the bare living room floor in front of the flat screen television. Quietly, he crossed the room and set the box on the carpet. How long would it take her to choose living furniture? It was late. He'd tell her about his new will in the morning.

She came alive as he lifted her. She jerked, punched and kicked. He barely held on to her thrashing body. Her fist connected with his chin. "Cindy, wake up. It's me."

A sharp gasp snapped her eyes open. "Cole."

"Are you all right? I didn't mean to startle you."

She blinked twice, and the fear was gone. "I...I must've been dreaming."

Another nightmare. Caution lingered on her face.

He cradled her close as he walked to their bedroom. Gently, he lowered her to the comforter and went to the kitchen for a glass of water. When he returned, his sweet wife slumped against the headboard. "Here. Sip this." After a cool drink, he pulled her into his arms. Her whole body trembled. He pressed a kiss to her temple. "I love you."

Her shoulders rose, and she snuggled close. He wrapped the covers around them and cradled her like the precious gift she was. "You want to talk about it?"

"'Bout what?"

"Whatever you're afraid of. Whatever steals your sleep. Whatever the devil uses to haunt you." Several times in the middle of the night, she'd cried out in her sleep. Cole had lain awake by her side, praying. Did she remember the dreams? Or was she hiding something?

She leaned back against his forearm. "Can you read my mind?"

"No, but I wish I could."

Her hair tickled his chin as she snuggled against his chest. "Elliot won't leave me alone. He needs money, and he thinks I should give it to him. He keeps calling and threatening me."

He smoothed her hair and held her tight. Today, he made her a very rich woman. His maternal grandfather had left Cole a sizable trust when he'd died a few years ago. Maybe Cindy didn't need to know how much money she had. Not that he didn't trust her. He did. It was his own mother and Cindy's father that he didn't trust. "Do you want to give him money? Would that help?"

"I mailed Maria some money to fix Granny's old car, but I don't want to give Elliot anything." Her face tilted. "I know I should pray for them, but I just want to forget everything they remind me of." Misery lined her eyes.

Cole dipped his head for a quick kiss. "You can pray now."

Cindy bowed her head, "Will you pray for my family?"

"Yeah." He struggled with words he didn't mean. He didn't wish them well. They had hurt Cindy, and he hoped the Avenger of Innocents was keeping score.

Chapter Eighteen

"Cynthia McDuffie?" The call came from an auto repair shop Monday afternoon. The male voice was gruff and no-nonsense.

"It's Maxwell. Cynthia Maxwell." She reached across the blue granite countertop for her purse. It was about time Maria fixed Granny's old car. How much could car repairs be?

"Yeah. Your sister is here and she says you're gonna pay her bill. What's your flavor of plastic?"

She pulled out her debit card and stirred the hamburger meat in her new skillet. "How much is the total?"

"Twelve fifty-nine."

That wasn't bad. "Twelve dollars?"

Laughter spewed from the phone. She held it away from her ear and switched the burner off. She'd never paid a mechanic before, but she heard stories of women getting ripped off. "Did she pay you any cash? Let me speak with her for a moment."

Cindy shredded half a head of lettuce while she waited for her sister's "hello." Cole would be home any minute. She got right to the heart of the matter. "I want to make sure the amount is right. Did you give the guy the money I sent you?"

"Girl, please. I paid the lights, the water, and the gas bill. I ain't got no money left over for no car. You said you'd help me. But if you don't want to pay the thing, then don't."

"Maria, I'll pay the bill. I'll feel better knowing you're not stuck with Elliot. Put the mechanic back on." Cindy gave her card information and disconnected.

Using the new knife set and cutting board from one of the church ladies, Cindy diced a tomato and placed it in a small serving bowl. At least now her sister would have a way to go, but handing out cash wasn't the answer.

The five thousand in her account was almost gone. She didn't want to ask Cole for money. He'd given her the gold card for apartment expenses, but she couldn't use his money to feed the street kids.

Sifting through her new kitchen gadgets, she selected a stainless-steel cheese grater. She wanted to tell Cole the truth. If he knew she wasn't in danger, surely he'd change his mind.

Someone grabbed her around her waist. She jumped and then relaxed against her husband. "You startled me."

He kissed her cheek and inhaled near her neck. "Something smells delicious."

"It's taco salad." She spun in his arms. It was time to come clean. "I want do something for God."

He pulled her close against his chest and ran a hand through her hair. "You could join one of Mom's charities."

She didn't want to insult him, but there was no way she'd join one of Rachel's pet projects. "Do you think giving someone a day at the spa makes a difference when the rent is past due?"

He reached around her and popped a black olive in his mouth. "Is that what they do?"

"Mostly. They call them self-esteem projects. They think it will give the moms incentive to find a job. But the right hair and clothes don't mean anything when you have no transportation to and from work. Or a babysitter. What about job skills? Why can't they give scholarships to the community college? Or something?"

He leaned against the counter. "The Lulu Scholarship Fund. I like the sound of it. You should check into it."

"Cole, I know what the Lord wants me to do."

"Who's stopping you?" He filled two glasses with ice and winked. "The Bible says we should please God rather than men. If He told you to help someone, I'm all for it."

The shrill pitch of the phone cut through the air. His wife flinched in his arms, and then cringed at a second ring. Cole reached around her and lifted her phone. His muscles stiffened at the name on the screen. HIM. "Do you mind if I answer this?"

Cindy stepped out of his arms. "Go ahead. Maybe it will do some good."

"Hello." Cole turned and walked out of the apartment. He stood on the landing, and shut the door.

"Who is this? And where is my daughter?" The worst example of fatherhood Cole had ever encountered spewed curses in his ear.

Cole fought to keep the anger out of his voice. "I'm the man who cherishes Cindy more than anything in this world. Something you've failed to do for the first twenty years of her life."

"Put her on the line. I've got nothing to say to you."

"Of course you don't. You'd rather abuse little girls who only want to be loved. She has that love now—from me, her husband—and I won't let you near her again. She's isn't a possession to be used. Lose this number. Anything you want to say to Cindy can be said through me, and you've got two seconds to say it."

"You can't steal my daughter away from me. She's mine! I'll get her back! I'm her father!" The additional words screeching through the phone turned Cole's stomach.

Until her father had visited his office, he'd had no idea the filth Cindy had to deal with. This was one time Cole could protect her. He slammed her phone against the edge of the banister. The screen shattered. A small satisfaction flowed through his hands. He pummeled the phone over and over again, taking all his frustration out on the electronic device. He wished it were her father who tasted his blows.

Satisfied the thing was inoperable, Cole sucked in a breath and entered the small apartment. The rubble bounced once as it landed in the empty trash can. "I think it's time we changed your number. After dinner, we'll shop for a new phone."

ഇറ

"Leather or cloth?"

Cole shrugged his secretary's hand off his arm and concentrated on his phone conversation with Cindy. "Hold on." He tilted the device away from his mouth. "That will be all."

"Are you sure?" The seductive tone in Juliet's voice was unmistakable. Ever since they'd worked late, or maybe before, she kept crossing the line. He had to tell her repeatedly to stay in front of the desk. How could he fix this?

Or was it his imagination?

"Close the door on your way out." He relaxed into his seat as the door clicked.

"Who was that?" Cindy's voice held a higher pitch than usual.

"That was Juliet, my paralegal." Cole didn't know how much he should tell his wife. He'd hired Juliet by Mr. Worthington's recommendation. Cindy's brother had returned to Atlanta, but Cole suspected Juliet kept tabs and reported to the man. "I think she propositioned me."

Cindy's laughter rolled. "Cole. Either she did, or she didn't. Which one is it?"

"I'm not sure."

"Fire the woman and move on to the next applicant."

Cole didn't want to do that until he found out what Zack was up to. "It's complicated. Where are you?"

"Reclining on a sofa in the middle of the furniture gallery, while your mother's interior decorator spies out the land. Back to the secretary thing. Do I need to come down there?"

All thoughts of his secretary's strange behavior fled. "You don't have to use a professional. You can decorate how you want."

"I know, but she's very helpful, and I make the final decisions. Besides, she loved the lounger and the dining table. The restoration shop delivered it while she was there this morning."

Cole smiled to himself. Hopefully, he'd come home to a comfy sofa today. "Are you almost done? Can you join me for lunch?"

୫୦ର

Cindy's heels sunk into the plush carpet. Thank you, God, for a good husband. Bless him in every way.

She opened the door to Cole's suite of offices and blinked. The secretary stooped at a file cabinet. Her rear end pointed in the air. Although the fabric was expensive, Cindy had seen longer miniskirts on the girls trying to earn money for a high that used to hang out at her place. The price might differ from an eightball to a luxury apartment, but the merchandise was the same. This woman advertised her body with the intent to sell.

God, forgive me for thinking Cole was overreacting. The woman stood and turned. If Detective Simmons saw her on the street, he'd arrest her on the amount of cleavage alone. Her eyes never lifted from the folder in her hand. Cindy stifled a gasp as the woman reached into her jacket and adjusted herself. Red nails tapped on the inner-office door and covered Cindy's huff of outrage.

"Coleman?" The secretary didn't wait for an answer. She opened the door.

Cole's exaggerated sigh filtered through the distance. "I told you to address me as Mr. Maxwell."

"Oh." The woman entered Cole's office. "I thought that was for the client's sake."

Cindy crossed the reception area and stood inside the doorway.

Cole had his eyes glued to his desk, and his torso leaned away from the pouty-lipped woman hovering over his shoulder. "No. And I've asked repeatedly that you wait on the other side of the desk." He glanced up, and when his eyes met Cindy's, relief bounced in his smile. "Well? What do you think?"

"Definitely a proposition."

The girl stood and tilted her head, clearly confused at Cindy's presence. "Excuse me." She skirted around the desk, but Cindy blocked her escape.

Cole leaned back in his leather chair and propped his hands behind his head. "How do I fix this? What can I do?"

His secretary tugged at the short hem of her skirt and pulled the ends of her jacket together. "Mr. Maxwell, if there isn't anything else…"

Cindy didn't back down. "There *is* something else. It's time you met Cole's wife. Have a seat." Cindy forced a smile and walked around the desk. She kissed the smirk from her husband's face and then shooed him out of his chair. "Go find something to do. Me and Little Miss Muffet need to have a girl talk."

ॐ☙

The soothing bubbles took away the ache in Cindy's feet and soothed the tight skin around her heel. She leaned back in the Pedi chair and closed her eyes. "I feel horrible. Everyone at Cole's office thinks I'm a crazed, jealous wife."

Andrea laughed a few feet away. A splash sounded. "Did you really threaten to kill her?"

Cindy giggled. "Only at the end. Poor Cole. No one wants to

work with him now. I can't believe Juliet told the receptionist that I caught them in a compromising position."

Joni's dainty feet splashed in the next chair over. "Did you?"

"No." Cindy sighed. "Cole did nothing wrong. I'm ashamed to say, I watched from the door for a few minutes to see how he reacted to her ploys. He did good. I'm proud of him."

Andrea's voice came from her other side. "Let them talk at his office. At least you have your husband."

Cindy sighed. "Not really. He's working late hours doing the work of a secretary and an attorney. The stress is exhausting him. Last night, he didn't wake me when he fell into bed."

Joni peeled the gel mask off Cindy's eyes and grinned. "So you fired the last secretary. Hire another one. There's got to be someone out there interested in a job. We'll pray about it."

"Excuse me, but I'd like to apply for the position." A woman on the other side of the salon lowered a fashion magazine. Her gray hair was in large plastic rollers. Wrinkles lined her face, but her eyes were kind and understanding. "I was a secretary for thirty years. I retired early to take care of my Edgar when he had a stroke." Sadness entered her smile. "He passed on to Glory six months ago. I've been thinking about returning to work."

"Thank you, ma'am. You're welcome to apply, but Cole is an attorney. He needs someone with legal experience."

∽∾

Somewhere under the mountain of paper was a deposition he needed for the Franklin adoption case. Cole turned and searched the documents on top of the keyboard, ignoring the continual beep of the fax machine. The pressure behind his eyes threatened to explode. He'd have to reprint the document. After a couple of clicks with the mouse, he stepped to the printer. A red light blinked in tune with the beeps.

The throb in his head kept time with the chaotic rhythm.

He reached into the cabinet over the broken copier and found the first aid kit. He downed four ibuprofen without the benefit of water. The office line rang. He turned to answer, but his cell chirped. His heart lightened as he ignored the landline and answered his wife's call. "Quick. Tell me you love me before I go insane."

The mess in his office disappeared with her laugh. "I love you." A heavy breath sounded. "But don't be mad."

She and her friends were having a girls' day at the spa and then they'd spend the rest of the afternoon shopping. "Why? How much did you spend?" He loved teasing her about her frugal ways.

"Cole." Her outrage made him chuckle. "I hired you a secretary."

He blinked out the window. "You did what?"

"Surprise. You're gonna love her, and she's has an excellent reference."

"Cindy, I appreciate the thought, but this is a specialized field. I need someone with legal experience, and as bad as I need help, you can't hire the first applicant that you find on the street."

Her deflated sigh echoed through his ear. "She's a very nice lady and she'll be there any minute. Be nice."

"Anything for you." He turned and found his dad frowning in the door. "I'll see you tonight."

"I love you, Cole. I was trying to help."

"I know. Thank you, and I love you too."

He ended the call and waved his dad in.

"Cindy hired you a secretary?"

He wanted to defend his wife, but her actions were outrageous. "It appears so."

"Son, I'm not big on office gossip, but you've caused quite a spectacle already by letting her fire Juliet. If you have a problem with your staff, you need to handle it personally."

"Cindy didn't fire anyone, though she should have. Juliet was a leech. I'm glad to be rid of her and her wiles."

"All the same. There's a certain political standard held by this firm. I want my son to excel and climb the ranks. I want you to make partner one day. That's not feasible when your wife manages your career. Or when you conduct business in an office of chaos."

His father wasn't saying anything that Cole hadn't already thought of. "Dad, I'm sure whoever Cindy hired is more than capable. If not, she'll be replaced."

"That isn't a very nice welcome." Mrs. Bevin—his dad's former paralegal who had retired three years ago—stood in the office doorway.

Cole hugged the woman who was like a second mother. She was thinner than she'd been at her husband's funeral.

She dropped a large black purse on the secretary's desk and handed Cole a résumé. "Should I consider myself fired?"

He was speechless.

His dad stepped into the reception area. "Mrs. Bevin? You've decided to leave retirement and accept my offer to return to your former position?"

"I'm sorry, Mr. Maxwell, but I don't want your office personnel to resent me, and I don't want to usurp anyone's authority. Besides, God has another plan." She smiled at Cole like the time when she'd caught him drumming with her stapler. "When Cindy told me of your predicament, the Spirit nudged me, and here I am." She turned and frowned at the disaster around them. "Where should I start?"

Cole blinked at the miracle standing in his office. The paper in his hand smelled like butterscotch candy. As a kid, he'd swiped many pieces from her desk drawer. "Mrs. Bevin." Relief colored his laugh. There wasn't a more qualified paralegal on the Gulf Coast. "Oh, thank you, God." He crossed the room and dug through the papers. "There's a deposition in here somewhere from Mr. Charles Bedford. If you could, locate it and correct the typos?" He straightened. "The printer's jammed, and I have no idea why the copier won't work."

She unplugged the fax machine, and the insistent beeping stopped. "I'll take care of it."

Cole grinned at his dad. "She'll take care of it."

His dad shook his head. "I can't believe you hired my secretary out from under me."

Cole's laugh freed the stress and cured his headache. "I didn't. My wife did." He laughed again. "I do believe I'll call her right now and tell her how wonderful she is."

Chapter Nineteen

Cole rolled across the carpet in his new desk chair and smiled. The most precious off-key singing he'd ever heard rumbled down the hall.

Despite her initial reluctance to buy quality furnishings, Cindy'd done a great job decorating. Even the lounger-thing in the sunroom with its yellow plaid cushions looked good, especially when he'd seen his wife in the thing reading her Bible this morning.

She had turned one of the two extra bedrooms into an office. In the master bedroom, above the headboard, she'd had their engagement photo enlarged and framed. Twin mirrors hung on its either side. She'd said she wanted to see God's blessings.

He slipped from his home office and tiptoed up the hall.

Cindy twirled across the living room without seeing him. Her oversized T-shirt billowed behind her, giving him a glimpse of long, perfect legs. She spun on her heel, and he remembered their wedding night. His arms ached to hold her. She fell into the recliner and yanked out her earbuds. Her eyes remained closed. "Thank you, Jesus, for the home you've given me with Cole. I promise to cherish him forever."

Cole quietly crossed the room and bent to kiss her. A dainty, bare foot pushed against the carpet, and the swiveling recliner caught him in the chin. "Oomph."

A hand covered her giggle. "Sorry. Did I disturb you?"

He shook his head and leaned near. "Nope. We have a couple more hours before tonight's service." He brushed her lips with his. She tasted of strawberries. He tugged her out of the chair and into his arms. "We have time to work on our nursery."

Her hand caressed his jaw, and a curious smile graced her beautiful face. "But we haven't decided on the colors."

๙๚

Cole claimed a good-morning kiss while straightening his tie, and then accepted the mug from Cindy. He inhaled the scent of caffeine—one of God's greater creations—and hoped she hadn't added too much sugar. He composed his expression and prepared himself to pour the concoction down the drain as soon as she turned her back. Thank God for the coffee shop around the corner.

The first sip surprised him. "This is delicious." He gulped another. The rich flavor wasn't drowned in sweetness. Nor was it bitter. "This is the best coffee I've ever tasted."

Her smile lit up her eyes. "Thank you. I bought a new coffee machine. I think I've figured this one out."

He drained his cup and held it out for a refill. She accepted the cup and turned to the coffee pot. As she measured with the small spoon, he wrapped his arms around her waist and kissed her neck. Would the second cup taste as great as the first?

"Pastor was right." Her words barely registered. "A half-truth is an entire lie. I know you misunderstood me the other day."

His cup filled, and she sprinkled something on the top. Something that dissolved and sank out of sight. "What was that?"

She turned and held out his mug once again. "My secret ingredient." She held the cup, and his hands enclosed around hers. Together, they brought the rim to his lips. He closed his eyes as the robust flavor rolled over his tongue. He swallowed and opened his eyes.

Cindy smiled. "I think I've figured out this wife business."

He took possession of the cup, abandoned it on the bar, and pulled her into his arms. "I've always loved the way you handle wife business. Your coffee, on the other hand, was…"

She leaned back and frowned.

"Your coffee was good. It was. But that..." He nodded to the cup on the counter. "That is awesome."

She reached up and pulled his head down for a kiss. Her lips teased his. It was a shame he had to go to the office.

"I can always be late." He lifted her in his arms, and she squealed. "I'm sure the DA won't mind waiting a few minutes."

Her gasp burned a hole in his neck. "The district attorney?"

His grip slipped on her silky robe. "Be still. I'll put you down."

She ran around the table as soon as her feet hit the tile. Mischief sparkled in her eyes as she lifted his coffee and held it over the sink. "Behave, or else I'll pour this down the drain."

He turned his back and reached into the cupboard for a bowl. "Go ahead. My beautiful wife will make me another one."

Her laughter crept close, and he waited until the perfect moment to turn and catch her. Their laughter mingled, and he was glad to see she left the cup on the table. She was hard to hang on to. He backed her against the cabinets.

"Cole, you can't be late."

"I know." He reached around her for the box of cereal.

She slapped his arm. "Did you choose cereal over me?"

He hooked an arm around her. Pulling her along with him, he crossed to the table and poured his cereal one-handed. "You said no. I settled for my next favorite breakfast food."

The morning sun highlighted her hair. "I love you."

Not trusting himself to stop with one kiss, he squeezed her hip and kept a firm grip. "I love you, too." He bowed his head and thanked God for his blessing.

Dainty fingers massaged his scalp. "Are you gonna let go?"

"No. If I could, I'd keep you in my pocket and take you out to kiss you a million times a day." He lifted his spoon to his mouth.

"Well, are you mad?"

He swallowed. "About what?"

"Weren't you listening this morning?"

Yes, he'd listened. He listened to love as she mastered the way he enjoyed his coffee. He heard the invitation in her kiss. The way her body leaned into his proclaimed sweet promises of the nights to come. "I heard every word."

"You're okay with me obeying God and helping the children?"

As long as it didn't place her in danger. "The church is looking for a new preschool teacher." He pushed back from the table and pulled her to his lap.

"Not those children." She bit her lower lip and he brushed his thumb over it, releasing her teeth's hold. Leaning against him she whispered, "Help me, Jesus."

Cole added his prayers. "Lord, bless the work of her hands, to bring You glory, that souls may be won for Your kingdom. Amen."

"Double Amen." Her lips brushed his lightly. "Thank you." She stood, but stayed close to his side. "Cole, I have a confession."

He hugged her close as they walked to the door. "What's that?" Pausing in the opened door, he waited. Her mouth opened and closed. He stole a kiss. She finger-combed his hair. "Don't be mad, but…I've been going to the same, old neighborhood and feeding the kids."

The knife of betrayal twisted in his gut. He reared his head back. "What? You went behind my back? Why, Cindy? Why would you endanger yourself?"

Her shoulders stiffened. "I wasn't in danger. I drove in, dropped off the food and got out of there. Piece of cake."

How could he make her understand? "Remember the first day we met and I waited for you outside your granny's house? A street kid approached me. He asked if I was buying or selling." Cole couldn't bear the thought of her in jail again. "You will not go back to those streets. I forbid it!"

His beautiful wife snorted and snatched out of his arms. "Seriously? You forbid it?"

"Yes." He held her gaze as icicles pierced his heart. Maybe he should have chosen his words more carefully. He swallowed the lump in his throat. "I love you too much to endanger your safety."

Her chin lifted. "I'm not an animal and I'm not endangered." She broke eye contact and stepped away. "You told me to obey God rather than men." She spoke as if she was soothing a child.

Cole gritted his teeth and leaned forward. "I meant mankind not me. You can't go back." He crossed his arms and stood his ground. "I am the head of this family, and you will do what I say."

He didn't like her smile or the smirk that followed. "Of course I will." She turned and walked down the hall.

"Cindy, wait!" The bathroom door slammed. His sweet wife was gone.

Chapter Twenty

"A good wife should know how to tie her husband's tie."

Cindy edged near Mrs. Maxwell so she might hear the rest of her comments while she loaded a plate with a banana muffin and a cinnamon pastry.

The Bible study portion of the meeting had ended, and the ladies lingered for morning refreshments.

"Not to mention, how to starch a shirt." They advised a girl Cindy's own age, who had recently announced her engagement in the art of wifely duties. Cindy eavesdropped.

"Forget the starch. That's what the dry cleaners are for." Joni licked icing off her fingers.

Andrea nudged Cindy's side. "But if you're planning on having a miniature Cole, you should know about ties."

A bit of muffin stuck in her throat. Cindy swigged her milk and hurried to the kitchen for a refill. Joni followed with an empty platter. "Are you okay? Anything I can do to help?"

Cindy had waited for this opportunity all morning. "There is, but it's not about men's clothes." Her friend nodded, so she continued. "I need some spiritual advice."

"I'll try to help, but I usually ask James when I don't understand the meaning of something in the Bible."

"Cole is good at that too, but this pertains to a woman's duty in marriage."

The pastry stalled on its way to Joni's mouth. "Oh, I assumed you and Cole were happy in your physical relationship."

Cindy laughed. She was making a mess out of a simple question, and she needed to hurry before someone overheard. "Our marriage is great, but lately Cole has gotten bossy and I'm a little confused. What if he says one thing and God says to do the opposite?"

Joni sighed. "I don't know."

Another church lady entered the kitchen, ending the conversation.

When Bible study was over, Cindy drove to her favorite thrift store and bought the male mannequin she'd seen last week. She also bought a dozen ties.

Back at the apartment, she stood "Fred" in the middle of the empty bedroom. Using her new phone, she searched the internet for a tie-tying tutorial.

Several mutilated knots later, she sank onto the floor and buried her head in her hands. Her stomach's growl echoed through the room. The kids on the street would be hungry too. Did they eat breakfast? She checked the time on her phone. One fifteen.

How could she eat knowing the children hadn't? Grabbing her keys and purse, she raced out the door. She'd be home before Cole suspected a thing.

The last time, she didn't have enough. The children multiplied daily. She ordered forty cheeseburgers, fruit cups, and chocolate milks.

At the same neighborhood, she pulled over at the curb.

The ringleader approached. "Didn't think you were coming." He reminded her of her brother, Zack. Always in protector mode as the children stood behind him.

She pressed a button and popped the trunk. He followed her to the rear of the car. "I had a conflicting obligation." She lifted the box of chocolate milks and handed it to the boy.

Blue lights flashed, and a siren tweaked once. From out of nowhere, three unmarked cars surrounded the BMW. The boy and the other children ran into the woods.

"Wait!" Cindy stepped toward the children with the cheeseburgers. An officer snatched the box while another slammed her against the car. Pain shot through her twisted arm as steel bands clicked onto her wrists. "Let me go. I didn't do anything wrong."

Jean-clad legs stepped into her view. "No visible signs of drugs. Take it to the dogs." Detective Simmons' voice crawled her nerves and created a deep tremor. He'd been the one to arrest her months ago. This couldn't be happening. *Jesus, help me.* Dogs sniffed the boxes. "Stop it. Those are for the kids."

Detective Simmons spun her around. "Sure they are."

He knelt and patted down her bare calves. His hands paused at her knee, below the hem of her skirt.

Cindy froze at his touch. Hatred welled inside her. "What? No pat-down? Isn't that the fun part of your job?"

He signaled a female officer, who took over the search of Cindy's person. Cindy kept her eyes on the detective while breathing a prayer of thanks. She couldn't bear the touch of any man but Cole. She had to get out of this mess, before he discovered where she was.

A uniformed cop held the dog's leash. "No drugs, boss."

Detective Simmons spit a sunflower seed. "Must have been in the other box." He grabbed Cindy's upper arm and steered her toward the car. "Haven't seen you for a while. We can get reacquainted on the ride downtown."

Oh. God. No. Her heartbeat jumped to her throat. "For what? All I did was feed some hungry children." She had no choice but to move her feet, either that or fall flat on her face. "Wait. My car. My purse is in there."

"Nice ride. Who'd you steal it from?" He paused. "Sid, call the impound lot."

Cole was gonna kill her. "I didn't steal it. It belongs to my husband."

Laughter surrounded her. "Yeah, right."

The metal cut into her soft wrists as the detective nudged her forward again. "Was your Mercedes in the shop?"

The radio clipped to his belt crackled. A female voice emerged from the static. "2005 BMW registered to Coleman Maxwell."

The uniform police officer dug through Cindy's purse and read her state identification card. "Cynthia LouAnn McDuffie. Not Maxwell. At the very least, we've got her on driving without a license."

The female voice came back on the radio. "Previous convictions of manufacturing and possession with intent to sell. Currently on probation."

Cindy bit her lip to keep silent. It was no use to argue. She was going to jail.

ℰℭ

Rachel smiled across Cole's desk as she signed the stock purchase agreement. "Are you happy, Cole? Truly?"

He leaned back in his chair and observed his childhood friend. How did he ever give her the wrong impression? "I'm happier than I've ever been. I love my job. My wife. Life couldn't be better."

Rachel fumbled with the purse straps in her lap. "I'm moving to Birmingham."

The tension in his shoulders relaxed. "You'll like it in the big city. There's a lot more culture to choose from. More fast-paced."

"Will you miss me?"

How did he answer without giving her hope for things that could never be? "I'll always remember my friend from childhood, but we all have to grow up someday."

She fidgeted and squirmed in the seat. "I guess that's my answer. If you ever need me… If things don't work out with Cindy…"

Hearing his wife's name made him smile. "Cindy's perfect, but if she weren't, I vowed to love her forever—good and bad times, richer or poorer, sickness and health, 'till death do us part."

Her eyes hardened. "I pray you don't regret those words."

Cole clamped his jaw. He didn't want to think about dying. "I'll never regret marrying Cindy. She's the best thing that ever happened to me." His computer flashed an urgent message from Mrs. Bevin. "Excuse me for one moment." Cole clicked the note and caught his breath. *Sorry for the interruption. Mobile Police Dept on line 1. They impounded your car during a drug bust.*

A groan escaped his lips, and he shut his eyes.

Rachel leaned forward. "What's wrong?"

He forced a smile. "Something's come up." He leaned back in his chair. "Mrs. Bevin!"

His secretary appeared in the doorway. "Will you see Rachel out while I take that call?" He wanted the troublemaker far away when he addressed the issues with his wife.

"Certainly, sir." Mrs. Bevin lifted Rachel's arm and led her toward the door.

Rachel called over her shoulder. "But we weren't finished with our conversation. There's something I need to tell Cole."

He forced another smile. "Whatever it is, I'm happy for you. Enjoy your new life in Birmingham. Mrs. Bevin, please close the door on your way out."

Cole counted to ten, giving himself a few minutes to calm down and to make sure Rachel couldn't overhear his conversation. How could Cindy have gone against his wishes? He had no doubt what she was doing when they arrested her. With a deep breath and a trembling hand, he lifted the receiver. "This is Coleman Maxwell."

A cocky voice answered. "Mr. Maxwell, we have your car at the city impound. The tow fee is two hundred twenty-five dollars. Additional storage is thirty bucks a day. It's not reported stolen, so you may be liable for any crimes committed—"

"Where is my wife?"

"Um, sorry. Who?"

"The woman driving my car—my wife. Where is she?"

"This is the impound lot. I don't know about the arrest."

"Thank you for calling." Cole disconnected and unlocked the bottom drawer of his desk. He tore off a blank check and folded it into his wallet. Long legs ate the distance to the door. He grabbed for his suit jacket, but knocked over the coat rack. He stepped over it and ran out the door. Whatever it took, whatever the fine, he'd pay for his wife's freedom.

୬୦୧

Cindy stared at the uniformed officer looming over her. "For the hundredth time, Cole Maxwell is my husband. I did not steal the car." She stood, but another officer pushed on her shoulders, forcing her into the chair.

"Get your hands off my wife!"

"Cole. Thank God." She bounced to her feet. "They wouldn't let me call you. They think that I was selling drugs, but it was food…"

The gleam in his eye and the set of Cole's jaw stole the words from her mouth.

"Mr. Maxwell?" Detective Simmons's brows arched, and his lips curled into a smile. "You're married to her?"

Her husband led her back to the chair she'd vacated. Rough hands urged her to sit.

"Cole, I'm trying to tell you—"

He placed a hand on either side of the chair rails and loomed over her. "Your attorney is advising you to remain silent."

"But Cole, they took the hamburgers and fr—"

"Your husband is telling you to *shut up*."

What? His jaw clenched and jumped. She'd never seen his eyes this clear. They were molten silver. She swallowed back the words she wanted to say and nodded.

Cole suppressed the urge to strangle his wife and turned to the snickering officers. "Why do you have Cindy in custody? What are the charges against her?"

A man a decade older than Cole leaned against a metal desk. "Technically, she isn't in custody, as no drugs were found."

Thank God. "Then she's free to go."

"Not yet. I want to know what she was doing in that area of town. It's dangerous for a woman alone."

Cole speared Cindy with an I-told-you-so look, and then focused on the man who seemed to be in charge. "I'll tell you what she was doing. She was feeding children. That isn't against the law."

"Without a permit, it is." The man crossed booted feet at the ankles. "And with her previous conviction, deliveries to an area known for drug trafficking makes her suspect."

Cole couldn't fault the man for doing his job. This was the main reason why he didn't want Cindy to feed those kids. "My wife grew up in a similar neighborhood. She feels it's her civic duty to help those less fortunate. Despite being warned against it, her intentions were good."

"And there's the matter of her driving without a license."

His wife shrunk into the chair and wouldn't meet his gaze. This whole time she'd been driving—illegally. "We'll take care of that first thing in the morning."

The officer nodded. "Good day, sir. Sorry to disturb your afternoon. You can take your wife's things." He pointed to two boxes on the desk.

Cole passed Cindy one box while he carried the other. A heavy burden lifted as they stepped into the sunshine. What could he have done if she was charged with a crime? With her probation status, would she have gone to jail?

She hovered close to his side. When they were on the sidewalk she peeked over. "Cole, I'm sorry."

He didn't want to visit his wife in prison. "Not now."

"But I want you to understand."

How could she have risked her freedom? "I said not now."

"Cole?"

He dropped the box in the bed and yanked open the passenger door. "Get in the truck."

Cindy didn't argue again and quietly climbed into the passenger seat. How embarrassing it must have been for Cole to leave work to bail her out of jail. She had to be more careful. What if one of his colleagues saw her in custody?

He didn't turn into the tunnel. "Where are you going?"

He drove down Water Street and hit I-165. His answer fairly exploded through the cab. "Cindy! Why? Why would you jeopardize your freedom and your safety? What was so important?"

∞∞

She leaned into the seat and closed her eyes. How could she make him understand?

"Tell me, Cindy. Do you love me? Are you deliberately sabotaging our life together?"

She scooted close to his side and rested her head on his shoulder. "Let me show you, Cole. Then you'll see what I see."

His sigh echoed through her soul, but he nodded and followed her directions. As the houses became smaller and more haggard, Cole's eyes scanned the trash-filled sidewalks. "No wonder they thought you were selling. A BMW on this street?"

"Yeah." She didn't hide the sarcasm in her voice. "Nothing like asking for the truth."

He squeezed her hand. "They were doing their job."

No they weren't. If the authorities want to shut down the crackhouses, they knew exactly where to go. Instead, they chose to play games with the dealers and users. She called it job security. "I forgot. You're on their side."

His frown bothered her. "You're on their side, too. Remember?"

"Of course. And that's why they threatened to lock me up." She escaped the question in his eyes. "Pull over near that oak tree."

"Cindy, it's getting dark."

"I know." She had to make him understand.

He hesitated, but did as she asked, parking on the curb. "Now what?"

Cindy released her seatbelt and reached for the door handle. Cole grabbed her wrist.

"It'll be okay. Trust me." She got out of the truck, and was surprised when Cole did the same. What would he think when he got a glimpse of the real world? "Grab a box." Together, they carried the food under the oak. "Leave it here. They'll find it."

"Hey, lady!" The ringleader appeared at the edge of some overgrown bushes. "How'd you escape the cops?"

Her near-arrest must have endeared her to the skittish children. Cindy waved her hand toward Cole. "My husband is an attorney. He got me out of jail."

"Cool. Can he get my dad out?"

Cindy smiled. "Probably not. We brought the rest of your lunch. Sorry it's cold."

The boy shuffled bare feet. "Don't matter to us none." He grabbed a burger and stuffed half of it in his mouth. "You coming back tomorrow?"

"No." Cole answered for her. "It's dangerous here."

"Don't worry 'bout that. We got her back." More than a dozen children hovered at the edge of the woods.

Cole's eyes widened. Did he see their ragged clothes? The dirt on their bare feet? Or did he see heathens, like his mother?

"She means a lot to me." A variety of emotions crossed his face during the exchange—sorrow, disbelief, and sympathy.

"The boys will take care of her."

"I'm sure you will. But I love her. I can't take the chance someone bigger will come along."

"Not us. The Boys." Three of the children pointed.

Cindy followed their grimy fingers across the street. Five young men, certainly not boys, touched three fingers to their foreheads and turned them to line up with their nose. With a flick of their wrist, they saluted. It was the sign of their gang.

"Desmond said to tell you that they like chicken nuggets."

Cindy eased toward the truck. "It's time to go." The Boys had been her biggest competitors. She didn't want to need their protection. Cole was right. This street was dangerous. She forced a smile as he started the truck and accelerated out of their territory.

Silence ruled until they entered the tunnel. Cole lifted her hand and pressed a kiss in her palm. "I'm sorry, but I don't want you in that neighborhood. What if you had a flat tire? The Boys might have offered their protection, but who would protect you from them?"

She scooted close to his side and forced a laugh. "Don't worry, Cole. I won't go back. I'd hate to think what would happen if I got their order wrong."

For the rest of the ride home, they discussed ways she could feed the children without endangering her own life. A food bank? Soup kitchen? The need was there, but Cole insisted she have the permission and full cooperation of the authorities.

At home, the open bedroom door reminded her of the tie lessons. "Sorry, Fred. I forgot about you." Cindy bent to retrieve the ties from the floor as Cole entered.

"Who's Fred?" His eyes widened and blinked at the life-sized mannequin. "What are you doing with this dummy?"

Cindy kissed Cole's furrowed brow. "I'm learning how ties work, so I can help my husband dress for work and church."

He loosened his top button and flipped up his collar. "I can tie my own knots. Fred has to go. I won't share you with someone else." Cole held out a tie. "If you feel the need to dress a man, here I am."

Chapter Twenty-One

An insistent knock woke her for the second time that morning. Cole's side of the bed was empty. Cindy smiled as she smoothed out the indention of his pillow. The knocking continued. "One minute."

She reached for her robe, tightening the cinch as she hurried to the door. Trouble was on the other side. "Mrs. Maxwell? Won't you come in?" She waved to the sofa. "Would you like some tea?"

Mrs. Maxwell's eyebrows arched into a deep V. "It's after ten." Her eyes pierced Cindy's satin robe. "Are you sick?"

Holding the lapels together, Cindy turned her back on the intrusion and wandered into the kitchen. She needed a strong dose of caffeine to deal with Cole's mother. If she loaded it down with cream, she could drink the bitter stuff. "Er, no. Cole and I were out late at a dinner party."

"I see." Mrs. Maxwell folded Cole's morning paper and set it aside. She brushed non-existent crumbs from the seat of the chair before lowering herself at the table.

Cindy breathed a prayer of thanks that she'd bought an elegant serving set from Belk last week. Serving traditional tea was a necessity in Mrs. Maxwell's eyes.

Balancing two delicate cups and saucers, Cindy inhaled deep and turned toward the table. Her nosy mother-in-law held a scrap of paper to her face. "Oh." She dropped the paper and it floated to the table.

Cole's handwriting landed face up.

Cindy rescued the letter and folded it into her pocket. She'd read it later, away from prying eyes. "So. Is there a reason for this visit? Not that you're not welcome anytime. It's just that you've never visited before, and I was wondering if there was something particular…" She was babbling. Cindy stood and removed Cole's used coffee mug and empty cereal bowl to the sink.

Behind her, Mrs Maxwell laughed. Laughed. Cindy turned and found the woman smiling. Genuinely smiling.

Settling back at the table, Cindy pressed her lips together. Of all the days she'd slept in late, Cole's mother chose this one to visit. "I'm sorry about the mess. The apartment is usually much cleaner…"

"No, dear." Mrs. Maxwell waved a hand. "The apartment is fine." A smile returned to her lips. "When Cole was a child, Marquetta would serve elaborate breakfasts with muffins, eggs, bacon, sausage, grits. But Cole? All he wanted was a bowl of Frosted Flakes."

Cindy was thankful for Cole's breakfast preferences. She didn't know how to cook eggs Benedict or how to make hollandaise sauce. "Cole does know what he wants."

Mrs. Maxwell sobered. "Yes, he does. That's why I'm here, to apologize."

Cindy's cup clattered against her saucer.

"Despite my efforts to convince Cole to eat a healthy breakfast, he wanted cereal. And I admit that I attempted to persuade him not to love you. I wanted him to marry someone like Rachel, someone who could help his legal career, not destroy it. But he wanted you. Rachel has accepted that marriage to Cole is no longer an option."

Thank you, Jesus. One prayer answered.

"You are Cole's wife. I cannot change that. But he must maintain a social standing. His career demands it, and as his wife you must conform to certain standards."

She wants to turn me into something I'm not.

"You cheated me out of a southern wedding. Allow me to host a small reception. To introduce you to Cole's family and friends."

Only Mrs. Maxwell could apologize and insult her in the same breath. "Your offer is generous, but I need to talk to Cole about it."

"We'll use the house. It was featured in *Southern Living* magazine. An intimate gathering." Mrs. Maxwell's countenance brightened. "Thank you, dear. I'll start on the guest list right away."

"But I haven't asked Cole yet."

Mrs. Maxwell poured more tea into her cup and stirred with a silver spoon. "My dear, Cole would do anything to make you happy. If he thinks you want a reception, he'd move heaven and earth to give you one."

The sharp lines of the cup handle bit into Cindy's finger. "But I'm not sure if *I* want a wedding reception."

Mrs. Maxwell waved a hand in dismissal. "None of your family will be invited of course. You have no idea how relieved I was, when Cole told me you'd cut all association with them, especially your dreadful father."

"How do you know Elliot?"

"I met him in Cole's office. The gall of the man, asking for money. Not that we blame you for your upbringing, dear. It isn't your fault you were a throwaway child."

Cindy redoubled her smile and twisted the napkin in her lap.

"No matter. You have a new family now. The Maxwells will adopt you in, and make you one of us." She tipped her cup and then sighed. "Now that that's settled, I must prepare the guest list."

"Of course." Cindy touched her stomach and faked sick. "I don't feel well." The words weren't a complete lie. Listening to her mother-in-law gave her a stomachache.

"Oh." Mrs. Maxwell stood. "Maybe you should lie down. Have you been experiencing morning sickness? Have things occurred on schedule? I'm not getting any younger, and I've resigned myself to accepting you as my grandchildren's mother."

"I'm fine." Cindy stiffened as Mrs. Maxwell hugged her.

"Go rest, dear. We can finish our talk later."

Cindy bit her lip and closed the door on her mother-in-law. The delicate tea service blurred as tears filled her eyes. She was a fraud. The real Cindy would never measure up to Mrs. Maxwell's expectations.

"God, I don't want to be a fake." Falling on her knees before the sofa, Cindy poured her heart out to the One who loved her before the fancy car and clothes. "Jesus, I don't want to go back to the slums where you found me." Tears streamed as she squeezed her eyes shut. "I'm grateful for every blessing you've given. I wouldn't trade Cole's love for anything, but Lord, this isn't me." Her heart constricted. "Who am I? Is this the life you'd have me live? Meaningless days filled with self-indulgence and hurtful gossip? You loved me when I was bad. Cole loved me without all the expensive trappings. Lord, who do you want me to be?"

Tears flowed unhindered as she prayed. Peace breezed through her soul as joy entered the room. An unseen hand etched words of love on her battered heart as a glorious mist covered her.

Her laughter echoed through the apartment. "I love you, Jesus." She didn't understand the pleas she spoke as she fell up in a rainbow of light. Giggles bubbled forth and happiness engulfed her. This feeling was beyond comprehension. Beyond time. She'd found a secret dwelling place for her and her Savior.

She emerged with strength to survive any storm. *Cole.* She wanted to share this unique experience. He often spoke in tongues while he prayed in the early morning. Was this what he felt?

A quick glance at the clock said she'd prayed longer than it seemed, but it would be hours before he'd be home. She rushed to her closet and ripped the tags off the jeans and a girlie t-shirt she'd purchase last week. As she pulled her hair back with a scrunchie, she stepped into her pink and orange flip-flops.

She turned up the volume on the worship CD and praised her savior during the drive across the bay to Cole's office. More than one head turned as she crossed the plush carpet in the bottom floor reception area. Would Cole be ashamed of her presence? Would her jeans embarrass him?

Mrs. Bevin wasn't at her desk, and Cole's door was slightly ajar. Cindy peeked in. His dark head bent toward a thick accordion folder as deft fingers thumbed through the papers while his brows furrowed.

She tapped on the doorframe. "Knock. Knock."

His surprise sparkled a welcome, and she stepped into his office. His loving gaze roamed her body. "You don't look sick."

His nosy mother must have called. "I'm fine."

His smile widened. "Close the door and come here."

"Am I bothering you?"

The steel in his eyes melted. The attorney was impeccable. The green button up shirt was wrinkle free. But she didn't drive to the office to consult with a lawyer. She wanted the reassuring arms of her husband. Instead of taking a seat across from his desk, she came around the side, and he swiveled toward her. Selfish in her own need, she crawled into the chair with him. Her lips greeted his, and he made her welcome. Safe in his arms, she told him about her new experience when she'd prayed. How she hadn't been able to stop laughing. "Has that ever happened to you?"

"Yes. Sometimes you need to be alone with the Lord." His breath caressed her temple.

Tilting her head, she stared into his eyes. "Your mother came by this morning."

"I know." A touch of mischief tugged at his lips. "That'll make anyone search out a place of refuge."

The door clicked. "Excuse me."

Heat flooded Cindy's cheeks as Mrs. Bevin's voice registered. What would the elderly woman think? Cindy pulled away, but Cole held her secure on his lap. Giving up on trying to escape, she hid her face in his shoulder as he thanked his secretary for a file.

Cindy peeked out from under her husband's arm. "Good afternoon, Mrs. Bevin."

"Good afternoon, Cindy." The smile on her face was kind. "It's so nice of you to visit Cole in the office. If my Edgar were alive, I'd find time to visit him every day."

Cindy's cheeks cooled as she read between the lines. There was no condemnation in the elder lady's eyes, only envy.

The door closed once again, and Cindy sagged against Cole. He kissed her hair and stroked her back. "Now that we've shocked my poor secretary, do you want to tell me what my mother said to make you doubt yourself?"

She toyed with the buttons on his shirt. "Your mother's in a higher class than I am. Most of the time, I don't fit in, and the other times, I don't want to."

His gold wedding band glistened in the sunlight streaming through the window as he caressed her cheek. "I love you for you. You don't have to fit some mold. Denim or diamonds, you're beautiful the way God made you."

"I know."

His eyes widened, and he chuckled. "Isn't that conceited?"

She laughed and played with his tie. "Probably, but I prayed and God told me I didn't have to be like everybody else."

"Then why did you come here?"

"Because I love you and I wanted a kiss."

"Mother's invited us to dinner. She wants us to approve the guest list. Thank you for agreeing to her party."

ဢ႟ႚ

"Cole?"

He dropped his spoon into his cereal bowl. He loved the way she said his name when she needed something. The love in her eyes made him feel like a superhero. He swallowed the last of his Honeycombs. "Yeah?"

"What does this mean?" She read a simple Bible verse.

His chair scraped the floor, and the bowl clattered in the sink. He reclaimed his seat and tugged her into his lap as he explained, "Jesus forgave us, so we must forgive those who sin against us."

"What if they don't deserve it?"

He shrugged. "Doesn't matter what they do. We're accountable for our own actions."

Tears trickled down her cheek. She blew the hair out of her eyes and snuggled against his chest. "What if I can't forgive someone? Will I go to hell?"

He caressed her back and shoulders. "Are you talking about your father?"

She nodded.

He sucked in a deep breath. "I have trouble forgiving him, as well. When I think about the life he forced you into, anger rises within me. But he has a soul, too, and I ask myself…do I want him to burn for eternity?"

"What's the answer?"

He chuckled. "Depends on the mood I'm in." He kissed the top of her head and closed his eyes. "Jesus, you've required something that we don't have to give. Help us forgive. Give us peace and open our eyes to the soul behind the crimes against us. Amen."

Cindy leaned her head back and tilted her face upward. Their lips were mere inches apart. Her soft fingertips traced his mouth. "Thanks. I love you, Cole. You always know what I need."

॰ঙ৶

From the safety of her car, Cindy stared at the green paint chipping off the front porch. She hadn't been back here since the day she met Cole. She suppressed a shudder. She wasn't a scared girl anymore. A squirrel disappeared through the hole in the eave of the house. Twisted wire-mesh encased the rotting front porch and concrete crumbled from the gray cinderblocks lining the lower portion of the house. Somewhere inside those walls, her father waited. Could she forgive him? Maybe saying the words would bring peace to her soul?

Memories swamped her. Unexpected ones. Her father laying on the floor as she and her sister played with their generic Barbies that they'd received from some charity. That was a good Christmas. Zack had gotten a cap gun. The dolls were wrapped in plastic, dollar store bags. Of course, there had been no tree, or lights, but Cindy and Maria had played for hours with those dolls. Wonder what happened to them?

Cindy lifted her chin and opened the car door. Halfway up the walk, a weak baby's cry alarmed her. What was a baby doing in her father's house? She navigated her way through the junk on the porch and cracked opened the door. She didn't bother to knock. The cry grew louder. "Elliot? Dad?"

No answer. Even the baby stopped crying.

Cindy crossed the small living room and bent near the sofa. Brown eyes blinked and bare legs kicked as tiny fists pummeled the air. What was this baby doing here? The same baby that was at Granny's weeks ago? Alone?

A bottle clogged with sour milk lay between the baby and the piles of pillows. The little face scrunched up and turned red. A wail pierced the air. Cindy reached with uncertain hands. From her downy hair, to the filthy shirt and down to the dirty diaper, the infant was soaking wet. Suspicious liquid poured down Cindy's arm as her hands pressed against the full diaper.

The baby wailed as Cindy sat in a battered chair and peeled off the soiled diaper. Tears pricked Cindy's eyes at the raw skin covering the baby girl's private area. She needed to dry the red, irritated skin. A quick glance around the filthy room produced no diaper bag.

Where was her sister and Rosetta?

Cindy tugged her phone out of her pocket. She'd locked her purse in the car. She texted Maria. *Where are you? Where are the clean diapers?* Cindy gently tugged the wet shirt over the soft head. Her heart flinched at each pitiful cry. Her phone chimed and she snatched it to read her sister's reply.

Danni's awake? We'll be there in 20

How could anyone leave a baby asleep in this house alone? The child needed a clean diaper and some ointment. Hadn't the girl's mother considered the dangers? Twenty minutes was too long to wait. *Diapers? And milk? Now!*

The reply was immediate. Baby bag is in the car. Oops. Be there soon. Drove dad to a friends. He'll be sorry you missed him.

Cindy relaxed against the chair, thankful she didn't have to deal with Elliot right now.

The baby on the other hand was another story. She cradled the naked baby and walked down the hall. The closet no longer had a door. She'd removed it herself years ago. Digging way in the back, Cindy found a clean pillow case. Back in the living room, she wrapped the baby in the linen as best as she could and wiped her own tears.

The next thirty minutes felt like an eternity. Her frazzled nerves couldn't take anymore. Her sobs echoed the little girl's. The children at Granny's? Were they alright? She called her sister. Over the babe's cries she asked, "Who's watching the other kids?"

"The state took 'em. Said I wasn't licensed." Maria swore and railed against the injustice of the social system.

Cindy had heard enough. "Where are you?"

"Oh." Surprise slurred her sister's voice. "We had an unexpected stop. Can you watch the baby for a few hours?"

"Maria!" The baby's cries intensified at Cindy's outburst. Danni was hungry. "I have no diapers, no milk and no bottle."

"Just leave her on the couch. We'll be back shortly."

Hours? Minutes? When high, the concept of time vanished. Cindy ended the call and carried the baby to her car. She couldn't leave her, and she couldn't let her go hungry.

She opened the driver's door and reached under the seat for her purse. She couldn't hold the baby and drive. A small fender bender would set off the airbags and kill Danni for sure.

The strip mall was three blocks away. The dollar store should have the things they needed.

၈၁၈

Cole tugged open the glass doors of the police station. Hopefully, this would be his last trip to see Detective Simmons, but Cole had to make sure the detective received Cindy's "proof of driver's license." He couldn't leave the paper on the desk and walk away.

Handcuffed to a chair, a familiar boy eyed Cole as he approached. The gangly teen straightened. "Hey. Where's your honey? I got hungry kids on the street. Thought she was gonna help out with that?"

He was one of The Boys. Was it coincidence he was here now? Or a God thing? "Despite your promised protection, it's too dangerous for my…" He smiled as Cindy's sweet face flashed before him. "…honey."

"You don't trust me." The cuffs rattled with his laughter. "That's all right. I get it. She's too good to walk my streets. Let the young'uns starve. It'll be less mouths drawing a check."

"If they're hungry, why don't you feed them?"

"Hey, dude. I ain't got no funds. I'm broke as a joke. Know what I mean? I could go for one of them burgers myself. Too bad you scared."

Cole read past the tough guy routine to the insecurities behind the façade. Were the kids truly hungry? If so, he should feed them.

Detective Simmons stepped around a cubicle wall.

Cole nodded to the boy. "What did he do?"

The detective shrugged. "Nothing that we can prove yet. He's free to go." Metal clanged and a click sounded as the cuffs released.

Desmond rubbed his wrists. "Ha. I knew you ain't got nothing on me. Better luck next time." He swaggered out the door.

Cole handed the cop the paper in his hand. "This should clear things up for my wife."

Detective Simmons accepted the offering with a grin. "Thank you, Mr. Maxwell. By the way, for the next few weeks, we'll be patrolling the area we found your wife. You may want to keep her close to home."

Cole nodded once and walked out of the precinct. Desmond leaned against the passenger door of his truck. He shouldn't befriend a criminal, especially with the shaky ground he walked with his father's law partners, but Cole felt a nudge from God. He cast a glance over his shoulder and found Detective Simmons staring through the glass door. Cole unlocked the truck with the push of a button and spoke to the insecure teen. "Get in. I'll buy lunch for you and the kids. You can help me deliver." He slid in the driver's seat as Desmond climbed into the passenger side.

"Nice truck." Desmond's dark eyes flickered about the interior.

"Thank you." Cole turned into a fast food restaurant and parked near the door. "Let's go eat."

Curious eyes stared as he and Desmond entered side by side. The boy wasn't shy. He ordered the biggest burger, and supersized it. Cole ordered the same.

The cashier glanced from Desmond to Cole. "Dine in or carry-out?"

Cole reached for his wallet. "We'll eat here. And give me thirty kids meals to go, fifteen with burgers and fifteen with chicken nuggets."

The cashier's hand faltered. "Yes, sir."

By the time Cole paid for the second purchase, Desmond had demolished half his food at a nearby table. Cole lifted his tray and followed. "Did you say grace?"

Dark eyes squinted. "Naw, man. I ain't into all that religious junk."

Cole bowed his head. "Thank you, Lord, for this food you've so graciously provided. Bless it and my new friend. Amen."

"You messed up, boy. Keep your voodoo to yourself. We ain't friends. This is business."

"What business do I have with you?"

Desmond lifted his burger and chomped down in silent salute. They ate in silence for a brief moment. Until Desmond said, "How'd you manage to steal the cook?"

"I don't know who you're talking about."

Desmond leaned back in his chair. "Naw, you don't. Do you? I'm talking about your honey. Her previous occupation."

"I'm not overly concerned with her past. It's over and done." Cole kept a wary eye on Desmond as they ate and then drove to the neighborhood. They placed the boxes of food under the oak. The children didn't appear until after Cole was back in his truck and Desmond was across the street.

Even the children knew to be afraid of The Boys. Lord, please help me protect Cindy. Help me keep her away from this place.

Cole parked behind his office and answered a call.

Zack's voice boomed through the phone. "You're supposed to protect her."

The greasy cheeseburger churned in his gut. "I am."

"Then why was she was almost arrested? And do you know that yesterday, her car was seen parked in front of Elliot's place?"

ꕥ

Stale cigarette smoke clung to her clothes. Cole leaned away from his wife in disgust. Confusion shone in her eyes as he pushed her away. "You stink. Where have you been?"

"Oh, sorry." He detected nervous energy in her laughter. "The baby threw up on me."

So that's what the stain on her shoulder was. He took another step backward. Yet it didn't explain the cigarette smell. Unless Zack was right. Had Cindy been back at her old house? Why? She hated her father and his business.

She stalked toward the bathroom, calling over her shoulder, "I'm gonna take a quick shower."

Her pace quickened and he followed. His stomach clenched into a strangle knot when the door slammed in his face. The knob wouldn't turn. Why lock him out? "Unlock the door. I'll wash your back."

"Um, no thank you. Go away, Cole. Some things in the bathroom are private."

He leaned his forehead against the door. "The bathroom? Yes. The shower? No. Let me in before I become suspicious."

The same nervous laughter as before answered. "There's no reason for jealousy. I was babysitting." Gushing water drowned her excuses.

He raised his voice. "For who? Sara or Andrea?"

"I can't hear you. Can we talk about this later?" The shower engaged, and Cole turned back up the hall.

He wasn't stupid. Either she'd been smoking, or someone near her had. No one in their circle of friends smoked. He sank into the couch and rested his elbows on his knees. She wouldn't go back to her old life. Would she? The story of Hosea and Gomer fluttered through his mind. He swatted it away. Lulu wasn't Gomer. She wasn't a prostitute. Cole gave her a good life. She didn't want for anything. She wouldn't go back to her old lifestyle.

The acrid scent of stale cigarettes stung his nostrils, and he jumped to his feet. Oh God, not his Lulu. She wouldn't.

හිල්

Cindy scrubbed her skin until it was raw. What else could she do? The disappointment on Cole's face hurt, but Danni needed her. The baby girl couldn't survive on her own. Cindy'd waited for her sister to return and then left enough formula and diapers for a few days. *Lord, keep Rosetta sober enough to feed her.*

An unseen hand squeezed her heart until her chest ached.

Torn between her love for Cole and a desire to help the baby, she begged God for an answer. Here in the shower, the water covered the sight and sound of her misery. *God, what do I do? The bible says to obey your husband, and I'm okay with that. Thank you for giving me such a godly man. But you also say to feed the fatherless. I can't do both. How can I choose?* She tilted her head into the spray and prayed until the hot water cooled.

In her haste to escape Cole's inquisition, she'd forgotten to bring clean clothes into the bathroom. She secured Cole's bathrobe around her, and wrapped her wet hair in a fluffy towel. Maybe she could sneak into the bedroom and dress for their dinner reservations without being seen. The news anchor's voice drifted from the living room as she opened the door.

Cole shoved off the adjacent wall and framed her face in his hands. Love and fear reflected in his eyes. "I won't let you leave me." His kiss possessed her. The towel fell from her head. Steel gray eyes captured hers, and she swallowed the guilt in knowing she caused his pain. "I know where you were. Promise me you won't go back there."

He would never understand the hardship of the people or her desire to help them. "You don't understand, Cole. Danni needs me. Please don't make me choose."

Firm but gentle hands gripped her shoulders. Thumbs caressed her collarbone as he backed her against the wall. "Promise me, Cindy." His warm mouth kissed a trail across her shoulders. Heat spread through her body. His lips found her ear and he whispered. "Promise me."

She shut her eyes forcing out a few tears. "I promise."

Chapter Twenty-Two

Cole lined the cue up with the three ball. Since he and Cindy had moved out of Sara's apartment, James had moved the pool table into his and Joni's basement. He leaned in to take the shot. A hand rubbed across his hip. The cue ball spun a few inches on the table.

James's laughter clanged throughout the room. "Thanks, Cindy. I needed an advantage."

Cole grabbed her hand as she dug in his front pocket. He turned his back to James, blocking his wife from the other man's view. Since seeing the private investigators report, Cole had watched his friend carefully around his wife. Neither had done anything suspicious, yet.

Sweet innocence laced her smile. "I need to borrow the truck."

"What's wrong with Joni's car?"

"She gets sick riding low to the ground." Cindy nodded across the room where James hugged his pregnant wife. His love for Joni seemed genuine.

Cole shook the thoughts from his mind and handed her the keys. "Be careful." As an afterthought he added, "Where are you girls going tonight? Shopping? Or dinner?"

She bit her lip and lifted a brow. "It's a secret." The love in her kiss eased his worry.

But Cole couldn't concentrate on the game after Cindy left.

James sunk the eight ball in the side pocket. "I can't believe the changes in her. She's different since meeting you."

Cole racked for another game. A thousand images of James and Cindy flashed through his mind. None of them were pleasant.

James shrugged as his cue struck. Solids and stripes swirled as the balls clacked and bounced from side to side. "I'm glad she found you. Cindy didn't deserve the life she'd been born into."

"It's interesting to hear you say that."

James studied the angle of the balls on the table. "Does it bother you that I knew her before you?"

He and James had been friends for a long time. "Depends on how well you knew her."

James circled the table and a hand slapped Cole's shoulder. "She was Kathy's dealer, but she protected Isaac once. I never slept with her." James readied for another shot. "In fact, I don't know anyone that did."

Cole needed the whole truth. "The deposit for the utilities at her granny's house is listed in the name of James Preston."

James propped on his cue stick. "They're still in my name? Man, I haven't stayed there in years. Wait. How do you know that?"

Cole shifted on his feet. "Doesn't matter how. The fact is that you lived with her."

The grin that splayed across James's face couldn't lie. James bit his lip and shook his head. "What you're thinking is all wrong. Kathy and Cindy lived together. Yeah, I stayed there for a short time to protect Isaac. But after Joni kidnapped him and arranged for his adoption, I never went back. I forgot the utilities were in my name. I'll take care of it first thing Monday morning."

"Don't bother. It's done."

James's explanation rang true. His words gave Cole hope that he was the only man Cindy thought of when he held her in his arms.

James leaned against the table. "I'm sorry. What you must have thought…Why didn't you ask me sooner?"

Cole remained silent. Could he have handled a different truth? Ever since he'd made Cindy promise not to return to her neighborhood, her nightmares had intensified. She called out a name more than once in her sleep. "Do you know someone named Danny?"

James shook his head. "Should I?"

"I don't know." Cole chalked his stick. His phone rang from his back pocket. A premonition hit him as he answered Zack's call.

"Do you know where your wife is?" The harsh words clipped through the phone. "Because my little sister just so happens to be at Elliot's place with a friend."

She wouldn't. "That's not possible. She promised not to go back there. Besides, how would you know where she is?"

"Apparently, I'm the only one watching out for Lulu. Go! Get my sister! And, take the kid with you."

The line went dead, and Cole pocketed his phone. He didn't bother hiding his anger from James. "For some reason. That I can't begin to fathom. The girls are at Cindy's old house. According to Zack, there's also a kid involved."

James ran a hand down his face and blew out a breath. "Let's take my truck."

Both men dialed as they rushed toward the driveway. Cindy didn't answer. James shook his head and left a voicemail for Joni. They made it across the bay in record time. When they arrived at the dilapidated house on Houston Street, Cole's truck was nowhere to be seen. He opened the passenger door, and a baby's squalls came from the house. Cindy's rough lullaby did nothing to quiet the sounds.

He was grateful for James's friendship, but this was something between Cole and his wife. He didn't want an audience when he confronted her. "Joni must have my truck. Can you give me a minute?"

"Yeah, I'll wait out here. Holler if you need me."

The baby's wails grew with each cautious step. He didn't bother to knock but snatched the door open. Cindy paced with the wailing baby on her shoulder. "Cole." Relief replaced surprise. "Help me."

The stench in the house turned his stomach. Filth was everywhere. A girl lay face down across the couch. Her arm dangled on the green matted carpet. Bruises lined her pale skin from the inside of her wrist to her elbow.

His feet wouldn't propel him forward. He recognized a bag of pot on the coffee table and assumed the variety of other things were also used to get high. He knew places like this existed somewhere in the world, but he'd never seen the cold reality.

"Where's Joni?" Cindy bounced the wrapped bundle. "Did she buy the formula?"

The baby was hungry. Headlights flashed through the window. "That must be her now." Concerned for the baby, he drudged through the filth. Careful not to touch anything, he pushed his way to his wife. Food containers in the kitchen were the same ones he thought Cindy had taken to the ladies supper at church. "What are you doing here?"

Tears rolled down her cheeks. "I'm sorry, Cole, but I was worried about Danni. Me and Joni were at the mall when the neighbor called and said she's been crying nonstop for two hours."

"She?" The baby was a girl. He wanted to throttle the unconscious girl on the couch. "Give her to me."

He took the baby from Cindy's arms and strode to the kitchen. Except for a fifth of whisky and a few beer bottles, the refrigerator was empty. He stepped to the sink and let the water run for a few seconds. Ignoring the dirty dishes in the sink, he stuck his finger under the flow and then slipped it into the baby's mouth.

The suction motion felt strange but quieted the babe's cries temporarily.

Joni waddled in, ripping the plastic off a new baby bottle as Cole repeated the motion. James shook a can of ready-to-pour baby formula and then popped the top. Cole continued to pacify the baby until Cindy pushed the bottle around his finger. The hungry baby slurped the milk and choked. Cole removed the nipple and set her up. When his forearm pressed against the baby's bottom, a pitiful wail replaced the coughs.

Cindy peeled back the pillowcase covering the babe's bottom. "Be careful. When I got here, her diaper was filthy."

The blisters—some festered and some broken—covered the baby's exposed lower back. Joni gagged, and James prayed, "Jesus, I can't do this again."

Cole echoed James's audible prayer as his friend helped Joni out the door. Keeping his touch light, Cole quieted the baby once again with the bottle and nodded to a hardback chair. Cindy cleared off a mountain of clothes and sat down.

He gently shifted the baby into her arms. "Don't let her take too much at a time."

She held the baby at an awkward angle.

Cole lifted Cindy's elbow. "There. Hold her like that."

He knelt before her and sighed with relief. "So this is Danni?

Why didn't you tell me?"

Blue eyes met his. "I'm not sure. I never wanted you to see the inside of this house. I never wanted to come back here." Her eyes shifted to the bundle in her arms. "But last week, when I came to forgive my father, I found Danni here alone. I waited hours for Rosetta to return."

That explained the cigarette smell. "Who's Rosetta?"

She nodded to the girl on the couch. "Danni's mother. I have no idea where Elliot and my sister are. Probably setting up a new stove."

Was there something else? She wouldn't look him in the eye. "But why didn't you tell me? Why didn't you trust me?"

"Look around you. Before we met, this was the life I knew. The life I was born in." The tears in her eyes didn't fall. "You are everything that is good. You were born with God's blessings and given His promise as a child. You don't deserve to know about this sinful world."

Cole nodded to the baby. "Neither does she." He was such a snob. Why had God given him a godly heritage, while others were born in poverty and abuse? The baby probably needed to see a doctor. How long had she been neglected?

From the living area, the girl moaned. Glazed eyes stared at him and then rolled back into her head. He wanted to beat the girl and take the baby far from this house, but the legal ramifications of those actions weren't feasible. A reddish-yellow stain on a pot on the stove claimed his attention. "What do they cook? Drugs?"

"Yes, the coffee pot makes small-scale amounts. You can smell it for miles. They need a remote location for large quantities." She gently inspected the sores on the baby's arm. "These are probably results of the chemicals in the air. She doesn't need to stay here."

Cole gathered the leftover formula. "Let's take her outside."

They walked into the jungle that should've been the front lawn. Joni was bent at the waist. A hand covered her mouth. James rubbed his wife's back and shoulders. "We need to get out of here."

"I know, but we can't leave the baby, and we can't take Danni without permission. We should notify the authorities."

"Cole, don't—" Cindy's words were silenced by his kiss.

James nodded. "Make the call."

As Cole and Cindy waited with the baby, James and Joni returned to the store for some diapers and ointment. Cole suspected James wanted his pregnant wife out of the neighborhood. He didn't blame him.

A county sheriff's deputy arrived first and took the girl into custody. A social worker from Child Protective Services arrived as the girl screamed, "My baby!"

Cole hardened his heart against her cries. She should have thought about the infant before she inserted the needle in her arm.

The female, social worker placed an arm around the girl. "Your baby will be safe in our custody."

Wild eyes twitched. "No! Cindy, take care of Danni."

A deputy forced the crazed girl into the backseat of a cruiser. Another deputy pointed the lady towards Cole's truck. He pushed off the fender and met the social worker halfway. Cindy sat in his truck cradling the baby girl.

Cole wished he was wearing a suit as he offered the woman his hand. "Cole Maxwell. I'm with Maxwell, Bedlight, and Jackson, Attorneys at Law."

"Sasha Covington. I'm familiar with your father's firm. It's nice to meet you."

Cole read between the lines. His youth was against him. What would Cindy think if he dyed his hair gray?

"I'm here to take the child into protective custody."

Despite the fact that he was wearing jeans and a ball cap, Cole stood his ground. "That won't be necessary. Before your arrival, the girl left the baby in my wife's care."

Mrs. Covington took a paper out of her satchel and clicked her pen. "Mr. Maxwell, I know you are trying to help, but there is an open case for this child. She has a grandmother that is very concerned for her welfare. Tonight's events will strengthen her custody case." She scribbled a local number. "She'd be delighted if you gave her a call."

Chapter Twenty-Three

The church's annual spaghetti supper raised money for missions. Cindy separated the cucumbers off her salad and watched in amazement as Mrs. Preston coaxed cooing noises from the baby. "I can't wait until Joni has the twins. I've bought two of everything blue that I could find." The elegant woman made silly faces toward Danni. "Yes. Yes, that's right. I'm gonna be a grandma again."

"So the last ultrasound confirmed James's theory?" One cucumber slid into the marinara sauce. Without thinking, Cindy forked the bite and crunched. The tangy taste awoke her senses.

Mrs. Preston's smile grew. "No. James refuses to allow the doctor to perform one. He said God's promises are more accurate than technology, and he doesn't want his faith weakened."

"Oh." Cindy forgot about James's stubbornness as she dipped another cucumber into the red sauce. Then she double-dipped. Why hadn't she ever thought to try this before? And then she triple-dipped. This was the most delicious thing she'd ever tasted.

Cole caught her hand on the forth dunk. "I thought you didn't like cucumbers?"

"I don't." Reaching around him, she dipped again and popped the remaining piece of the crunchy vegetable in her mouth. "But this is delicious. You want one?"

He stared at her now-empty plate. "No thanks. Danni's grandmother is meeting us in half an hour. We need to go, if we don't want to be late."

She savored the remaining bite, and then reached for the baby. "Mrs. Preston, thanks for holding her while I ate."

Joni's mother-in-law wore a silly grin. "I'm always available if you need a babysitter."

"Me, too." Sara wore the exact same grin as her mother.

Cindy didn't know how to respond to the women's strange behavior. "Uh." She placed Danni into an infant seat. "Thank you, but I doubt we'll see her again."

Cole lifted the baby and nestled her downy head against his chin. "I want to hold her one last time before we give her back." The baby cooed from Cole's embrace. "See, she likes me."

The hope in his grin scared Cindy.

Everyone in church knew about Danni's rescue.

They also knew Cole wanted his own baby girl.

Cindy had her suspicions, but what if the doctor said no? Is that why James wouldn't allow a third-term scan?

Cole had held on to God's promise for years. Cindy couldn't bear to fail him.

80C3

The smell of greasy burgers filled the truck as Cole slid into the passenger seat. Leaning over the console, he kissed his wife and then licked his lips. "Yum. Strawberry."

Her sweet laughter was precious. "Thank you." She slurped a large milkshake and steered with one hand. "Your lunch is in the bag on top."

He reached in the backseat and claimed the fast food bag amid the many kids meals. "Where are we going today?" He bit into his burger and wiped ketchup from his lip. Every weekday since they'd rescued Danni, they gave lunches to neglected children. So far, Cindy had kept her promise. She hadn't gone without him, and he loved spending his lunch hour with her. Today would be the last day. Tomorrow began the new school year. With the free lunch program, the children were guaranteed one nutritious meal a day.

Cindy slurped through an empty straw and then shook the paper cup. "I thought we'd drive down to tent city."

He offered her his own vanilla milkshake from the cup holder. "As long as I'm back at the office by two o'clock."

80C3

Other than having a constant hunger and a missed cycle, she had no symptoms of pregnancy, but today she'd find out if Cole's promise lived inside her womb. She straightened the purse strap on her shoulder and entered the automatic doors of the three-story doctors' complex. The obstetrician Joni recommended had an afternoon cancellation—blind luck or divine providence?

Joni had said the office was on the third floor. Cindy followed the signs to the elevator and pressed the up button. She smoothed her skirt and breathed. *Lord, help me not to cry if they say no.* The elevator dinged, and she straightened her shoulders.

The doors swung open.

Cole blinked from the interior.

Her stiff spine deflated. "What are you doing here?"

His stricken expression wasn't an answer.

"Oh, wait. Let me guess. Joni told James, and her blabbermouth husband couldn't keep a secret." A few people stepped around her and into the elevator. Cindy hurried in before the door closed.

Cole hadn't said a word. His expression was void and his eyes were rimmed in red. Had he been crying?

This was why she didn't want him to know. He'd get his hopes up. She pressed close to his side and kept her voice low. Three other people shared the elevator. "I didn't want to tell you yet. I have my suspicions, but I could be wrong."

His hand latched on to hers and squeezed. The elevator stopped on the second floor, and a nurse stepped off. Why didn't Cole say anything?

"Don't be mad 'cause I didn't tell you about the appointment. I knew you'd want to come, and I couldn't bear to disappoint you."

The bell dinged again, and Cole snapped out of his stupor. Both of his hands caught her around the waist and pulled her in front of him. His voice was scratchy. "You're here to see the doctor?"

What was wrong with him? "Yes. Joni's obstetrician had a cancellation. Why did you think I was here?"

His knees bent and his forehead landed on her shoulder. "Oh, God." His breath heaved. And then he shuddered. "Lord, forgive my doubts."

She'd barely heard his whispered words. Unease stirred nausea in the pit of her stomach. Cole was a Maxwell and Maxwells never showed emotion in public. Ignoring the curious glances, Cindy wrapped her arms around him and held tight. *Lord, please let there be a baby.*

ɞ◯ᒫ

"Mom, Cindy and I have a surprise for you." Cole kissed his mother's cheek and held out the frilly wrapped gift.

The wrinkles lining his mom's face puckered into a frown as she glanced over at the loveseat where Cindy fidgeted.

Hopefully their gift would entice his mother to accept Cindy into the family.

His mother placed the professionally wrapped box in her lap. "Thank you both very kindly."

"Dad, this is for you, too."

His dad leaned up in the recliner. "Open it up, Bev. Let's see what we've got."

The elaborate bow was bigger than the box. Graceful hands untwined the loops and refolded the ribbon on the coffee table. Tired eyes met his.

"Go ahead, Mom. You'll love it."

Cindy smiled at his father. "I wanted to choose a different color, but Cole insisted it should be this one."

A soft gasp mingled with the crackle of tissue paper as his mother lifted a frilly pink baby dress. "Oh, my."

His dad moved to the sofa and placed an arm around his wife. Though tears streamed down his mom's cheeks, her hands caressed the laced hem. Both his parents stared at him in expectancy. He finally did something that made them proud.

"So." He stretched his legs out on the coffee table and wrapped his arm around his wife's shoulder. "What should little Lulu call you? Gramps and Gran? Granny and Papa? Or Mawmaw and Pawpaw?"

His mother huffed and rose to her feet. "Coleman Alexander Maxwell, you know perfectly well that Grandmother and Grandfather will do fine. Oh, thank you, Jesus!"

The baby was cause for excitement. Cole stood and allowed his mother to squeeze off his breath.

"I prefer Papa." His dad shook his hand and then hugged him.

Cole reached down and pulled his wife into the celebration. To his amazement, his mother reached for Cindy's hand. "How are you feeling, dear? What did the doctor say? When is my grandbaby due?"

ℬↄↃℭ

Seagulls squawked above the fishing pier as waves crashed against the wood pilings. Cindy lifted her face toward the sun as the wind tossed her hair. She should be shopping for baby furniture, but Cole's mother was driving her crazy. Cindy needed a break from all the *suggestions*. This past weekend, Cole had taken them out into the gulf, and she longed for the freedom experienced on Cole's sailboat again.

Walking down the long pier, she sidestepped the fishermen and their stinky bait. The clean scent of salt was stronger in open water. Her phone rang, and she reached in her back pocket.

A sob breezed through the earpiece. "Mrs. Maxwell? This is Danni's grandmother. I need your help. Yesterday, Rosetta showed up and wanted to see the baby while my son was at work. I didn't have the heart to refuse. I went in the kitchen to fix a bottle and they disappeared. The police can't get involved in a custody issue without a judge's order. Please, will you help me?"

Cindy's heart ached for the babbling woman, but nothing could entice her to break her promise to Cole, especially now that she was expecting. "I wish I could, but there's nothing I can do."

"Your sister was with Rosetta. Do you have a number I could call? My son can legally take Danni as neither parent has lost custody, and he's listed on the birth certificate."

Cindy stepped off the pier and turned toward the beach.

"Please, help me."

Her sister was probably laid up at the house. A seagull squawked overhead, and Cindy thought she heard a baby cry. "I'll make the call and then give you directions, but that's all I can do."

"Thank you, Mrs. Maxwell. Thank you."

Leaning against the seawall, Cindy unblocked her sister's number and called.

"Hey, Big Sis. Glad you changed your mind. You know Dad's hands aren't steady. He needs your help."

"He's cooking with the baby in the house?"

Laughter cackled through the earpiece. "No. We're at the lodge. Danni's outside in the car."

"It's ninety degrees outside. She'll die of a heat stroke." Cindy shoved off the concrete and hurried toward the parking lot.

"No she won't. Rosetta parked in the shade, and we have the windows down. What's your problem anyway? It's your recipe that Elliot is using. Are you coming to help or not?"

Cindy's motherly instincts kicked in. She had to rescue Danni. "Where are you?"

"We're at the line shack."

෨෬

Cole jogged down the office steps as Cindy pulled up in the BMW. She was too early for a lunch run. He loved it when she visited the office, but today her timing was horrible. He opened the driver's door. "Kiss me quick. I'm late for a meeting."

Her nervous laugh and desperate kiss put him on guard.

He pulled back. "What's wrong?"

"Nothing. Everything. Can I borrow the truck?"

The last time she'd borrowed the truck, she'd ended up in her old neighborhood. But she promised she wouldn't ever go back. He pulled the keys out of his pocket. "Here. I parked around back."

A trembling hand offered him the keys to the car.

Something wasn't right. He brushed her lips again and slid in the driver's seat of the BMW. The nagging suspicion returned as he adjusted the seat. Cindy wore long sleeves and tennis shoes in ninety-degree weather. Why? "Are you sure you're okay?"

"I'm fine, Cole." The straps on her purse tangled between her fingers. Her breath and words burst forth. "Rosetta and Maria have Danni. Her grandmother called. I'm taking her to them."

"Where?" He got back out of the car and slammed the door. His meeting could wait. "Not at the house."

"No." She leaned in and kissed him. "They're at an old hunting lodge in the north corner of the county. It's used for making large quantities." Her hand rested on her abdomen. "Danni's father and grandmother are following me. I'm pointing them to the baby, and then I'm out of there. Piece of cake." Her chin lifted, and she wet her lips. "Cole. I'll be fine."

He grabbed the hand holding the keys. "Wait half an hour and I'll go with you."

"I can't. Maria said they left the baby outside in the car."

The thought of Danni trapped in a hot car crashed over him. "Call the police. Let them handle it."

Her brilliant smile cinched the knots in his stomach. "The cops won't get involved in a custody dispute."

She was his wife. He'd have to trust her?

₧ℂℝ

The truck's tires crushed small pine branches as Cindy pulled off on the side of the country road. There wasn't a house around for miles. Secluded, it was the perfect place to hide. She left Cole a voicemail saying she had arrived and that she'd call again on her way home.

Danni's father ran up to the side of the truck.

Cindy pressed a button to lower the passenger window. "Look to your right. There's an abandoned trailer about three hundred yards down that dirt road. Maria said the baby was in the car. It should be parked out front." Cindy's eyes widened as the guy opened the door and slid into the passenger seat.

He cocked a 9mm and nodded. "Let's go get her."

She swallowed against a dry throat. "I'm not going with you. What are you doing with that gun?"

"Making sure no one stops me from taking my daughter." He palmed the pistol in one hand. With the other, he touched his curved knuckle to his nose and sniffed deep.

"You've been snorting." She should've known. "Get out of my truck. I'm not helping you." Her freedom with Cole was too precious.

He sniffed again. "It was half a line. I needed to calm my nerves. I'm good. I just want my baby."

In the rearview mirror, Danni's grandmother waved from the driver's seat of her car. She seemed like a decent person, but her son was obviously a user. Big surprise there, since he had a child with Rosetta. Cindy lifted her phone, intending to tell the woman to control her son, but hard steel pressed into her side. The barrel pointed straight at her womb. She froze and then slowly placed the phone in the door pocket. "Don't shoot. I won't call."

"Good." The hand holding the pistol trembled. The gun could go off any second. "I don't want to hurt you. So drive, okay?"

He sniffed again. "Just drive."

Jesus, protect me. As she prayed, an unexplainable calm settled in her soul. Cindy shifted into gear and traversed the deep ruts in the dirt road. One jolt and she'd never see Cole again. The rusted trailer looked abandoned. The truck rolled to a stop behind Granny's old sedan. How ironic. The repairs she'd paid for would now transport death in crystal form.

The barrel jabbed into her side. "Go find my baby, and no sudden moves. I'm watching you."

Cindy eyed the pistol and then glanced into wild eyes. Heart beating in her throat, she eased out of the truck and gently closed the door. The heavy-metal guitar blaring from the trailer confirmed Elliot's presence. He'd always claimed the music soothed him. She wiped her sweaty palms on her jeans and crept near the car. All four windows were down. Cindy's stomach clenched.

In the backseat, Danni lay on a folded blanket. No safety seat in sight. Her cheeks were red, and sweat soaked her downy hair. Cindy held her breath and opened the door. The squeak couldn't be helped, but she doubted anyone inside the trailer would hear.

A cool wind blew as she lifted Danni from the backseat. The baby's shirt was soaked and her breath was light, but at least she was alive. Cindy didn't have time to cool her off. She had to leave before Elliot spotted her. If he was cooking, he couldn't walk away from the stove—unless he had a death wish. Tucking the baby against her chest, she hurried away. Her heartbeat pounded in her ear. Which way should she go? Danni's father and his gun waited in the truck, but she couldn't walk back to the city.

"Hey, you made it." Her sister's voice stopped Cindy in her tracks. "Dad didn't think you were coming, so he's already started. Where you going with Danni?" Maria stood on a rotten step.

Cindy breathed easy and forced a smile. "She's burning up. I'm cooling her off a bit."

"She has a tea bottle in her bag. Milk sours in the heat. When you put her in the car, there's a blanket you can use to prop it up."

No way would she leave Danni. "I'll be in there in a minute."

Her sister looked over her shoulder once and then disappeared into the trailer. Cindy hurried toward the truck. Danni's daddy jumped from the passenger side and ran towards her. The pistol was nowhere in sight. "My God, what did they do to her?"

Cindy didn't have time to explain. "Take her and go."

The baby never changed hands. Danni's daddy marched toward the trailer as the grandmother pulled her car behind the truck on the narrow path. Cindy was now blocked in.

"Rose!"

Little Danni cried at her father's outburst. The trailer door banged open. Rosetta screamed and wailed.

This isn't happening. "This was not the deal. You've got your daughter. I won't be caught in the middle."

He reached behind his back and untucked the pistol from his belt. "When I'm done, I won't have to worry about her anymore."

Sirens sounded in the distance, but grew in volume. The cops? She had to escape. Fast. Cindy handed the baby to her grandmother. "Move your car or I will run over you on my way out."

Tears clogged the woman's eyes as she cradled the infant.

"Hurry?" Blue lights flashed. Doors slammed. "Great!"

A SWAT team swarmed through the woods. Cindy reached for the truck's door handle. Someone grabbed her arm and slung her against the hood. "Ouch. Get off me. I'm on your side."

Steel cuffs pinched her wrists. Pandemonium broke out as Rosetta and Maria ran out of the trailer.

Scorched sulfur polluted the air. Seconds later, an explosion shook the ground.

Heat rolled over Cindy and darkness descended.

Chapter Twenty-Four

It was Cole's worst nightmare come true. *Jesus, help us.* Cole and his dad stood behind the media barrier as a deputy helped Cindy out of the backseat of a cruiser. Handcuffs bound her hands in front of her.

Her gaze met his over the open door. Sorrow lined her eyes and a bruise marred her chin. She mouthed, "I'm sorry."

His numb feet moved forward, but his dad laid a hand on his shoulder. "No, Cole. Not yet."

"But Dad, that's my wife. And my baby."

Sympathy stared back at him. "I know, Son. I know." They had hired the best criminal lawyer in the state. He was due to arrive this afternoon. "Let's go. We have a lot of work to do if we want her released anytime soon."

ഇൻൻ

Lying on her hard bunk, Cindy stared at the stained ceiling. "Jesus please help them through this. I've been where they are, Lord. They need you."

Yesterday, they'd been brought to the detox ward. A nurse kept watch from outside the cell. Periodically, she'd check their blood pressure as most drug related deaths occurred while coming down. The heart simply stopped beating.

Rosetta stooped in the corner of the cell and rocked on her heels. "Oh God, kill me now. Just let me die. Let me die." Pitiful groans overshadowed the prayers and echoed through the cell block as sweat plastered her bangs to her pale forehead.

Cindy remembered the awful pain left in the wake of poison. Thank God she no longer suffered through the shame of addiction. But she worried about her sister. Maria shivered in a blanket, wild-eyed, flinching at every sound.

A girl Cindy had never met, battled an upset stomach on the open toilet situated in the middle of the cell. Jail afforded no privacy. It stole your freedom, your dignity, and your pride. Cindy hid her face in the scratchy, disaster-relief blanket and hid from the sounds and smells.

℠ℝ

Cole stood to his feet as they led Cindy into the courtroom wearing an orange jumpsuit. Shadows lined her tired eyes. She graced him with a sad smile as she walked in front of the bench.

Her defense attorney addressed Judge Pierson. "Your Honor, I respectfully request the handcuffs be removed from my client. She poses no threat to anyone here."

The judge nodded to the deputy.

Cole wanted to kiss her as Cindy lifted her chin with her hands. When the cuffs were released, she rubbed the red marks on the delicate skin that encircled her wrists. He couldn't reach across the wood banister. Her attorney advised that he not be included in her defense. Cole had reluctantly agreed. His bad choices brought them here today. He hadn't trusted her and had called Detective Simmons. But why had they arrested Cindy? She'd done nothing wrong.

Judge Pierson rapped the gavel and nodded to Harry, who paced in front of the bench. "Your Honor, the state presents a case against Cynthia LouAnn McDuffie Maxwell for manufacturing an illegal substance. As the defendant is on probation from a previous conviction and her familial connections deem her as a flight risk, we ask that she be held without bail until the grand jury convenes."

Cole jumped to his feet. "Harry!"

Judge Pierson rapped the gavel. "Refrain from such outbursts, young Maxwell, or I will remove you from my courtroom."

Cole sat and rubbed his forehead. His dad shook his head. Cole blew out a breath. He wasn't helping Cindy. He needed to keep a cool head. *God, please don't take her from me.*

The judge turned to the defense attorney. "Proceed."

"Your Honor, my client was in the wrong place at the wrong time. Other than a previous mistake, there is no evidence of her guilt, nor will there be. Her scheduled check ins with her PO have been timely, and her drug screens negative. The charges against her are a blatant attempt to embarrass the Maxwell name."

Harry interjected. "Your Honor, manufacturing doesn't necessarily include personal usage. The state has verified that no drugs were in the defendant's bloodstream at the time of arrest. However, we have an eyewitness who testifies that Mrs. Maxwell was the"—Harry glanced at a piece of paper—"best cook in the county."

"That was not submitted to me. Therefore, it can't be used in this arraignment. Who is this witness?"

"Maria McDuffie, half-sister to the accused."

Cindy gasped, and her head slumped. She turned, and their eyes met. "It's not true, Cole. I would never risk our life. Or Lulu's. Maria's mad because I wouldn't give her any more money."

The judge hammered on the wood.

Cole wanted to believe her. Betrayal buzzed with the courtroom noise. He forced himself to hear the judge's bail order.

"Given the witness's question of character, and the charges pending against her, this court will consider the evidence as hearsay and not permissible." He turned to Cindy and removed his glasses. "However, I cannot fathom why a woman of intelligence would submit herself to suspicion without some measure of guilt. Therefore, the defendant will be held *without bail* until the Grand Jury convenes," He turned to the defense attorney. "*Or* an agreement is reached with the state."

Cole left her. Her husband walked out of the courtroom without looking back. *God, I've never wanted to bring him shame.* Her chest ached at the thought of him seeing her in handcuffs. Why hadn't the officer removed them before he walked Cindy into the courtroom?

The jailer led her by the arm through a side door.

Her attorney followed. In the hall, he stepped up beside her. "I need a moment alone with my client, if you please."

The guard unlocked a small room. "A room has been arranged for you, sir." As Cindy entered the doorway, Cole pressed a finger to his lips from the shadows in the corner. Her attorney nudged her and she stepped in.

The jailer spoke, "Knock when you're finished."

The door closed, and Cindy fell into Cole's open arms. His steady heartbeat soothed her frazzled nerves. Warm lips brushed her hair, and gentle hands massaged her back.

She knew then everything would be all right.

"Excuse me." Her attorney was strictly business. "You don't have much time. If you need to say anything, do it quickly."

She didn't hesitate. "I love you, Cole. I'm sorry your truck blew up. I had to help Danni. Is she okay? Have you heard?"

"She's with her grandmother, but I'm concerned about you and our baby. Does the jail have electricity?"

"Yeah. I miss you, Cole. I want this nightmare to end."

"Soon. And then I'm locking you in the apartment and I'm never letting you out."

Cindy memorized his smile. "That's fine with me."

Gentle hands framed her face, and the brush of his thumbs wiped her tears. "Your father's in ICU. He may not survive."

"I don't want to talk about him." She snuggled close into Cole's protective embrace. She should forgive her father. Maybe with God's help, someday she would, but it wouldn't be today. Cindy gasped. "My wedding rings. They took them."

Warm lips brushed her temple. "I've got them. I'll keep them safe until you come home." He turned to the attorney. "Whatever Harry wants, give it to him. I don't trust myself to negotiate with the man. I don't care what it takes, or what it costs. I want my wife out of here and safe at home where she belongs."

The attorney glanced at Cindy. "Give me a few days. I'll try to plea-bargain with Harry."

She tilted her head at Cole. "A few days? I'll be out before the wedding reception."

Cole stiffened. "Mom canceled, given the circumstances."

"You told your mother I was in here?"

His chest rose, and she braced herself for his next words. "The explosion was big news. All three local channels covered it."

Her knees buckled and his arms supported her. This is the one thing she never wanted to happen. She'd humiliated Cole in front of the whole world. "I'm so sorry."

&)CR

Footsteps echoed down the corridor. Cole paused outside the waiting room and prayed. "Lord, make me a light to show others your love. Amen." He pushed the door open. The room was empty.

With Cindy in jail, he felt an obligation to visit her father and offer to pray with the family. He paused at the volunteer desk. "Excuse me. Can you direct me to the McDuffie family?"

The elderly lady shook her head. "I'm sorry, sir. There isn't anyone by that name in the waiting room." She flipped through a clipboard. "The family members usually leave contact information in case they miss a doctor's consultation."

Perhaps he had the wrong hospital. "Is Mr. McDuffie in ICU?"

She checked the computer. "He's in 1208. Are you family?"

The sad truth prevailed. "Yes. He's my father-in-law. When are visiting hours?"

"Now." She waved at the empty room. "There's seven minutes left, if you want to visit."

"Thank you." Cole entered the east wing. The double doors opened, and a lady wiped tears as she walked out. Cole smiled hoping to encourage the woman as they passed in the hall.

A round nurse's station centered several rooms. He found the one he sought. No one questioned his presence.

The sight on the bed turned his stomach. A bloated body was blackened beyond recognition. Tubes protruded from his nose and mouth. Machines beeped and huffed near the bed. Cole leaned over the prostrate body. Could Elliot hear him? Would he remember?

"Mr. McDuffie, it's Cole, Cindy's husband."

The charred flesh, where his eyebrows should've been, bunched into what might've been a frown.

"I want to pray with you."

A lone tear leaked from the corner of one eye.

Cole reached for his father-in-law's hand, but gripped the bedrail instead. The burns covered the man's entire body. Cole didn't want to think about the pain he must be suffering. The man deserved it, but Cole bowed his head. "Jesus, I ask that You grace us with Your mercy, though we are all sinners and none deserve Your favor. You died on a cross and suffered the lash of the whip to not only heal our bodies, but to save us from eternal torment. Heal Mr. McDuffie's body. Spare him the pain of his injuries. Love him, Lord, like only You can. In Your name I pray. Amen."

ഇൗരു

A knife sliced through her stomach and slammed Cindy in the gut jarring her awake. Sticky moisture coated the inside of her thighs. "The baby." Another pain hit her.

She screamed, and Maria rushed to her side. Rosetta paled as she stared at the sheets.

Maria turned to the other girl. "Yell for the nurse."

Another unseen blade stabbed into her, destroying her last hope. "No. Lulu? I can't lose her."

"Shhh. Cindy, it'll be all right." Maria squeezed her hand and Cindy held tight.

Voices came and went.

"Cole, where are you?"

Sirens and red lights flashed.

"Cole!"

Something pricked her arm. Once again, darkness took control.

ഇൗരു

A shrill ring woke him. He reached for Cindy and encountered an empty bed. She wasn't here. It was her third night in jail. How long would they be apart? The ringing persisted, and he fumbled in the dark for his phone. "Hello."

"Mr. Maxwell? This is Mobile County Metro Jail."

He sat straight up in the bed and reached for the lamp. "Is there something wrong with Cindy?"

"I'm sorry to be the bearer of bad news, sir."

"Out with it! What's wrong with my wife?" Cole stood and yanked on the pants hanging on Cindy's vanity chair.

"She's in an ambulance in route to USA Medical Center. The staff nurse suspects she's miscarrying."

His knees buckled, and he collapsed on the bed. "Oh, Jesus."

"We're sorry for your loss, Mr. Maxwell, but with your being an attorney, we thought you should know that an ambulance was dispatched the moment we were made aware of her fragile condition."

The phone trembled in his hand, and then blurred into obscurity. A wave of pain rolled over him and threatened to drag him under. His little Lulu. His sweet baby girl. His promise from God. She couldn't be gone. He fell to the floor and curled into a ball. Sobs racked his body. "God help me. Help me." The room swam into nothingness as his tears soaked the carpet. He wanted to crawl under the bed and hide from the cold reality of the moment. *Why, Lord? Why? You promised, Lord. You promised.*

He questioned the pain. He questioned God. He questioned himself. Unrest answered.

A slim, empty sandal focused. Cindy. Dear Jesus, she was alone. *Hold her, Lord, until I can reach her.*

₧₧₧

Emptiness beeped beside her. Her hand went to her flat abdomen. Lulu? Pain stung her eyes and she rolled onto her side. Long, jean-clad legs were bent at an odd angle. Cole's head was tilted sideways on the back of a stiff chair. He was here. Tears streamed down her face as she reached for him. "Cole." Her whispered word stirred him from sleep. Red-rimmed eyes met hers, and she knew. Lulu was gone. "I'm sorry, Cole. It's all my fault. I should've stayed home. I've should've said no. I would never do anything—" Her voice broke on a sob. She closed her eyes. She didn't want to see the pain on her husband's face.

Footsteps sounded. The chair was empty. Her tears doubled.

Movement rustled behind her. Cole lowered the safety rail and lay on the bed. Gentle arms embraced her. She leaned into his strength. Wrapped in the love of her husband, she cried for the promise they'd lost.

Cole whispered words near her ear and kissed her forehead. "It's not your fault. You are the best mother. Shh. I love you. Rest now, I've got you."

₧₧₧

Prayer seemed too little a thing to do.

He wanted to shake his fist at the heavens as he held his trembling wife in his arms. His faith was shaken. He didn't understand why God had taken Lulu. Knowing God had good intentions didn't lessen the pain. Bright light blinded Cole as the door opened and the morning nurse walked in.

She frowned. "Do you need a cot?"

"No, thanks. I'm fine."

The nurse smiled. "Love is often the best medicine." She inserted a needled in Cindy's IV. "I'll be back to check on her later. Use the call button if you need anything."

His wife snuggled into his left side. Cole cradled the curve of her arm and brushed a thumb over her soft skin.

Cindy's breathing slowed. She was asleep. God would heal her, but it would take time. Cole wished his father were here. He hadn't known what to say to his wife. "I'm sorry" seemed so inadequate. He held her for a while longer and then slipped from the bed.

Out in the hall, he checked the time on his phone. His parents would be eating breakfast. He called their landline.

His dad answered. "Good morning, Son."

"No, Dad, it's not." He sucked in a breath. "We lost the baby."

"Cole. I'm so sorry. What hospital? Your mother and I will be right over."

As much as he needed his father's support, Cindy's needs came first. "No, Dad. Cindy's hurting enough right now without having to deal with Mother's subtle insults."

Pregnant silenced ensued. Then his dad spoke. "At times like this, family comes together."

"Pray for us, Dad. That's what we really need."

"All right, Son. I'll talk to your mother. Remember that we love you and Cindy. And don't forget, Lulu was our grandbaby."

"Thanks for understanding, Dad. I gotta go now. Cindy could wake any minute." Cole made one more phone call.

Mrs. Bevin's soft cries lingered in his ear long after he'd disconnected.

∞�◊

Cindy didn't want to smile, but Cole insisted on telling her every funny thing that ever happened at church. She winced and shifted on the bed.

"Are you in pain?" Cole kissed her hand. He had scooted a straight back chair close to the hospital bed. "Do you want me to call the nurse?"

The dull ache in her body was manageable. The hole in her heart may never heal. "I'm fine, Cole."

The door swung open and the doctor sauntered in. "I'm glad to hear that."

Cole stood and shook the man's hand.

"Mr. Maxwell, your wife is doing wonderful. Last night, I was able to stop the hemorrhaging, and there was no damage to the uterus. I expect a full recovery."

Not true. Cindy lost a part of them last night that she couldn't recover. She sucked in a breath as the doctor's cold hand pressed on her abdomen.

"Hurt?"

"Your hand is cold."

Cole peered around the doctor. "Cindy?"

"I'm fine."

Kindness flickered in the doctor's eyes. "The psychological effects of a miscarriage vary from patient to patient. I could prescribe an antidepressant, but with your addiction history, I don't think that's wise. I suggest you rely on prayer to help you through this." He turned to Cole. "Both of you." He faced Cindy again. "There is no known medical reason that you can't carry a baby full-term. You'll be going home tomorrow. Give your body a few weeks to heal. Then I suggest you give this baby-making thing another go." He paused at the door. "Let God heal you from the inside out."

When he was gone, Cindy raised her eyes to find hope shining in Cole's. "He was wrong. I can't go home tomorrow. I have to go back to jail."

Cole lifted his chin. "We'll make it through this."

Her heart shattered into a thousand pieces. "I don't want to go." She covered her face in her hands. The sobs couldn't be contained. "I want to go home." Cole held her as she cried. "I need to go home. I need you to hold me." Her babbled words stopped making sense to her own ears as her sobs grew louder. She was so tired of fighting. So tired.

Cole settled on the bed beside her. The skin under her eyes was almost translucent. Slightly curled lashes rested against her pale skin.

He had to protect her. "I promise. I won't let them take you back to jail."

"You can't stop them." With a final sniff, she drifted to sleep.

There had to be some way to convince Harry to drop the charges. Perhaps if he knew the loss she'd suffered. Cole had until tomorrow, and if that wasn't enough time, he'd bribe the doctor into keeping Cindy at the hospital. He dialed his office. "Mrs. Bevin, I need you to do some research for me." He laid out his wishes, glad that his secretary was capable enough to handle his instructions. He had Cindy to thank for that. The door opened as he ended the call.

His mom and dad entered. Why couldn't they do as he asked? His father carried a potted plant fit for a funeral. If his parents made his wife cry, he'd toss them both out.

"Place it there." His mother indicated a corner near the bed.

Cindy woke and pressed a button on the side of the bed. Slowly the bed lifted until she surveyed the occupants of the room. Her eyes landed on the white flowers in the middle of waxed greenery. Her bottom lip trembled, and tears pooled in her eyes. She raised her eyes to his mother. "Thank you." Her chest heaved, and tears fell. "Thank you so much."

"Mom." Cole's warning died in his throat as Cindy lifted her arms and his mother rushed to her side.

The women clung to each other as they both cried. What was going on here? They parted slightly, and Cindy stared at the plant. "Lulu would've liked peace lilies."

His mom nodded. "I thought so too, dear."

Cindy cried again and his mother hugged her tight.

Cole looked to his father for answers. His dad shrugged and whispered, "Sometimes a woman knows things that a man can't comprehend. Come on, Son, let's leave them alone."

Cole wasn't so sure. "Cindy?"

His mother turned. "Shoo, Cole. Take your father with you."

Chapter Twenty-Five

That same afternoon, Cole slapped a file on the District Attorney's desk.

Harry glanced up. "What's this?"

Cole narrowed his gaze. "The biggest lawsuit Mobile County has ever seen."

Harry flipped through the file. "I can't believe this. You're suing the county for medical negligence? You'll never prove this."

"During the explosion, Cindy was rendered unconscious for six minutes. Yet, she wasn't offered medical care." Cole's heartbeat thundered in his chest. He couldn't afford to mess this up. "I may not win, but I might. Regardless, it'll cost the taxpayers millions in legal fees, because I'll file so many motions and contingencies, I'll have this thing buried in court for years."

Harry swore and dropped the file. "Fine. I'll switch Cindy's case to Drug Court and move her out of the general population to the women's barracks."

"I want my wife's freedom." Cole leaned across the desk. "Drop these ridiculous charges and the lawsuit will never be filed."

"Yeah." Harry laughed. "How can I be certain of that? Overplayed your hand, haven't you?"

Cole refused to back down. Zack agreed. Bluffing may be a bit underhanded, but it was their best option. "I've spoken with my father, Uncle Kyle, and Grandfather. I have the Maxwell name and fortune at my disposal. If you don't drop the charges against my wife, I'll make your life a living nightmare."

Harry grinned maliciously. "Fine, but I want the boat. Sell it to me, and you've got a deal."

He should have expected this. Harry had wanted the boat since Cole defeated him in a sailing competition years ago. But to demand the boat now when Cole was at his lowest reeked of desperation.

Harry licked his lips. "You postdate a bill of sale for one month's time, and the charges disappear today."

Cole swallowed. He'd give everything he owned for Cindy's freedom. "Two months." He held out his hand and the deal was made. "It'll be on your desk before the end of the day."

ജൠ

Cindy refused all narcotics, but something in her IV made her sleepy. She dozed in and out until Cole's voice penetrated her dreams. "Cindy." Warm lips brushed her cheek.

He was at his office trying to keep his promise, but she was afraid to hope. "Cole?"

"I'm sorry it's taking me so long. Harry needed some extra persuasion. Sit up. I need your signature."

Strong arms lifted her back. The overhead light flickered on. "Can we go home now?"

His smile strengthened her faith. "Not yet." He pressed a pen in her hand. "Sign right here. Cynthia LouAnn Maxwell."

The legal words swam before her. Blue outlined the white paper. She signed her name where he indicated, and again after he turned the page and pointed. "What am I signing?"

"Don't talk. Just trust me." He flipped the pages. "Initial on all three lines."

She did as he asked but scanned the pages before doing so. She didn't know a lot about the law, but knew enough to know he was selling something to Harry Buruger. The District Attorney? She dropped her voice, not wanting the nurse to overhear. "Is this legal?"

"Loopholes." Cole winked. "Go back to sleep. I'll be done in a few more hours."

ജൠ

Zack stood as Cole strode into his office. "How's Cindy?"

"Sleeping mostly. She didn't want anything for pain, but I convinced the doctor to give her something anyway." He rounded the desk and claimed his chair. "Did you call the courier service?"

"No." Zack pointed to his bodyguard who lingered in the corner. "George will hand deliver the package."

Cole nodded and double checked the documents. Not long

ago, his sailboat was the only thing he valued, but Cindy meant more than material possessions. Everything was in order. He slipped the papers into a legal envelope and passed them to the giant. "Tell Harry that I want confirmation today."

"Yes, sir."

The office door closed behind Zack's personal assistant. Cole leaned back in his chair and folded his hands behind his head. "She needs the support of her family. She needs you."

Cindy's brother sank into one of the two chairs across the desk. "I can't."

Cole leaned forward. His feet hit the floor as he caught and held Zack's gaze. "You can. My wife is drowning in guilt. She's lost her baby. Her sister's in rehab and her reprobate father doesn't deserve to live. I can't change any of that. But I can give her the truth—her brother is alive and he loves her. That he's been watching and taking care of her from a distance."

Zack circled his thumbs around his temples. "She's suffered enough these past few days, and I can't put her through another shock. I have to take care of some business in Atlanta. I'll be back in a few weeks. I'll come for dinner or something." Zack closed his eyes and winced. "Let me tell her myself. Let me explain why…"

Cole saw through Zack's flimsy excuse, but he couldn't force the man. "Fine. But if you don't tell her soon. I will. And then you can explain why you've been hiding from her. I know my wife. She'll think it was because you didn't want her."

The office phone rang. Cole nodded at Zack. "This is it."

Mrs. Bevin's voice came through the intercom. "Sorry to disturb you, sir, but Cindy's attorney is on line one."

He pressed the speaker button. "Yes?"

"The District Attorney must have a heart after all. All charges against your wife have been dropped. When the hospital releases her, she's free to go home."

ഔൽ

Two weeks later, she woke in an empty bed. A tear slipped down her cheek. Her palm caressed her flat belly.

How could she miss someone she'd never met?

Why did it hurt so much?

Tears fell in earnest now. She curled on her side and hid under her pillow. Cole had abandoned her and returned to the office. Not that she blamed him. She'd killed his Lulu. She'd destroyed his promise from God. Maybe she should've accepted the prescription from the doctor?

A memory of his voice floated on the breeze. "Cindy, you're the strongest person I know. God will help us through this."

It was a lie. She was weak. She couldn't do anything. She'd tried to be good. She'd tried to fit in church. *Please, Jesus. Help me.*

The doorbell rang. Hiding under the pillow, she cried. She didn't want visitors. She didn't want to hear the well-meaning words. No one knew the pain. No one understood. Not even Cole. The bell chimed again, and she groaned, "Go away."

"Cindy?" Joni's voice floated in the abyss. "Are you awake?"

"Maybe we should come back later." Andrea's whisper came from beyond the bedroom door.

How did they get inside her apartment? Cole would never leave it unlocked. Cindy rolled over and propped on her elbows. "What are you guys doing in here?"

Both her friends crossed the room and sat on the end of her bed. Joni's rounded stomach reminded Cindy of her loss. The well of tears she'd thought had run dry sprang a new leak. Gentle hands caressed her back and shoulders as the prayers of her friends' penetrated heaven. Tissues materialized in front of her. She blew her nose and dried her eyes.

"Don't give up on life, Cindy. Cole needs you."

"Cole?" Sun shone through the window. Cindy sniffed and choked on her tears. "Cole's little Lulu." She gasped for breath. "He was so excited. I don't know if he can ever forgive me."

Joni gripped her hand. "Sweetie, Cole loves you. He knows you're not to blame. No one knows why God does what He does."

Andrea opened the closet door. "You need some fresh air. Let's go to the spa."

Joni smiled. "Yes, my feet are killing me."

Cindy didn't want to leave the bed, but the girls wouldn't take no for an answer. She caught her reflection in the mirror. How could Cole think her beautiful looking like this? "My hair could use a deep conditioner."

"That's the spirit. Now shower and dress. We'll wait in the living room."

"How'd you get in?"

Her friends paused in the door and Andrea held a single key. "Cole is worried about you. When we told him you weren't answering the door, he gave us this, but he made us promise not to upset you." Her friends smiled and left the room. The door clicked shut.

Cindy left the bed and stood at the window. Seeking the warmth of the sun, she tilted her face. Her hand automatically went to her stomach.

The fog in her mind lifted with the rays of light. She didn't want to worry Cole. Gathering the clothes that Andrea had draped on the bed, she turned for the shower.

≈

The office walls closed in. Cole had to escape. He lifted the phone and buzzed Mrs. Bevin. "Can you handle our appointments this afternoon without me? I need some space."

"Of course." His secretary paused. "Please, tell Cindy, I'm praying for her, and give her a hug for me."

His insurance had totaled the truck, but he hadn't had a chance to replace the vehicle. On the way home, he stopped by the storage unit and exchanged the car for the Harley.

Could he talk Cindy into going for a ride? Was she physically able? Unsure, he brought out his phone and texted. Played hooky this afternoon. Looking for my biker chick. If she doesn't feel up to it, we can be pirates instead ?

He paced the unit with his helmet in his hand. Was it too soon? He wheeled the bike out of the unit as his phone sang her ringtone.

"You're on speaker. Joni and Andrea dragged me to the spa." Coarse laughter flowed through the phone, but it wasn't Cindy's. He missed her musical laugh. "Stop, you guys. I can't hear."

How long would she blame herself? "Did you read my text?"

"Yes. Either one sounds good, but I prefer the first."

"Are you physically able to do it? I mean… Can you take me off speaker?"

Andrea's voice muffled. "She tells us everything anyway."

Joni's laughter followed. "It's a girl thing."

Irritation entered Cindy's voice. "Don't say a word. They're fishing for clues. My nails will be dry in a minute. I'll call you back."

"Tell me where you are. I'll meet you there."

Ten minutes later, the Harley rumbled into the spa's parking lot, and Cole pulled close to the building near the bench where the girls waited. He cut the engine. Cindy walked to his side, kissed him, and then claimed her leather jacket folded in his lap.

Joni's eyes widened. "Is that Cole?"

"She better not kiss anyone else." He winked and turned to free Cindy's helmet from the back of the bike.

Andrea stepped near. "Does Derek know you have this thing?"

Cole couldn't resist teasing the girls. "What? You didn't know?" He snapped his fingers and then buckled Cindy's straps. "And here I thought girls shared everything." They gawked in silence as Cindy climbed on behind him. He saluted the women. "If you'll excuse me, my biker babe wants to go for a ride."

He didn't want to overexert Cindy, so after a short jaunt in the country, he cruised into the marina. "Next stop. I thought we could use a dose of sea air." He hadn't told her what her freedom had cost. Hopefully, he could purchase a new boat before Harry took possession of this one.

She kissed his cheek. "You read my mind."

Out in the open water, Cindy's arms wrapped around him from behind. It was nice to be held for a change.

"I love you, Cole. I'm sorry I lost your Lulu."

He let the boat ride the waves and pulled her around him. Gathering Cindy in his arms, he held tight, and watched the clouds gather. "Look up."

"Cole, I'm not ready." She scurried to the bow and leaned against the pulpit railing.

He secured the wheel and followed her. With a gentle hand, he caressed her shoulder. "God keeps His promises."

She whirled around. Anger flashed in her eyes. "Where are they?" Her voice rose against the wind. "I'll tell you where they are. They're dead. Dead! Just like Lulu!"

Cole grabbed her close. How could he make her understand without causing her more pain? "My promises from God are fulfilled. He gave me you. He gave me Lulu. Like I've always imagined. She's up there. Swimming the clouds with Jesus. Waiting for her daddy to join her."

Sobs shook Cindy's frail body. "I want her here. With us."

He leaned back and captured her gaze. "No matter what happens down here, God's promises are real. He gave me a promise years ago, that if I waited, He'd give me an angel to love. You. I will never regret waiting. I will never regret loving you. And one day, we'll join Lulu, and our family will be complete."

Tears streamed down her face. There was more he wanted to tell her, but her faith was shaken.

"Hold on to Him, Cindy. Let Jesus be your strength. He knows what He's doing." Cole hooked his finger under her chin, nudging it up with his knuckle, tilting her face toward the heavens. "Look at those clouds. Before, she was a dream, but you made her a reality." He could almost see his little girl. "Knowing she's up there waiting for me makes for a sweeter heaven."

೮೦೧೪

Sunday morning, Cindy held tight to Cole's hand as they walked into the sanctuary. For once, Cindy was glad he came early to pray. She couldn't have walked into a crowded church after everyone had seen her in handcuffs on the local news. This was the first time she'd been here since the explosion. Since she'd lost Lulu.

James gestured from the platform, but Cole lingered at her side. "Are you okay for me to play for the worship service?"

She loved to hear Cole's drums. "Go ahead. I'm fine." He kissed her brow and hurried up the aisle. Cindy glanced around the church. A few people wandered in. Her gaze found Mrs. Briggs.

The elder woman snarled and turned away.

Cindy stared at the carpet and sank into the pew. She opened her Bible and pretended to read while the others prayed. *Jesus, help me get through this day.* Did everyone think badly of her? Did they think she was guilty of the crimes she'd been accused of? She blinked past the hurt and willed her eyes not to cry.

A shadow fell over her.

Sara hugged Cindy tight. "I'm so glad you're here. I've missed you so much. How are you doing?"

Somehow Cindy managed to choke out the words, "I'm fine."

Mrs. Preston was next in embracing her. "I'm praying for you, sweetie. I've been where you are. Losing a baby is devastating, but God will see you through this and you'll be stronger in the end."

The hug was awkward with Cindy sitting and Joni's mother-in-law standing. Cindy came to her feet and accepted the offered comfort.

Several ladies in the church gathered around her, sharing hugs and words of encouragement.

Cindy couldn't stop the tears that welled in her eyes and spilled down her cheeks. "Thank you. You guys have no idea how much you mean to me."

The musicians played, and one by one the women returned to their own pews. Cindy met Cole's smiling gaze. She wiped her cheeks and nodded. When Joni sang of God's amazing love, a tingling sensation fell over Cindy. She raised her hands toward heaven. Angel wings fluttered through her mind as a gentle voice spoke healing into her soul.

Chapter Twenty-Six

"James Preston, get that camera out of my face." Joni's cheeks puffed as she exhaled. Relief flashed across her face as Cindy and Cole hurried down the corridor toward their friends. "Cole, take James's camera and throw it out the window. Cindy, help me walk. The doctor said it will speed the labor process."

Cindy offered her arm. They'd made five steps when Joni's fingers dug into her flesh. Joni cradled her stomach with her other hand and cried out in pain.

"Yes!" James zoomed in. "That's a good one, beautiful. A few more like that and we can say hello to our boys."

Joni batted her hands at the camera. "You better hope its twins. I'm not going through this again."

James handed the device to Cole and reached for his wife. "You're doing great." He leaned in and brushed a kiss across her forehead. "Hold on to me. I've got you."

Cindy stepped back, and Cole's arm encircled her. His other hand pointed the video camera toward the miracle unfolding before them. "Try to smile, Joni. This should be a happy occasion."

Murderous eyes zeroed in on Cole. "I'd like to see a man puke for nine months, and then smile while his body is ripped apart." She froze. And then pleading eyes met Cindy's. "My water broke."

"Hey!" James yelled at the nurses' station. "Our water broke." He swooped Joni in his arms and carried her toward a smiling nurse who held open the delivery room door.

An unexpected wave of sadness washed over her.

Cole lowered the camera. "She was a little crazy." His goofy grin softened his words.

"James was a nutcase. Would you have been like that?"

"Absolutely not." His arms tightened, and she lifted her face for his kiss. "Maybe we'll find out one day?"

The elevator dinged. The doors opened and Mr. and Mrs. Preston rushed toward them. "How is she? Do we have a baby yet?"

Cindy couldn't find her voice. Cole answered, "They just took her back. James is with her."

Mark and Sara appeared and the waiting area filled quickly. Joni's parents were the last to arrive. A nurse escorted her mother to the delivery room at Joni's request. Andrea leaned near Cindy and whispered, "Are you okay?"

Cindy forced a smile. Despite her own pain, she was truly happy for her friends. "I'm great."

"Good."

Sara squealed. "This is so exciting. I've never been on the outside of the delivery room before."

Speculation circled the waiting room for hours. Was James right? Did God promise him twins? Cindy wanted to believe, but it was hard to have faith when the facts testified to a different truth.

Cole's arm draped around Cindy's shoulders. "You okay?"

She turned into her husband's arms. "I don't want Joni to be disappointed if she doesn't have twins. I'm worried about her."

Mr. Preston leaned up in his chair. "If James was promised twins, that's what he'll receive. God always keeps His promises."

Cindy stared at the scuff marks on the floor. "Not always."

Cole squeezed her shoulder. "Yes, He does. Maybe not like we think He should, but He isn't a man that He should lie. James will have his boys. Count on it. God doesn't do things halfway."

His kiss landed on her temple.

Oh how she wished his words were true. "For Joni's sake, I hope so." But she couldn't believe them.

Until, James appeared in the hall. "Haha. Look what Daddy's got." Dressed in yellow scrubs, he held two blue bundles. One in each arm. "You can't tell me that I don't serve an awesome God."

ഔ�

Three days later, Cole cradled one sweet baby against his chest. Fully dressed, Joni reclined on the made bed. "Where's Cindy?"

"She's visiting her father. She'll be sorry she missed your homecoming." Cole traced a finger across the downy head. "He's so tiny." A thought hit him. "Should I have gone with her? She insisted that she go alone, but…" He looked to Joni for advice. "Now, I'm not so sure. What do you think?"

"No offense, but when a woman says something, that's usually what she means. Cindy doesn't want you tainted by her past."

"She said that?"

"Not in so many words, but yes." Joni bit her lip.

He had a feeling she wanted to say more, but a knock sounded and a familiar guy walked into the room. "Hey, there now. How're you feeling?"

Joni lifted her arms and accepted a kiss on the cheek. "I'm good." She nodded across the room. "Cole, this is Ray Simmons, James's friend."

The guy was surprisingly quiet on his feet to be dressed in jeans and work boots. Cole balanced the precious bundle in the crook of his elbow and shook the calloused hand. "We met at the wedding."

"Yeah, I remember. You're the drummer, right?"

"Right." Cole vaguely recalled Ray hiring a stripper at James's bachelor party. Thankfully, James had instructed the girl to stay clothed and called her a cab. If he remembered correctly, Ray was James's friend from his construction days. He certainly looked the part, until he gently lifted the other twin.

"There's Uncle Ray's construction worker." His smile aimed for Joni. "Do this a few more times and I'll have a whole crew."

Joni's laugh startled the babies.

The twin in Cole's arms bunched up his face and turned red before letting out a loud cry. He bounced the little one against his chest and glared at Ray.

The man grinned. "They've got a good set of lungs. It's a good thing, too. Uncle Ray can't have any wimps on the job." He laid his forehead against the baby's head, and miraculously the babe hushed.

"Don't get them all wound up. I'm hoping they sleep during the drive home." Joni readjusted the pillows surrounding her. "You should find a wife and have your own crew."

"Oh no." The guy paled and eased the baby into the crib. "I wouldn't mind having a kid or two, but who needs the nagging woman that comes with them?"

Cole's heart lightened at the thought of Cindy.

"Finding a wife is a good thing." James struggled through the door with two infant seats. "But stay away from mine." He set his burdens by the wall and slapped Ray's shoulders. "How long can you stay? We might need help with diaper duty."

Ray cast a longing look toward the cradle. "I'd love to, but I'm just passing through on the way to New Orleans. I'll stop back by in a few weeks."

James nodded at the car seats. "Before you go, you and Cole can help me carry my blessings to the car."

There was no manly way to tote an infant seat. Ray hooked one on his arm and propped against the stainless wall while James wheeled Joni into the elevator. Cole suppressed a smile.

The guy wasn't dumb. "What?"

"You look like an old lady toting a purse."

Laughter echoed in the chamber, and Ray gave a good-natured grin. "At least I do it with flare."

Joni scolded both of them. "Now, now boys. Behave."

Under the patient pickup canopy, Cole secured his twin into a base anchored to the backseat of Joni's car. When the Honda pulled away from the awning, Ray grinned. "Man, can you imagine the poop those two are gonna spit out?" He shook his head. "I'm glad I'm not the one changing diapers."

∞

The old man was pale as death. Hopeful, Cindy walked straight for the hospital bed. Unfortunately, his chest lifted and fell quickly. She stopped out of reach. "Don't bother sitting up. I'm not here for a friendly visit. I came to forgive you."

A frail hand lifted the oxygen cup from his face. "What for?"

"You didn't protect me. You didn't care for me. And we won't talk about the times you sold me, locked me in the closet, or forced me to mix dangerous chemicals. It's a miracle I'm still alive."

Indifferent eyes stared back at her.

"Regardless, I have a new life now, and I won't have unfinished business with you polluting it. So…you're forgiven."

The frail body slumped into the pillow. "Good." The hand holding the mask trembled. "I need your help. Now more than ever."

"Elliot, I'm not helping you. I'm not visiting you. I don't want anything to do with you or your sinful life. You do need help, but Jesus is the only Man for that job." She turned for the door.

"Your husband prayed." She barely heard the raspy words as her feet kept moving. "Why should I?"

She didn't answer. If Elliot repented, Jesus would forgive him. But, Cindy secretly hoped her father burned in hell.

෩൞

A few weeks later, as Cole drove them home from church, peace flooded Cindy's soul. The pastor had once again admonished the congregation to do something good for the Lord. She was tired of living in her past. "Cole, if Elliot makes it out of the hospital, he's bound for prison. Right?"

His hand covered hers. "Yes, and Dad asked the judge for the maximum sentence."

"Good." She turned in her seat toward her husband. "But what happens to his house? And Granny's? Who owns them?"

His grip tightened around her palm. "Until he dies or sells it, Elliot owns the green house, but since your granny didn't have a will, the three of you share ownership. Why?"

Three? "Who?"

"You, Elliot, and your sister. And even though he wasn't blood kin, Zack may be entitled to a child's portion."

"Oh." Disappointment rang through her. "I wanted to open a brown bag mission." He lifted his brows, so she added, "It's like a soup kitchen, except you hand out lunches-to-go. The green house is in the perfect location, but I don't want to share it with Elliot."

He lifted her hand and kissed her knuckles. "That would be a lot safer than dodging The Boys. I think I can buy his signature, but what about your brother and sister?"

"Maria needs a home. I don't mind her keeping Granny's house if she agrees to give me use of the green one." She curled into her husband's side. "As for Zack, since your investigators haven't found him, can't we declare him legally gone or something?"

Cole stopped at a red light. "No. I couldn't in good conscience do that. Especially knowing that he—" Cole cleared his throat as the light changed. "Knowing that he might be alive out there."

She'd once dreamt that her brother would return and rescue her, but she'd given up that fantasy long ago. "Is there anything you can do?"

"Maybe. Let me make a few phone calls." He released her hand and fumbled with the radio controls. The closer they got to their apartment, the more distant he became. Since she'd been home, Cole had waited on her hand and foot, but it wasn't enough. She needed more than friendly hugs and the occasional kiss. She wanted her husband back. Sometimes, she'd catch him staring into the distance with deep sorrow etched on his face. Did he miss Lulu, too?

His hand rested on the console between them. She scooted close and placed her hand beside his. Her mind drifted back to the day they'd met. He'd seduced her heart with a simple touch. Could she do the same?

Using her pinkie, she traced circles around his knuckles. His hand turned, palm up. He didn't take his attention from the road, but the twitch of his lips gave him away. She entwined her fingers with her husband's, never intending to let go. "I love you, Cole."

"I know." He lifted her hand to his lips and kissed every finger.

The twins were precious, but she wanted a baby of her own. She could never come right out and ask Cole to love her, but the nightgown in the pink and white gift bag would convey her wishes.

Heat flushed her face as his lips curled. How did he know what she was thinking?

"I can't explain it." He gently squeezed her fingers.

Resting her head on his shoulder, she enjoyed his closeness as he drove them toward home.

Chapter Twenty-Seven

The clouds were perfect for swimming. This was the first time he'd been out in the boat alone since he'd met Cindy. And the last time he'd ever sail the *Lulu* again. Harry would take possession tomorrow, but Cindy's freedom was worth the price paid.

In her, Cole had a love he'd only dreamt possible. He leaned into the wind and counted his blessings. With the church's funding, Cindy's brownbag mission was well under way. Maria was clean and living in Granny's house. With her father bound for prison, Cole no longer worried about Cindy's safety.

He secured the wheel and let the boat ride. Cumulus clouds floated by. Cole moved to the bow and lay on the cabin roof. He closed his eyes as the boat rose on a swell.

Oh, how he longed for heaven. He opened his eyes.

The clouds appeared closer than they'd ever been. When would he join little Lulu? The doctor had given him weeks, months ago. The day of Cindy's initial obstetrician appointment. He inhaled the salty air and thought about diving into the waves. He wished she were here, but Cindy didn't know he'd sold the boat. He'd never found the words to tell her. About a lot of things. *Lord, give Cindy the strength to accept the promise you've given me.*

A wave folded over him and a sweet giggle floated in his ears. He almost glimpsed his angel, but the sun blinded his eyes. Pain shot through his head, and he became weightless. Unexpected joy engulfed him as he swam through a rainbow of light toward his ultimate promise.

Epilogue

Losing the baby hurt. But this new pain wrenched both her heart and her mind, leaving numbness in its wake.

Cole looked so peaceful, like an angel. People swarmed in the church, most of whom Cindy had never met. Their conversations buzzed in her ears. Mrs. Maxwell's cries came from her right, Rachel's from further down. Everyone wanted to claim part of her husband, but he was hers. At least until God had taken him.

Cindy wanted to crawl into the casket with Cole.

She threaded her fingers together and stared at the carpet. Pain rolled over her in suffocating waves. She gasped, inhaling the sickening smell of gardenias.

Someone hugged her. Another shook her hand. The tide of pain ebbed, leaving emptiness in its wake. *Why Lord? Why did you take him?* A shoulder jostled into her, and she found herself further down the casket—further away from her husband.

Who were these people that flocked into the church? Why didn't they go home and leave her in peace?

No one knew him like she did. No one saw him intimately. His playful side when they were alone. The bossiness when he thought he was right. His stubborn streak. How he liked his coffee in the morning. His favorite cereal bowl.

Anger rose in her, and she choked. *Where is my promise, God? Where are the comforting arms to hold me? Who's left here to love me?*

A commotion came from the front, and the sea of people parted. She raised her head, and her breath caught as her eyes met those she'd never expected to see again. How had he found her? How did he know she needed him?

Her hands lifted as her knees collapsed.

Zack caught her in his arms. She buried her face in his chest and hid from the judgment surrounding them. Safe in her brother's embrace, pain burst forth, and erupted. Deep-gutted wails surfaced. Uncontrollable cries racked her body.

"Mr. Worthington?" Mr. Maxwell's voice barely reached her. "What are you doing?"

Strong arms tightened around her, and she prayed he'd never let go. "Where can I take her? She needs a few minutes alone."

Wrapped in her brother's love, Cindy cried through the pain. She cried through the loneliness of the empty bed waiting at home. She cried through her anger at Cole for leaving her.

Cindy blinked through the tears. They were in the pastor's office. She sniffed. "You're Cole's Mr. Worthington?" Everything clicked into place. "You changed your last name. Did he know who you were?"

"Not at first. I tried to hide it. But your husband was one smart guy. He figured it out." A kiss landed on her temple. "Shhh, Lulu. Don't be angry. I made him promise not to tell."

Her chest heaved as fresh pain rolled over her. She pushed the words passed her trembling lips. "Cole believed in promises."

"Yes. And he made me promise to take care of you. So dry your eyes and we'll go back out there."

Fresh tears fell. "I want to be by his side for as long as I can. I want to say goodbye privately, but his mother won't let me."

"Sweetie, you're his wife. You have the power to kick them all out if you choose." He cried with her, and then wiped her tears. "Cole left you in a position of security. What do you want to do?"

She struggled to her feet and smoothed the wrinkles from her black dress. "Cole would want me to honor his parents, and to welcome his friends."

Her brother opened the door and held out his hand. "Then that's what we'll do."

She had a million questions, but for now, all that mattered was that her brother was here. And she needed him. She gripped his hand and led him into the sanctuary. More than one pair of eyes glared at their joined hands.

She didn't care. Nothing she did would stop them from judging her. Mrs. Briggs turned her nose up as Cindy walked past. She pushed Rachel aside. "Excuse me." Cindy took her place near Cole. His hand was cold. She'd give anything to see his gray eyes open. To see his lips twitch into his secret smile. The one he reserved for her. Cindy turned to her brother. "When everyone is gone, I want to stay here. Just for a while."

"You got it, Lulu."

The endearment stole her breath.

"Cindy, are you okay?" Mr. Maxwell and James stepped near. Both glanced inquisitively at her side.

Cole's father had been good to her and Cole. Cindy didn't want to taint her husband's memory. "Mr. Maxwell, I'd like you to meet my brother."

Mr. Maxwell blinked. "Mr. Worthington is your brother?"

Joni appeared in front of the crowd. "Of course he's your brother, who else could he be?" She shook his hand. "It's so nice Cindy's family could be here in her time of grief." Joni released him and hugged Cindy. "How are you holding up?"

Cindy nodded and wiped fresh tears. She was one step away from shattering into a million pieces. "Thankful for good friends."

Tears shimmered in Joni's eyes. "I'm here when you need me."

A long line of mourners waited to pay their respects. Keeping Cole's hand in hers, Cindy shifted slightly, making room for his friends to say goodbye.

Joni's smile wavered as she peered into the casket. "Cole was the best drummer I've ever heard. He kept us in rhythm. I'm gonna miss him."

Cindy would give anything to have him at home, banging away on the set of drums in their apartment. "He loved to play."

Joni stepped aside and raised her voice. "Mrs. Briggs, have you met Cindy's *brother*?"

The faces blurred together as people slowly made their way to the front. Each offered sympathy and shared a small memory of Cole. With her brother on her left, and Mr. and Mrs. Maxwell at the head of the casket, Cindy endured the awkward hugs as friends and family related their fondest memories.

"My name's Peter."

Cindy blinked at the man in front of her.

"Cole and I were dorm mates." He smiled sheepishly. "All of us guys"—he waved his hand at three men beside him—"we're glad he found you, before he…" He blinked and then swallowed. "Out of curiosity, Ms. Lulu, what's your real name?"

Through his college years, Cole had waited for his promise. Love for her husband overwhelmed the pain of loss for a brief second. Then reality returned. "My name is Cindy. Cynthia LouAnn Maxwell."

One of the men peered in the casket. "She's beautiful, my friend. And you were scared she'd be ugly."

She wished she'd married Cole the first time he'd asked her. The day they'd met.

He really was her superhero.

He'd rescued her, gave her love, taught her how to find God, but then he'd flown off into the heavens without her. She wiped the tears from her cheek, and smiled through the pain.

One day they'd meet again. Until then, she pictured him flying. Or swimming. Swimming in the clouds with their little Lulu.

Dear Reader,

You may question Cole's death. Let me reassure you. I cried more while writing the last scenes than you did while reading them.

I fought the direction God led the story. I didn't understand why Cole had to die. But God in his wisdom sees the future, and He always works for our good. We have many promises in the Bible, but occasionally God will give us a specific promise unique for us. This is demonstrated through the lives of Noah, Abraham, David, and Paul.

You may not think that Cole's story has a happily-ever-after, but he stood firm in his faith and received his promise on earth. Because of that, he reached his ultimate promise in Heaven.

As for Cindy, God promised her a good life. One without fear. As a bonus, He restored her relationship with her brother. In the back of this book you will find a sneak peek of Whatever Is Done, the third story in this series. It continues Cindy's journey of finding and accepting God's blessings.

What has God promised you? The devil tries to trick us into walking away from our promises. As Cindy learned, some things are worth fighting for. Don't give up. Hold on. Because…"The Lord is not slack concerning his promise, as some men count slackness; but is longsuffering to us-ward, not willing that any should perish, but that all should come to repentance.~ 2 Peter 3:9" If you haven't received the promised gift of eternal life, please do so today.

A preacher I greatly admire has said many times, "If God promises you the moon, you better clear off a place in the backyard to put it." This is so true. God always, always keeps his promises.

If you have any questions, or just want to chat, I'd love to hear from you. Send me an email at bridgett@bridgetthenson.com

May we all swim in the clouds with Jesus,

Bridgett Henson

Discussion Questions

1. How did Cole's promise from God effect his sexual purity?
2. Does God have specific people in mind for marriage? Why or why not?
3. Could the church ladies have done more to welcome Cindy? Should they have addressed Rachel's jealousy?
4. Should Cole have intervened more between his mother, Rachel and Cindy?
5. Why couldn't Cindy save her sister, Maria?
6. How does jealousy and suspicion of Cindy's past affect Cole's decisions throughout the book?
7. Did Mrs. Maxwell show the love of Christ to Cindy?
8. Should Cindy have kept the sock money? Do you agree with her decision to give it to the church?
9. How does Cindy's childhood affect her ability to accept God's blessings? Was Cole spoiled?
10. Should Cindy and Cole have invited his parents to their wedding?
11. Why is Cindy so concerned with her choice of clothing?
12. Do you agree with Cole's decision to keep Cindy's brother a secret from her? Do you agree with Cindy's decision to feed the children behind Cole's back?
13. Why didn't Cole want her to visit her old neighborhood?
14. In the end, does Cindy have a good life without fear?
15. Could Cole have gotten his promised Lulu another way?
16. Does God always keep his promises?

He longs for a family. She doesn't want a husband.

The Whatever Serie
Whatever Is Done
Book 3

One small boy crouched alone at the grassy edge of the water. Around the perimeter of the huge pond, adult-child, two-person teams competed for the best catch. The kid frowned at the toddler-sized rod and reel in his hand. Ray searched the crowded bank for the boy's dad and then waited for someone to lend the little boy a hand.

No one stepped forward.

A little brow wrinkled in concentration as the boy peered about ten feet to his right and watched James demonstrate how to press the button and release the line.

Curious what the boy would do next, Ray eased nearer with his own pole. Little fingers struggled with the release button and then slumped in defeat.

As Ray moved closer, the boy gritted his teeth and squeezed with both thumbs. A hard plastic fish splashed into the water's edge and sank six inches to the sandy bottom. The line had no hook, no weight, and no cork.

Ray shook his head. There was no way possible for the boy to catch a real fish.

Yet the little cherub face grinned as he yelled over at James. "I did it."

James—Ray's oldest friend in the world—cast a line into the water and handed the pole to one of his sons. "That's great, Trevor. Don't fall in or your mom will kill me."

Trevor stared into the water at the plastic fish attached to his line. "Yes, sir."

Why didn't James rig up Trevor's line?

The kid wasn't much younger than the twins. And the rod he held was way too small for a boy his age.

"Ouch." James howled and pushed the end of a pole out of his face. "Be careful with that son. You 'bout caught your dad."

Both twins giggled. One peered up at James and said, "Sorry, Daddy."

Ray laughed at his friend's terrified expression.

"They do it all of the times." The little fisherman's gray eyes sparkled with mischief.

"Oh, yeah." Ray grinned. "What do they do?"

"Break stuff."

Full blown laughter escaped from Ray. That was one way to describe the twins. He stepped beside Trevor and whispered, "That's why I call them the Twin Terrors."

Little giggles floated off into the morning sunshine. Trevor lifted his pole and tilted his head at the fake fish. He sighed and dropped it back into the water.

James's voice boomed along the breeze as he removed a fish from a line. "Great job, son."

The ripples from Trevor's pole spread out into deeper water.

"Your dad must be at the office, huh?"

"He doesn't go to work." The little boy concentrated on the water.

"Oh." A dead beat dad? Ray glanced at Trevor's well-kept appearance, designer clothes, and the bulging backpack at his feet. "Well, your mom must take good care of you."

"Yep." Trevor nodded. "She loves me." The line was pulled up again and plopped back into the water. He squinted over at Ray and then leaned around him. "Where's your kid?"

Ray dropped his tackle on the shore. "I don't have one." Over the years working construction, he'd carefully insured that he'd not become a weekend dad like so many of the men on his construction crew.

"Not even in heaven?" Trevor peered into the bright sunlight.

Ray's heart dropped. "Is that where your father is?"

The sad little smile pierced Ray's gut. "Sometimes he swims the clouds with my sister. Momma says he watches me." He jiggled his pole again. "If I catch a fish and win the prize, he'll see me and say it."

"What will he say?"

The little head tilted as Trevor tucked his chin and mimicked in a low voice. "Good job, Trevor."

The steel cage around Ray's heart melted. Every boy should have a dad, and every man should have a son. Maybe that's why Ray had empathy with the kid. Neither one of them had either of those things. The modern-day, father-son fishing tournament included a few women and girls. Ray didn't see any reason for him and Trevor not to enter the competition. "James!" Ray waited until his friend turned his way. "Is there a rule against non-related fishing partners?"

"No." James looked pointedly at Trevor. "But if you're thinking what I think you're thinking…don't. His mom will stroke out if you put a real H-O-O-K on that line."

Ray rubbed the hairs on his chin and eyed the little boy. "Well, we don't want to upset your mom."

The little boy swung his line out of the water. Animated sparks flew from his eyes. "Grandmother says if momma ain't here, she don't matter."

The cutest smile pleaded with Ray. Was the mother really that bad? He looked back at James.

His friend shrugged. "Go ahead. She can't kill you if you're half way around the country on another job."

Yeah, but he'd be in town for at least six weeks. The boy grinning up at him in expectation was skinny as a steel beam. Was his mom just as petite? Few women worked construction and none on his crew, but there were some stout women out there who could heft twice their weight. He'd never raised a hand toward a female, not even in self-defense. "Trev, what's your mom do for a living?"

"She feeds people."

A waitress? Some could be tough, but he'd never met a woman yet that he couldn't sweet talk. "What's she look like?"

"Don't go there, Ray." James shook his head. "She's an old, widow woman. She's not your type at all. Come over here, Trevor. And leave Mr. Simmons alone."

If the crestfallen look on the little boy's face didn't cave Ray in, his next words would have. "But Mr. James. He don't got a kid. He needs me."

"Yes. I do." Ray reached out and ruffled the silky red hair. He wanted to help the boy, especially if his mom was one of those paranoid freaks that didn't let their kids get dirty. He called over to James, "What do you think? Should Trevor and I fish? Or are you and the boys afraid to lose?"

James laughed. "Fine. Enter the competition, but promise me you'll stay away from his mom."

Why would James think he'd want a widow saddled with a kid? Cute though he may be. Ray shrugged. "What's one woman in a vast sea of females?"

Ray ignored James's pointed look and focused on his new fishing buddy. "Well…if we're gonna catch something…you need some bait. Swing your line over here."

Using his pocket knife, Ray cut the fake fish off Trevor's line. "Hand me my tackle box behind you."

Trevor hefted the box over and Ray rigged up the pole. Then he showed Trevor how to cast. Without thinking, he said, "Catching fish is like catching women, Trev. Keep your hook sharp, your line tight, and your bait fresh. Then all you have to do is sit back and reel 'em in."

Around the curve of the pond, a group of teenage boys high-fived and laughed. James's face had turned a purple hue. He hissed, "This is a church fundraiser."

Ray'd been watching his words real close to avoid saying any profanity. What did he say wrong?

He welcomed the buzz of his phone. He reached in his pocket. The last time he'd been in town, he'd split his time off work enjoying the company of two waitresses. He just arrived in the city yesterday and made that knowledge public via social media. He'd wondered who'd make the first contact. He smiled as he read Shelia's comment.

Glad you're in town. Buy me a drink?

"Where'd it go?" Trevor peered into the water. His cork had gone under.

Ray lay his phone on the grass beside him. "You've got a fish. Pull him in." He crouched down beside the boy and helped Trevor reel in a bream the size of a man's hand. "That's a nice one." Ray grabbed his phone. "Hold it by the string and smile." Women loved pictures of their kids. If the widow got too ornery, Ray'd show her this. He took several shots, and then a selfie with Trevor and the fish. "We'll win this thing yet."

℘℘

The new shingles and fresh paint may have changed the appearance of the old wood house, but Cindy's mind's eye saw the prison of her youth. She pushed past the memories as she bustled through the commercial glass door, and went to work preparing sandwiches for the needy.

Minutes later, the empty stare of the bruised child standing in front of her reflected Cindy's own childhood. The little girl couldn't be more than thirteen. Yet the hand reaching for a brown bag trembled. The girl winced and then touched her swollen lip. "Can I have two? Dad'll freak if there isn't food when he wakes up."

"Sure." Cindy dropped a second sandwich and another apple into the bag. She wanted to do more. "I can help. If you let me." She softened her voice. "Did your father hurt you?"

"No." Panic flashed in wide brown eyes. "He didn't. Please, don't tell."

A sour odor reached across the stainless steel countertop and stabbed Cindy through the heart as the girl pivoted away. She smelled of bodily fluids that couldn't possibly be her own. Cindy gagged as the girl rushed out. She wanted to protect the child, but unless the girl confessed the truth to the authorities, the abuse would continue.

The back door slammed.

For the next thirty minutes, the line of hungry people continued through the doors of what once was Cindy's childhood home—the house she, her brother, and her sister had shared with their abusive father. The new varnish on the old hardwood floors couldn't cover the dirty feeling in the bottom of Cindy's stomach every time she stood in this room.

Five years ago, Cole had paid to convert the wood building into a distribution center for the hungry. Part of her was glad the dwelling was used for good. Another part of her—the part that couldn't escape the haunted look in a young girl's eyes—wanted to burn the place to the ground. Instead of striking a match, she smiled at the helpless people trickling through the lunch line.

She nodded encouragement to a young woman with two small children and shoved the memory of trying to feed her sister to the back of her mind. Grubby hands reached for the brown bags that held lunch for the hungry family. Cindy wished she could offer the woman a place to rest from the southern heat, but the permit Cole had gotten for her, prohibited consumption on site. Since his death, she'd knocked down a few walls, but the minor remodeling didn't give her room to grow.

She missed him.

Blinking away the nightmare of her youth, she recalled the good memories of her deceased husband. Cole had saved her. He'd given her love and a home.

He'd given her a son.

Cindy prayed that Trevor would never taste the pangs of hunger. After a horrible miscarriage, her son was an unexpected blessing. One that arrived eight months after Cole's funeral. He was her reason for living. Her motivation to survive. Cindy thanked God for him every day.

"That's the end of the line." Maria, Cindy's sister shut the commercial glass door and twisted the lock. One hand smoothed her pixie cut, dark hair as she crossed to where the kitchen used to be—where their friend Joni stood counting leftover bags.

Cindy drummed her knuckles on the bar. "What's today's totals?"

Joni held up a finger. Her golden head bobbed in rhythm with the flip of the bags. Then she looked up. "Two hundred twelve." She stacked the empty bags into a perfect rectangle. "I saw her too. Should I dial up Detective Simmons, or did you want to make the call?"

"While you're at it, tell the detective to quit hanging around here. He makes our clients edgy." Maria swigged from a water bottle. "DZ's Boys came in, snatched two bags and lit out the back door knocking Mrs. Peterson off her walker."

Cindy joined in the cleaning by replacing unused loaves of bread in the pantry. "The boys need to eat." She leaned close to her sister and whispered, "If you'd stop hitting the green stuff, you could tell the detective yourself." She swiped a wet rag across the countertop. "But, if I was gonna call someone, it wouldn't be him. Besides, there's nothing he can do. We all know without proof, notifying the authorities will make the situation worse."

Joni's smile disappeared with a grim nod. "Proving a parent unfit in the Alabama court system is next to impossible. If his biological mother hadn't voluntarily signed consent, James's son would still be on the streets. I'll be so glad when we open our intervention clinic." Joni moved to the other side of the room.

Maria leaned close to Cindy and whispered, "I'm not using. It's just sometimes I need a smoke to calm my nerves."

Cindy blew out a breath and wished her sister would give her life to God. "I don't want to know details."

ಬಂಡ

Ray held tight to the wiggly, little boy with one hand and knocked on the blue apartment door with the other.

No one answered.

Skinny arms latched around his neck. "Am I back by five?"

With one hand, Ray checked the time on his phone. "We're early." He lowered Trevor's feet to the landing and hunkered down beside him on the cool concrete. "We'll have to wait."

Trevor blew out an exaggerated breath. Little legs scampered to the rail and peered through the bars to the luxury cars below. "Where's momma?"

From where Ray sat, the welds appeared solid, but the landing was thirty feet high. "She'll be here in a minute. Move away from the edge."

Curious feet wandered further down the landing. Ray opened his mouth to call Trevor back to his side when singsong music danced from the parking lot below.

Little eyes widened and his mouth opened as he gasped. "Ice cream." In a flash, the little boy disappeared down the stairwell.

Ray scrambled to his feet and ran to the top of the stairs. His heart dropped as Trevor rounded the corner out of sight. "Trevor!" All day the kid had been an angel, why did he all of a sudden go rogue? Pulse racing, Ray descended the steps three at a time. He left the brick building and spotted his target following a crowd of children toward the parking lot. In two strides, Ray snatched the little boy off his feet. "Don't ever run off again."

Gray eyes morphed like drops of mercury as tears gathered. Each of Trevor's sobs punched Ray in the gut. Maybe he'd been a little rough. He cradled the boy close and whispered, "It's okay, Trev. You scared me. Please don't cry."

One final sniff and it was over. Ray caught a glimpse of an innocent smile before Trevor rested his forehead against his. Eye to eye. Nose to nose. "Uncle Ray, I want ice cream."

Uncle Ray? His heartbeat tripped. The Twin Terrors claimed him as an uncle, although they weren't blood related. Trevor probably thought Uncle Ray was his name.

A sweet kiss fluttered against Ray's cheek. "Please."

Warmth flooded through his coldblooded veins as he hugged the little boy close. "Sure thing, Trev. Uncle Ray will buy you as much ice cream as you want."

A precious giggle was thank you enough as they waited their turn in line. Across the small crowd of parents and children, more than one pair of eyes glanced his way. Nothing new there. He was used to the appreciative looks from women. One stared with open admiration. Ray ignored her and lifted his wiggling bundle onto his shoulders.

Little hands propped on top of Ray's head. "I see the big chocolate."

He kept a firm grip on Trevor's ankles. "Go ahead and pick which one you want."

"Excuse me." The woman had maneuvered to their side and brushed her hip against his leg. "Hi, Trevor. Where's your mom? And who's your friend?"

Ray recognized the invitation in her eyes, but the gold band on her finger answered for him. He stepped to the side ending the bodily contact. "Ray Simmons."

"You're Trevor's uncle. You must be Cindy's…brother?"

At least a dozen pairs of ears besides her two pierced ones leaned close. He kept his answer short. "No."

Gold hoops dangled beneath her short bleached hair as she laughed. "Brother-in-law?"

"Nope." His rude answer didn't seem to faze her. Thankfully, two preteen girls waved from the front. "They're waving for your attention."

She huffed and rolled her eyes. "My girls." Her eyes violated him once more. "I'm in the apartment below Cindy's, if you need to borrow a cup of sugar or anything. I'm always available." With one last, wide smile, she turned and walked away. The heels on her sandals sank into the soft lawn as she moved to the front of the line. The exaggerated sway of her ample hips did nothing to flatter her rounded figure.

One of the few men in the crowd whispered, "Her husband is a good man, unfortunately, he travels a lot. My guess is she's lonely."

Lonely meant clingy. Ray didn't want a lonely woman. And he definitely didn't want a married one. Soft fingers tightened on Ray's chin. He glanced upward and a little face pressed against his.

"Momma says she's a floozy." Several snickers sounded near them. An elbow bit into Ray's skull. "Momma says we don't like people who—"

Ray flipped Trevor over his head and swung him around his back. Giggles erupted, drowning whatever the little munchkin had planned to say next. Ray tossed the little boy high into the air and caught him airplane style. Disaster avoided, Ray perched the giggly, little boy on his forearm and stepped to the counter. "Okay, Trevor. Choose."

"The big one."

Behind the opened, sliding-glass window, the ice-cream man's hat twisted at an odd angle. A wrinkled hand offered a frozen yogurt bar. "This is what Miss Cindy buys."

"No thanks. Real men don't eat fluff." Ray pointed to a large cartooned head on the chart of gooey confections. "Give us two of those." He set Trevor on his feet and reached for his wallet.

The man hesitated but palmed the offered bills. "His mom isn't gonna like this."

Trevor grinned and accepted the opened package. The ice cream was three times the size of Trevor's hand. One bite and both cheeks were smeared.

Ray held his little elbow, and steered him away from the crowd.

A few feet later, a pretty blonde blocked his path. She was cute, but too young for his taste. He searched his brain for a polite refusal as her smile trembled.

"Hi." Color infused her cheeks. "My husband and I attend church with Cindy at Bible Tabernacle." Long slender fingers threaded and a knuckle popped. "We would love to see you this Sunday."

He lifted one brow. The husband wasn't in sight.

"I'm sure Cindy's already invited you." Sweat beads materialized on her forehead. "James Preston and his wife sing most Sundays." One huff feathered the hair out of her eyes. "Except when they have other engagements."

"James and Joni are friends of mine."

"Oh." Her eyes widened against her pale skin. She ducked her head. "Sorry for bothering you."

He studied the strange creature who'd issued an offer he'd never encountered. "It was no bother." What did her husband think of her asking men to church? "I doubt I'll make it Sunday, but thanks."

Kind eyes met his. "You're welcome. Tell Cindy I said hi." She turned and with a little wave, pushed a baby stroller across the neat lawn. "Bye, Trevor."

Melted from the hot evening sun, ice cream dribbled down Trevor's arm. "She's nice."

"Yeah. A little weird though." Ray's mawmaw had forced him to attend church every Sunday morning. As a child, he'd sat on the hard pew in starchy clothes while a man talked forever.

Mawmaw would pinch his side when he'd fall asleep. So he studied the architecture of the building and decided to build things. Though, then, he'd never suspected he'd work industrial construction. He'd dreamed of building his own house for years. Maybe he'd start on it while he was working local.

The invitation to church surprised him. James and Joni asked him occasionally, but they'd never waited for an answer like the shy girl had.

At a young age, Ray'd said the required prayer to make it through the pearly gates. He believed in God and His son, Jesus. What was the point of listening to a boring sermon?

"Let's head back. Your mom could be here any minute."

Sitting on the bottom steps, Ray bit into his treat. The ice cream had gumballs protruding from the etched cartoon face on the front. "Trev, check this out." Ray chewed and then blew a bubble. A loud pop echoed in the stairwell.

"Me too." Trevor plucked out the eyeballs made from gum and chewed.

"Like this." Ray demonstrated again. Trevor giggled as the bubble deflated on one side.

His phone buzzed and he read the text from Charlotte. *You in my neck of the woods? Let's get together.*

Charlotte? Who was Charlotte? Was she the teacher or the dancer? Oh, wait. She was the girl that drove the Jeep.

Beside Ray, the little boy blew on the gum but no bubble formed. "Keep trying. You almost got it."

Ray replied to the message on his phone. *Sorry my schedule's full.*

⁎⁎⁎

Long, jean-clad legs ended at scruffy work boots. Cindy sucked in a breath as she rounded into the stairwell and pressed a hand to her fluttering abdomen. The unknown man looked far too comfortable sitting on the step above Trevor.

Green eyes lifted to hers and widened in surprise. A hand holding an ice cream paused halfway to his open mouth. Full lips curled as he stood, and then tossed the treat in the nearby trashcan.

She stalked toward him. "Who are you? And what are you doing with my son?"

"Momma!" Trevor vaulted from the bottom step and shoved something behind his back smearing a mess along the side of his shirt.

The gorgeous hunk of man towered above her. His smile elevated the foreign heat in her belly. "Mrs. Maxwell, relax. Trevor's safe with me."

Cindy lifted her chin. Ignoring the sizzle in the air, she stepped closer and focused on his jade colored eyes. "Where's James?"

"Ah, you see, Mrs. Maxwell." The man ran a hand through his short, sandy brown hair. The unabashed little-boy-lost look that covered his handsome face seemed genuine. "James had a run-in with a fish hook. And then one of the twin terrors dropped his knife and well…Mr. Preston drove James and the twins to the emergency room. To save 'em some time, I volunteered to bring your son home."

Sitting on the bottom step, Trevor's eyes widened. "Mr. James bleeded." And then he pulled his hand back around and licked what little remained of an ice cream.

She didn't doubt Joni's twin boys created the chaos described, but that didn't answer her original question. "Who are you?"

His stance widened and his voice rose an octave. "I'm Ray. Ray Simmons. I'm a good friend of James's. I was with them when the accident happened."

Her nerves untangled as she searched her memory. "The friend from James's construction days that always gets him into trouble?"

He shrugged and muscles bulged beneath his brown tee shirt. "Well…"

He definitely looked like trouble. "Joni's mentioned you."

~ Whatever Is Done
Now Available
www.filledbooks.com

About the Author

Bridgett Henson was raised in the Deep South by a Baptist mother and a Mormon father. During her teen years, she abandoned the Christian faith altogether. Now, she and her husband minister at a small Methodist church, while holding membership in a local Pentecostal assembly where they raise their three children.

When she's not writing fiction for all denominations, she attends short mission trips, youth conferences, rallies, and summer camps.

Bridgett has a special burden for the youth of today, especially those bound by sex, drugs, and alcohol. She often speaks to those recovering from these addictions.

She hopes that her readers will come to know the God who created and loves them, understand the merciful grace found in the blood of Jesus Christ, and be introduced to the sustaining power of the Holy Ghost.

Visit her website for more information.

www.bridgetthenson.com

www.ingramcontent.com/pod-product-compliance
Lightning Source LLC
Chambersburg PA
CBHW060856250626
47159CB00008B/2766